DEADLY
BLIND

SIOBHÁIN BUNNI

POOLBEG
CRIMSON

Blind
(noun)

a. an obstruction to sight or light

b. a subterfuge; a person, action, or thing that deceives or conceals the truth

c. a camouflaged shelter used for observing or hunting wildlife

This novel is entirely a work of fiction. The names,
characters and incidents portrayed in it are the work of the
author's imagination. Any resemblance to actual persons,
living or dead, events or localities is entirely coincidental.

Published 2018
by Poolbeg Press Ltd.
123 Grange Hill, Baldoyle,
Dublin 13, Ireland
Email: poolbeg@poolbeg.com

1

A catalogue record for this book is available from the British Library.

ISBN 978178199-8236

Printed and bound by CPI Group, UK

www.poolbeg.com

About the Author

Siobháin was born in Baghdad in 1968 to her Irish mother and Iraqi father. Educated by the Benedictine Nuns at Kylemore Abbey, Connemara, she went on to graduate from the College of Marketing & Design in 1992. Writing became an accidental passion some ten years later and has remained such ever since. Juggling her writing with raising three children while managing a full-time career is the constant challenge that keeps her alive and on her toes.

Siobháin lives in Malahide, Co. Dublin, with her three children and a very cheeky Golden Retriever called Milo.

Also by Siobhán Bunni

Blood & Water

Dark Mirrors

Published by Poolbeg

Acknowledgements

It's daunting writing about something you know very little about and what little you do know is learnt from shows on TV. To find someone who is willing to invest their time in you is both rare and invaluable. I am hugely appreciative of the precious time Fionnuala Olohan afforded me. Her insight and guidance into how things work in our police force, I hope, have helped make this a credible and dynamic crime novel. Thank you, Fionnuala. Thanks also to Aidan Ford for his technical advice and for pointing me in the right direction in the first place. Not forgetting the Gardaí on the front desk at Malahide Garda Station! Thank you for entertaining me and my burning questions one late evening.

Thank you also to Shelly Horan for her astute logic and legal advice.

As always to Paula Campbell and her dedicated team at Poolbeg – thank you for your patience and ongoing support.

I am incredibly grateful to my editor, Gaye Shortland, whose opinion I trust implicitly. Thank you for your patience and your encouragement. I'm also thankful that at least one of us has an incredible attention to detail, and it's not me!

I'm lucky enough to be surrounded by an amazing family and great friends. Their names appeared in the acknowledgements for both *Dark Mirrors* and *Blood and Water* and I am honoured to once again be able to include them here.

First and foremost, my dad and mum, Nael and Anne, have been an unrelenting constant that I will forever be grateful for and will probably never be able to thank enough.

Once again, I'd also like to thank my siblings who despite our squabbles and scraps, of which there have been many, when it comes down to it are always there – whether it's a call for a natter or a cry for help they always answer. Each, however, deserves a special mention.

To Nadia, my eldest sister, thanks for being there for me but this time I insist you actually read this book!

My brother Layth and his wife Sarah Jane – the inseparable duo – whose support and mentoring has been unconditional and unfailing. For that I am acutely grateful.

To Lara, the whirlwind that never fails to tell you how great you are, lest you should ever forget, and Layla, the legal eagle with an eye on my best interests.

To Lydia & her hubby Fred, thanks for responding so quickly and giving me Shelly.

To my godson Karl McCabe, for his enthusiastic naming assistance over a roast chicken dinner!

And to my friends:

A massive thanks to Andrina who despite having a hectic life of her own always finds time to check in and make sure all is well.

To the foxes, Ais, Jo, Aoife and Cathy – thanks for the laughs and the wine and more laughs. To the lovely lads and the ginger at TonedFit as well as my fellow spinners and boxit-ers, thanks for keeping me sane despite the sweat, tears and whinging.

A mention also to Niamh Mc Loughlin – you know why you're here, thank you very, very much.

And finally to Daniel, Lara & Lulu. Nothing has given me greater pride than to watch you grow into the incredible individuals you are today. You guys are the essence that keeps me strong and gives me the impetus to fight each and every single day for you. Thank you for being the curious, funny, slightly crazy bunch that you are. Never mind to the moon and back, I love each of you much farther than that.

For Daniel, Lara and Lulu

Be brave in your head and in your heart, in your desires and in your dreams. Have faith in yourself and your abilities and always stand tall for what you believe in. Mind each other always and remember to show respect for yourself by having respect for those who have shown themselves to deserve it.

Prologue

Camouflaged behind her beaming smile were the teeth of a snarling tiger, preparing to bite in defence of its territory. Karin returned to her table amidst spotlights and rapturous applause, her ballgown delicately caressing her ankles, her inner cynic incensed by the hollow sound of their praise.

With all eyes in the room still watching, she felt the warmth of her husband's hand at the base of her spine and caught the sweet smell of whiskey from his breath as he leaned in to politely kiss and congratulate her.

'That was amazing. Honestly. Well done,' he told her as she reclaimed her seat, although she knew it was unlikely he'd understood a word she said.

Across the table her business partner Seán, his elegant wife beside him, sat back and slowly nodded his head in approval. He had stopped clapping a while ago, even though he was the one who should be clapping loudest of all. He knew her success was his too but, unlike Karin, he wasn't willing to place himself in the media firing-line, no matter what class of a buzz it generated. Given the attention that their latest deal was attracting, he was lucky that Karin was a natural. She had fleetingly considered telling him about the two threatening letters she had received but decided against it. She wasn't the kind to be intimidated.

To his left sat Gordon and his wife Sive, Karin's friend from their university days. 'I'm so proud of you!' Sive cried openly. 'Really, why can't I be more like you?'

'Well, you certainly try hard enough,' Gordon muttered under his breath while shifting uncomfortably in his seat.

Karin and Sive had graduated together, Karin at the top of her class and Sive by the skin of her teeth due largely to the patient tutelage of her friend. That was the way it was, and had been through the years, a silent understanding that Karin helped Sive and in return received the only thing Sive could afford: her friendship and, Karin assumed, her loyalty.

'I'm so looking forward to this weekend,' Sive told her with a broad smile. 'It'll be nice, just the two of us.'

From across the table, Karin tipped her glass in a silent toast to her attentive friend.

'Fantastic job!' Minister Devaney boomed as he approached.

Karin got to her feet to turn and greet him.

'Glad I was up first,' he said. 'You'd be a hard act to follow. Captivating speech – you really are an inspiration – we could do with people like you on our team.'

Bowing her head and lowering her eyes in mock modesty, Karin graciously accepted his compliment. If only he knew he was the only reason she was even there. He was, in her opinion, a smart politician – one of the few – and tipped as the frontrunner in the race for party leadership. A worthy man to share the podium with.

'Why don't we have lunch?' he invited.

'I'd be delighted to, Minister.'

'Minister!' he howled. 'Please, call me Nigel. Why don't I give your office a call on Monday and we can agree a time?'

'Perfect.'

'Good! But be warned I'm looking forward to getting a real sense of what makes that brilliant mind of yours tick.'

She smiled in response as he was ushered away by his minders, knowing he was unlikely to ever comprehend what was really going on in her mind.

Chapter 1

Naomi Fox tried her best to calm the first-day butterflies that fluttered wildly in her stomach. You'd think at this stage, seventeen years and ten new posts into her career, that she'd be used to it by now. She'd had more leaving do's than she cared to remember. Mounting the steps of the station, she was eager to get the awkward introductions over and done with as soon as possible and get herself stuck in. It was time to start something new.

Just as she lifted her hand to push the heavy door, it was opened for her. A rotund balding Garda in uniform stood there, smiling at her.

'Detective Inspector Fox?' he asked.

'That's me,' she replied.

'Fantastic. Don't bother going in, you're coming with me.' He let the door go and made his way past her towards the waiting squad car, expecting her to follow. 'Looks like you might have your first case,' he told her over his shoulder while opening the car door and gesturing for her to get in.

She climbed into the back seat.

'Oh, and welcome to Galway,' he finished with a chuckle, slamming the door shut after her before getting into the passenger front seat. 'Garda Sergeant Anthony Joyce,' he said, twisting round to throw a welcoming hand over the back of the seat. 'AJ for short.' He nodded at the driver. 'And this is Garda Paulie McBride.'

'Great to meet you, AJ, Paulie,' she replied, taking the proffered hand. 'Most people just call me Fox.'

'Fox it is,' he said with a smile.

'So where are we headed?' she asked, noting their exit on the roundabout was taking them out of town.

'One of your own,' he said, shifting back in his seat so he could steady himself with the overhead handle. 'A Dub,' he qualified. 'But she's a regular visitor, has a house out beyond in the valley, beautiful spot right on the lake.'

The car careered wildly to the right.

'*Jaysus, Paulie, will you slow it down a bit!*' he roared to the driver, hanging onto the overhead handle. 'Paulie here thinks he's the feckin' Stig.'

Paulie smiled at her in the rear-view mirror but said nothing. She was sure he was a little heavy-handed with the wheel on purpose.

'Me brain is rattlin' in me skull,' AJ huffed as they rounded a bend at speed. 'Anyway, I assume you know Karin Bolger?'

'Karin Bolger? *The* Karin Bolger?'

'The very one. Well, we have a report she's missing.'

'Missing? How? When?'

'That is what we're about to find out. Seems they have the husband in Dublin saying she hasn't come back after the weekend.'

'It's only Monday. Maybe she didn't want to come home,' Paulie offered, slowing to take a sharp bend.

'Well, there is that,' AJ said with raised eyebrows, 'but I'm not sure it's that simple.'

'She owns the house?' Fox asked, hanging on to the front seat.

'She spends a lot o' time this neck o' the woods. You'd see her the odd time in the town.'

They took the turn off the main road and headed into the valley.

'It's beautiful here,' Fox remarked.

AJ glanced out the window without comment. 'Problem is, we were already here on Friday night.'

'Why?'

'She reported a break-in and we responded.'

'And was it?'

'Oh, it was, alright – but it seemed fine when we got there and they were certainly fine when we left.'

'They?' Fox asked.

'Ms Bolger and her friend.'

'Who was the friend? A man?'

'Nope,' he said with a single shake of his head. 'A woman. Sive Collins.'

'And where is she?'

'We don't know as yet.'

'Are we worried we missed something?'

AJ's responding shrug was noncommittal.

'OK,' she said. 'Let's take a look and see.'

'Baptism of fire, Fox, baptism of fire,' he muttered.

Nothing like a good first case to distract the butterflies, fuelled now by adrenaline rather than fear.

This was a part of the world that Fox had never seen and, as they travelled further into the narrow valley, she honestly wished she'd experienced it sooner. Following the ribbon of road as it wrapped its way around the edge of the lake, the mountains on either side grew steeper as each mile passed until they loomed over them like giants, separated by a body of water so still it reflected the crisp blue sky above, like a carpet of shimmering blue sapphires. On each side a dense blanket of trees covered the steep inclines in a kaleidoscope of breathtaking autumnal colour, orange blended to chocolate brown mixed with yellow gold and ochre.

'Bloody hell!' she whispered, its vista so rich, her senses so overwhelmed by the beauty that she could hardly speak. I'd come here every week too if I could, she mused, then realised she could, now she was stationed locally.

They slowed and turned into a gap in the trees. A discreet gatepost bore the name *Silene Cottage*. Remote and secluded, there wasn't another house for miles. They drove up a steep lane that divided the trees until the stone cottage appeared before them. Like something out of a storybook, it had a yellow door and window frames, and yellow window boxes with the remains of summer blooms doing their best to survive the changing temperatures.

'It's absolutely incredible around here,' Fox said. 'So remote and gorgeous.'

'That's why they come,' AJ said. 'To get away from the strife of the city.'

'No better place.'

'We've a few big names living down this way,' AJ boasted, 'but we're blind to their prestige – we don't care who they are or where they come from – they're guests with us and we're supposed to keep them safe.'

Outside the house, a squad car was parked. Its doors opened and two uniformed Gardaí got out to greet them.

Beside the squad car was a midnight-blue Jaguar XJ.

AJ and Fox got out.

'Nice car,' Fox remarked, bending over to take a look through the passenger window. Apart from the two paper cups in their holders, as expected the car was both exquisite and immaculate.

'Well?' AJ enquired of the Gardaí. 'Anything?'

'We've checked the house and the grounds – no one's here,' one replied.

'OK, wait here,' he instructed and handed Fox blue plastic shoe-covers and a pair of latex gloves. 'This is our new detective – Detective Inspector Fox,' he told the young officers as he snapped on his gloves. 'It's her first day, so be nice.' He flashed a cheeky smile at Fox. 'Now, let's take a look.'

Fox nodded to her newest colleagues and followed the determined sergeant into the house. Having paused to cover her boots and put on her gloves, she scanned the scene from the door.

'The break-in?' she asked, pointing to the new lock on the door.

'Yes, ma'am,' both Gardaí chimed in unison.

The house was dead quiet, the air heavy and still. As soon as Fox entered, a comfortable sense of calm washed over her, her heart rate slowed, and her senses tuned in to high alert, aware that she was standing at the heart of the incident, where it all happened. Like a snapshot in time, the place stood eerily still. The silence of the crime scene teased and tested her, as if reluctant to offer up the answers to what had happened without a fight.

The more she looked, the more she saw, and the more the theatre of the last scene began to play out in her head. Slowly she walked the small, refurbished house, so sensitively and lovingly restored with its small square windows, thick walls, spacious open-plan living area and quirky mezzanine accessed by a spiral staircase.

She stood still to get the bigger picture and felt the chill from the now-dead fire that three nights earlier probably burned bright and high in the old stone hearth. At a glance she posed the riddle that belonged to this scene: a cosy empty cottage, the remains of a meal, personal effects untouched, a chair overturned but no damage done – what happened? That was her challenge to solve.

On every available surface picture frames of all shapes, sizes and finishes hung and sat. Smiling faces beamed at her from every corner of the room. Certificates were mounted proudly on walls between shelves and trinkets mashed with collectibles on the mantelpiece and wherever else they might fit. This was a collection of much-loved and favoured possessions and the apparent inner sanctum of Karin Bolger.

To the right of the front door, two black coats were hung on the row of hooks. Two hard-shell overnight cases on wheels were tucked into the corner. Further in were two handbags, one hanging on the back of a chair near the fireplace and the other, an expensive-looking Prada that she guessed wasn't fake, sitting on the small bureau beside the door. Beside the bag lay keys she assumed were for the Jaguar outside.

Starting with the Prada, appreciating the designer quality of the leather, she emptied the contents onto the bureau. The bag was perfectly clean, containing only the essentials. This was a woman who changed her bag regularly, giving herself no time to amass the usual rubbish that ordinarily collected in the corners. Picking up the matching wallet, she counted one hundred and fifty euros cash and what appeared to be a full complement of cards. Putting it back in the bag, she then picked up the plain burgundy Filofax. She smiled as she flicked through it. Karin, it appeared, much like herself, liked to write things down. Meetings, lunches, notes-to-self and remarks to remember, the diary told the story of the last eight months, including the last week and the schedule for the weeks coming. A small Lulu Guinness make-up pouch held a hairbrush, a miniature perfume bottle, lipstick and a few other cosmetic items. Her phone, which had lost power.

By contrast Sive's bag was more of a satchel than a handbag, lacking all the finesse and elegance of the Prada and without the add-on embellishments. Sive Collins, it appeared, was more chaotic than her friend. As well as a bulging make-up bag, she carried a weight of rubbish around – everything from old tissues and rubber bands to notebooks, an array of pencils and pens, and a smaller bag with painkillers, Tampax and cotton buds. Messy. Sive's wallet was also there, with cash and cards, apparently untouched, along with her phone, which just like Karin's had lost power hours before. But no diary.

Fox circled the dining table, set for two, with almost-drunk wine in crystal glasses and a half-finished meal – shepherd's pie, it seemed – on bone-china plates with the cutlery placed carefully at the sides as if the diners had only left for a minute and planned to return shortly. The twin candles were burned down to the silver candlesticks. She wondered who was sitting in the place where the seat had been turned over – Sive or Karin? She made her way around the counter that divided the living area from the kitchen, noticing that despite what appeared to be a home-cooked meal there were no pots in the sink and no mess around the kitchen.

'Is there a housekeeper?' she asked.

'There is,' AJ replied. 'A local lady from the town, Mary MacGarry, a lovely woman – I know her well.'

'Was she here?' she asked.

'Yes, but earlier, before Karin and Sive arrived.'

'I'll need to speak with her myself.' Fox started up the skinny spiral staircase to reach the mezzanine tucked high into the rafters.

'We can drop in on our way back to the station.'

A single Velux window overhead shed plenty of light on the small area. Bookshelves lined one wall with a desk nestled efficiently amidst a skirmish of fiction and non-fiction, where authors and genres mixed haphazardly. On the desk sat an open laptop and a neat pile of papers. With everything going on in Karin Bolger's world, Fox was in no doubt that there were people who would pay good money for even a quick glance at the information on that computer. If nothing else, it would give an interesting insight into the business deal that had the whole of the country up in arms. Her fingers itched to log in but, until she was sure that a crime had actually taken place, she would have to hold off.

Making her way carefully back down the stairs, she called out to AJ, 'So what do we know for sure?'

Immediately standing upright, adopting an official stance, AJ filled her in.

'They arrived at approximately nine thirty pm on Friday last. We got a call to say there had been a break-in. The door had been jimmied alright but there were no other signs of a break-in and nothing, Ms Bolger thought, had been removed from the house.'

'So you spoke to her?'

'We did. I took the call myself but it was Gardaí Nealon and Ward who responded.' He indicated towards the two outside. 'You can ask them, they'll tell you what they saw.'

He called them in.

'How did Ms Bolger seem?' she asked.

Nealon took out his notebook.

'She seemed pretty calm although her friend was a little upset.'

'Well, more freaked out than upset to be honest,' Garda Ward offered.

'But Karin – she wasn't nervous or even a little scared?'

'Not at all – it seemed pretty routine to her. She kinda went about her business and left us to it really. Her friend, though, wouldn't even come into the house till we'd given them the all-clear.'

'Any idea when it might have happened?' Fox asked.

'No, but Mary MacGarry had been here all morning,' said Nealon. 'She said she left the house set and ready for the women at about four or so, so any time between four and nine.'

Fox nodded pensively, puckering her lips while processing what she'd heard. Still pacing the room, looking, touching, and seeing, she stopped again at the turned-over dining chair that was the only indication that a struggle had taken place at all.

'Did you check the windows and doors?' she asked, careful of her tone.

'We did,' Nealon assured her with a defensive hint to his response. 'And did a full perimeter walk. Checked the two outhouses. And made sure the ladies were locked in before we left.'

'And who fixed the lock?' she asked.

'Paul Cleary from the village. He came pretty quick, had them sorted in no time. He secured the jamb too but they'll need to get that sorted properly.'

Again Fox nodded. It was a peculiar scene, like a world interrupted. They were gone but not absent, their departure so fresh their shadows remained.

'I'm assuming the bedrooms are down here,' she asked, turning to open the door onto a narrow, dark corridor.

Positioned opposite each other, they were pristine and untouched. Noting in each room that the curtains hadn't been drawn, she looked under the beds, pulled out the drawers and opened the wardrobes.

'Doesn't look like they even ventured down here,' she said to AJ who had followed behind her.

'Not a bad place, she's done a lovely job,' he remarked, admiring the smooth plaster finish on the walls.

'It's pretty nice alright,' Fox replied from the bathroom where she was checking out the bottles of potions and lotions on the windowsill. 'She's got great taste too.'

Closing the doors behind them, they made their way back to the living room and the two idly chatting Gardaí.

'Nothing was taken … no sign of break-in after they arrived,' she said to no one in particular. She turned to Nealon. 'Is there a chance,' she asked cautiously, 'that whoever broke in might still have been in the house when you left?'

'Hiding, you mean?'

'Yes.'

'Maybe,' he said doubtfully. 'It's a possibility. But the place is so small …' He gestured around the room.

She nodded, lifted one of the wineglasses to her nose and sniffed. 'We should get this checked, and the shepherd's pie too.' She turned to AJ. ''Prints?'

'Forensics are on their way,' he replied. 'We'll get them on the system as soon as we can.'

'Perfect. We'll need to speak to the husband.'

'Well, you'll have to go back to Dublin to do that.'

'Great. I've only just arrived and I've to head home again!

Set up the incident room in HQ and I'll see what the story is with the husband.'

'Will do.'

'We'll need to brief the Commissioner,' she said as she and AJ made their way back to the car. 'This'll be all over the media – he'll need to be involved in that. But first, can we drop in to the housekeeper?'

'Absolutely,' AJ replied approvingly.

Chapter 2

Mary MacGarry lived in one of the cottages that looked out onto Main Street in the local village. Having been served milky tea and scones straight from the oven, AJ and Fox sat in her front room on the edge of the floral three-seater sofa with a portrait of Jesus Christ looking down piously on them from above the fireplace. Fox felt an involuntary shiver run down her spine. Somewhere in the room a clock ticked while silhouettes of passersby could be seen through the thick white net curtains.

Mary sat opposite them, her eyes red and swollen, having cried when she heard the news. Fox gave her a sympathetic smile and told her they were doing everything they could but needed her help to piece together the hours before the women arrived at the house together. Maybe she'd seen something without realising that could help their investigation.

'That poor woman,' she said, wringing her handkerchief tightly in her hands. 'That poor, poor woman.'

'Well, we don't know that anything's actually happened to her,' Fox tried to reassure her only to be rewarded with a look that screamed *do you think I'm an eejit?*

'Really now, in this day and age,' Mary scowled, 'who in

the name of God goes out without their coat or their handbag or their car, for feck's sake? No one, that's who.'

Fox retreated immediately. Mary wasn't going to be fooled, nor was she going to be polite about telling them so.

'It's those damn Dublin bastards!' she blasted passionately, shaking her hankie held tight in her fist.

Fox felt her eyebrows rise involuntarily and threw AJ a look to question his earlier assessment of this 'lovely woman'.

'I mean, really, she's only tryin' to make an honest bloody livin', creating jobs and nice homes for people and all they can do is give out, ungrateful bastards the lot of them! Well, let me tell you she wasn't scared, no sir, not one jot. They can send her all the poison letters they want but she won't be pushed around!' Mary's voice trembled as she realised the irony of her words and the implications of Karin's disappearance.

'What do you mean *poison letters*?' Fox asked, suddenly interested in Mary's rant.

'Those letters, they said some terrible things.' Mary clutched her hands to her chest and shook her head.

'What letters? Did you see them?' Fox asked, leaning forward.

Mary responded with a nod. 'I wasn't supposed to but she had them in her workbook thing and they just fell out when I was cleaning up around her desk – she makes an awful mess sometimes.'

'Did you ask her about them?'

Again Mary nodded eagerly, gulping back the rising sobs.

'What did she say?'

'She said it was nothing to worry about, that they were just angry, that they wouldn't dare touch her.'

'Can you remember when this was?' Fox asked, keeping her tone level and calm.

'A few weeks back.' She thought for a minute, her eyes closed tight. 'August Bank Holiday,' she then said decisively. 'The weekend of the festival – Ms Bolger had been down for the whole week. I was rushing, wanted to finish to make evening Mass – that's how come I dropped the stupid book.'

'Did you not tell anyone about them?'

'She told me not to, said we'd only be playing into their hands. She didn't want a fuss.'

'Did she put them back where you found them – are they still on her desk?'

'They won't be there still,' she said anxiously. 'Ms Bolger took them back to Dublin. You'll need to ask Mr Williams about them.'

'Who's Mr Williams?'

'That's Tom. Lovely man.' She wiped her eyes, calmer now. 'He takes care of her, well, he's supposed to – not doing a very good job of it.' She huffed crossly and would likely tell him as much when she saw him again. 'A bit like her security man type of thing.'

Fox made a note of his name before tentatively asking about the previous Friday, hoping not to set her off again.

But, having composed herself, Mary gave them a calm and thorough rundown of her usual routine when Karin was coming down, which was always on a Friday it seemed. As always she set the fire, filled the pantry, and prepared supper, leaving it ready to heat in the oven when she arrived. And that Friday was no different to any other, apart from the fact Sive had been with her. Mary was asked to set up the spare room and set the table for two. Aside from that, there was nothing that caught her attention, nothing unusual at all.

'What about the wine, did you choose that?'

'No. Won't touch the stuff – the devil's drink – Ms Bolger

knows I won't. Anyway, I wouldn't know the first thing about it. No. She picks that out herself. She keeps a few bottles in the roundy shelf-thingamajig under the counter in the kitchen.'

'Tell me, does Mr Bolger accompany her often?'

'Mr Bolger?' She looked confused, 'Her father? Sure he's dead these last years.'

'Her husband, Finn,' Fox corrected herself, trying not to laugh.

'Ahh, he's not a Bolger – he's Ellis, Finn Ellis.'

Fox nodded her understanding as Mary continued.

'No, not anymore,' she told them almost sadly, 'but he used to, in the beginning but ... oh, I don't understand him.' She gave a pensive shake of her head, looking from Fox to AJ. 'Calls himself an artist! I mean, look at the place, it's an inspiration.' Her arms waved dramatically above her head. 'All you have to do is walk out the front door to be wanting a bit o' paint. Christ, I wished so many times to have the gift, but it's an affliction.'

'An affliction?' Fox asked, curious as to what she meant.

'I've heard those stories about those mad fellas on the Continent cuttin' off their ears.'

'Is Finn like that? Mad, I mean.'

'I bloody hope not.'

'Do they fight much?'

'Can't say I've been round them much lately to notice – but I can say she isn't happy,' she said with a wise purse of her lips, crossing her arms under her breasts. 'I've seen her come down here with a face as long as January, not a smile to be had out of her. She sits in that house all on her own, not a soul to talk to ...' Then her eyes widened and she asked, 'You don't think this was him, do you?'

'No, we don't,' Fox replied with what she hoped was a reassuring smile.

'Oh, good God!' Mary exclaimed, blessing herself twice. 'You do, don't you?'

'No, Mary, we don't. We're just trying to get a picture of what was happening in her life. What about Sive, has she been here before?'

'Not to my knowledge. I've never met her. Heard of her alright, but never put a face to her.'

'Anyone else come here with her?'

'Not really, no. This was her place, her sanctuary. No one bothered her here. Nobody round here minds her money – she could just be herself.' She suddenly picked up the pot with its knitted cosy. 'More tea?'

'That woman is absolutely bats,' Fox declared, getting into the car while waving to Mary who stood in the doorway, handkerchief in hand.

AJ smiled. 'She's a ticket alright.'

'A ticket? A safe pass to the asylum more like!' She laughed, ignoring the curtains that twitched as they drove away. 'I wonder who this security guy is – what did she call him?' She looked down her notes. 'Tom Williams. Surprised he hasn't made contact himself.'

'Not a very good security lad to let this happen,' AJ remarked, and he was right.

Chapter 3

Fox knew she'd be back in Dublin soon but couldn't have predicted that it would be this quick. As the miles passed she threatened never to travel this road again. Her first day, despite the case she'd been assigned, hadn't gone well. You're being an idiot, she told herself, knowing it was only her ego that was hurt. Unable to stop it, she let the first conversation with her new boss rerun again in her head.

He was waiting for her when she and AJ returned to the station from Mary's.

The Western Region Headquarters was housed in the same building as the Galway City Centre Garda station, taking up the third and fourth floors of the newly constructed building. It still smelt of fresh paint and newly laid carpet. Superintendent Moyne's office was on the top floor with glass doors that opened into the open-plan office and a window looking out onto Eyre Square.

'They'll be all over this,' Moyne had warned unnecessarily. 'We'll need to keep this tight until we know more.'

Fox nodded in agreement as she stood in front of his desk, her hands clasped behind her poker-straight back.

'Are we one-hundred-per-cent certain that this is a genuine abduction?' he asked for the second time.

Fox tried not to let her impatience show on her face. 'Well, sir –'

'This could very well be just a tired wife who left of her own volition,' Moyne interrupted. 'Maybe she doesn't want to be found? Perhaps the pressure of all this filthy media coverage got to her?'

'I really don't think so, sir, but even if that is the case it doesn't explain her friend Sive Collins' disappearance.'

He looked up at her with raised eyebrows. 'Maybe it does.'

Fox lowered her head and squeezed her fists tight behind her back.

'I really don't think so, sir.'

'Well, it's unfortunate this has happened on our doorstep,' he moaned, giving Fox one more reason not to warm to him. 'Set up an incident room here but I suspect, given the profile, this will be managed out of Dublin.'

Fox shifted from one foot to the other. 'Yes, sir,' she responded, biting her tongue. Her experience told her exactly how and from where this would be managed, as did AJ who was already taking over one of the assigned rooms on the floor below.

'Organise full forensics from this end and set up the house-to-house team,' he ordered. 'We'll need CCTV footage, street cams, dash cams, anything that might have caught sight of these two ladies wherever they went.'

'Yes, sir, I've already got that covered.' She knew exactly what to do and didn't take kindly to being treated like a rookie.

'Good,' he remarked with a sideways glance. 'You'll need to speak to her husband and the other one. We don't know for sure who's the actual mark yet.'

'Yes, sir, I have both men waiting to be interviewed in Dublin. I'm heading there now.'

'Make doubly sure you watch what you say – we don't want egg on our face if she turns up from some girlie shopping trip.' He twirled his hand in the air dismissively as if this was just some bored housewife they were dealing with.

'I will but I don't think that's the case, sir.'

'And what about the media briefing?' he fired at her.

'I know, sir, I –'

'Call Caroline in the press office from the car,' he interrupted. 'We can't afford to waste time on this. Once the media get a whiff of this, if they think we've stalled at all –'

'Sir,' she interrupted, unable to disguise the huff in her voice, 'I've got it covered. I've already left a message …'

She saw his eyes widen and nostrils flare and knew she'd made a mistake and wished she'd kept her mouth shut. Panic made her heart race and her muscles tense as she braced for his reprimand. He and his chauvinistic rebukes were notorious.

'Detective Inspector Fox, this is my briefing to you. Listen and learn. This is what *I* want from you.' He leant forward with both knuckles on his desk. He looked as if he might lift his legs and leap at her. 'I've only heard third-hand about you – now don't get me wrong – it's all been good, excellent in fact, but I want to find you out for myself, understood?'

Standing at six-foot five he was intimidating enough but, combined with the punch his booming voice packed, he made her knees tremble. But instead she nodded, doing her best to keep her face neutral and not give away the fear and loathing she felt for him. In all of her career none of her

23

superior officers had ever spoken to her like that. This was a whole new experience for her and she didn't like it.

'So, you can either like it …' he paused and looked to the ceiling as if searching for the right thing to say and, finding nothing, he looked back at her, 'or like it. Got it?'

'Yes, sir,' she replied, focusing on keeping her voice level. 'Will that be all, sir?'

'Yes. But keep me briefed.'

'Yes, sir,' she replied with a hint of a nod before turning and leaving the room, taking the time to calmly close the door behind her and walk away as if completely unfazed by this behaviour. She could feel his eyes on her as she returned to her new desk which was devoid of her personality, picked up her phone and left the office.

Behind the wheel of her car, heading back to Dublin and the Garda Headquarters that she'd only just celebrated leaving, she felt her cheeks flush.

'Fuck,' she muttered, hating not making a good impression. Hating to have her reputation as a smart, savvy and successful policewoman disrupted by a grumpy misogynist and, for the first time in as long as she could remember, doubting her next step. Even if she wasn't already aware of Moyne and his reputation – there wasn't a female in the force that wasn't – she'd been warned often enough in the past couple of weeks. At her leaving do they presented her with a handmade *'Break in Case of Emergency'* box containing a muzzle – they obviously knew her well and she got the hint. Thumping the steering wheel between expletives, she wished she'd taken their advice.

Oblivious to the autumn sun that lit up the road in front and the fields around her, she debated the options in her head: to go straight to the husband or first to the Commissioner?

This definitely wasn't the best start.

Detective Simon Callaghan was waiting for her with a smile when she pulled up outside Wild Wind, an impressive contemporary villa perched at the summit of Cliff Road. Overlooking Dublin Bay, it was one of the most coveted roads in Dublin, boasting at least one politician, two pop stars and an actor – there was no denying Karin Bolger was in good company up here. It was impossible not to be awed by the sheer scale of the house which was revealed as the electronic gates pulled back. With its angled roofs, cantilevered verandas and tiered lawns giving way eventually to the cliffs beyond it, it was stunning and worthy of its *Best House on the Street* accolade. The bluster of this edifice in comparison to the simplicity of the cottage buried in the country was not lost on Fox.

She got out of the car, trying her best not to be distracted by her colleague who stood, hands on his hips, grinning from cheek to cheek at her. Returning his smile, she braced herself for the inevitable slagging that she knew was about to follow and she didn't have long to wait.

'Jesus, Fox, what do we have to do to get rid of you?'

Throwing her eyes up to heaven, she prepared to bat back.

'Very funny, Callaghan. I know you missed me – you're just too shy to admit it.'

'Yeah, right!'

Their banter was interrupted by the sound of the front door being opened by a short balding man with a comb-over that, despite the generous smearing of gel, refused to stay still on his head, insisting instead on lifting with the gentle sea breeze. Completely oblivious to it, he smiled and lifted his hand in welcome.

'Tom Williams,' he introduced himself as he approached, his shoes crunching heavily on the gravel driveway. 'Spiro Capital Group Head of Security.' His long arm extended, taking Fox's hand into his firm but gentle single-slice handshake.

'Detective Inspector Naomi Fox,' she returned. The words sounded peculiar coming out of her mouth – she'd only ever said them on her own in front of the mirror. Saying them out loud now felt both alien and delightful, sending a shiver of mild excitement down her spine. 'And this is my colleague, Detective Simon Callaghan.'

'We've already met earlier when I arrived,' Callaghan offered with a respectful nod of acknowledgement towards Tom.

'Sorry about that again.' Tom laughed confidently like a man with the upper hand. 'Just doing my job.'

'I'm sure,' Callaghan huffed and, turning to a silently enquiring Fox, explained, 'He thought I was a journalist, he called it in, I was almost arresting myself.'

Fox grinned as Tom turned towards the house.

'Finn Ellis, Karin Bolger's husband, and Gordon Collins, Sive Collins' husband, are waiting for you inside,' he told them, making his way to the door.

'How are they doing?' Fox enquired as they entered the house.

'Good, considering,' Williams replied, leading the way. 'Nervous to be honest,' he added after a pause. His voice echoed in the vast square hallway.

'Have you heard anything from any would-be abductors?

Any demands?' Fox asked, admiring her surroundings.

'Nothing yet, which makes me nervous.'

'When did you last hear from Ms Bolger?'

'We spoke on Friday afternoon while she was en route to the cottage, I believe, but not since.'

Fox nodded then stopped at the closed door.

'Before we go in,' she said, 'I understand Ms Bolger received some threats recently.'

'She did. Do you mind me asking who told you about them? I understand they were …' he paused to find the right word, 'confidential.'

'Her housekeeper in Galway found them so I'm not sure how confidential they are now,' she told him with a rueful smile. 'What did they say?'

'Well, they were pretty nasty actually. Abusive. Personal. Amateur.'

Fox wondered what he meant by 'amateur'.

'No doubt you've heard about Spiro Capital's latest development involving Kings Brewery?' he said.

Karen nodded.

'I don't mean to gloss over the detail but in short the old brewery will close down and move to a new modern facility that needs less than half the staff. The job losses will be substantial, in their hundreds, and basically the staff are pissed off. You've seen the demonstrations on TV.' He shrugged.

'But the brewery will still exist, albeit in its new home,' Fox said.

'There are generations who live, sleep and breathe that brewery – they don't want to up sticks and leave. The brewery, the beer, the community, it's theirs.'

'You sound like you're defending them,' Fox remarked quietly.

'I understand, that's all. I'd be pissed off too. But these notes that were sent,' he shook his head solemnly, 'they're amateur. Angry people with angry words and no voice.' He paused to heave a weighty sigh. 'They've been signed by a group calling themselves Justice for the Workers. First they warned that if she doesn't stop the deal going ahead, if she doesn't keep the brewery open, they'll cut out her heart and feed it to the pigs – and the second, well, let's just say it was a little more intimate and sexually charged. Not pretty.'

Fox winced. 'I assume you still have them?'

Williams nodded.

'Can we have them?'

'Absolutely.'

'Did you not think to report these threats to us?' she asked.

'Unfortunately, for whatever reason, Ms Bolger was adamant that we kept them to ourselves. They're in my safe at the Spiro building in town. You'll want to meet the team there too, I can take you once we're done here.'

Fox looked at her watch. It was almost four. She was tired, hadn't eaten and needed to pee.

'That would be great,' she replied.

Williams opened up the heavy oak door into the most magnificent kitchen Fox had ever set foot in. Like something from a magazine shoot, there wasn't a pot or a cup or a dishcloth on view. It was pristine with only a tall stem lily reflecting on the centre of a polished granite island that housed a hob and prep top on one side and a breakfast bar complete with high-top dove-grey bar stools on the other. Charcoal walls, grey high-gloss cabinetry with polished silver door handles and a built-in coffee machine completed the state-of-the-art kitchen. Thirty, maybe forty grand, Fox priced in her head – but a nightmare to keep clean, she concluded, counting the numerous shiny surfaces.

At the end of the room in the living area, seated side by side on one of the matching charcoal-leather sofas, were two men who stood as the others approached. Both, as if rehearsed, wiped the palms of their hands on their thighs.

Williams stepped forward. 'Finn Ellis, Gordon Collins,' he introduced them, gesturing. 'Detective Inspector Fox and Detective Callaghan.'

Side by side but worlds apart, Finn and Gordon were almost complete opposites. Both men stood tall at just under six foot and were roughly the same broad build, although Finn had a more defined and toned physique. Five years younger than Gordon's forty-four, he had a generous mop of chestnut-coloured hair while Gordon had salt-and-pepper short back and sides. Finn, despite his nerves, looked relatively comfortable in his jeans, loose fitting T-shirt and bright pink socks – this was his home after all. Gordon, on the other hand, oozed tension in his beige slacks and khaki-green polo shirt. His handshake was limp and his palms sweaty.

'Thanks for coming,' Finn offered quietly, extending his hand to shake theirs. 'Do you have any news about Karin? And Sive, of course,' he added, glancing apprehensively at Gordon who Fox suspected wasn't making the day any easier for either of them.

'Not as yet,' Fox said, indicating that they should sit.

She and Callaghan sat opposite the two husbands who leaned anxiously towards them.

'I've just come from the house in Galway,' Fox said, 'and I can assure you that whatever happened it wasn't violent – there is no sign of a struggle or physical injuries whatsoever.'

Finn had lowered his eyes to inspect his hands as she spoke.

'So, what? They went of their own free will?' Gordon asked, his tone laced with sarcasm.

'Perhaps,' Fox answered, ignoring his abrupt manner. 'But, if I'm honest, I don't think so. Obviously, we need time to investigate and, well, if a demand is made then we'll know for sure.'

When neither man said anything, she continued, looking at Callaghan for support. Nodding, encouraging her to proceed and hoping to appear empathetic, he mirrored their lean.

'We're conducting door-to-door enquiries and we've set up a team to see if we can track them on CCTV.'

'So, what do we do?' Finn asked.

'For the moment we need you to stay put,' she said. 'Whoever has Karin and Sive will make contact soon so we need you to be ready. We also need to take your prints, just so we can identify and eliminate your prints from the scene.'

'I can't sit here and do nothing!' Gordon stood up and circled the couch, running his hands through his hair, his frustration getting the better of him. 'There must be something, *anything* we can do.'

'I appreciate you're both anxious,' Fox said, standing to meet Gordon's eye, the control in her voice unmistakable. 'This is obviously extremely tough and I promise we'll do our very best to get Karin and Sive back to you as quickly as we can, but these next few hours are critical so we'll need your full cooperation.'

'Gordon, sit down please, you're making me nervous,' Finn pleaded, his tone tired but diplomatic.

Like a petulant child Gordon sat down, his face like thunder.

Fox thought it was ironic that, of the two, Gordon

probably had the best upbringing with a private-school education – he probably played rugby, maybe a bit of cricket – but he was by far the worst behaved.

She liked Finn. He was handsome in a manly, messy kind of way in contrast to the well-manicured and polished Gordon who sat bolt upright on the edge of the couch.

Still standing, Fox continued. 'I understand the media are already asking questions so you can expect contact from them too. The Commissioner will be making a statement this evening.'

'And what's *he* going to say?' Gordon asked.

'How long do you think they'll make us wait?' Finn asked calmly.

Fox chose to answer Finn first – he seemed to deserve it more. 'I can't tell you that. We just have to sit tight and wait.' Taking a deep breath, she then turned her attention to Gordon. 'The Commissioner will tell them what they need to know and what we want them to know.' Then to both men she said, 'We've assigned each of you a family liaison officer – Sam Reilly and Becky Thomas – they'll be here shortly and with you every step of the way. If you have any questions, if you need anything, just ask either Sam or Becky.'

Again, both men nodded. Gordon looked sceptically through his long lashes at her like he didn't really think she was up to the job while Finn sat quietly, twisting the wedding ring on his finger.

'Do you mind if I use your bathroom?' Fox asked, suddenly conscious of her bladder. She really needed to pee and, with the tension building, now was a good time to let the mood settle.

'Let me show you,' Williams offered and led her from the kitchen.

The house truly was an opulent statement of wealth. Pools of sunshine poured into the hall from the circular glass roof-lights overhead, bouncing warmth off the luxurious deep grain of the stained white-oak floor and reflecting in the chrome-and-glass console dressed with tall white lilies, their scent sweetly pungent. The downstairs bathroom was equally stylish and contemporary. Having wandered around Karin's home in Galway and established a certain impression of the woman, this contradiction was intriguing – and also very much at odds with her impression of Finn.

Curiosity piqued, she returned to the kitchen where the conversation in her absence had moved to golf. This, she knew, was Callaghan's tactic to relieve the tension and it rarely failed to work. He, Gordon and Williams were lightheartedly debating the merits of the recent success of the Ryder Cup team. Finn sat silent – it obviously wasn't his game.

'You don't play?' Fox asked.

'Jesus, no! I'd rather watch paint dry,' he said with a fleeting smile.

Fox used the moment to ask him about the last time he saw his wife.

'It was last Friday morning – she was leaving for work when I came down. She's normally well gone by the time I'm up.'

'How did she seem?'

'Fine. The usual really.'

'Had something delayed her?'

'No idea. I didn't ask and she didn't say.'

'Did she tell you her plans for the weekend?'

'Not really. She did say she was going to the West but that's about it.'

'Did she come back home before she left?'

'No – I don't think so anyhow – she usually just heads straight from work.'

'Would she go every weekend?'

'Not every one but most – well, maybe every other.'

'And what about you? Do you not travel with her?'

'Sometimes. Not often. It's her thing really. She loves the house. It's in the middle of bloody nowhere. She likes the quiet.'

'And did you hear from her during the day?'

'No.' He shrugged, looking straight at her, his eyebrows slightly furrowed. 'We don't really talk during the day.'

Fox nodded. 'And do you mind me asking what you did?'

'What do you mean?' he asked, lifting his chin ever so slightly.

'You – what about you? How did you spend your day?' She held his gaze for a moment longer than perhaps was necessary.

'Me? I spent the day here, in my studio.'

'All day?'

'Mostly. I'm working on a show,' he said with a quick glance at Tom Williams who had turned his attention away from Callaghan and Gordon. 'I started about ten and finished about seven.'

'No lunch?'

'No,' he answered with a hint of caution, glancing again towards Tom who gave him an encouraging nod. Finn ran a hand through his hair and sighed.

'I worked in the studio, ordered pizza.' He paused, throwing a quick glance at Callaghan whose interest in golf had now also waned. 'Check if you want. Domino's. I ordered the Meat Feast and a Coke.' He turned back to Fox.

'I worked through the afternoon – great work, if I'm honest – and about seven I finished up and washed. I heated the lasagna Aggie, she's our housekeeper, had left out for me, polished off the last of a bottle of wine and after that,' he paused with a shrug, 'I guess I fell asleep.'

'You fell asleep?' Fox repeated.

'Yep. I fell asleep.' Finn slapped his hands on his knees. 'That's about it. Wine does that to me. Sometimes. Sends me right out.'

'That's OK, Finn, you're allowed to sleep!' Fox quipped and, turning to Gordon, asked, 'And what about Sive, how was she? Anything out of the ordinary?'

'No.' Gordon dropped his eyes to the floor and coughed. 'My wife and I weren't speaking. We'd had an argument the night before and, well, she wasn't talking to me.'

'OK,' Fox replied, taking mental note. 'Can I ask what it was about?'

'I don't see how it's relevant. It was a stupid squabble, that's it. I slept in the spare room and left for work before she woke up. End of story. That's all you need to know.'

'I appreciate your situation, Mr Collins, really I do,' Fox responded with a don't-mess-with-me lift to her eyebrows, 'but let me be the judge of that, if you don't mind.'

'My apologies,' Gordon replied, suitably chastised. 'I actually can't be sure. Something trivial, aren't they always?'

'Do you fight often with your wife?'

'No more than most,' he defended himself, regretting, Fox was sure, his cocky approach to her questions.

Eager not to be late for her appointment with the Commissioner, she checked her watch, making sure she'd left enough time to take a look about the house. Right on cue, the doorbell rang and Tom left to answer it, only to return a few minutes later with both the assigned liaison officers, Becky and Sam.

Fox stood up, and after introductions had been made, said, 'Let's leave it at that for the moment.' Taking business cards from her pocket, she handed them to Finn and Gordon. 'It may be that the abductors will try to make contact with one or other of you. We'll need to be able to trace that call if it comes through, so we'll have to put a monitor on your mobile and land lines – is that OK?'

'Yes,' they replied in unison.

She turned to Tom. 'Same applies to Ms Bolger's office. We'll need to speak with whoever handles the switchboard and post.'

'That can be arranged,' Tom replied efficiently.

'So, what happens next?' Gordon asked.

'I suggest that Becky take you home. Sive may be trying to contact you so stay close to your phone. And, in the meantime, we'll keep going. Becky will talk you through the Commissioner's statement once it's ready to go and please don't talk to any reporters until we're ready. Is that OK?' She looked at each of them and nodded towards Becky and Sam.

Finn escorted them out. In the hall, she turned to him to ask, 'Do you mind if I take a look around before I go?'

'No, please do,' Finn acquiesced. 'I'll show you around.'

'I'll head and see you back at base, if that's OK?' Callaghan said to Fox before shaking hands with the men and leaving.

The house was truly stunning. It was as if she had stepped into the centerfold of an international design magazine. Walking from room to room, she couldn't help but notice the collectible furniture and gallery-worthy art works. This, by comparison to the warmth of the Galway cottage, was obviously the show home, the place Karin took people she needed to impress, or maybe intimidate. A combination of flamboyant wealth and elegant styling, the house was designed to trigger envy from the very first moment guests walked through the door, with comfort playing second fiddle to prestige.

She recognised a few names on the art works, including Finn's own.

'This is one of yours?' she asked, taking a step back to admire the only burst of colour in an otherwise neutral guest room.

'It is.'

'It's amazing.' Fox was genuinely impressed and tilted her head for a different perspective.

'Thanks,' he replied with a blush, 'Karin was, I mean is,' he stammered, 'my best customer.'

Fox let the error of his past tense pass without remark and they continued on the tour, moving from one room to the next: living room, billiard room, library, study, gym, cinema … the house went on forever. But, for all its splendour – the plush carpets, the sumptuous furnishings, lavish curtains and matching cushions – the house was devoid of any personality, saying everything and nothing at the same time. There were no stories or journeys on display, no parties or weddings or celebrations. No faces, no smiles, no people. It was a contemporary emptiness in stylish shades of grey.

Only when they reached the master bedroom did she get a sense of the woman she had met, albeit only in spirit, in Galway. Without denying the fashionable flair of the rest of the house, this room took it to the next level by adding colour and a little bit of romance. There were no lights in the ceiling, just an array of floor and table lamps that cast a warm hue even on this, an unseasonably warm and sunny autumn afternoon. Frames with photos of a man and child in varying degree of growing up dotted around the room, some replicated from the pictures she had seen on the walls in the cottage.

'Her dad,' Finn confirmed as she wondered, picking one up to take a closer look. 'He died not long after she graduated.'

'And her mum?' Fox asked.

'She left when Karin was much younger and never came back.'

'Left?'

'Yes. She's in the States somewhere, I think. Karin has two brothers though but she's lost touch – can't remember the last time she spoke to either of them.'

Fox nodded slowly.

Above the bed was a painting entitled *Love's First Kiss*.

'Yours, too?' Fox asked.

'Yep. That was the first painting she ever bought of mine.'

'You're really quite good.' Fox stood absorbing the emotion of the abstract image of two shapes facing each other, male hands resting gently on a female face that tilted to one side, eyes shut, blushing cheeks and scarlet lips.

'Don't sound so surprised!' He laughed self-consciously.

'Are you with a gallery?'

'Not yet, but I hope soon. I haven't really needed to up to now, but I've a show coming up at Solo and I'm hoping they'll represent me permanently.'

'Nice. So what's changed?' Fox asked casually.

'What do you mean?'

'Well, what's changed that you need it now?'

'Dunno,' he replied with a shrug and a pout. 'I just think it's time.'

'Well, with work like this you won't be long getting noticed. Good luck!' She crossed the room to the dressing table and pulled open the centre drawer.

'Do you mind?' she asked, taking out a purple-leather notebook so he could see it.

'Be my guest,' he said with a wave.

She opened what appeared to be an expenses record of sorts, last used six days earlier, a neat hand in blue ink filling the pages.

Returning it to the drawer, she picked up the wastebasket.

'Aggie cleans every day,' he said, explaining the emptiness.

Fox made a mental note to ask her about any discarded papers.

An oversized and well-used armchair sat in the corner with a fleece thrown over its arm, a table by its side and a tall freestanding lamp hanging over it. It had the feeling of a frequently occupied spot, the impressions on the cushions and dog-eared books on the table evidence of a much-loved corner. And Fox wasn't surprised, given its aspect in front of the full-length window and a view over the sea towards Howth Head.

'Her favourite chair?' she asked.

Finn nodded.

She moved into the ensuite.

'You don't share this room then?' she asked Finn who was standing at the door, knowing his answer would be no – there wasn't a hint of a man anywhere in this room.

'No,' Finn replied with a blush.

'Has that always been the case?'

'I suppose we just drifted into it. I like to work late and she likes to go to bed early so it just kind of happened.'

'So, where do you sleep?'

'My studio. It's on the other side of the house. I've set up a makeshift bedroom, nothing special and, well, that's where I live.'

An interesting choice of words, she thought. The other side of the house, as if they had split it in two: His and Hers.

Unconsciously he shifted from one foot to the other, uncomfortable she reckoned at the truth of their relationship being revealed. She checked her watch – if she didn't leave now she'd be late for her meeting. She'd have to come back – she was curious to see his studio.

They made their way back to the stairs.

'It must be amazing, living in a house as beautiful as this,' Fox said as they descended the stairs.

'I don't really notice it anymore. I'd be happy anywhere really.'

She eyed him sceptically, not believing him for a minute.

'Keep your phone on and let us know if you hear from her,' she told him.

'What are you going to be doing?' he asked.

'Looking for them,' she told him simply.

Tom Williams was waiting for her outside, leaning against her car whilst scrolling on his phone.

'That's a pretty comprehensive security system,' she remarked as she approached him, nodding towards the sensor-activated cameras. 'I didn't see anything like that at the cottage.'

'No. She never wanted or needed it over there or so we thought.' He sighed. 'As for this baby, we were only just beginning the upgrade here. It hasn't been commissioned yet but when it's done it'll have full digital capability. We're just testing it now. Another week or so and we'll be up and running properly.'

Fox took one of her cards from her pocket and handed it to him.

'You're staying here, right?'

'Yeah. I'll stay until, well, until whoever's got her makes contact.' He looked back at the house. 'One other thing … I didn't want to say anything in front of everyone and I'm not even sure it's relevant, but I'd best mention it to you anyway. A few weeks back Karin asked me to trace the source of an internal leak.'

'What kind of leak?'

'Someone disclosed details of the brewery deal to the media.'

'Was that the story printed as the exclusive in the *Indo*?'

Tom nodded.

'How sure are you that it was an internal source?'

'One hundred per cent. It had to have been. There was information handed over that could only have come from the inside.'

'And have you found out?'

'We have a pretty good idea where it came from – we just need to confirm who actually sent it – but we're close.'

'And?' Fox prompted.

'I'd rather not say, not until we're sure.'

'And I'd rather you did.'

Williams shrugged and sighed. 'We believe an email was sent from an Internet café in the city. The documents that were attached were highly confidential and only five people had access to them – Karin herself, Seán her business partner, her PA Nathan and Sophie, our head of communications.'

'Have you spoken to them about it?'

'No. Karin didn't want to approach any of them until we knew for sure who it was.'

'Even Seán?'

'Even Seán.'

'OK, well, let's leave it that way for the time being.'

Williams nodded.

'Keep me posted,' she said. 'As soon as you figure it out, let me know – and anything else you think of, doesn't matter how trivial, let me know.'

'Absolutely,' he promised, shaking her hand firmly.

'I'll meet you first thing tomorrow at the Spiro Capital office,' she said as she got into the car. 'Nine OK?'

'Suits me,' he said, closing the car door for her. 'Talk to you then, unless … how long do you think they'll wait?'

'If she has been abducted, I'd expect you to hear from them any time now, so let me know as soon as they do.'

'Will do,' he promised.

There seemed to be an awful lot going on for Karin Bolger between media leaks, threatening notes and now abduction, Fox thought. Was it all coincidence? She pulled away and waited for the gates to slowly slide open. Instinctively she glanced back at the house through the rear-view mirror. Standing at the living-room window, Finn was watching her leave. Fox wondered what was going through his head. He had been nervous, stressed almost, during their discussion but quite relaxed as they walked the house. He didn't seem the type to fret and she speculated if, like the cat with nine lives, he'd landed on his feet.

Chapter 4

The ransom demand took two days to come and, just like the threatening notes before it, it was old school. Posted from the city centre the day before and curiously addressed to Karin's PA Nathan Smyth, it was typed on plain white paper with no significant distinguishing features. It was a curious thing to do, Fox thought, to send it to Karin's assistant and not either of the husbands. And if there was any doubt before, it clearly identified Karin as the mark, so making Sive the unlucky bystander: wrong place, wrong time. Simply written, its message was very clear: a five-million-euro transfer along with assurance that the brewery would remain open and operational. It was a ridiculous demand, made apparently in support of the Justice for the Workers campaigners. Whatever about the money, any assurance about keeping the brewery open would be worthless and doubtless temporary. And what exactly, Fox wondered, were they going to do with the five million euro if their supposed objective was to keep the brewery open? Was this nothing more than an aggressive display of tokenism or a genuine opportunistic ransom? What was the ransom deal-breaker: the brewery remaining open or the money being delivered? And who would make the call to keep the brewery open but Karin? And how could she make such a promise while they had her? Complicated and bizarre, it didn't make sense.

Aside from the brewery workers, Fox was curious to know who else had it in for Karin. She wasn't, it seemed, short of enemies. Clinical and cutthroat, she had over the years upset more than her fair share of people, some as losers to the deals she won and others as excess to requirement in companies she'd bought. She filled column inches in the daily newspapers with the constant stream of lawsuits, objections and complaints, sufficient to demand an in-house legal team as well as Tom as head of security. Up until now her adversaries were visible, out in the open and vocal. They would attack her in the courts or the papers or at times in the political arena – but this, this was different – this was personal and took things to another level.

Fox's meeting with Tom and the rest of Karin's team in the offices of Spiro Capital took the best part of the day. Taking up the top two floors of an unassuming glass-and-concrete office building on the periphery of the Financial Services Centre, it was not what either Fox or Callaghan had expected. Probably one of the last blocks to go up, in its day it was more than likely described as state-of-the-art but today it just looked a little tired.

They took the lift from the soulless entrance lobby and Tom was waiting for them when it arrived on the seventh floor. Passing along the timber-clad corridors, with news of her disappearance only two days old, it wasn't surprising that they were greeted by a hushed almost scared atmosphere filled with whispers and nervous looks.

Tom escorted them into Karin's corner office. From up

here Karin had a perfect view over the best parts of the low-rise city below.

There was nothing on her desk apart from the plain black mouse mat, wireless mouse, the cable from her recently unplugged laptop and a desktop phone-charger.

'Is she always this neat or was she planning to move out?' Fox asked.

'Nope, that's Karin. Everything has its place and, besides, we have a strictly enforced clean-desk policy – everything must be locked away before home time. So much of what we do relies on absolute confidentiality.'

Nodding her understanding, Fox noted that, like Wild Winds, the office was a contradiction to the homely Silene Cottage. She sat into the chair and pulled at the drawers in the pedestal under the desk, but they were locked.

'Can we get a key?' she asked.

'Do you really need to do that?'

'Afraid so.'

Tom left and returned a couple of minutes later with a master key.

'You know, I'd like keep this visit quiet,' he said nervously as if the words had been teetering on his lips since he'd greeted them but he'd been too scared to let them out. 'As head of security it's my job to be discreet.'

Fox laughed up at him. 'Seriously? Tom, there isn't an icicle's hope in hell that this will be kept quiet. Your boss has been kidnapped. Karin Bolger is probably one of *the* most hated women in our country at the moment. Do you think, even if we wanted to, we could keep this quiet? If it helps I won't tell anyone I looked in her drawers, how about that?' She gave him a sarcastic grin before pulling out the first drawer.

Everyone had an opinion about Karin and not all of it complimentary. Focused, determined, scary, hardnosed, ballsy, brave, outspoken and plenty more forthright adjectives were offered up, but what Fox extracted from the often frank conversations with Karin's colleagues was that she was both fair and generous to those who worked for her, and in return she demanded their respect and loyalty. But all seemed to agree they wouldn't like to cross her. Even Nathan, who as a faithful assistant defended her honour with gusto, said she wasn't someone he'd like to get on the wrong side of. In fact, he'd rather extract his own teeth than cross her on a bad day.

A tall handsome lad dressed in a sharp suit with a slick haircut, Nathan surprised Fox the moment he literally opened his mouth. By his own admission he was misplaced in an office full of private-school graduates, but he, in his own words 'worked me bollix off to get this job and deserve it more than half the posh-boy arseholes in here'. And he was right – his thick Dublin accent stood out like a blizzard in July but then so did he. The only one in his family to go to college and his mother's pride and joy, Nathan was unique. He had to work harder than most to be accepted in this corporate world and took nothing for granted.

'I get on with Karin,' he told them. 'It's hard bloody work sometimes but we actually have a bit of a laugh. She can be a tough ol' bitch, but then no one is perfect.' He shrugged. 'I understand her. I know what she wants and I don't muck about. She hates waffle so I get straight to the point, she fuckin' hates excuses so I don't give her any, and she can spot a fudger a mile off so, well,' he finished with a disarming grin, 'I say it the way it is. She appreciates honesty.'

'And what about the others?' Fox asked, indicating the rest of his colleagues beavering away in the offices beyond.

'Anyone around her who would do her any harm?'

'Harm? Depends what you mean. Would anyone bitch about her behind her back or online? Plenty! As I said, she can be a real cow and not everyone appreciates her style. She does things her way and not a lot of people like that. But this? Like, kidnapping – that's mental shit, that is, and no, I don't think so. And, anyway, none of them here would have the balls to take her on.'

'Anything out of the ordinary happen over the last few days?' Fox asked.

'Nope, nothin' strange at all,' he replied but his eyes glanced away from hers.

She could see he was ambitious and knew which side his bread was buttered. He wasn't a snitch but he was holding something back. One thing Fox prided herself on was her instinct and it told her there was more to Nathan than he was letting on.

Against the advice of the police, Finn paid the ransom.

'*Just send the goddamn money, it's not like you can't afford it!*' Gordon had shouted at him as he hummed and hawed in the plush boardroom of Spiro Capital the morning the ransom demand arrived. Delivered with the daily post, Nathan had opened it along with all the other letters. He did as he was told and called Tom as soon as he realised what it was. He too sat in the boardroom alongside Finn, looking like he didn't belong and would rather be anywhere else but there.

And Gordon was right. Finn could well afford the money, or rather Karin could. But Finn's reluctance to fork out wasn't because he didn't want to or didn't have access to that amount of money. It was that he didn't know who to listen to. On the one side the official Garda position was absolute:

we do not pay terrorist demands and that was exactly what this was, a terrorist demand. On the other side he had Gordon snarling like a starving hound – who nevertheless hadn't yet offered to contribute even though the demand was as much his as it was Finn's.

And then there was Williams, a trusted advisor who for all his promises to protect and counsel was useless, telling Finn this was his call.

'Finn,' he advised, 'no one can guarantee that they will let either Karin or Sive go free. Or that they'll be released unharmed. Moreover, there's no guarantee that they won't demand more money in a week's time. So it's a gamble, whatever you decide.'

Finn looked at him with equal measures of confusion and disappointment. He'd been sure Tom would know what to do and would tell him straight out, but it seemed he was wrong.

'But what if it was you, Tom? If you had to make this decision, what would you do?' he asked from the stylishly ergonomic chair behind his wife's desk.

'Me?'

'Yes, if you were *me*.'

Williams shrugged. 'I can't answer that, Finn. This has to be your decision.'

'Tom, please!' he begged.

Fox felt for him. With so much at stake it was a tough choice.

'Can you stop me? Paying it, I mean?' he asked her, like it was a lifeline or his excuse. *I wanted to but they wouldn't let me …*

'No, I can't stop you,' she replied, 'but I can advise you strongly that it is not the right thing to do and we can't and won't support any such decision.'

'All right. All right. Just give some space, please,' he begged.

They left him alone in the boardroom, looking down on the busy quays below. It took him almost half an hour to decide.

'Pay the ransom,' he instructed.

'What took you so long?' Gordon demanded. 'She's your wife, for God's sake!'

'Well, I didn't see you offering to pay.'

'I can't afford it and you know it.'

'No,' Finn sneered, 'you can't, can you, and we all know why, don't we, Gordon?' Fox noticed Gordon visibly recoil. So Finn had hit a nerve. Parking the questions that instantly came to mind – now wasn't the time – she watched the exchange There was apparently no love lost between the men.

'It's funny,' Finn remarked quietly as he and Fox descended in the lift. 'You think it'd be a no-brainer. But when it's you, when you have to decide and they're telling you no and you don't know ...' he took a deep breath and let it out slowly, 'you actually begin to doubt yourself.'

'Well, thankfully it's not every day you have to make that call.'

'Yeah, and I don't ever want to have to do it again.'

'It's done now and hopefully you won't have to do it again, but you have left yourself and Karin exposed. Now they know you'll pay. There's no reason for them not to ask for more or even take her again.'

His head dropped.

'Are you *sure* you want to do this?'

'I'll have to take that chance.'

The doors of the lift opened into the lobby.

'What helped you decide?' she asked.

'I asked myself what would Karin do. And then I did the exact opposite.'

It was a harsh truth. Seán Cusack, Karin's business partner, had quietly remarked that she would not be happy with the proposed payout, expecting the authorities to be focusing on hunting the bastards down not paying them off. That was why he wasn't happy for Spiro Capital to put up the money. She wouldn't do it for him and he knew it.

'That's business,' Seán had said with a shrug.

Fox and Callaghan had met him in the sales suite on the eighth floor the morning before and, regardless of which side of the fence you sat on, Fox had to admit the development of Kings Brewery would a spectacular transformation of the area.

'Talk me through the project,' she'd said.

Seán, happy to oblige, led them through to the conference room. It was laid out like a cinema with comfortable tiered seating. He invited them to take a seat, then taking up the controls pressed a button on the wall and immediately the windows darkened. He pressed another button and the large screen at the back of the room came to life.

A deep voice from all sides filled the room. *'Welcome to Kings Brewery, a new dimension in city living.'* On screen a fully animated virtual production of the development, as close to reality as you could imagine, began to unfold. It walked through buildings that existed today only on paper, showed real people enjoying a leisurely lunch and shopping in restaurants and malls that weren't yet there and lazing in imagined parks on sunny afternoons. The movie created an experiential journey so incredible that if Fox had the money she would have bought into it there and then herself. The power of the imagination, Cusack remarked, as quadrant by quadrant, zone after zone, the voiceover took them on a futuristic and breathtaking journey through the development.

As the movement on screen slowed down to the scene of a thriving village going about its daily lives, it was down to business. Timed to perfection with a soulful springtime soundtrack in the background, Cusack stepped up to the front. And, as if they were the targeted investors, he delivered the rehearsed speech that ordinarily would close the deal. Planning permission, he said, was secure. The project was ready to go. The site was vast, the opportunity huge and the returns considerable. So convincing was the presentation that Fox almost stood up and applauded.

'That's incredible. It felt so – so real,' she effused, amazed at what technology could produce.

'Thank you.' Cusack accepted her words with a small bow. 'If only others had your enthusiasm. This really is a game-changer for the area and, yes, there will be jobs lost at the brewery but the number of new jobs this will create overall will be treble that amount.'

'So, how many bricklayers or electricians or carpenters do you think you can make out of the guys at Kings?' Callaghan asked. 'People don't like change and this is an entire community obliterated. Sure it creates a fresh start for new communities to grow, but that will take years, generations potentially, and what are they supposed to do in the meantime? The brewery workers are nothing more than collateral damage to this fantastic project. Are you surprised they're pissed off?'

Cusack remained at the top of the room, the springtime

soundtrack sounding ridiculous as Callaghan's remarks hung heavy in the air. But he wasn't fazed. He'd heard the arguments before – he and Karin, along with their media people, had rehearsed the potential questions and answers to death.

'We could dress this up any way you like,' Cusack replied pragmatically. 'But the reality is the brewery is relocated to Dundalk, reducing its overheads significantly and thus securing its future. Appropriate staff, as many as possible, will be retrained and offered new positions at the new location. This is progress.' He opened his arms wide. 'The alternative,' he continued in a sombre almost patronising tone, 'is that we do nothing, let the plant continue on its current trajectory and it'll close anyway within a year, eighteen months tops.'

'So I get that it's a no-brainer, but what would it take to delay the project?' Fox asked, convinced by his pitch.

Cusack sniggered at first – then, realising she was serious, his laugh grew deeper and stronger.

'We can't do that!' he snorted. 'We have people relying on us. Investors for a start, contractors, architects … we've gone too far to stop now … well, certainly not without incurring hefty fines.'

'What about for Karin? What if it means getting her back?'

'And then what? We get things back up and running only to have them return to take her again. I don't think that's a very wise strategy, do you?'

'No. No, I don't. But my objective is to get both women back safe and as such I have to look at the options.'

'Well, delaying *that* is definitely not one of them,' he said, pointing at the rotating million-euro virtual model on screen.

As an answer it was a resounding no. She had no words. She wanted to tell him that he had a responsibility, but he stood defiant at the top of the room, his hands held casually in his pockets, confident in the knowledge that she could do nothing.

But Fox had other ideas.

'I'm afraid, Mr Cusack, that you might not have a choice.'

Chapter 5

The apartment was like ice. She hadn't thought to let her neighbour know she would be back, albeit temporarily, and ask her to go in and turn on the heat. Throwing the bag of groceries on the counter, she peeled back the film of the ready meal and stuck it in the oven. She hated the microwave – things never tasted the same – they always had that nuked, slightly soggy not-quite-cooked texture.

Looking around the familiar environment that was her home, she sighed, relieved not to have succumbed to the lure of Airbnb. Although tempting, she couldn't face the logistics that seemed to come with the renting territory. Maybe it was her instinct telling her she'd be back sooner than she thought. Whatever it was, as she pulled the cork on the wine and poured a glass before hitting the shower she was glad she didn't bother. Taking a leisurely first gulp, she kicked off her shoes and headed for her room, closed the curtains and switched on the bedside lamp. Connecting her phone to the speakers, she ran her finger over her short playlist, selected the edgy Paolo Nutini to match her mood, and turned up the volume. Stripping off her clothes, she stepped into the steaming shower. There was nothing quite like that first warm spray of water when it hits your body following days of drought. It had been a long and busy week travelling between Galway and Dublin and she was starved for sleep. She thanked God for the Dunnes around the corner from the station – at least she'd been able to run in during the week and buy fresh underwear.

But despite the cathartic cascade, her mind refused to stop and still ticked over furiously. Over forty-eight hours had passed since Finn had made the transfer to pay the ransom. Twenty-four hours after that, Spiro Capital had released a media statement to the effect that progress at the brewery was delayed due to technical difficulties at the site with the completion date postponed indefinitely. It might not have been true but it bought Fox time, the only compromise Cusack was willing to accept.

And the media ran with a report hour after hour, using new words to say the same thing over and over. They had camped out at Karin's home and office and were calling the station daily looking for a source. But, despite the promise of release, there was still no sign of Karin and Sive. Patience was wearing thin and results eagerly sought.

There was as much work in managing her peers as there was in working the case itself. Fox was relying on help from wherever she could take it, to do jobs she wished she could at least oversee herself but just didn't have the time.

'The price you pay for promotion,' Callaghan had teased and he was right.

With daily briefings, progress meetings, reports to write, business cases to draft, there was little time left to do what she enjoyed most: investigate. Even now, despite her lack of sleep, she was tempted to head back in to her Dublin-based incident room, but her body screamed *no!* Letting the shower spill down till the water ran cold, she wished time to stand still for just a few hours.

Refilling her glass before burning her fingers on the foil dinner tray, she curled into the sofa and switched on the telly. Once upon a time she would have proclaimed that this was the life, but her head was still running the race and her feet were itching to do the same. Even Graham Norton couldn't distract her.

She checked her watch. It was only eight o'clock and, accepting it was pointless trying to ignore her conscience, she got up to retrieve her notebook from the hallstand. Putting Graham on mute, she didn't want to turn him off completely, she took a sip of her wine and forkful of her pasta bake, plucked the pencil from its noose and began her list. She had learnt over the years that there was nothing like a good list to help clear her head. As the page filled line by line she could feel her shoulders relax and the stress transfer from pencil to page. When she was done there were twenty-two things for her to do: the first, *Call Ken Stanley* and the last, *Get Some Sleep*.

A sergeant at the station local to the brewery, Ken Stanley was a terrier. Having worked with him a few years back, she knew that if anyone would know anything about the demonstrations and protestors it would be him, and she guessed he'd be only too happy to help. Given the activity over the last few months, he probably had a few of them already in his sights. Neither, she reckoned, would he mind her phoning him so late on a Friday evening.

And she was right.

'Thanks for doing this for me, Ken – you're a star,' she told him once he'd agreed to pull together a *Who's Who* report on the demonstrators for her. He knew some but not all of them.

'No problem, Foxie,' he said, making her cringe, a telling

sign of how long it had been since they last spoke.

As a young Garda in uniform it was a name everyone tried to christen her with and she despised it. Over her career, with great effort she managed to stifle it, which wasn't easy and had at times caused her much grief as colleagues took offence at her offence – *sure, weren't they were only messin' with her?* But she was shrewd enough to know it was the kind of name that had the potential to stick and pay her future ambitions no favours. She wondered if Stanley remembered and was using it on purpose. Nevertheless, he was doing her a big favour, so he could call her what he liked.

'Anything to help,' he said, 'but to be honest I'd be really surprised if they had anything to do with this. They're just a bunch of angry workers looking to keep their jobs – sure, half of them are over fifty, the brewery's all they know – they don't have it in them.'

'Yeah, I kinda think that myself,' she confided, 'but there must be a link back to her somewhere. Whoever did this knows her and knows her well.'

'Well, leave it with me. If there's a connection here, I'll track it.'

It was the truth – she didn't believe the kidnapping was a stunt pulled by the campaigners – they couldn't be that stupid. But whoever did take the women claimed to have done so in support of them, so the link had to be found. And no better man than Ken Stanley to find it, whatever *it* might be.

The case needed a break or at least something meaty enough to get them going. The door-to-door had come up with nothing, which wasn't surprising given the remote location. There weren't that many doors to knock on. And they were still waiting for a full report on the traffic-camera footage recovery. Located at almost every junction on all the major and some minor routes across the entire road network, it made it almost impossible for a car to travel anywhere in the county unnoticed – they just needed to know what they were looking for.

What they did have was footage from the service station only twenty miles from Dublin. As soon as the manager heard about the abduction he had called in. She was one of the regulars who would come in on a Friday evening to stock up on coffee and snacks, hoping to make the rest of their journey without stopping. He liked to spot and classify the celebrities who came into his station. Apparently he'd served some great ones over the years, Bill Clinton being the best and 'yer one off the news', whoever that was, being his least favourite – apparently she was a real bitch. Karin wasn't on his A list, more like his C. Often chatty, never rude, she bought the same things every week: a large skinny cappuccino, a banana and a cereal bar, always the same with a full tank of petrol and a smile. He liked her and wanted to do his bit to find her. This was his contribution, the tape from her last visit.

Her usual stop en route to the West, the silent footage watched her as always fill the car first then go into the store, make a coffee at the self-service counter, pick up the banana and the bar then go to the till. The only unusual thing about this visit was that this time she had Sive with her. Both ladies were clearly visible on the small screen happily chatting, completely unaware of what was to follow.

Fox, still scribbling and adding notes to her list, felt her eyes grow heavy. She was tired, her body fighting her brain for sleep. Setting her notebook to the side she curled her legs underneath her, let her head drop to the cushion and closed her eyes. Somewhere between being asleep and awake she thought of Oisín and let the memory of his smile take her the rest of the way to sleep. Even though he was gone now almost five years, she missed him every day, but more at moments like this when tired and worn out she wished to feel his strong arms wrapped around her shoulders, his soft lips on her cheek and hear the beautiful lilt of his voice caress and warm her aching heart.

Chapter 6

'Itinerant bastards,' he muttered to himself as he stepped out of the jeep and into the pouring rain, the ground soft and thick beneath his feet. This was as far as he would go by car – he didn't fancy getting stuck in this muddy sludge. He hadn't been up this way in months. The fields were waterlogged from the recent rains and the lane almost impassable. Why anyone would want to mess around here was beyond him. It was Bridget in the post office that first alerted him, telling him that Joe from the pub had passed last week and saw lights over this way. At the time he paid no heed to her – she was known to be a nosey old bat sticking her nose into everyone's business – but then Mattie from the garage said he had seen a car up here yesterday. It was the last thing he needed right now what with his wife, Eileen, coming down so ill and the harvest as good as washed out. He was stressed enough as it was and could have done without the extra worry, but in the end he decided to put the niggle at the back of his head to rest.

'Probably those young wans up here ridin' again,' he huffed.

He'd caught them at it last summer, filthy bastards. As long as it wasn't those Jesus freaks – he'd heard stories about them coming in and setting up altars and sacrificing donkeys, attracted by the ancient so-called 'fairy forts' and standing stones around this area on the Cork–Kerry border.

'Better not be them,' he said to himself as he prised his wellington-clad boot from the mud. 'I'll feckin' sacrifice *them*!'

He wished he'd come up a bit earlier when the light was better. Cautiously he made his way up the lane to the small stone building. One of those old abandoned cottages, it was on a part of his land he couldn't do much with – it wasn't even up to sheep. Letting it lie was his only option for the time being anyway. But squelching up the marshy overgrown lane, he admonished himself for letting it get this bad.

His heart sank when he saw that Mattie was right. The muck-splashed bushes, broken reeds and tyre grooves in the mud were sure signs there had indeed been someone around here – up to no good he was sure – why else would anyone come to this muck-fest other than to cause trouble? And how, he wondered, had they managed to get in and out without getting stuck? Stopping short of the cottage itself, he saw that a path had been trampled into the reeds and grass approaching the door which no longer hung off the frame but was closed tight and snug. Light was fading as dusk approached.

He tried to recall if he had anything close to a weapon in the jeep. He took a step closer to the door to see if he could hear anything. The windows were still blocked up and he thought about pushing the door to see if it opened but taking one more step forward and seeing a new lock on the door changed his mind. Maybe it was his imagination or his mind playing tricks, but he thought as he turned to leave that he heard a whine, like an animal in need of attention.

Stepping up his pace, he hotfooted it back to the jeep, slipping and sliding in the mud, pulled his mobile from his pocket and dialled 999.

They surrounded the house, armed and silent. Dressed in black, they melted into the darkness as skillfully they closed in. Like night itself, they wrapped themselves around the house. Quietly, slowly, they edged nearer, their leader using only hand-signals to communicate with his team. Arms primed, they readied themselves to make the final move. All they needed was the go-ahead. Fox and Callaghan stood a distance away and waited. Without realising it, Fox held her breath, waiting, listening but hearing nothing. She dropped her head and closed her eyes, hoping the darkness would heighten her senses. She didn't move a muscle, but her heart thumped furiously, fuelled by the adrenaline that surged like a dam released through her veins.

This had to be it. Come on! she silently encouraged.

Callaghan stood behind her, holding on to his earpiece – she could feel his breath on her neck and willed him to say the words. Finally …

'They're in position,' he whispered.

Fox held her breath.

'They're going in.' he said.

Instantly the night burst alive with shouts, loud bangs and heavy thuds. They could see nothing from where they were, but the sounds were deafening, heightened by the darkness in this place at the back end of she didn't know where. The seconds passed in what felt like hours, waiting for the all-clear to approach.

'*Clear!*'

'*Clear!*'

'*Clear!*'

And then almost immediately the urgent words she'd hoped for …

'*In here!*'

Fox hurried up to the cottage, Callaghan at her heels.

She looked pathetic, lying on the floor, her knees tucked up to her chin, still dressed in her designer shift dress with her pearls wrapped tight round her neck and her face black with dirt. Flesh-tone channels made by rivers of tears crossed her cheeks as she looked up and squinted into the bright torchlight. Her tied hands were cuffed to the leg of a steel-frame bench that had been bolted to the wall. Her stockings were loosed and torn at the knees and beside her sat an empty stainless-steel dog bowl.

Her parched lips moved but nothing came out of her mouth while her red eyes blinked wildly. She was in a bad way. As soon as her eyes focused and she realised who was standing in front of her and why, she started to cry.

'Thank God,' she whispered, looking up at the Emergency Response Unit team leader, who bent down to release her hands. 'Thank you.'

Carefully he helped her up. Unsteady on her feet, she swayed, but he held her up. Karin Bolger let her head fall onto his shoulder and sobbed. Instinctively he put an arm around her and hushed her gently. Seconds later the ambulance crew pushed through, taking her into their care.

Fox could see the outline of a crude doorway through the gloom.

'Did you check that other room?' she asked the ERU leader.

'Yes. Some piles of excrement visible. Human. No one there but …' He moved his headlamp to the opposite side of the room.

An overturned dog bowl and a set of black cable-ties that hung empty but closed came into view, attached to what looked like a handrail coming out from the wall.

Fox sighed, the euphoria of the find instantly losing its edge.

Taking a moment, she swallowed and approached Karin who, wrapped in a foil blanket, sat slumped on the bench.

'Karin, you're safe now,' she assured her, kneeling down so she could catch her eyes. 'We're going to take care of you.'

Unable to speak, Karin's head, heavy on her shoulders, nodded weakly.

Trying to conceal the urgency in her voice, Fox asked, 'Karin, where is Sive?'

The ERU leader and Callaghan were standing by, listening intently.

Karin croaked, her throat as dry as her lips.

'What happened to Sive, Karin?'

'She … ran …' Karin managed.

'But she was tied up too, wasn't she, Karin?'

Karin nodded and whimpered.

'Did someone free her?'

Karin's chin sank to her chest and her eyes closed.

'Karin!'

Her eyelids flickered then opened.

'Who freed Sive, Karin?'

'She did,' she croaked.

Fox hesitated. Karin was clearly in no fit state to answer questions, but some were vital.

'Karin, when did Sive escape? How long ago?'

'Yesterday … the day before … I don't know,' she sobbed weakly, her voice barely audible.

Fox's heart sank. If Sive had got away they would have

heard by now. Did she have an accident? Had she been caught by the kidnappers? If so, why hadn't they brought her back here?

One of the ambulance team spoke up abruptly. 'I'm sorry – we need to take her now.'

'Yes, of course.' Fox rose to her feet.

'We'll conduct a search outside immediately, ma'am,' said the ERU officer.

'I didn't catch your name?'

'Sergeant Keith Murphy,' he said and, ducking his head under the low lintel, left the cottage.

Fox and Callaghan followed him outside, then stepped aside as Karin was carried past on a stretcher, her eyes closed.

They stood and watched as, using headlamps and torches, the team began to scour the area around the cottage.

Callaghan shook his head. 'It's impossible, Fox – it's just too dark – they can complete the search in the area around the cottage but they'll have to wait till morning to go farther afield.'

'We can't wait,' Fox grumbled.

Murphy approached.

'Can you get some lamps out here?' Fox asked. 'To extend the search.'

'By the time we get the lights it'll be almost dawn.' Murphy argued. 'We can get a full team here first thing.'

'That might be too late. If she's here we need to find her. Now. She may have had an accident. I want her found tonight.'

'Yes, ma'am,' Murphy replied, knowing it was pointless arguing with her, and left.

'We need to secure the area,' Fox said to Callaghan. 'And get forensics out here asap – we need to process this site before it rains again.'

'With this many people tramping around in the dark, it's probably messed up already,' he said with a grimace.

'True. I'll follow Karin to the hospital,' she said. 'You stay here. I'll call Becky and have her meet me there with Finn.'

'What about Gordon?'

Fox hesitated, trying to formulate in her head the best way to tell him that they had Karin but not Sive.

'He'll want to come here, you know that, don't you?' Callaghan said. 'Well, I would anyway.'

Fox nodded. 'We'll let him,' she decided, 'if that's what he wants. I'll talk to Becky and see how he responds. I'll keep you posted.'

Being so far from Dublin, they took her to the University Hospital in Tralee. Fox arrived there amid a flurry of activity. Knowing who they had in their care, there was a mix of overexcited urgency and fear about what state Karin was in. Fox briefed security as well as the hospital management team, advising them to appoint a spokesperson and prepare for a media influx. She instructed them neither to confirm nor deny Karin's presence. It was essential that the families were properly informed before they put anything out to the media and they still hadn't managed to contact Gordon. He wasn't answering either his mobile or landline and a patrol car was waiting for him at his house.

Fox met Finn at the hospital door as soon as he arrived and took him straight to the nurses' station where she introduced him to the attending doctor.

'I'm Dr Ita O'Brien – I'll be looking after your wife over the next few days,' she told him with a sympathetic but tired smile that, despite the dark circles, seemed to reach her eyes.

She was young, younger than Fox anyway, and attractive

too even in those god-awful oversized blue scrubs. Fox knew a thing or two about working late and long hours, but doubted she'd have the stamina or confidence to care for people after a fourteen or fifteen-hour shift.

'How is she?' Finn asked, almost tearful.

'She's deeply traumatised and dehydrated,' Dr O'Brien told him, 'but we don't think she'll suffer any long-term physical damage. How she copes emotionally, we'll just have to wait and see. We've given her a sedative and we'll monitor her through the rest of the night, but we're happy she'll make a full recovery in no time.'

Finn returned the reassuring smile and let out a deep and long sigh of relief.

'Any news on Sive?' he asked then, turning to Fox who shook her head.

'Not yet,' she replied, offering nothing more.

'Can I sit with my wife?' he asked the doctor.

'Absolutely,' she replied. 'She's right here. We're going to move her to a room shortly but for the moment she's in here.'

She led him into a curtained cubicle only a few feet away from the nurses' station.

'Can we have a word in private?' Fox asked when the doctor returned.

'Certainly,' she replied, pointing to the emergency department manager's office.

'I don't think I need to tell you how sensitive this situation is,' Fox told her once the door was closed. 'Karin has been through an extremely traumatic experience, and, for the time being and until we have a better idea about what happened, I'd appreciate if you could keep the details of her condition confidential.'

'It goes without saying. We'll move her to a private room the minute one becomes free. We'll take good care of her and she'll be safe here, I promise.'

'I'm sure she will but, just to be sure, we'll have a Garda on duty at her door round the clock.'

First light came and with it an exhausted Fox arrived back to the scene, armed with coffee and day-old doughnuts – it was all they had left in the last petrol station she'd passed.

The floodlights were still on as she approached, their glare visible through the trees for miles while they continued their search.

She had called Callaghan from the car as she left the hospital but there was still no sign of Sive. Gordon, he said, was at the scene.

She took the car as far as she could and pulled in behind one of the Garda vans.

Gordon was sitting in the front of the Garda 4X4 nearest to the scene. Fox got into the driver's seat beside him and offered him one of the coffees in the tray.

'It's probably a bit cold by now, but it might help keep you awake,' she said.

'Thanks,' he said quietly.

'Where's Becky?' she asked, looking into the empty back seat.

'No idea. She got out about twenty minutes ago.'

Fox nodded and took a sip of her coffee.

They sat in silence, watching the activity outside.

'How's Karin?' he eventually asked.

'She's good. Traumatised and a bit bruised, but she's OK. She's asked to be transferred to the Saol Private Clinic in Dublin.'

'Doesn't surprise me – only the best for our Karin, eh? Did she say what happened?'

'Not really. She wasn't able – she could barely speak – and I didn't ask much. She's really not in any fit state. We'll have to wait but I'm hoping later today we'll be able to speak to her properly.'

He nodded and stared out the car window.

'You don't have to be here, you know,' Fox told him gently. 'We can keep you informed by phone.'

'I do have to. I want to be here when you find her.'

As the darkness brightened and the new day dawned, more personnel began to arrive. The view from the jeep was depressing. Red-and-white-striped tape surrounded the derelict cottage which was swarming with officials wrapped head to toe in disposable white body suits. In the field beyond, through the galvanised steel gate, Gardaí slowly combed the marshy field, and beyond into the trees dogs sniffed and scoured.

'Don't you want to help?' she asked, slicing the tension, intrigued by Gordon's lack of desire to participate. If it were her partner out there no one would stop her digging back the undergrowth.

'Not really. I'm afraid of what I might find,' he replied, calmly sipping his coffee which she knew for sure was at this stage stone cold. His stare remained focused but his hand trembled when he lifted the cup to his lips. He was scared.

'She might not even be here,' Fox told him, feeling the need to be positive despite the circumstances. 'Karin says she ran. She might have got away.'

He shook his head. 'Nope. She's here all right. I can feel it.'

As soon as he said it her whole body filled with dread and she had to admit she felt it too. She let the previous hush settle back in, his breathing heavy and slow, and watched and waited as the minutes ticked by.

'Today is our wedding anniversary,' he said bluntly, taking Fox by surprise. 'We've been together twenty-two years.'

She wasn't sure if she should congratulate or commiserate with him so she didn't say anything, but felt her cheeks flush as the uncomfortable tension heightened in the car.

When it happened, she knew by the formal nod of the Garda's head that they'd found her body. Instinctively she looked at Gordon. He'd seen it too. His head dropped and eyes closed.

'Stay here,' she told him.

She got out of the car and trekked across the field in the direction of the activity.

Face upwards, fully clothed and partially covered by the falling leaves, she lay in a shallow ditch. Fox had seen some pretty gruesome crime scenes in her time but this was one of the saddest and most depressing. Vermin had already started to pick at her fragile body that had lain, Fox guessed, for at least two days in the soft dirt. Her heart immediately reached out to Gordon and how he would react when he saw her. Feeling an urgent need to protect him, she turned in the direction of her car only to find him standing silently behind her, his eyes brimming with tears.

Standing on the edge of the ditch, he wept.

'Take her out, please, take her out of there!' he begged, moving to go down to her.

'We can't, Gordon,' she said, grabbing him as he pushed past, holding his arm tight. 'I'm so sorry.' She searched for the right words that would explain without sounding heartless. *We need to gather evidence, the coroner needs to process her*, just didn't cut it.

'At least cover her up,' he whispered, turning away.

'We will, I promise,' Fox assured him and, still holding on to him, she placed her arm around his back and tried to lead him away.

But he wouldn't be moved, as if his feet had rooted to the ground. His upper body went to move but his feet just wouldn't budge. Gently he swayed like a reed in the breeze, forwards and back, until eventually he doubled over, his chin almost touching his knees. His grief was a quiet one. No sounds came from his mouth which was opened wide, his eyes shut tight while his arms formed a cross with bunched fists in front of his chest. Around him everyone stood still and stared and then, as if granting him a moment of privacy, averted their eyes to the ground. Overhead birds sang in the trees whose softly swaying leaves seemed to whisper a mournful melody.

She watched Gordon watch them set up the tent to conceal Sive's body and preserve the scene. He would have better days, she thought to herself, leaving him in the care of Becky so she could turn her attention to the crime scene.

The frequent autumn showers had washed away any potential clues that might have been there. And, while the sodden ground still held the impressions of footprints and tyre tracks, most of the detail was gone, unable to hold its shape in the soft melted muck.

Fox walked the house, inside and out, inspecting every detail – the newly hung door, the filthy second room, the freshly sealed windows and the newly installed handrail and steel-frame bench that had helped contain the women.

And what the rain took away on the outside, it offered up on the inside: obvious footprints, size eleven, she guessed, with a definite impression from the soles of runners or well-worn walking shoes. It wasn't much but at least it was something, she acknowledged, taking a snap of it with her phone. She knew forensics would scour the area for the micro-evidence but it would take time to process so for the moment this was a start.

Looking around and taking stock of what was a very well-planned set-up, she asked herself just how had they, whoever *they* were, been able to set all this up without being noticed?

She looked at her watch. It was only eleven and, although anxious to get to the hospital in the hope of being able to speak with Karin, she would wait for the coroner to arrive to get her first assessment.

'She's on her way,' Callaghan told her when she asked how long she'd be.

In preparation Fox took a pair of disposable white overalls from the boot of her car and pulled them on over her jeans. This was going to be messy.

As efficient as ever, Amanda Stynes arrived and greeted everyone as if what she was about to see was normal. Dressed head to toe in disposable overalls, she carefully climbed into the ditch and disappeared into the tent.

While Fox waited patiently for Amanda to make her first-sight assessment, others around her had begun to dismantle the lights and pack away the generator.

Finally, Amanda's hooded head appeared from the cloth tent entrance and she climbed out of the ditch to where Fox stood waiting.

Pulling down the hood of her white paper suit, she swept the stray blonde hairs from her eyes and sighed. 'She has a deep laceration to her forehead, cuts to her wrists, as well as multiple bruises on her wrists, arms and legs. But,' she stated confidently, 'they were not the cause of her death.' She stopped for a moment and, hands on hips, surveyed the surrounding area before continuing. 'My guess is she was running and, having reached this ditch, turned to face her pursuer and either fell or was pushed, hitting the back of her head on ...' She let the sentence hang as she clambered back down and into the tent, only to re-emerge seconds later offering up a dirty great big rock with a bloodied sharp edge. 'This thing. See here,' she pointed to a spot on its surface, 'we've got traces of hair and blood. We'll have to test it of course but I'd safely say the blood, the hair, it's hers.'

'But, if she was being chased,' Fox said, 'why did that person let her lie here? Make no attempt to hide her?'

'Your job, not mine, to figure that out,' said Amanda with a shrug.

Fox nodded to the uniformed Garda standing sentry at Karin's hospital room door before knocking and entering. Finn jumped up, his face flushed, and gawping like a startled rabbit.

'Sorry, didn't mean to startle you,' she said.

'It's OK. I shouldn't have been snoozing anyway – it's the heat, can't help it.' He smiled, embarrassed.

'How is she?' Fox asked, nodding towards Karin who was asleep.

Finn turned to look at her lying peacefully, thinking before answering, and when he did it was with an air of solemn resignation.

'She's fine. I don't know if she actually realises what she's been through.'

'How do you mean?'

'I'm not sure ... she seems, I don't know, normal? The doctors say she's in some kind of denial.'

Disturbed by the noise, Karin began to stir.

'Karin,' Finn said gently, sitting down by her bedside, 'this is Detective Inspector Fox. She was there when they found you.'

'I remember,' she said, trying to push herself up in the bed.

'Here, let me.' Finn stepped forward to give her a lift.

Karin's flinch was almost imperceptible, but Fox noticed.

'It's OK,' Finn assured her, letting her go and tending to her pillows instead. Feeling like an intruder, Fox watched. They seemed uncomfortable with each other, awkward almost, as if they hardly knew each other.

'How are you feeling?' Fox asked once Karin was settled.

'Fine. Still a bit groggy,' she replied with a weak smile.

She looked different. Although still pale and a little gaunt, she looked stronger, more alert.

'I need to ask you a few questions if that's OK.'

'Why don't I leave you to it?' Finn offered, getting up – delighted, Fox suspected, to be handed the excuse to get away. 'I'll go get a coffee. Can I get you one, detective?'

'That'd be great, thanks, milk, two sugars,' Fox told him.

'Karin?'

She shook her head.

Fox waited while he shuffled around her towards the door. Then, changing his mind, he returned to the bedside, leaned in to give Karin a kiss on the cheek and with a quick smile left the room. It seemed contrived and clumsy. He was trying hard, too hard, to show affection that judging by his delivery and her response was obviously misplaced. Why would that be? Fox asked herself.

'Sorry about that,' Karin joked, mortified. 'He's driving me crazy.'

'I can imagine. He was pretty worried about you, you know.'

'Really?' She sounded surprised.

'Of course.' Fox paused, taken aback. 'Karin, you were kidnapped, he had no idea what to do, he was worried for you, for your safety.'

She moved the visitor chair towards the bed and sat down but, before she had a chance to ask her first question, Karin got there first.

'What about Sive?' she asked quietly.

Fox pulled the chair a little closer to the bedside.

'Yes, we've found her,' she told her. 'This morning – a few hundred yards from the house.'

For a split second it seemed that Karin's whole body froze. The colour drained from her face and her eyes closed. Without opening them, she calmly asked, 'Is she OK?'

Fox hated this part of her job. There was no nice way to break bad news like this to anyone and no matter how much training or how many times she had to do it, it never, ever got easier.

'I'm afraid not, Karin. I'm so sorry but Sive – she didn't make it.'

She neither opened her eyes nor uttered a word but, nodding slowly, let her head fall back onto the pillows.

'Karin, can you tell me what happened?' Fox eventually asked and, when she didn't answer, continued. 'I know it's hard, but if we want to catch whoever did this we need to know everything you can remember.'

'I know, I'm sorry,' she murmured, 'it's just … this is all my fault.'

'No, it's not. This is not your fault. You couldn't have stopped it, nor could you have known it was about to happen.'

'But I did. I assume Tom has told you about the letters.'

'He has, yes, but –'

'I should have been more careful. He wanted me to install a security system in Silene too, but I wouldn't let him. That's my space. It's where I go to get away from it all. I thought it was safe.'

'Look – these guys, whoever they are, they planned it so well, security system or not, Dublin or Galway, they would have found a way to get to you one way or another.'

'I'm sorry,' Karin repeated, taking a deep breath and wiping her eyes.

'Look, Karin, I know how difficult this is, but I need you to focus and tell me what happened.'

'What happened to her?' Karin sobbed, either not hearing the question or choosing not to answer. 'She ran, she said she was going to get help, she said she'd be back.' Tears flowed slowly down her cheeks, her eyes searching for answers.

'I need you to start from the beginning – can you do that? We're still trying to piece it all together – that's why what you can tell us is so important. But we need to know everything right from the start.'

Karin nodded and swallowed. Taking a deep breath, she exhaled slowly from between her pursed lips and braced herself as if going back there mentally meant returning physically.

'We were late. Nathan, my assistant, he delayed us. We should have left by five but it was closer to six before we finally got in the car. I was livid with him.' She spoke through gritted teeth and looked down at her hands. 'Traffic was pretty OK so we made good time getting out of Dublin. We stopped where I always do to fill up the car and get a coffee and then drove the rest of the way without stopping. But when we got to the house the lock on the front door had been smashed. Someone had broken in. Well, that's what we thought at the time. I called the Garda and they were there in no time.' She paused to take a breath. 'Sive wouldn't come into the house, she was really scared – she thought someone might be hiding under a bed or something and refused point blank to go inside. So I went in on my own to see if anything had been taken. But nothing was. I tried to tell her it was alright, but she was having none of it. I could hardly leave her out there on her own so we sat in the car together and waited for the Gardaí to arrive. They did a walk-about and didn't see anyone but, even after I had walked through the house with them, she still wouldn't go in. She wanted to drive back to Dublin.' Karin stopped, took a breath and smiled sorrowfully, her eyes wide and sad. 'We should have just gone home. But I didn't want to waste the weekend, you know?'

Fox nodded. 'You weren't to know.'

'Why didn't I listen to her?' she asked herself quietly.

'This isn't your fault, Karin.'

'Well, it certainly feels like it is,' she cried, shaking her head.

Fox waited for her to pull herself together before asking, 'Are you OK to go on?'

Karin nodded, wiped her nose with the back of her hand and continued.

'Mary, our housekeeper, had left a shepherd's pie in the oven for us – she's fantastic really – knows it's my favourite. She's a bit like my mammy, if you know what I mean.' She laughed a sad, sweet laugh and, having met the woman, Fox knew exactly what she meant. 'So we sat down to eat but that's about the last thing I remember. I do remember feeling dizzy and a little sick in my stomach. I thought it was the wine and how maybe it might have been a bit off.'

She stopped to rest her head back on the pillow. Her eyes closed and a small sob escaped her but she didn't cry.

'You're doing great, Karin, this is great. Really, you are,' Fox encouraged her, wishing her to continue, praying the nurse wouldn't come in, sure she'd be sent away if she did.

Karin was visibly struggling. 'When I came round it was dark, black almost, and really cold. My hands were tied and the floor was hard and freezing. My leg hurt. I was kind of twisted, I don't know, I couldn't sit up as my wrists were tied up sideways so I just kind of lay there. I have no idea how we got there. I called out for Sive. I couldn't see a thing and then I think I yelled a bit. I don't know. It's all a bit of a blur really.'

'Did she answer?' Fox asked. 'Was Sive with you then?'

'Yeah. She was there. I think we were drugged – that's why I can't remember so much.' She looked at Fox with raised eyebrows.

'That is what we think, yes – we're just waiting for the toxicology report to tell us exactly what and how much.'

'Well, whatever it was, Sive took much longer to wake up. I thought she was dead.' She gasped, realising what she'd said. 'But she wasn't. She cried a lot.'

'Was she hurt?'

'No, I don't think so. She just panicked, couldn't take being locked up like that. It was really, really freaky.'

'Did you see your kidnappers?'

'It was really dark in there. At first I couldn't see a thing but then in the morning the sun came up. There were no windows – well, not open anyway, but there were small holes in the roof so we could see a little bit. She was on the other side of the room and like me she was tied but at least she could sit up and lean against the wall. Her hands were tied over her head. She cried a lot. I saw blood run down her arms — she kept pulling and twisting at her wrists trying to get them free. I begged her to stop. She kept saying if she could just free her wrists we'd be OK. I was sure he'd come back and find out what she'd done and kill us both.' Karin closed her eyes and gently massaged the still red lines and welts on her wrists. 'It stank. Really stank.' Her voice had dried to a jagged rasp. She swallowed, cleared her throat and, finding her voice again, continued. 'And there were mice or rats or something anyhow.'

She shivered and Fox couldn't help but mirror her action. It was horrific. She didn't need to explain. Fox got it.

'At the end of that first day, I think, we heard a car. I screamed my heart out. I roared so loud my throat hurt.'

Fox could see the defiance in her face then that turned to a bitter sneer.

'When he came inside he was really pissed off. He told us to shut the fuck up.'

'What did he sound like?' Karin asked hopefully. 'Did he have an accent?'

'I couldn't really hear. His voice was muffled — his mouth was covered. I thought maybe he had a Dublin accent but not a strong one — but I couldn't be sure.'

'What did he look like?'

'I couldn't see his face. He had one of those scarf things that you wear skiing pulled up over his nose and to his eyes and a baseball cap with a hoodie pulled up over his head. He was tall though, maybe about six foot and pretty fit — he wasn't fat anyhow. He wore those ridiculous tracksuit bottoms — you know, tight on the calf and then the crotch is all sloppy to the knees. Pig.'

'You could see his eyes?'

'No – no – they weren't really visible in the shade of the peaked cap and it was dark anyway.'

'Were there any logos on his clothes that you recognise or any words on them?'

Karin's eyes closed as she tried to recall the image. 'It was a Nike top, I think.'

'Colour?'

'Black, I think, black bottoms and his hoodie was grey and there was a logo on the cap too. I can't remember what though.'

'Good. That's a start. So, what did he do while he was there – did he hang around long?'

'No. He didn't stay long, just enough to give each of us a bowl with water in it – we were like dogs trying to lap it up. And a plate of this muck, like a granola or dried lumpy porridge or something. It was awful.' Her face squirmed. 'I tried to eat a little but …'

'And then?'

'We both begged him to let us go even into the other room to relieve ourselves so he freed us and took us in there one at a time … I'm sorry … I don't mean to be disgusting.' She flushed, and tears began to spill.

'Don't distress yourself, Karin. I'm not disgusted and you're doing very well.' Even by criminal standards, this kidnapper was a brute, Fox was thinking. 'Was there anything else about him that you remember?'

'He smelt nice. Like spice.'

'Would you recognise it if you smelt it again?'

'I'll never forget that smell as long as I live. It was cheap, nothing fancy, but yeah, I think so.'

'Did he come every day?'

'I'm not sure, I slept so much I don't really remember the

days or the nights even but when I did wake up there was always this confusion, like I forgot where I was and then I'd remember. It was a nightmare. I'd try to scream but nothing would ever come out of my mouth.' She put her head in her hands and pressed her fingers to her temples. 'I think he came back twice after that first time but I can't be sure. It was like I was drunk or something. He left water and more of that food muck but I just couldn't eat it, I wasn't even hungry anymore …' Her voice trailed off, lost in that last moment of despair.

'How did Sive get out?' Fox asked.

Karin smiled. 'Only Sive could do a Houdini on it. Have you seen her? She's tiny. Eventually she did manage to get her wrists free. They were bleeding but she got them out of the ties. I wanted her to stop. But she wouldn't. She tried to get my hands free too, but I'm a little bigger. There was no way my wrists were coming out of those ties. And then, there she was searching for a way out but the door was locked or bolted from the outside and the windows were blocked up – she did try to push them open, really she did, but it was pointless. And then she thought she could fit out through one of the holes in the roof but she couldn't reach. She was like a bloody rabbit bouncing up and down, falling all over the place trying to reach that hole, but she couldn't do it. I knew she wouldn't. I told her so. But she just kept at it and at it. It was terrible, watching her desperately jumping. In the end she just sat back against the wall and waited. I've no idea how long it was until the sound of the car stirred us. And then she was up. She crouched low beside the door, the side that opened in and she was lucky, he stepped in a few steps first. It took him a couple of seconds to get used to the dark but she was ready to go.' There was pride in her voice now.

'What is it they say – fight or flight? Isn't that it? She just nipped behind his legs and ran out that door like lightning. Jesus, he went mental, screaming all sorts of names as he went after her. His voice faded away and it was quiet as hell. I tried to listen I couldn't hear anything but then he went at it again, shouting like a lunatic, fuck this, fuck that. He didn't come back after that, well, not inside. He locked the door and drove away. After that I slept a lot. Sometimes I was sure I heard a car. I kept thinking "She got away, she's gone to get help, she'll bring someone". But she didn't. I don't remember much else.' Karin looked at her hands like they were the most interesting things in the world, like there was nothing else quite like them. 'I don't even know how long I was in there.'

'Six days.' Fox told her softly. 'You were gone for six days.'

Karin had had enough and as if on cue Finn returned with the coffee, his eyes red and cheeks flushed. In trying to avoid making eye contact with Fox, he only made it more obvious that he'd been crying.

'I'll leave you two to it,' Fox told them, focusing her attention on Karin but curious about Finn. 'You need to rest. But if you remember anything, please give me a call.' She put her card on the bedside table.

Finn followed her out the door.

'Have you any idea yet who did this?' he asked.

'Not yet,' Fox replied, which was true – they still had no solid lead. Under pressure from all sides she had been really hoping that Karin would be able to give her something to follow up on, but there was very little there. 'We're working on it.' Which was also true. From the hospital she was going to see what the CCTV footage would uncover, and Ken Stanley had sounded positive when he'd called her. 'I'm hoping we'll have good progress to report by the end of the week.' This she prayed would turn out to be true; otherwise she'd be in trouble.

At the nurses' station, Fox was asked to see Karin's doctor, who it seemed had been waiting for her.

'Ketamine,' she told Fox bluntly as soon as the office door closed behind them. 'Simple but very, very effective and almost impossible to detect by an unsuspecting user.'

'How much was she given?'

'Can't say exactly how much but I suspect it was administered regularly. Most likely it was mixed in the water because I don't think she ate much while she was held. It works like an anaesthetic, disconnects the brain from the body so to speak. They call it the date-rape drug because it confuses the victim who has no idea what's going on, making it easy for the attacker to manipulate her or him.'

Fox nodded. Better at least for Karin who wouldn't remember the worst of it but from her own perspective it meant Karin wasn't likely to remember anything concrete that might help with the investigation.

Chapter 7

With a firm grip Gordon squeezed the arms of the secateurs, snipping the dead head of the rose clean off. Fox and Callaghan stood beside him and watched and waited. He didn't seem in any great hurry to interrupt what he was doing.

'You have a beautiful garden, Mr Collins,' Fox complimented him, admiring the perfect lawns and tidy flowerbeds filled with the last blooms of autumn.

'Gordon, please. And thank you. It's very therapeutic, especially at this time of year … and it helps to take my mind off … things.' He continued to snip as if they weren't there.

Callaghan and Fox looked at each other uncomfortably, sure Gordon was well aware of the difficult impression he was making.

'I don't mean to draw you away from your roses, but we really would like a chat,' Fox insisted gently.

'Let me just finish this one branch and then I'm all yours.'

They waited, patiently watching as Gordon precisely placed the secateurs just below the last growth and with one tight clench of his fist snipped the branch clean off.

'There!' he declared as the last remaining brown and tired bud hit the floor.

He pulled off his thick gardening gloves, one finger at a time. 'So what progress have you made?'

'May we sit?' Fox suggested, pointing to the cushioned rattan seats on the patio.

'Good idea. Let me just get Harry – I'm sure he'd like to be here also.' He disappeared into the house and reappeared minutes later with his son.

At sixteen Harry was a replica of his mother. Tall and slender with her beautifully defined features, he was destined to grow up to be a handsome man. But today his eyes and nose were red and swollen and in his hand he held a crumpled tissue, suggesting he wasn't quite done crying yet.

Leaning forward to shake their hands, he did his best to smile but failed miserably. He didn't need to smile, not for them. They understood. And even though she didn't possess a maternal bone in her body, Fox's heart melted a little.

They sat at the table.

'I know Becky has been with you,' Fox started, referring to their appointed family liaison officer, 'but I wanted to come and speak to you myself, just to let you know how things are going and, of course, to bring you Sive's things from the house.' She pointed to the overnight case and satchel, and handed Gordon the large brown envelope she held in her hand.

'Thank you, we appreciate it,' Gordon said, taking the envelope from her. Placing it on the table in front of them, he let his hand rest on it and closed his eyes for a moment. Then, placing his hand gently on his son's knee, he blurted out, 'So, are you any closer to finding out what happened?'

'We have the toxicology report from the hospital which indicates that Karin and Sive were drugged before they were taken,' Fox told him.

Harry's head dropped and Gordon tightened his grip a little around his knee.

'We're still waiting on the report from the coroner.'

'You're an experienced officer,' Gordon said. 'Surely you've some idea of what happened. I was there, I saw it. Even I can put together a scenario. What do you think happened?'

It was an uncomfortable scene, especially in the company of the young boy, and Fox couldn't help but wonder why Gordon was behaving like this.

'I have an idea,' she confirmed honestly, glancing at Harry. 'But really I think we should wait for the facts rather than me speculating and potentially getting it wildly wrong.'

'Well, here's what I think,' he said, his calm demeanour disintegrating as he started into an almost manic rant. 'I think, as was typical of her, she refused to do what she was told and I think she ran and when she ran I think she –'

'*Stop! Please!*' Harry shouted suddenly, standing up. 'Can I please be excused?' His breath was catching in his chest and his eyes were brimming with tears.

Gordon nodded and watched him go.

'Do you need to go to him?' Fox asked, worried about the young man whose heightened anxiety was palpable.

'He'll be fine. I'm sorry. He's finding it very hard to come to terms to this.'

'No need to apologise, although I'm not sure your speaking like that was necessary,' Callaghan responded without attempting to disguise his disdain.

'It's important he knows the truth,' Gordon reasoned flatly.

'I agree, but maybe not just yet – he's grieving for his mother.'

'If you don't mind, I'll be the judge of what's best for my son. You just concentrate on finding who did this,' Gordon bit back.

Callaghan dropped his head and raised his hands in mock surrender.

'This is her fault,' Gordon muttered.

'Whose fault?' Fox asked.

'That Bolger woman!' he spat, his face twisting into an ugly sneer. 'If it wasn't for her, none of this would have happened.'

It was a difficult statement to argue against but, rather than get tied up in an unpleasant and slanderous diatribe, Fox moved on to the point of their visit.

'The last time we spoke you mentioned that you and Sive had had a squabble. Can you remember any better now what that was about?'

'Yes,' he sighed, holding his hands tight in his lap, 'and I said some pretty horrific things. If I could take them back I would.' He shook his head sadly. 'It was all about the money for Sive – always about the money – but she had absolutely no idea how to manage it when she had it. If she'd just kept her feet on the ground maybe she'd still be here.'

'What do you mean?'

'Sive, well, she was the eternal entrepreneur, always trying, always failing, but unlike most entrepreneurs she never learned from her mistakes. Never. She lost so much money I wish I could lose count but I can't. And then, at that stage, we found ourselves back to square one.' He lifted his hands in exasperation. 'Another idea, another few thousand euro down the drain – and, well, I'd just had enough. I told her so.'

'How did she take that?'

'Not very well.' He let out a strained chuckle. 'She told me to mind my own bloody business so I told her she had to choose. This family, *her* family or Karin's money.'

'Karin's money?'

'Yes, Karin once again was putting up the cash to start *a-bloody-gain*!'

'And?'

'Well, it seems the lure of the great Karin Bolger was just too much for her to resist.'

'Did you try to stop her?'

'God, no. When she got something into her head there was no stopping her, but I did go to Karin. I asked her not to interfere, to keep her money to herself ...'

'Why?'

'Because she was feeding a beast with a voracious hunger to be as good as her – her idol.'

'And what's wrong with that?'

'Nothing, if it works. But no matter how hard Sive tried she was never going to be another Karin Bolger. But there was just no telling her, and Karin just seemed to be this endless source of investment, almost as if she *wanted* Sive to keep failing, proving her point she'd never be as good as her.'

'And you know this how?'

'I don't know it for sure but it's what I think.'

'So you asked her, Karin, to stop giving her money.'

'Yes. I went to see her at her office.'

'What did she say?'

'Pretty much the same thing as Sive: to mind my own business.'

'Did that upset you?'

'Damn right it did!' he replied forcefully. 'Who the bloody hell does she think she is? Did it upset me? It bloody well infuriated me. Sive is or was my wife, not some plaything for her to toy with!'

'And why do you think Karin was so generous?'

'Are you not listening to me? I've just told you. She loves to be the best. Has to be the best. I think she enjoyed seeing Sive fail and fail again. Sadistic pleasure.'

He was shaking visibly and Fox let him settle before asking what she knew would be an incendiary question.

'Can you account for your movements on that Friday night?'

He didn't answer immediately but considered her through slightly squinted eyes, observing her and pondering her question. He looked like he might not answer, like he was weighing up his options but wisely he gave her the straightforward, uncomplicated response she was looking for.

'I can,' he said smartly. 'As I told you before, I was here on my own.'

'Can anyone verify that?'

'No. *I was on my own.*'

'Did you order pizza? Did anyone call the landline? Anything?'

'No. Nothing, I'm afraid.'

'And Harry?'

'He was at school – he boards and doesn't usually get home until mid-term.'

'Are you sure you made no calls? Did you order a movie online perhaps?'

'No, I did not – and I'll be honest, I'm not sure I like the insinuation behind your line of questioning. Are you accusing me of something? Am I a suspect?' His tone was even and body language neutral.

'No, sir, we are not accusing you of anything. These are

merely routine questions we ask everyone – to rule you out rather than implicate you.'

'I'm relieved to hear it.'

'But,' she warned with a note of caution, 'until we find who did this, everyone is a suspect.' She let her statement hang in the air before asking, 'Can we also ask that you come to the station to allow us take DNA samples? Again, only to rule you out.'

'You can and I shall. Is this afternoon convenient?'

'Very,' Fox replied politely, fully aware that the conversation had moved quickly from free-flowing to stiflingly courteous in a matter of sentences.

'Bloody hell!' Fox groaned, pulling her collar up against the chilly night air as they left the house. 'That was hard work.'

'He's a dick.'

'Yes, but he's also a grieving husband – he's bound to be cross, I would be. But, oh my God!' She sighed then, thinking of Harry. 'That poor boy. How shit must he be feeling!'

'Come on, let me buy you a drink – it's been a long week.'

'It sure has, but I'm not really in the mood.'

'Don't be ridiculous – come on, I won't take no for an answer.'

'Oh, all right,' she said with a laugh. 'You've twisted my arm. But just the one.'

'Just the one,' he repeated without an ounce of conviction but with his signature charming smile that many of the younger officers found impossible to resist.

'And we're not going anywhere near Coppers, right?'

'Right.'

Three hours and five pints later they were sitting in the

middle of the flashing and heaving den that was Coppers where every inch of every surface jigged and reeled in time to the music. Although they were the oldest there by about twenty years, no one seemed to care or notice. In Callaghan's case, being in the company of another female only seemed to make him more attractive. They were like moths to a flame.

'I'm too old for this shit!' Fox moaned, looking round her.

'You say that every time we come here.'

'Then why do we keep coming here?'

'Tradition,' he said with a shrug and a smile.

'Time to break it, I think!' she said into his ear.

'I think not. What would we do without this place? Where would we go?'

'Home, maybe?' Fox suggested.

'Not a chance! Jesus, you are getting old.'

'Good God, man, when are you ever going to settle down?'

'Me? Settle down? You've gotta be kidding! Why would I want to do that?'

He smiled at a poor drunk girl who, wobbling like a newborn gazelle with legs up to her neck, sucking the life out of her alcopop through a straw, fell into his lap to declare, 'You're cute!'

Callaghan beamed, patting the young girl away on her perfectly round backside. 'Unlike you,' he said to Fox, 'I have a life and I'm making sure I enjoy every damn minute of it.'

Seeing Fox's face drop, he realised his mistake.

'Oh shit. I'm sorry, I didn't mean …'

'Yes, you did – you're only saying what everyone is thinking,' she retorted while trying to decide whether she should slap him or laugh at him but, when he didn't dispute what she'd just said, she decided there was no point in doing either because he was right.

'We're different, that's all I'm saying, and I'm happy with my pace,' he told her with a frown, trying to make it more about him than her, but the damage was done. 'You're on a mission, I get that, but I'm not – not yet anyway. When I'm done having fun then I'll consider it.'

They sat foot-tapping, surrounded by people but alone in their own thoughts.

'How long has it been now anyway?' Callaghan asked her, breaking through their noisy silence.

'Nine years and three months.'

'Do you miss him?'

'Every day. Not one goes by that I don't think about him.'

'Isn't it time you got yourself back on track?'

She shook her head, disappointed but not surprised by his train of thought. She didn't expect anything else. He didn't understand, how could he?

'I'm neither ready nor interested,' she defended herself a shrug.

'Christ, Fox, you're only what – forty-five? You're smart and you're not that bad looking, even by my standards! Don't give up on yourself yet. At least try and have some fun. You might surprise yourself and actually enjoy it.'

'Am I supposed to be flattered?' she replied with a forced but good-natured laugh. 'What do you think we're doing right now? Anyway, can we drop it, please?'

Callaghan threw his eyes up to heaven. 'For now, but this conversation isn't over, not by a long shot – it's time to get you to shift your priorities, park the career and get back in the saddle. Oisín wouldn't mind. He was my mate too, you know, and I can tell you this much: he'd never condone this celibacy crap. He'd be on my side.' He thought for a second then asked, 'What about yer man Murphy? He's a bit of a looker – would you not go for him, just, you know, like a first step?'

This time her laugh was real. 'I'll tell you what, you look after getting the drinks in and I'll look after my love life, OK?'

She was glad the following morning that she had declined Callaghan's chivalrous offer of a pillow on his couch but was deeply sorry she'd agreed to the kebab that seemed like a good idea at the time but this morning threatened to come back to haunt her. The inside of her mouth was like dry cotton and her head spun like a wheel. On top of that, she was probably still way over the limit to drive but, with her early-morning briefing scheduled for ten, she took to the coffee and burnt toast and prayed for sobriety.

Chapter 8

'You get away with very little these days,' AJ told her as he gathered up the data to show her.

And he was right; between traffic cameras, street surveillance, shop CCTV and taxi dash-cams, surveillance had become very sophisticated and very little went unnoticed. You really had to try hard to be invisible.

'You can run but you can't hide.' AJ whistled to himself proudly, rubbing his rotund belly. While the door-to-door hadn't been hugely enlightening, the callout for information locally was bountiful.

The report took the best part of two weeks to collate but it was worth the wait.

The incident room in Galway Garda Headquarters was a hive of activity. True to his word, AJ had put forward the best team he could to trace the steps of Karin and Sive before and after their abduction. Two mobile whiteboards were positioned at the top of the room, taking centre stage. On one AJ had mounted a large map of Ireland. On it two thick lines, one blue and one red, represented both journeys the women had made. The blue line was their drive from Dublin to Galway and was direct and easy to track with a confirmed departure and arrival time noted in blue marker both on the map and on the opposite board. The red line was their exit from the Galway valley and, although unconfirmed, it also had an approximate departure and arrival time documented on both the map and the whiteboard.

'They're informed guesses,' AJ told her confidently, inviting her to sit down so he could present his team's findings to her.

Armed with his ruler and a smile, he took a deep breath before beginning his presentation.

'The beauty of a remote location such as this is that, not only is there only one road to travel, there is only so much traffic using it.' He pointed to X that marked the location of Silene Cottage then swept the ruler up and down the road that ran through the valley and along the lake. 'We know that the ladies arrived at the house at approximately 9:30pm because we have their logged call.' From the table beside the whiteboard, he picked up the first in a neat row of documents and handed it to her. 'That's the call log and report from Garda Nealon.' Turning back to the board he continued. 'We know they were alive and well when Garda Nealon and Ward left them at eleven thirty pm. Between the hours of eleven pm and eight am the following morning only forty-one cars passed through the valley.' He turned to pick up the second document and handed her the stapled list of car registrations and their owners. 'We have successfully tracked all of these cars and only one remains of interest. Curiously, this is the only one that isn't registered to a domestic owner but rather to a secondhand car dealership.'

'Interesting,' Fox murmured, flicking through the report.

AJ, using his ruler, traced the journey along the map.

'This same car left the valley, travelled to Galway along the N59, turned on to the N6 here, eventually hit the M18 and turned south towards Limerick. It then took the M20 which becomes the N20 heading for Charleville and Mallow. Still with me?'

Fox nodded, fully immersed in the journey.

Satisfied, AJ continued. 'This is our last sighting on this route but we pick it up again about forty-five minutes later travelling on the N72 west from Mallow – about fifteen minutes away from where the women were held across the Cork-Kerry border.'

'What is it, the car – what make?'

'A 2010 Volvo Estate.'

'Registration?'

'10MH 33602.'

'Do we know where it is now?'

'Unfortunately not. It hasn't been spotted since.'

'And the timing works?'

'It does,' he replied, checking his notes. 'We have a statement from a fisherman, John Milne, who was fishing that night and was positioned almost opposite the entrance to Silene Cottage, he says he saw a car leave the valley just after ten past one in the morning. He's quite precise about the timing because he'd just got off the phone from his wife who checks in with him every hour when he's out on the lake.'

'What the hell was he doing out there at that time?' Fox asked, almost aghast at the notion.

'That's the best time to fish for trout,' AJ said with an everyone-knows-that look on his face before returning from his notes.

'He wasn't able to give us anything more, couldn't remember for sure if the car turned left or right, but it does give us a timeframe to work off.'

Fox nodded in agreement and let him go on.

'If this is our man then he's an absolute amateur,' AJ said in disgust, standing back to look at the marked-out route. 'He did very little, well, nothing in fact to cover his tracks. Took all the main roads to get there.'

'Do we know where this car started out from initially before it reached Silene Cottage in Galway?'

'We focused on the journey after the kidnapping first. But, now we know what we're looking for, it shouldn't take so long. Plus we also have this ...' AJ picked up a remote control and pointed to the screen mounted on the wall. Immediately it came to life and a grainy static CCTV image appeared on it. 'This, we think, is him.' He stood aside to let her examine the slightly blurred but definite shape of the man on screen. 'Assuming the Volvo is it. This is taken from the cameras at the service station at Loughrea on the Dublin side of Galway on the M4 at 17:40.'

He pressed play and they watched the man dressed in tracksuit bottoms, peaked sports cap, hoodie with its hood up and over the cap and a neck-warmer wrapped high around his neck, up above his chin. He kept his head down, obviously aware of the cameras, and walked to the till where he picked up a packet of chewing gum, paid cash for it and a full tank of diesel, then left again, head down. The image on screen switched to an outside camera and the same man walking with a heavy hunched gait back to the Volvo, same registration, get in and drive away.

'Go back to him,' Fox said, 'and let's take a look.'

She stepped up the screen, hands on hips, to scrutinise the image. Although impossible to see his face, he wore a very distinctive ensemble with a Boston baseball cap, a grey Nike hoodie and black tracksuit bottoms, tight at the ankle and loose at the backside, just like Karin had told her.

'What are your thoughts on a description, AJ?'

'From this, all I think we can say is he's maybe six foot, average build …'

'Average – I hate that word,' she moaned. 'Print that picture off and I'll take it to Karin, see if we can get her to identify him, but it certainly looks like this is our guy. Was he alone?'

'We believe so.'

'Is it possible that one person did this? That this was one person acting on behalf of the entire Kings workforce?' Karin tapped her pen to her lips. 'We have a link, the threatening letters signed *Justice for the Workers* who clearly have it in for her, and then this …' She paused and turned back to the board. gazing at it with squinted eyes, 'It's an obvious line … a little too obvious maybe. We as good as know who's in this Justice for the Workers group – they're all over the bloody media. They're not hiding anywhere. They couldn't be this stupid.'

'Or maybe he's just one loose cannon off on his own private mission – maybe these justice guys aren't in on it at all?' AJ threw in.

'*Hmm.*' She shook her head.

'Or, it could be both – you know, a bit of a maverick taking on the establishment, make a quick buck at the same time.'

With one eye closed, Fox considered the possibility. 'It would go a distance to answer the question about *why*, if the objective was to save the brewery, the cash was added into the mix. Greed? Opportunism? Yes, maybe he is one of them but acting on his own wit.'

Fox switched her focus back to the image on screen as if it might speak to her and reveal all.

'No,' she declared decisively. 'We need to look at this a little differently. Outside the box, so to speak.'

'Like how?'

'If I knew that …' she mused and, as if to refocus, took a breath. Turning again from the screen to the map, she asked with renewed energy, 'So this Volvo then, when you say it's owned by a car dealership, what do you mean?'

'It was last registered to a Mr Brian Ryan from the city here in Galway. He sold it to McKeevers Skoda dealership in Sligo and then they sold it on for cash to a small-time dealer in Kildare, *A1Autos*. That was …' he checked his notes again, 'June nineteenth this year. But they never transferred ownership to the new owner, so it's still in the dealer's name.'

'And we're sure this is the car?'

'Ninety-nine-point-nine per cent. It makes sense. It would be a massive coincidence if it wasn't,' He turned towards the screen. 'The timings work. 17:40. It's only an hour's drive to the cottage, plenty of time to get in, do what he has to do and leave before the women get there.'

She couldn't argue with him – it did make sense.

'Yep, I think you're right,' she announced and prayed he was because it was all they had to go on. 'Thanks a million, AJ, this really is fantastic work.'

'No problem, that's my job,' he modestly replied.

'Well, I'd best go and have a word with this car dealer then, hadn't I?'

Looking at her watch, she clocked the time. She'd only just got back and she was off again. She could, she supposed, ask Callaghan to check it out since he was nearer but decided against it. This was the only good lead they had – she wanted to make sure she got the best from it.

'You're off again then?'

'Yep. I'm going to pay this garage a visit but I'll be back later for the briefing.' There was an afternoon conference call with the Assistant Commissioner and her wider team. If Fox had known she'd be back in Dublin she'd have arranged to meet her in person there. 'Hopefully we'll have something solid to report.'

On the drive back to Dublin, Fox called the lab to see how the results from the crime scene were coming along. The end of the week, they promised.

'Christ, guys, what's taking so long?' she moaned.

'Yours is not the only crime in this country, Detective Inspector,' came the curt reply.

Hanging up, Fox knew that after a call like that she could probably add an extra day on to her wait. She should have kept her mouth shut.

Her conversation with Sergeant Ken Stanley was thankfully more productive. 'There's a lot to learn,' he told her with relish and a hint of warning.

She listened eagerly while picking up her speed.

'There are some interesting names and characters involved here but I've still got a good way to go. Let me email it to you once it's done and you can give me a shout once you've had a chance to go through it.'

'At least give me some clues,' she pleaded.

'Patience!' He laughed and hung up with a playful 'Cheerio!'.

Her last call was to Amanda Stynes.

'Sorry, pet,' she apologized. 'I know I promised I'd be done by tonight but it's been manic here – but I'll get it to you first thing tomorrow.'

'That would be great, Amanda, thanks. Should I expect any surprises?'

'No, I don't think so – it's pretty much as we figured when we got her.'

'OK, well, we'll chat tomorrow so.'

'Yep and drive safe,' Amanda said before hanging up.

She made the rest of the journey in silence, unable to think with music blaring or the banal daytime radio voices. She thought about Karin and Finn, curious about the irrefutable tension that simmered between them at the hospital. What was their story, she wondered – what was it that kept them together? Too many couples remained as such out of the fear of being alone and she wondered if that was the case. What a waste, she concluded, assuming the worst of both while feeling a pang of jealousy. She'd do anything to have Oisín back and here they were, two people who very obviously didn't want to be together but were. Not fair, she childishly sulked.

As soon as she turned into the narrow parking lot of the backstreet car lot, Fox knew exactly what to expect and it didn't disappoint.

Bill Baxter sauntered out of the Portakabin as soon as she pulled up. He was wrapped in a long black overcoat with a beaming smile, a jet-black-dyed off-his-head comb-over and whiter than white teeth.

Trying not to laugh or gag, Fox prepared herself for a charm offensive.

'Don't say a word,' he said dramatically with his hand faced forward. 'I have the perfect car for you.'

Amused, she played along and let herself be led to the heart of the make-do forecourt where a red Porsche was parked, dented side to the fence, with a price tag of two-and-a-half thousand euro.

'But for a *bee-ute-ee-ful* lady such as yourself,' he gushed, 'I'll do it for two.'

'Why, thank you,' she replied, anticipating how his face would look when he realised she wasn't a punter but the law. 'That's very generous. On any other day perhaps, but not today.'

'*Awhhh!*' he moaned, putting on a mock sulk. 'Well, then, what *can* I do you for today?" he asked through lowered lids, the innuendo apparent even if it was in jest.

'DI Naomi Fox,' she answered, taking her badge from her hip pocket.

'*Ah for feck's sake!*' he moaned with a real pus on him this time, throwing his hands in the air. 'What have I done now?'

Fox smiled, well used to disappointing men like this.

'I just want to ask you a few questions, that's all.'

'Well, go on then,' he replied, walking back to the cabin at a great pace. 'I'm all bloody ears.'

Fox followed him into his dingy office and stood while he settled himself behind the desk.

'This car.' She showed him a picture and registration.

'What about it?'

'It's registered to this garage, at this address. Can I see it?'

Grabbing the piece of paper he looked at it, taking his time before handing it back. He shook his head and went to the filing cabinet in the corner.

'I sold that car months ago,' he said, sifting through the files.

She was surprised he kept any at all.

'There!' he said eventually. 'Here's the paperwork. See, sold it back in March.' He handed it to her.

Fox looked straight for a name, and there it was, in black ink.

'*John Wayne?*' she asked, incredulous.

Snatching it off her, he growled, 'Let me see that.'

She watched his cheeks puff.

'Great name,' he told her, hiding his annoyance with bravado. 'We get all sorts in here.'

'Did you take a copy of his licence or passport?'

'Look, he paid cash,' he said, poking at the form as if that was an excuse for his laziness.

'Can you at least remember what he looked like?'

'Are you for real? That was months ago – there's no way I'm going to remember that.'

'Well, perhaps you can tell me why the car is still registered here?'

'Must have forgotten to send this,' he said smartly, holding up the transfer-of-ownership form that was still in the file.

'You do realise that you're obliged by law to complete all required registration details?'

'I am.'

'But you didn't.'

'I'll do it today.'

Fox considered him for a minute. He wasn't worth her while. She took down *John Wayne's* mobile number even though she knew it'd go nowhere and turned to leave.

Pausing at the door, she asked, 'I don't suppose you've got CCTV?'

Lifting his arms wide and cocking his head, he replied, 'What do you think?'

'No, didn't think so,' she muttered and mentally made a note to talk to the boys in Vehicle Registrations – they'd have a field day here.

Back in her car she rang Mr Wayne's mobile number and threw her eyes to heaven when, as expected, the line beeped annoyingly back at her. No such number.

'*John bloody Wayne*,' she again muttered while spitting gravel as she drove out of the car lot.

By the time she got back to headquarters the conference call had already begun. Superintendent Moyne, AJ and his team sat around the incident-room table.

'Apologies,' she whispered as she took her seat.

On the phone the Assistant Commissioner was looking for the facts of progress so far.

'Ma'am,' Moyne interjected, 'DI Fox has just joined us.'

'How good of you, DI Fox,' she responded sarcastically.

'Apologies, ma'am. I've just come back from interviewing the owner of the car lot where we believe the car involved in the abduction was sourced.'

'Have you got the actual car?'

'Not yet, ma'am, but now that we have the licence-plate number, it won't take long to track it down.'

'Good. What else?'

'Well, we also believe we have a visual of the abductor. Sergeant Jones and his team have completed extensive work tracking both the women and the abductor, using a sighting of the car leaving the property as a time-indicator.'

'Do we need to take this to the general public?' the Assistant Commissioner asked.

'No, not yet. I'd like to be one-hundred-per-cent sure we have the right man before we do that.'

'We have a slot if we want it on *Crimeline* and we're looking at doing a reconstruction, once we have the car,' Moyne reported, which was the first Fox had heard of such a plan.

'Excellent. Well, again, keep me posted. When's the funeral?'

'I believe the morgue are releasing Sive to her family tomorrow so –'

'Have we seen the autopsy results?'

'Not yet, ma'am, but I've set up a conference call this evening with the coroner,' Fox told her, glad she'd called Amanda from the car to see how things were moving.

'What's the delay? Have they found anything?'

'Initial findings are that she died from blunt-force trauma to the back of the head having fallen or been pushed backwards into the ditch.'

'And what about the ransom? Have you got any sight of that payment? It's a significant amount of money to lose.'

'Not yet, ma'am,' she replied, darting a furtive glance at Moyne to see how he was reacting to the question, 'but we are continuing to put pressure on the bank to assist. They're reluctant though.'

'Well, keep on it. As I said, keep me posted.'

'Will do, ma'am,' Fox and Moyne replied in unison, eyeing each other sceptically as she hung up.

'Don't be late again for your own conference call, Fox. Got it?' Moyne said, and left the room taking the tension he created with him.

Counting to ten, Fox folded her arms on the table and pinched the skin of her biceps hard.

'You OK?' AJ asked. 'You look shattered.'

Fox smiled. 'That's because I am shattered.'

'Why don't you come back to ours for some supper? Sandra's made one of her stews – can't say it's gourmet but it won't kill ya.'

'Thanks but I'll give it a miss. I wouldn't mind just working through this one. I've spent the day chasing my tail.'

'Well, if you change your mind …'

'Thanks, AJ, I appreciate it.'

Making herself a mug of coffee strong enough to hold up her spoon and guaranteed to keep her awake and alert for another few hours at least, she went back to the incident room to focus on the whiteboard and all the information AJ had stuck to it.

Confident that AJ's assertions were right and the man in the hoodie, still static on the screen, was indeed their abductor, they needed now to find the car. She'd asked AJ to circulate its details and hoped he was correct when he said it wouldn't take long to locate it. Once they had it they'd be more than a few steps closer to finding him. Sipping her drink, she took a long look at the screen-shot pinned on the board. He could be anyone – average height, average build, fit but not remarkably so. His cap, hoodie and the angle of his head meant she wasn't able to see his face and while AJ had painfully pointed out he hadn't tried very hard to conceal his movements, he knew what he was doing in making sure his face was never caught on camera. Not that much of an amateur after all. There was nothing else to glean from the image.

Silently she asked his image the questions that needed answers. Was he hiding in the house when Karin and Sive arrived? Why make the break-in so obvious? Did he want Karin to know he'd been there? Surely he'd be worried that, freaked by the intrusion, they might not stay? Or worse still the Gardaí might have hung around. But the image on screen offered her no answers.

'Working the late shift?'

Startled, she jumped. Moyne stood in the doorway, his coat on, ready to go.

'Jesus, you scared me!'

'Sorry. You should go home – you've had a long day.'

'I know, I'll head shortly.'

'Where are you staying?'

'I've rented a place on Moss Street.'

'Nice?'

'It'll do. Sorry about earlier.'

'Just don't make a habit of it. You're making good progress. Now go home, get some sleep – you'll be no use if you're exhausted.'

He was right. She was wrecked.

She sat down and closed her eyes. It was quiet. Night-time, despite the late-shift activity, brought with it a peaceful hush usually until about closing time. She liked this time of day in the station – the phones tended to stop and it gave her time, valuable time, to think. Still holding her mug, she let her head rest on the back of the chair and her breathing settle into a gentle rhythm.

'I'll rest my eyes just for a minute,' she promised no one in particular, savouring the moment, the bang of doors and chatter of voices almost a million miles away while the constant hum of the radiator lured her towards sleep. But, like a siren, the ringing of her phone shattered the peaceful comfort of her snooze. Grabbing wildly at the offending article she looked but didn't recognize the number.

'Detective Inspector Fox, it's Tom Williams here, Karin Bolger's head of security.'

'Hi, Tom, what can I do for you?' she asked, hoping her voice didn't give away what he had interrupted. She sensed from the controlled urgency in his voice that another potential gem was coming her way.

'I hope you don't mind me calling so late but I have something I think you need to see.'

She sat up, instantly alert.

'How urgent? I'm in Galway and I don't plan to be back in Dublin for a few days.'

'You need to see it. I could email it if you want.'

'Sure, send it to me now, I'll just log on.' She pulled her chair towards her laptop and called out her email address.

'You know I told you we were upgrading the security system at Wild Winds?'

'Yeah.'

'Well, after what happened we brought forward the date for full installation, bypassing some of the testing phases.'

'OK.' There was nothing like CCTV footage. Fox could feel her pulse rise in anticipation.

'What with Karin coming home, I wanted to make sure everything was up and running as it should, so I ran a couple of checks myself and found some recordings from the original test phase, before Karin was taken, when we first put in the cameras.'

'Good – and?' she asked breathlessly.

'Well, take a look and see for yourself. I've just sent you a link – you should get it now.'

Within seconds his email appeared on her screen. Opening it, she clicked on the link.

'OK. Got it. It's spooling,' she told him, watching the small wheel spin as the machine got to work.

'I couldn't isolate the frames so you'll have to fast-forward until the picture kind of flickers, then stop – it's only a few seconds after that.'

She did as she was told and waited. On screen the front entrance of Wild Winds was visible as seen from the gates of the house. It was bright outside, the time on the bottom right-hand side of the image said 13:52. The only movement came from the shrubs and plants that bent and swayed in what appeared to be a gentle breeze. Two cars were visible. One she recognised as Finn's, the other she hadn't seen before. The front door of the house opened sharply and someone rushed out. At first Fox didn't recognise her.

'Who is it?' she asked Tom.

The woman was dishevelled with her shoes in one hand as she scampered barefoot across the gravel to the car, her shirt half in and half out of the band on her high-waisted skirt, one arm in the sleeve of her cardigan.

'That's Sive,' she realised, answering her own question before Tom had a chance to respond. It was surreal watching her move on screen. Apart from her photograph, she'd only seen the woman dead. 'But she's half dressed.'

'Wait, there's more.'

A man could be seen coming to the frame of the door. He too was barefoot with only his boxers and T-shirt on. As he emerged from the house, he called to her.

'Where's the sound?' she asked, frustrated, but like a black-and-white silent film the gist of the unfolding scene was pretty clear.

'There is none. Not yet anyhow. Once it's fully installed there will be.'

'Can you retrieve it?' she asked, watching Finn rush towards Sive and take her by the shoulders.

He was pleading with her but she was having none of it. Had he just assaulted her or were they having what appeared to be a lovers' tiff? It was unclear.

'*Wow!*' Fox said, glued to the screen as Sive tried to shrug free but he wouldn't let her go. Whatever she was saying, she was pretty animated. His features weren't that clear and she was standing at an awkward angle to the camera. Again, she tried to pull free, reaching out to the car, but he held her firmly by the shoulders. Turning in to him fully she lifted her knee sharply. As it connected with his groin Finn let go and dropped to the ground. Fox winced, feeling his pain. Free, Sive got into the car, almost reversed over him and blasted out the still-opening gates which must have been triggered by their movement.

'Bloody hell!' Fox whistled.

'I know. Some head of security I am. I didn't know this was going on.'

'When was this?'

'It would have been the Wednesday before they went missing.'

'It's the middle of the bloody day!' Fox exclaimed, not sure whether to be impressed or appalled. 'And two days later she's off on a jolly with Karin, her lover's wife?'

'Looks like it.'

'Look, let's not jump to conclusions, there could be a simple explanation,' Fox suggested, more for her own benefit than Tom's. 'Hey, maybe she was posing for him? He is an artist after all. Maybe he made a move she didn't like?'

'Maybe,' Tom replied, unconvinced.

'Well, whatever's going on, it looks like we need to have a chat with Finn. And Karin is home now?'

'Yeah, she was discharged from the Clinic a few days ago and she's back to work too.'

'And Finn?'

'I haven't seen him but that's not unusual. I'm assuming he's back at the house, most likely in his studio.'

'Thanks, Tom, and please don't mention this to anyone. We'll take it from here.'

'No problem. I'll organise a disc copy for you.'

'Thanks, Tom, this is really helpful.'

She hung up the phone and looked at the image of Finn clutching himself while rolling like a dog on the paved driveway of the house.

'Idiot,' she whispered, utterly disappointed by what she had just seen.

Chapter 9

Rain hammered down on the roof of the car, the wipers struggling to keep up with the deluge of water. Never a great day for a funeral but this was the worst.

Gordon and Harry stood at the graveside dressed identically in black suit, white shirt, black tie and overcoat, with their hands clasped and heads bowed. Despite being protected by a large umbrella they were still drenched by the rain that bounced inches off the ground. Fox doubted if they even noticed.

A crowd of about three hundred family, friends and colleagues had filled the Dublin suburb church to say farewell to a woman who, according to the eulogy, was both liked and respected in the community. Described as a successful local businesswoman, Sive was involved in the local Chamber of Commerce and Enterprise Board. Hearing all this from the pulpit, Fox realised she knew nothing about her victim, having focused so hard on Karin and her activities. The ransom note had pointed them in the direction of the brewery and the Justice for the Workers group. But listening to the tender words spoken about the wife and mother whose life they were celebrating, she wondered if she'd made a mistake. The video of Sive with

111

Finn had taken her by surprise. Were they lovers? Did Gordon know about his wife's affair? Did Karin?

Watching Finn out there in the rain, unguarded, while holding up his still fragile wife, thinking his secret was still secret, she wondered what was going through his head. She'd find a moment to talk to him at the reception later. She was curious to know how he would behave, confident the degree of his grief would expose him.

Watched over by Tom and held up by Finn, Karin looked elegant in her black trouser suit and dark glasses. She kept her head low, discreetly lifting her glasses every now and then to dab her eyes. From where she stood, Fox could tell that Karin was causing a stir amongst the mourners. Some looked at her with sympathy, others with disgust. They blamed her. Fox checked the locations of both the uniformed Gardaí on the peripheries and the plain-clothes officers mingling in the crowd but close enough to Karin, just in case. Gordon had declined the offer of security, mocking Fox and her concern for his and his son's safety.

'It wasn't us they were after in the first place!' he spat, his voice laced with bitterness.

'We don't know that for sure,' Fox told him, doing her best to convince him to change his mind. 'At least let us put someone outside on the street – we'll keep them at a good distance.'

Gordon would not be moved but he could do nothing about them at the graveyard where Karin's presence secured theirs.

TV cameras from the national stations held a respectful distance. Fox had already requested all footage and placed her own photographer to be sure everyone present was captured, even those that may have lurked in the trees.

And so 'Poor Sive', as she had been referred to so many times that day, was buried in the pouring rain under the watchful gaze of many.

Her last few days were not kind. She had suffered. A lot, of that there was never any doubt. Drugged, kidnapped and held hostage for days, when she finally escaped she was chased like a dog and run down. They didn't know yet if she died instantly, Fox hoped she did and shivered at the idea that perhaps she hadn't. For Sive this funeral, despite the rain and the overwhelming sadness, was the calm after her storm.

Fox breathed deep and promised, no matter what was going on in Sive's personal life, she would find out who did this to her. No one deserved to die like that. She was too young to die. Watching as the crowd gathered and the casket was lowered into the ground, she felt a familiar cold shiver make its way down her spine and clutched her collar tight around her neck.

'You OK?' Callaghan asked.

She nodded. It was going to be a long day.

Gordon and his son hosted the funeral reception in the four-star Waybury Manor Hotel only a few miles from their home.

Fox waited for the right moment to engage with Finn. She took her time, wanting it to feel as natural as possible so she could really get a sense of him. If they were having an affair he'd have some interesting insights into Sive and her relationship with her husband for a start. The less their conversation felt like an interview the better. Without scrutiny he'd be less inclined to massage, embellish or fabricate the truth. Biding her time, she spent most of the afternoon just watching people and how they behaved, listening to what they said and what they didn't say. Same as in the graveyard, Karin was treated with a mix of pity and disdain, but Finn never left her side and Gordon never came near her.

She wouldn't have orchestrated it any better if she'd had the chance. Their paths collided, literally, as she entered and he left the bathroom lobby.

'God, sorry!' he gasped, having almost knocked her off her feet. Playing up, she *fell* into him. He helped her to the bench beside the door and knelt to make sure she was OK.

'My fault,' she told him with a smile. 'I should have been paying attention.'

'And I shouldn't have pushed the door so hard,' he joked.

'No harm done,' she assured him, taking a moment to catch her fictitiously fraught breath. 'So, how is she doing?'

'Karin? She's doing fine,' he told her, his eyes looking anywhere but at her.

'And what about you?' she asked. 'How are you doing? This can't be easy on you either.'

'Me?' he asked, immediately standing. 'I'm fine. What have I got to be upset about? I'm not the one grieving for my wife.'

'Sorry, I just meant looking after Karin must be draining too. It can't be easy to comfort her after what she's been through.'

He must have realised he sounded unnecessarily defensive and now looked as if he were searching for words to repair the damage.

His unnatural response had let him down just as she knew it would.

'I feel like a fraud being here,' Fox told him by way of a distraction. 'I didn't even know Sive. What was she like?'

Looking over at Karin – either to make sure she was in good hands or a safe distance away – he sat down beside Fox and pondered the question.

'She was a nice lady. Good fun, didn't take life too seriously, always up for a laugh. I wasn't surprised when I heard she'd made a run for it.' He let out a small laugh. 'Impetuous to the end.'

'You've known her a while then?'

'Yeah, they've know each other for years. Herself and Karin were in college together. Best friends, I suppose.' He swallowed and looked away.

'Did you guys see her often?'

'Often enough, maybe once a month – they were in business together too. Karin sank a good bit of money into Sive's businesses over the years but they never really worked out for them.'

'Interesting. And what about Gordon, what's he like?'

Finn shrugged, instinctively looking up to find him.

'A bit stiff, I suppose, not really my type. A real south-side boy.' There was a hard edge to his words.

Jealousy? she wondered.

'How did they get on?'

'Who?' he asked.

'Gordon and Sive.'

'Grand, I suppose. But then what would I know? They were very different people really. Different interests. I don't think he actually knew what he had in her.' He coughed suddenly to disguise the crack in his voice.

'And how about you, how did you get on with her?' Fox asked, afraid if she let a silence settle he'd walk away.

Resting his elbows on his knees, he smiled down at his shoes then looked up at her.

'You know, don't you?'

Smart guy, thought Fox.

'Yes, we do.'

'I'm assuming it came from Tom. I kind of thought he had us sussed – he's been pretty cold the last few days.'

'You gave yourself away by all accounts,' she told him. 'Caught on camera.'

Finn wrapped his hands around his head. 'Does Karin know?'

'I was going to ask you the same question.'

'I don't think so. Well, she's never let on if she does.'

'Things seemed a bit tense before, in the hospital.'

'That's the norm.' He laughed. 'She can be a tough woman to be around.'

That didn't surprise Fox. She was appeased by that fact that Finn didn't try to hide his affair but actually seemed glad to be able to talk about it.

'So you and Sive, how long?'

'God, I don't know – over a year – maybe eighteen months.'

'That's a long time.'

'Tell me about it!' he replied smartly, his eyes dropping again.

'This must be really tough,' she said with a small sweep of her hands.

He nodded but said nothing.

'Did you love her?' she asked.

Again he nodded, only this time he couldn't raise his head for fear someone might see his tears.

'Look, let's not do this now – this isn't the right time or place,' she told him.

'Thanks,' he responded appreciatively.

116

'But we do need to talk more.' In the back of her mind Fox considered the statistic that over half of women murdered in recent times were killed at the hands of their partner. 'Can you come down to the station and we can finish our chat there and in private?'

Finn agreed and scheduled it for the following morning.

Finn arrived on time and as agreed at nine. Dressed casually in blue jeans and a long-sleeved white T-shirt with paint splashes decorating the backs of his hands and strands of his sandy red hair, she didn't think he was aware of the attractive picture he presented – if that was your type – and again she couldn't but help wonder what he was doing with Karin. No disrespect to Karin but she didn't seem like his type, even less so now considering he was having an affair with her best friend. Talented and handsome, he could have any woman he wanted. What was her appeal? Money maybe? Influence possibly? Sex? She doubted it, Karin didn't seem the type.

She told them at the front desk to take him through to the interview room and offer him coffee, then she let him wait half an hour before joining him, letting Callaghan take up position in the adjoining room to watch through the two-way observation mirror.

'Sorry about that,' she lied as she entered the room. 'I got caught up in a meeting.'

Recently decorated, it still smelled of paint and new linoleum. Although the windows were frosted, the brightness outside still managed to filter its way in.

'Not to worry, I got coffee.'

'Working?' she asked with a smile, sitting down opposite him and pointing at the cobalt-blue paint that he was unconsciously rubbing off his skin.

'Yeah,' he sighed. 'It helps me relax.'

'How're you doing?' she asked, placing her notebook on the table and opening up a fresh page.

'Grand, but yesterday was bloody awful.' He scowled and slouched into the back of the chair.

'And Karin?'

'She's doing OK, I suppose. Can't sleep though – I heard her up in the middle of the night – but she's in good enough spirits.'

'Can't sleep either then?' she asked.

'When I'm on a roll I'll just work through till I can't keep my eyes open.'

Fox nodded, knowing exactly what he was talking about.

'So, you and Sive,' she said, picking up where they left off the day before, 'you'd been together quite some time. Seems more like a relationship than an affair?'

He shrugged. 'I suppose, maybe.' His demeanour was more like that of a petulant child than a grown man. 'We didn't mean for it to happen, it just did.'

Fox held her tongue, itching to tell him that that's what they all say, but she held back on her condescension and just let him speak.

'Karin and I, well, we're different. I'm afraid I'm more of a checked box than her husband,' he told her with an accepting shrug.

'A what?'

'A checked box,' he repeated, 'as in: fine house in an amazing location, check; successful business that makes good money, check; a commanding reputation and almost celebrity status, check; beautiful car, check; a dutiful husband that keeps his mouth shut, check … see what I mean?'

Fox was a little taken aback by this lifeless, hollow

approach to his relationship with his wife.

'Then why did you get together in the first place? Surely there must have been something there, in the beginning?'

'Absolutely,' he said with a sad smile that spoke volumes about the once genuine affection. 'There was something quite flattering about having someone like her interested in me. Genuinely – I mean Karin-bloody-Bolger! Even then she had a reputation. I *knew* who she was. And then she knew me and *she* wanted me. When everyone else was kissing her ass, her eyes were stuck on *me*, a complete nobody. And that I suppose is the truth of it. Who the hell was I? Some idealistic painter with fantastical ideas of changing the world, just me and my trusty paintbrush!' He gave a manic laugh. 'What a fuckin' eejit!' His laugh quickly turned to a sneer. 'What a fool,' he muttered under his breath.

There was a sorrowful stress in his voice, a hard-done-by tone that caught Fox by surprise but she wasn't there to either comfort or contradict so she let him continue on his self-deprecating rant.

'I think she fell in love with my talent, not with me.'

'What about you?' Fox asked, genuinely curious. 'Did you love her?'

'I did. Although she never really took me seriously. I've asked myself so many times how she became so hard, so full of self-loathing. I don't know if it goes back to her parents, maybe her mom abandoning herself and her brothers is what makes her work so hard, like she has something to prove, that there's nothing else to like or be proud of beyond her work achievements. I've never really said this out loud, I don't think anyone would believe me, but on the outside she's this hard-nosed bitch who takes no shit from no one. Put her in a boardroom and she'll own the room, give her a euro and she'll make a million, but take that away, peel those professional layers back and she has nothing. No confidence, no personality, nothing. She doesn't know who or what she is or, if she does know, she sure as hell doesn't want anyone else to know, not even me.'

Fox was amazed by Finn's emotional demolition of his wife and in such a peculiar fashion. He appeared to be genuinely saddened by the prosaic state of his marital relationship but had come to accept it as inevitable.

'She has some pretty serious issues, you know. For such a smart woman in the boardroom she's a complete thick at home.' His tone had a bitter edge. 'Nothing I did could convince her I actually loved her. It was like she couldn't believe it possible. So I gave up, I'd had enough.' He wiped his palms together. 'I stopped trying altogether and she got paranoid. She's insane. Really, she started accusing me of having affairs. Apparently I had an affair with one of my customers. God, she made such a scene. That woman paid almost two grand for a piece and the only piece of work she got was my fucking wife. In the end I had to give back her money. It was so embarrassing.' As if reliving the humiliation, his shoulders dropped and the colour rose on his face. 'And then she cut my allowance.' He laughed. 'Like a bold child, I was being punished. I wouldn't mind if she cared emotionally but it was more that I was hers like a possession and even if she didn't want me physically or intellectually, no one else could have me either.' Realizing the conversation had descended into a rant he stopped and, folding his arms protectively across his chest, let out a long and desperate sigh.

'If you loved her so much why did you do it?' Fox asked. 'Why the affair?'

'There comes a point where you just … I don't know …

' He struggled to find the works to explain. 'It's like if someone's convinced you're stealing from them but you're not but you might as well go ahead and do it anyway because that's what they already believe. Does that make sense?'

'Ish.'

'Look, nothing I could say or do could convince her I was faithful, so I had nothing to lose, did I?'

'So you started the affair she already thought you were having?'

He shrugged. 'I suppose, yeah.'

Again Fox bit her lip, irked by the so-it's-her-fault attitude. She had so many questions, the biggest one being why on earth did he stay, but she had a good idea what the answer to that would be. Instead she chose a different tack.

'But then how did you do it if she was so suspicious? Surely, if what you're saying is true, she was watching you like a hawk?'

'She was.' He shrugged. 'But we just kept ourselves out of sight. We let Karin's schedule dictate when we met up, sometimes here during the day when she was away or there's a small hotel on the Northside we go to when she's home.'

'What about Aggie? And Tom?' Fox asked.

'They're not here all the time. And Tom tends to track Karin not me – he couldn't care less what I get up to.' He stopped talking and let his head drop to massage his temples with his thumbs. 'Sive was so vivacious,' he said into his lap, his voice almost a whisper. 'Up for anything, she really enjoyed her life. Even though she failed so many times at so many things, she always picked herself up and started again. Always.'

'And Karin, she was supposed to be her best friend,' Fox threw in.

He let out a deep and sorrowful sigh and shook his head.

'She was, I think. Sometimes Sive did get bit weird about her. I know she admired her, looked up to her but actually I think she might have been a bit jealous. Karin was really good to her. Too good, to be honest. I didn't agree with what Sive took from her – she kind of took the piss sometimes and sometimes I'd take her up on it, but they were Karin's choices at the end of the day and Karin is well able to look after herself. She didn't need me to fight her battles.'

'And you, Finn, are you her friend?'

'I used to be. I used to be her only *real* friend. Karin has lots of people around her but you wouldn't call any of them her friends. They don't care about her, not really. They're nothing but parasites, the lot of them. Most of them don't even like her but they sure as hell love her money. Miserable bastards!' Then, noticing Fox's sceptical lift of an eyebrow, he admitted with a shrug, 'Yes, I know how it looks. I'm no better than them, I get it. Yes, Sive took advantage and, yes, we betrayed Karin but we didn't set out to. And for what it's worth I feel like a piece of shit but …' He shrugged but said nothing and they both knew he had no words because he had no excuse.

'You didn't have to stay. No one was forcing you to.'

He shook his head. 'I know that. You don't think I've thought about it? Thought about packing my things and leaving? We talked about it, Sive and I…'

'So what stopped you?' Fox wanted to hear him say it, hear him admit it. Finn wasn't ashamed about his relationship but he felt hard done by, like he was the underdog.

'Come on, you know what!' Finn scoffed with an embarrassed playfulness.

'No, I don't. Why don't you tell me?'

She held his stare, her eyebrows raised in anticipation, waiting for him to reply, refusing to fill in the blanks for him.

The silence stretched out like a lonely road and he knew he had to go it alone.

'Where else would I find a place like mine? I have it good, I know it, and I don't want to leave. Simple as that.' He leaned back in the chair as if the confession had taken the air out of him, leaving him deflated and limp. 'Don't judge me. I put up with a lot. I deserve my space.'

'I'm sure you do, Finn, I'm sure you do,' Fox replied, looking down at the still-blank page of her notebook. 'I have to ask this, Finn, but where were you on the night Sive and Karin went missing?'

Finn let out a cynical chuckle. 'I knew that was coming.'

Patiently Fox waited for him to answer, her impressions of him fluctuating between pity and disgust.

'I think I told you the day we first met. I worked through the whole of that Friday. At about seven I finished up and ate the dinner Aggie had left for me, finished off the bottle of wine and then I fell asleep.'

'Can anyone verify this?'

'Nope,' he told her with a single but decisive shake of his head. 'I was all on my own.' He sat bolt upright now with his shoulders held back and his chin ever so slightly lifted.

She hadn't intended to be so direct with her next question but there was something in his tone that smothered any sympathy she might have felt at his loss. 'Finn, can you tell me about the argument you had with Sive the week of the kidnapping?'

He looked at her sharply, his features tensing into a questioning furrow.

'What argument?' he asked as if he didn't know but the instant flush on his cheeks gave him away.

'The CCTV footage I mentioned to you yesterday was

123

recorded while testing the cameras at the front of the house the week before Sive and Karin were kidnapped.' She paused and waited for the penny to drop. 'It shows you and Sive arguing. No sound, I'm afraid, but it's pretty clear what's going on.'

Finn's face turned a bright crimson, but he didn't deny it.

'I wasn't happy about her going away with Karin,' he admitted.

'Why not?'

'Why do you think?' he asked sarcastically. 'I wanted her to move away from Karin, not get stuck in deeper, that's why.'

'Go on.'

'This trip, this wasn't some nicey-nicey girls' weekend away in the country – this was Karin getting involved all over again in another one of Sive's mental business ideas. I have no idea why she kept funding her but she did, and I wanted Sive to stop. I was uncomfortable with her going away with Karin, not when we were, well, not while we were involved – it didn't feel right. I wanted her to stop but she said no, said it was none of my business and actually accused me of being jealous. *How ridiculous is that?*' He slumped back into the chair, realising he had raised his voice and a few people were looking. 'Sorry,' he whispered.

'That's OK, no need to apologise. This can't be easy.'

'It's a bloody nightmare.'

'And Sive, she didn't have a problem obviously with the trip?'

'Not at all. It didn't seem to bother her at all. '

'So you fought her?' Fox asked, leading him, and he nodded. 'Did you speak to her again before she left for the West?'

'I tried but she wouldn't return my calls.' There was no denying the quiver that had developed in his bottom lip.

'That must have really upset you.'

Finn nodded, too afraid to speak.

'I'd say you were pretty hurt?'

Again Finn gave a quick nod.

'Hurt enough to want to hurt her back?'

'I know what you're thinking,' he replied quietly.

'What am I thinking?' Fox challenged.

'That was not me. I did not harm anyone, especially not Sive,' he said, stressing each word as he spoke. 'I didn't hate her. I *loved* her.' He let his head drop into his hands again. 'Really I did but I can't show it, can I? I have to pretend while that knob prances around like the poor grieving widower. He's some piece of work. He didn't love her.'

'How can you be so sure?'

'I know. Sive told me what he was like, how he didn't appreciate her, called her a waste of space.'

'Did he ever harm her?'

'No. Not physically anyway. Not that she ever told me. But he could be pretty cruel when he wanted to be. Some of the things he'd say would really upset her.'

'If he was that bad why did she stay with him?'

'I don't know,' Finn huffed. 'Security? I told her to leave him often enough.'

'Were you never tempted? To take her away from all that?'

'It was never part of the plan.'

'So what was the plan?'

He stopped, as if holding his breath, before declaring, 'It doesn't matter, not now.'

'No, seriously,' Fox insisted, 'what was your plan? I'd like to know.'

But he simply shook his head and pressed his lips together in a sour-faced grimace. 'It just doesn't matter.'

'So, what will you do now? When you leave here?' Fox asked, an element of sensitivity returning.

'Go home, I guess.'

'And Karin?'

'What about her?'

'Well, are you going to tell her?'

'About what? Tell her that I was having an affair with her best friend? I don't think so. I can't. Not now.'

'You may have to.'

'Well, I'll cross that bridge …'

'How can you live that lie?' Fox asked, genuinely wondering how he could pull it off, how he could live with one woman when plainly he was in love with another.

'Unless my hand is forced I'll not tell her until I'm ready to go and I know she can cope.' He looked at her. 'You're not going tell her, are you?'

'It will come out eventually, so if you don't plan to tell her then, yes, I guess we will.'

'At least give me time,' he pleaded.

'We'll be in touch,' she told him, terminating the interview.

From the window of the top-floor office Fox watched him leave.

'What do you think?' Callaghan asked, coming to stand beside her.

'I don't know, I can't tell,' she replied, perplexed. 'Did you get the DNA sample?'

'Yep.'

'Good. If he was there we'll soon find out.'

'I feel sorry for the poor fucker. They should have run away, the two of them. Karin and Gordon sound like an absolute nightmare.'

'*Hmmm.* He's got motive, I think, and no alibi and along with half the bloody country fits the 'average' description of our abductor.' With her hands stuck into the pockets of her trousers she stared out the window. 'We need to find that bloody car.'

'Well, that would help,' Callaghan replied smartly and, looking at his watch, declared, 'Come on, I'm parched, let's grab a cuppa.'

Chapter 10

Just as she took the first bite of her jam-covered scone Ken Stanley's number came up on screen.

'Hi, Ken, please tell me you've got something great to tell me,' she said, almost choking on her food.

'I might do,' he replied and she could hear the smile in his voice.

'*Fan-bloody-tastic!* Just what I need.'

'Happy to oblige. I've popped it into the secure server and forwarded to you on the link. I'm assuming you've got access, but, if you don't, let me know and I'll get you a password.'

'Brilliant, Ken, yes, I've full access. Thanks.'

'No problem, just gimme a call when you've had a chance to look at it.'

'Will do – you're an absolute gem.'

Frantically looking for something to wipe her greasy hands on, she pushed her chair back and grabbed her coat.

Looking aghast from her almost untouched and still steaming tea and scone to the woman herself, Callaghan moaned, 'Where are you going?'

'Back to the office – come on!'

'*What?* I haven't finished.'

'You stay, I'll see you back there then.'

Throwing his eyes to heaven he took a last slurp of his tea and grabbing the remainder of his toast ran out of the café after her.

'What's the rush?' he asked, sitting into the passenger seat. 'It'll still be there in half an hour.'

'Seriously?' she asked, pointing with a grin to the melted butter on the side of his mouth. 'No time to eat, buddy.'

The hot sweet tea burned her lips as she settled at the conference-room table, waiting for her laptop to link with the screen, full of anticipation of what Ken had managed to find out. Logging into the server, she couldn't help but smile at the familiar and anal filing conventions that she and her colleagues used to tease Ken about.

'Jesus, would you look at that!' Callaghan remarked as she selected the first of six files in the folder and double-clicked. 'He really is a bit peculiar, isn't he?'

An Excel spreadsheet opened up with multiple tabs across the bottom. Picking up her phone, she rang Ken. She put him on speaker while she clicked through the folders and he explained the content of what she was looking at. In it he had documented the names of everyone who had, to the best of his knowledge, based on pictures and screen footage, participated in the various demonstrations over the past few months. Noting their name, age, address and connection to the Kings Brewery, the dossier was comprehensive and thorough, but most interesting were the notes in a separate tab marked *Summary*. In it he pulled out three names, three people who stood out in the context of Karin's abduction and their special connection to her.

Desmond 'Dessie' Smyth. A fifty-nine-year-old master

brewer, Dessie had been made redundant after forty-four years of service. Having left school at fourteen he joined Kings Brewery as a troubled teenage apprentice where he learned to respect his peers and master his trade. He always said the brewery saved his life – left to his own devices he didn't care to think what institution he'd have ended up in. But, being made redundant at fifty-nine, he would not be moving with Kings to its new home and despite the sizeable payout he was facing the remainder of his working career unemployed. Too old, he thought, to retrain – sure who'd want him, at his age? – and too young to be put on the shelf. Dessie, the report stated, led the first parade of protestors and held aloft the now iconic banner that made world news declaring *Justice for the Workers*. Interviewed on TV for the *Nine O'Clock News* he openly proclaimed his disgust for Spiro Capital, the brewery development and Kings management team. He was an angry man but he was also a calm man. Ken surmised that Dessie was the dangerous kind of protestor, simmering dangerously beneath the surface with the potential to explode unpredictably at any moment.

Michael 'Mikey' Smyth was Desmond's brother. Following a couple of years later, he too earned his stripes at Kings. Like his brother he was a very angry man but unlike his brother he had no control over it. Belligerent and mouthy, he had form, the grievous bodily harm kind of form, and used his burly weight and stern features to get his way. And while Dessie spent his years at Kings taking pride in his work and honing his craft, Mikey went to work to earn his money, nothing more, nothing less. Active at all three protests, Mikey had tried but failed to organise a sit-in at the plant, doing his best to incite aggression and destruction amongst his younger, passionate and more impressionable colleagues. When the Gardaí were called there were a few scuffles and more than a few arrests but Mikey wasn't one of them. Somehow he got away with it, leaving the others to take the blame.

Kings Brewery also employed John Smyth, another brother of Dessie and Mikey. He, if he was willing, was offered a promotion at the new facility, which would mean relocating with his young family. Dedicated and hardworking, John, according to his line manager, showed great promise and was worth hanging on to. With fifteen years between them, John was a different breed to his older brothers. A quiet chance conversation between John and one of Ken's officers suggested that he was delighted with the offer but was being put under pressure by his older brother to stand and fight. His bruised cheek and black eye said it all. Conflicted and petrified that supporting his brothers would jeopardize his promotion, John knew he had to choose. Ken suspected John had his head screwed on and, not having seen him for a couple of weeks, believed he had chosen well.

Fox was a little puzzled and a little disappointed. 'So what is it about these men, Ken? They're belligerent and likely suspects, yes, but no more so than many of the other demonstrators, surely?'

'You do realise who they are, don't you?' Ken asked.

'Not a clue.'

'Seriously?'

'No, Ken. Seriously.'

Even when Ken pointed out their surname she still didn't join the dots.

'Smyth? Sure, half the bloody country's called Smyth!' she complained, wishing he'd just come out and tell her.

'With a Y?'

'With a Y, with an I, what is it?' she begged, throwing her eyes to heaven and grimacing at an equally confused Callaghan.

'Smyth, Nathan Smyth, ring any bells? Executive Assistant to Karin Bolger?'

'*Bloody hell!*'

'I knew you'd like it.'

As unconvinced as she had been by the idea of the protestors being the perpetrators of the crime and Justice for the Workers as probable cause – it just seemed too obvious, more like an afterthought than a motivation – there was no denying this was a distinct and relevant line of enquiry.

'Jesus, where do you start with this one?' she asked.

'Well, that's your job, my work here is done,' Ken told her smugly. 'If you need anything else, you know where I am.' And he signed off.

Taking stock of the situation, she quickly replanned her day and called AJ in the West headquarters, telling him she wouldn't be back till later and he should move the conference callout by a couple of hours.

'All this driving is doing my head in,' she grumbled while ringing Tom Williams' number. 'It's just not sustainable.'

'Well, talk to the Super and see if you can temporarily transfer the incident room to Dublin – it might get yourself back to Dublin for a few weeks,' Callaghan advised her while trying to navigate his way through the files on screen.

'Don't think it'll fly,' she said doubtfully with the phone still to her ear, waiting for Tom to answer.

'DI Fox here,' she introduced herself when he did. 'A quick question for you – what can you tell me about Nathan Smyth – he's Karin's PA, right?'

'That's right. Nice guy, been here a little over three years,

132

Karin likes him so he must be all right as she doesn't take to everyone. I'll send you over his file. Why?'

'Were you aware that half of his family on both his mother's and father's side were employees at Kings?' She could tell by the length of his pause that he hadn't.

'No, I wasn't. Is he involved in this?'

'I don't know yet but we're looking into it.'

'Do I need to do anything on this end?'

She could hear his military authority kick in. She could bet he wouldn't be impressed with himself at missing that nugget. But then how or why would he know?

'No. Not yet. Keep things normal. By the way,' she asked hurriedly before he hung up, 'have you had any luck tracing that press leak you mentioned before?'

'Funny you mention it, I've only just confirmed the address of the Internet café where we believe the email was sent from.'

'Where's that?'

'SurfCity, just off Grafton Street. We have the date and time so hopefully they keep good records and we'll be able to find out who pressed the button.'

'Fantastic – let me know as soon as you have a name,' she replied with a good idea who it was most likely to be.

Within minutes of putting the phone down Nathan's employment record arrived into her in-box.

A graduate of Dublin City University, Nathan graduated top of his class with a degree in property economics. He won an internship with Ingram, an international commercial property firm based in London. With a starting salary just above minimum wage it didn't take him long to secure his first and quick second step up the ladder. References from his past employers were glowing, applauding his ingenuity and innovation in getting the job done. Obviously a very smart young man, he was one of ten candidates who fought for the chance to return home and work with Karin. Scoring top of the group, hands down, Nathan secured the position and started a little over two years ago.

Fox doubted if either Tom or Karin were aware of his connection to Kings and wondered on which side of the loyalty fence he sat.

One of five children, Smyth was the only one of his siblings to go to college. Of the remaining four the first was a carpenter, the second an electrician and the last two did their apprenticeships alongside their father and uncles on both sides of the family and their grandfathers before them, in Kings Brewery. It was in their blood. It had paid for every Christmas turkey eaten in the Smyth family for years. Generation after generation earned their stripes behind those iconic high stone walls.

Even before the Kings sale this wasn't a background Nathan was likely to share with his work colleagues. He had said it himself when they met, that he was an anomaly among most of his peers. She'd bet none of them knew where he lived, never mind what his father and uncles did for a living and she didn't blame him for keeping quiet. People could be unnecessarily judgmental when it suited them.

Placing the ransom letter and two previous threats back into the case file, she grabbed her coat and left the building with Callaghan hot on her heels.

Nathan Smyth, middle child of Theresa and Dessie Smyth sat calmly across the boardroom table. He was the duck that glided effortlessly across the water but underneath his feet flapped wildly to keep him moving and afloat. She knew the signs, the slightly flushed cheeks, the tiny beads of sweat that formed on his upper lip and the whites of his knuckles from the grip that held his hands tight so as to deny the shake that might give him away. Calm but scared, he smiled politely, looking from one to the other, waiting for the conversation to begin.

'So, Nathan, you remember Detective Callaghan, don't you?' she asked, looking at him with what she hoped was a friendly smile. When he nodded she asked, 'And how are you today?'

'Grand. You?' he replied, returning her smile while bravely holding her stare. 'What's this about?'

'Nothing to be nervous about, we just want to have a chat,' she said, opening up her folder to take out the three notes protected in their individual plastic sleeves.

'I'm not nervous,' he said. 'I've got nothing to be nervous about.'

'Take a look at these.' She watched his face as she laid the sleeves out in front of him.

Looking down, he took a minute to look at each of them as if seeing them for the first time.

'What about them?'

'Have you seen any of them before?'

'You know I have. This one came to me,' he told her, pointing at the ransom note.

'And the others?' she asked.

'No,' he replied with a slight lift to his voice, like a question, testing her to see if she'd believe him. 'Why are you showing them to me?'

'Do you know what they are?'

'Not these two.'

'These,' she said, pushing two of the sleeves towards him, 'are two threats sent to Karin when the deal with Spiro Capital was first announced.'

Nathan shrugged and shook his head, his face fixed with an exaggerated look of confusion.

'Nathan,' she said, fixing the sleeves one by one in a neat line. 'I understand your family has a long history with the Kings Brewery.'

He swallowed. 'Yeah, we do. My da works there, so do my brothers and two of my uncles. What of it?'

'Well, given what's happened recently along with the fact that you are employed by the company that has effectively closed the brewery down, I'd say that is an important route for our investigation to take, don't you think?'

'Off you go, don't let me stop you.'

'Don't be flippant, Nathan, this is serious.'

'Do I look like I'm laughin'? What's it to do with me?'

'That's what we're trying to figure out,' Fox responded, making sure to hold his defiant stare as long as she could.

'Are you sayin' this was me?' he asked with a forced laugh.

'Look, Nathan, we're not saying anything – just that both threatening notes and the ransom have obviously come from someone who is pissed off and declaring justice for the workers. Sound familiar?' She lifted the ransom note and a picture from the case file of his father holding his now internationally famous banner aloft.

'And?'

And her patience was wearing thin.

'*And,* we find out that half your family earned their living at Kings Brewery, that the slogan *Justice for the Workers* was first coined by your father and it's your boss that's as good as closed it down. Are you beginning to see the link here?'

'Conflict of interest, I'd say,' Callaghan added.

'Only if you are actually interested,' Nathan retorted.

Fox took a moment to consider him, imagining those feet frantically working double-time.

'Does Karin know about your family ties to the brewery?'

He gave a slow shake of his head.

She hadn't thought so.

'I assume your family know you work for her?'

With his eyes closed, the first sign she was making progress, he nodded.

'Can you at least see why we'd be suspicious?' she asked, leaning forward, trying to appear reasonable while appealing to his good conscience, which she was sure he had.

But Nathan gave her nothing. It was time to be a bit more specific.

'Let's change the subject, shall we?' she suggested, placing a well-read copy of the *Sunday Times* on the table. 'Remember this?' she asked. 'Eleventh of August, I believe.' She turned it around for him to read the headline.

Nathan shifted in his seat. 'Yes, I do.'

'I'd say Karin went ballistic when this came out.'

'She wasn't happy,' he replied.

'You know she still has Tom Williams trying to find out who leaked the story?'

He nodded slowly.

'"*Exclusive*",' she read. '"*Reliable source*" – any idea who that might have been?'

'It was going to come out anyway.' He shrugged.

'Really? Karin didn't seem to think so, or so she told me. Seems that some of the things they printed weren't ever meant for public consumption. They printed information that was both sensitive and private which came from a set of documents that only you and three other people had access to and now there's lawsuits coming from all sides threatening to stall the entire project. It's a terrible thing, to bite the hand that feeds you, isn't it?'

'How would I know?'

'Because I think the leak was you.'

Nathan shook his head and smiled. 'You're miles off the mark.'

'No, Nathan, I don't think I am. I think it was you. I suspect you may not have had much choice. Maybe you were told to do it? Am I right?'

'No. Sorry to disappoint you but you're not.'

'Well, we'll soon find out,' she told him, taking back the newspaper without taking her eyes from his face and, even though his features remained neutral, there was no mistaking the panic she saw rise up in his eyes.

'You didn't think she'd let it go, did you?' she asked with a patronising lilt in her voice and a tilt of her head. 'Not a chance! But I'll bet she never thought it would be you though.'

She'd struck a chord and she knew it. His head dipped in shame.

'It seems the email was sent from the SurfDock on Grafton Street. Tom is there as we speak going through the logbook and internet history for all its computers over the last six months.' She watched intently for a reaction. 'So it's only a matter of time really before we get the details of exactly who logged into that computer that day and hopefully a good image of who was using the machine at the time.'

'That's bullshit – it could have been any one of a hundred customers that go in there every day.'

'True, but there's only one you, isn't there? Now wouldn't

that be a coincidence, if you were there that very same day?'

Nathan shifted uneasily again.

'I didn't leak that information and I had nothing to do with the kidnapping. I'm not a murderer either, by the way.'

'So who do you think it was?'

'How the hell do I know? All I'm saying is that this has nothing to do with me. If you've got a problem with my uncle, go speak to him, not me.'

'Who said anything about your uncle? Why would we talk to him?'

'Oh, for God's sake!' he moaned, throwing his arms in the air, his calm beginning to unravel. 'Look, this is a great job. I'm lucky to be here. Karin can make or break someone like me. I get on well with her, she likes me. Why the hell would I fuck it all up?' There was a strong whiff of desperation in his voice. 'This has nothing to do with me and you know it. I don't know what my uncles might or might not have done. It's a free world.'

'Nathan, are you telling us that this had something to do with your uncle?' Callaghan asked. 'You might as well tell us because we'll figure it out pretty soon anyway.'

'I'm not saying anything.'

Calling time on the interview, Fox got up to go but Callaghan laid a hand on her arm and she sat again.

'Before we let you back to your work, can you tell us your movements on the night of the abductions?' he asked.

'I was home, with my ma and da, watching *Late Night Live*. Katie Taylor was on it and that yoke from *Fair City*,' he replied firmly and standing up he fixed his shirt, for the first time giving Fox a chance to properly assess his build. He too was a good fit.

'Convenient, that you would be each other's alibi, isn't it?'

'Oh piss off, would ya! You've got nothing on me except that I work here. So if you want to, then go ahead and arrest me and I'll get myself a lawyer and sue the shit out of you for harassment.'

'Are you willing to come down to the station to give us a DNA sample?' Callaghan asked, choosing to ignore the threat.

'Do I have a choice?'

'Depends on what way you look at it, but for your own sake I strongly recommend that you do.'

'When?'

'This evening, if possible.'

'Fine, after work,' he huffed, storming out of the room.

They let him go.

'Nice job,' Fox complimented Callaghan as they descended in the lift. 'He's shitting himself.' She smiled, feeling only a smidgen of pity for the young man whose world they had just rocked. 'OK, all set,' she said into her phone. 'Let's see where he goes.'

They didn't have long to wait. Within forty minutes they saw him exit the office, dash across the road and stride at a great pace up the street with his phone stuck to his ear. From the safety of their parked car they watched him march on, with the first of their trackers following a safe distance behind.

Callaghan drove them back to the station. Getting out of the car, Fox checked her watch. She was under pressure and cutting it fine. She still had to call to Karin's before hitting the road back to Galway.

'You go on in,' she told Callaghan, digging the keys to her own car from her pocket. 'I'm under pressure so I'm going to just head from here.'

Climbing into her own car she fired up the engine and

called to Callaghan out of the open window, '*Let me know where he goes, yeah?*'

'*Sure thing!*' he called back to her with a salute, running up the steps and into the station.

Nathan banged on the door three times and when there was no answer he pressed his finger firmly on the bell, looking over his shoulder with venom in his eyes.

'Jesus Christ, lad, what the hell's up with you?' his father cried, pulling open the door with a scowl.

Nathan pushed past him to storm down the hall into the kitchen without saying a word.

'*This is all fucked up!*' he howled, throwing his jacket on the floor and his arms in the air. '*I knew this would come back to me! I told you it would! What the fuck have you done?*'

Mikey took the cigarette from between his lips to flick the ash into the overflowing ashtray.

'Calm the fuck down, would ya? You're givin' me a pain in me bloody face with yer yellin' like a big girl's blouse.'

'*I knew this would happen! I told you, but oh no, you wouldn't listen! Well, let me tell you this, asshole, they're on to you!*'

'*You*, ya mean.' His uncle smirked.

Unable to control himself Nathan dived at his uncle, knocking over the chair and his overweight uncle with it. Pinning him to the ground with his knees, he raised his fist above his head, his intention to bring it down hard and direct on his face.

'Get the fuck off him, ya big eejit!' Nathan's father growled, grabbing his son's fist with one hand and the scruff of his neck with the other. 'Get up *now*. Both of youse!' He hauled a heaving Nathan off the floor and threw him towards an armchair in the corner. '*Don't you ever come into this house throwing your weight around like that again, do ya understand?'* he roared. *'This is my house!'*

Nathan panted without answering, steadying himself against the arm of the chair while casting an evil eye at his uncle. His whole body shook, disgusted that his father seemed to be protecting his brother.

'You have no idea, have you? He's got us all involved.' Nathan pointed to his uncle 'He's a fucking thug and you know it.' And when his father didn't reply, he asked, 'Do you even know what he's done?' He turned again to his uncle, 'Was it you? Did you do it? Did you?'

Mikey stood his ground, his arms slightly wide from his overworked torso.

'Answer me, fucker!' Nathan roared, incensed by the taunting grin that filled his face.

Taking his son by the scruff of the neck, Dessie dragged him back down the hall, opened the front door and threw him out on the street.

'Don't come to my house an' think ya can throw yer weight around!' he growled.

'Ask him, Da. Ask him did he do it?' Nathan shouted, pointing to Mikey who appeared behind his brother.

'Look at ya, with your airs and graces and your stupid fuckin' poufter haircut!' Mikey sneered down at him. 'Who do ya think ya are? Ya fuckin' traitor!'

'That's enough,' Dessie told him, putting an arm across his chest, stopping him from crossing the threshold.

'I did nothin' that wasn't coming to her!' Mikey shouted as Dessie closed the door on his son.

Chapter 11

It was a different woman Fox met when she visited Karin at her home. At Karin's request, preferring not to conduct their conversation under the busybody scrutiny of her entire office, Fox called to her house just after six. Gone was the helpless, vulnerable woman she had helped pick up off the floor. She had been replaced by a smart, confident and stylish businesswoman who stood tall and proud while pouring herself a very large glass of Merlot. Even though Karin's taste wasn't akin to her own – she was more of a cheap and cheerful Zara girl – Fox had to admire her effortless regal elegance from her incredible Louboutin shoes to the beautifully tailored Victoria Beckham dress suit complemented by the delicate diamond stud earrings with matching solitaire drop pendant.

'Are you sure you won't join me?' Karin offered from behind the marble counter.

'No, thanks, but tea would be great. I have a long drive ahead of me,' Fox replied, momentarily intimidated by the transformation, and took a minute to retune her assessment.

'I heard you were at the office today,' Karin remarked while leaning over the sink to fill the kettle.

'That's right – we had a few questions for Nathan Smyth.'

'May I ask why?'

'Well, we're following a specific line of enquiry. It seems Nathan come from a family of Kings employees – his father was a master brewer there and he also gave us the *Justice for the Workers* slogan.'

Karin nodded. 'Tom mentioned it to me earlier. He doesn't talk much about his family – Nathan, I mean.' She shook her head. 'You don't think he's involved in this malarkey? He's a smart kid. I like him – I don't think he'd be that stupid.'

'I'm not so sure,' Fox replied, surprised by Karin's apparent lack of concern. 'His father and uncle seem to be a pair of heavyweights. He may not have had an option.'

'I see,' Karin pondered, putting her glass on the counter. 'Pity. I really liked him.' Fox noted her use of the past tense and felt a short pang of guilt for Nathan who had just, she guessed, become unemployed.

'How are *you* feeling?' Fox asked as she followed Karin to the lounge area and the sofas.

Karin switched on the collection of floor lamps as she passed and although the kettle had long since boiled there was no sign of tea.

'Getting back to normal, I suppose,' she replied, sinking into the sofa, crossing her legs and throwing an arm over the back of the chair.

Finding it almost impossible not to be distracted by her shoes, Fox took a sneaky glance while Karin settled herself with another sip of her wine.

'I have to admire your determination – I'm not sure I'd be able to get right back in the way you have,' Fox remarked.

'You'd be surprised,' Karin told her with a tilt of her head. 'It's amazing what strength you can draw from defiance.

Anyway, you don't strike me as someone who would be knocked down that easily.'

Fox smiled at what she took to be a compliment – she certainly was not and was proud to be recognised as a tough individual.

'People like you and me,' Karin said, 'we're resilient. Rebellious almost or tenacious, I don't know. Out of utter stubbornness we refuse to go down, not without a good ol' dogfight anyway.'

'Am I that easy to read?' Fox asked, almost embarrassed by Karin's exact interpretation of her without having ever talked to her properly.

'Yes and no. I recognise myself in you. We haven't got as far as we have by being pushovers, have we? Ours is a man's world. To survive we need guts, stamina and balls.' She laughed, raising her clenched fist dramatically in front of her.

'So I take it you haven't changed your plans or timing for the brewery then?' Fox asked, eager to shift Karin's attention away from her.

'Absolutely not. We have had challenges through the courts but, no, as far as I'm concerned we're on track and ready to go,' Karin declared firmly. 'No one pushes me around like that. It would be a dishonour to Sive's memory to do anything but deliver what we set out to do in the beginning.'

'Are you at all concerned that whoever did this might come back?'

'Let them try. They can come to get me again and this time I'll be ready and waiting. They won't know what hit them.'

Fox admired her courage but, even with Karin's bold and audacious war cry, she was glad of the Garda presence outside both front and back doors.

'What are your thoughts on the Justice for the Workers campaign?' Fox asked.

Karin considered the question. 'It's a tough question,' she admitted. 'But honestly, I think if I were an employee losing my job I'd be out there campaigning and protesting alongside them. I get they're unhappy, really I do, but this is progress. This plan is commercially sound. The plant is outdated and in bad need of modernization and the business can't do that efficiently in its current location. It makes sense to move.'

Fox listened to what was probably part of a media-trained hard sell.

'And if it's not me there are plenty of other investment developers out there who'd give their left testicle to get their hands on the site,' Karin went on. 'Now, they wouldn't give a toss or a single thought to the workers. It's a terrific opportunity for the community if they'd get their heads out of the sand. They'll have parks, playgrounds, sports fields, restaurants, shops and a centre to be proud of. Sure the brewery will be gone but not completely. It will just move, that's all – a new future for a new generation – it's called evolution.'

There was no denying the passion in her voice or the belief in her attitude but, despite her conviction, Fox was sideswiped by Karin's response to the protestors.

'So you don't blame them?' she asked.

'Of course not – it's their right to protest. It's refreshing to see people stand up and be counted, isn't it? As a nation we don't protest enough. Look at us, sure we rolled over and let ourselves be kicked by the banks and Europe and the IMF.'

'Even if it's led to what happened to you and Sive?'

'I'm sorry, Detective Inspector, but I don't believe what happened to Sive and me had anything to do with these protestors – they're not up to it – have you seen them? Half of them have one foot in the grave, for God's sake, and anyway if it was all about saving the brewery what in the name of God are they going to do with five million euro?'

Fox was intrigued to see that she and Karin had arrived at exactly the same conclusion.

'So, if it wasn't them, who do you think did it?' Fox asked, tempted to ask about Nathan but deciding against it for the moment.

'I have no idea, really. I can't imagine who or why. I am a businesswoman, an entrepreneur – nothing I do is personal, ever.'

'What about Sive and your business deals with her, were they not personal?'

'Well, yes and no. Sive was my friend. My only *real* friend if I'm honest. And even then, I suppose even she took the mick sometimes.' She stood up and went back to the counter and the bottle of wine and paused to fill her glass. 'I'm happy to admit it. I'm not stupid. I know a bum deal when I see it. That's the thing. I *see* it. I don't go into any deal blind. I like to see it first, visualize it, know it inside out, understand its DNA and then, only then, do I decide. That's the way I do things and it's stood me well.'

'Makes sense,' Fox said.

'I also know I'm not very, what's the word …' she put a hand to her chin, 'popular, I suppose. I don't have many friends – tons of acquaintances but very few friends.'

Fox was about to contradict her, to tell her not to be ridiculous, but thought better of it. Karin was right. From what she had learned about her so far she didn't have any friends. To pretend otherwise would be disingenuous.

'Have you ever been in a room full of people where everyone wants you, to be near you, to talk to you? They point and nod and gravitate towards you and you know damn well that when they get home they'll bitch as passionately about you as when they loved you only hours before.'

'I can't say I have.' Fox felt a little uncomfortable.

'Well, I have – it happens all the time. And in that room full of people you're completely alone. I know if I woke up in the morning penniless, all those people would simply disappear.' She snapped her fingers, making Fox jump. 'Just! Like! That!' Her honesty was tinted by bitter acceptance.

Again Fox chose not to answer, she had no credible rebuttal to the statement.

'Yes, many of my acquaintances, if you ask them honestly, will have a duplicitous opinion about me, one they keep for my face and the other for my back.' Her tone became matter of fact as if speaking of someone else unknown to her. 'They couldn't give a rat's ass about me – they're only interested in progressing themselves – self-serving – what's in it for them.'

She was beginning to sound a little drunk, Fox wasn't even sure if she was still engaged in conversation or just muttering to herself.

'Not one of them I could depend on personally, none I would call on in a crisis, none I could ever rely on to be discreet.'

'What about Sive? You said she was your real friend.' Fox was hoping to steer the conversation back to something that was useful.

'Yes. Sive was different. I knew what she was at, most of the time. She wasn't so smart that she could hide it, but she really was a friend and she was harmless. If I was in trouble, *real* trouble, there are only three people I'd call on: Finn, Tom and herself. Not that I've ever needed to, until now. And now she's gone it doesn't matter anymore, it's too late.'

Topping up her glass for a third time she walked over to the window and looked out over the bay. At dusk the evening sun cast a surreal haze over the crisp blue sea but Fox wasn't sure Karin even noticed. She felt sorry for her. Despite her bravado, she exuded an underlying tinge of sorrow not just for the loss of her friend but for the absence of a single contender willing to step up and comfort her. She was completely alone What a sad existence! All that money but very little happiness and even less pleasure. She wouldn't trade places with her for all the money in the world.

'I'm neither a stupid nor a naive woman,' Karin declared eventually, turning back into the room. 'I can see what's going on around me. Finn thinks I don't see them for what they are, but I do. I did find it difficult to accept at first, but it is the way it is. I'm not an easy person to get along with, I know that. I like things done my way and I say it the way it is. I don't believe in lying for the sake of it but that doesn't mean that I don't have feelings myself. I do get hurt – some of the things they say about me in the press are pretty damn awful but I get over it.'

Even though she'd only just met the woman, Fox knew that the last thing Karin would either want or appreciate was her pity but there was no denying the empathy she felt because, as Karin had so astutely pointed out, they were alike in more ways than one. Apart from her obvious strength of character and powerful determination, they could both count their friends on one hand. And although the reasons may have been different, the result was the same.

For Fox it didn't help that her job was so demanding and occupied so much of her time when she was both on and off duty, or that her friends were by now mostly married and had moved on leaving her behind, comfortable in her bijoux one-bed apartment. As one by one her friends, mostly male to be fair, got married, the invitations to hang out dwindled until they just stopped altogether. No woman wants her man hanging out with a single woman no matter how platonic the relationship.

'And what about your business relationship with Sive?' Fox asked, refocusing both herself and the conversation.

'I've invested in Sive and her various businesses over the years,' Karin replied casually.

'So you bought her friendship?' Fox said, because that's exactly what it sounded like.

'Not in so many words, no,' Karin sighed. 'Sive and I were in college together. I don't know why really but we just clicked. Not many of the others wanted to hang out with either of us, well, me anyway, so we just kind of gravitated towards each other. Well, anyway, I was the brains and she was the looks. I helped her with her college projects and she flirted and got us into parties. Simple.'

'And when you left college?'

'We just stuck. Look, I know she was hung up on becoming *someone*,' she said, making air quotes above her head, 'and my success didn't actually help. I think I just made her feel bad and that made me feel bad.'

'But from what both Finn and Gordon tell me, you've funded her attempts for years.'

Her eyes dropped. 'You could say that.'

'I don't understand why, to be honest. You're a shrewd operator, you must know when to stop but with Sive …'

'She asked.' Karin shrugged, like it was that simple.

Fox pulled back, unconvinced. 'Really?'

And again Karin shrugged which in Fox's opinion was the guilty man's way of making sure they didn't give anything away. Fox wondered what it was Karin had to be guilty about.

'If you don't mind me saying, for someone who claims to be and indeed has proven herself to be such a good businesswoman, you didn't have much success with Sive's businesses, did you?'

'Fair point.' Karin grinned. 'But the point is, they were Sive's businesses, not mine. But,' she sighed, 'in the end that was what we were supposed to be doing that weekend. I'd told her I wasn't giving her any more money unless she let me help her with her strategy and planning.'

'And Gordon asked you to stop, didn't he?'

'He did. But I didn't.'

'Why not?'

'Because it wasn't his business.'

'Did he threaten you?'

'Gordon? Good God, no!' she cried, almost aghast at the suggestion. 'He asked, I said no and that really was that.'

'Did he say why he wanted you to stop?'

'Yes, he thought I was enabling a loser, which I found offensive. Everyone deserves a chance to succeed.'

'Even those who demonstrate no talent whatsoever?'

'Yes, even them.'

By the time Fox got up to leave Karin had polished off the bottle of wine and was opening her second.

'Sure I can't tempt you?' she asked, pulling the cork with a pop.

'Positive, thanks.'

'There's a spare bedroom all made up.'

Fox laughed delicately, unsure what to make of the offer, and wondered if Karin was looking for a drinking buddy or something else entirely. She was curious to know where her husband was.

She cut through the two-and-a-half-hour drive in less than two. With her favourite Spotify mix to keep her company and her thoughts to distract her, the miles melted away without her noticing the distance.

On top of that, Oisín was on her mind. For whatever reason, he seemed to find his way into her thoughts a lot more often these days. She didn't mind really, she liked the warmth the memory of his handsome face gave her.

As she navigated the last roundabout before pulling into the station car park, her phone rang. It was Callaghan.

'So, our pal Nathan dropped in not long after you left.'

'Surprised it took him that long. And?'

'He's really rattled.'

'What did you do?'

'You know me, I rattled him some more,' Callaghan teased.

'For God's sake, I wish you wouldn't! You know it could work the opposite way to what we want, don't you?'

'No, seriously, he needed to be told.'

'What exactly did you say?'

'I told him he was our only suspect so, if he'd anything to say to prove otherwise, he should spit it out now before we come to arrest him, which was anytime soon.'

'But we're *not* going to arrest him, not yet anyway.'

'Yeah, but he doesn't know that,' he said with a chuckle.

'You're an evil bastard, do you know that?'

'I'll take that as a compliment.'

'*Hmmm*,' she replied dubiously. 'He'll be back.'

'I know, I'll give him twenty-four hours, max.'

'Less,' she wagered, getting out of the car and taking the steps into the station in twos.

She surged into the incident room out of breath, seconds before the Chief Inspector.

'Sorry,' she said with an apologetic grimace to AJ, knowing his shift finished hours ago.

Throwing her a sideways glance, Moyne sat down and slid a file across the table towards her.

'We have the car,' he told her.

'Seriously?'

'In Tipperary. About 130 kilometres from the kidnap cottage.'

'That's fantastic,' she replied, wondering how and why he had the information before she did. She'd spent so much of her time driving across the country she hardly knew what day it was. Mentally she made a note to check her messages – maybe they'd called her first but she missed it. Opening the file, she flicked through the handful of photographs of the abandoned car.

'Well done, AJ,' she said as she scanned the images. 'You were spot on and by the look of things it seems pretty much intact.'

'You'd imagine they'd have set it alight or something, wouldn't ya?' AJ remarked, looking over her shoulder. 'Thank God for amateurs,' he muttered.

'You're not the first to say that,' she said. This was good. They'd definitely be able to harvest some good evidence out of this. 'Where is it? I wouldn't mind taking a look at it myself.'

'They've taken it to The Park.'

And another journey back to Dublin! The driving was killing her. I'd have had to go back tomorrow anyway, she silently reasoned, pushing aside the logic, or lack thereof, in being based here in the West.

The dial tone over the speaker rang out. Fox looked at her watch. It was almost nine. She'd be impressed if the Assistant Commissioner answered. The fact that Moyne was still here was impressive. He, she had been told, was normally gone by seven at the latest.

But the Assistant Commissioner did answer and, not one for small talk, got straight to the point. Coming under pressure from the media and as a consequence the Commissioner, she was anxious to get a result.

'Where are we, people?' she asked.

'We've located the car,' Moyne repeated.

'Excellent. How fast can we turn around forensics?' she asked.

'We'll give this priority – it shouldn't take more than forty-eight hours.'

'Well, make it so.'

'Yes, Assistant Commissioner.'

'What about suspects?'

Fox gave her the update on both Finn and Nathan.

'Good work. What are your thoughts on these protestors? Are they a solid line?'

'I'm not sure,' Fox told her. 'But we'll take it as far as we can and see what comes out of it.'

'Good, because there's obviously something going on there. Related or not, this has to be part of our investigation.' She didn't ask for the detail, only reiterated her faith in her team. Then, with a hint of a warning, she said, 'I want this closed off

154

as soon as possible. Track these people down and make it stick.'

'We're already on it,' Fox said with a sideways glance at Moyne.

'Is there anything else I need to know? I have a press conference in half an hour on this latest inner-city crime feud and I want to be covered if anything comes up.'

'No, Assistant Commisioner, I think you're fully briefed.'

'OK, well, keep me posted on the forensics and as soon as you make headway with these suspects I want to know.'

And then she was gone.

'OK, well, let's see where we are.' Moyne sighed, looking first at his watch and then down at his notes. 'As I said forensics have committed to getting back to us with their initial findings tomorrow evening at the latest. Whether they can actually deliver is another thing, but let's wait and see.'

'Did they say anything about what we're likely to find?' Fox asked.

'It's an old car with plenty of history so we should expect a lot of profiles to emerge.'

'But no immediate signs of our occupants, no blood …'

'Nothing obvious, no.'

'I'll head over and take a look at it in the morning. But how did you manage to get them to agree to turn around the forensics so fast?'

'Good friends in high places, comes with the job,' he told her without looking up. 'Now, what about the money?'

'I beg your pardon?'

'The ransom? The five million he paid out for her?'

'Oh. Sorry. Yes, the money was transferred but we're still waiting on the bank to get back to us. It's an international account that was set up online so it doesn't really belong to any one branch that we can actually call into and check. I suspect we'll be told we need a warrant.'

'I'll make a call, see if I can move things along.'

'That would be great, sir,' she replied awkwardly, knowing he had no option. The Assistant Commissioner had made it clear she expected results, so it was as much his head on the line as her own.

'And this Nathan fellow, tell me about him,' he said.

Fox gave him her assessment of his character, his family connections back to the brewery and back again to Karin.

'It was his father, we believe, who coined the *Justice for the Workers* slogan,' she said, pulling out and handing him a range of stills from the television footage of the various demonstrations.

'It could be a coincidence, but –'

'I don't believe in coincidences,' he dismissed flippantly, flicking through the images.

Fox could feel her blood begin to heat up. Did he really have to be so rude? She didn't mind if he didn't like her as long as his behaviour towards her remained professional – she wasn't here to be his friend. Choosing to keep her misgivings to herself and take care of her own professional etiquette, she ignored his manner and continued regardless.

'We have a potential suspect in his uncle who seems to be a bit of a loose cannon.' Taking her pen, she circled Uncle Mikey in each of the pictures. 'He's been pretty vocal and once Nathan comes back to us we'll be able to make a judgment on the extent of his involvement, if any.'

'You seem confident Nathan will offer him up.'

'Definitely. Nathan's too success-hungry to let even his family get in his way.'

Moyne was so absorbed in the pictures he didn't respond. She wasn't even sure he heard her. She watched the slow rise and fall of his shoulders, listened to the slight rasp in his breath, and wondered if it was just her or was he always this cantankerous? She was that little bit too old to be scared of her boss but he definitely unnerved her and she didn't like feeling that vulnerable.

'Sir?' she said, taken by a sudden impulse inspired by her earlier conversation with Callaghan. 'I'd like to request that I base myself in Dublin just for the time being.'

'Really?' Moyne asked smartly, his too-good-for-us-here tone very much apparent. 'Not exciting enough for you here in the West then, is that it?'

'If you don't mind me saying, sir, I really don't think that's a fair assumption,' Fox replied curtly, feeling her shoulders pull back. 'As you know, I specifically requested a posting to this part of the country and I like very much being stationed here.'

'Don't I know it,' Moyne muttered.

It was an unusual remark for him to make. Only for the fact that she was on a roll she might have asked him to explain it.

'The challenge is that I'm spending half my time driving between here and Dublin. All of our leads and evidence are coming out of Dublin. It just makes sense.' She knew he knew she was right but, rather than admit it, he chose to knock her down instead.

'To you, perhaps, but not to me and mine is the opinion that matters. I appreciate you're spending a considerable amount of time on the road but that is part of your job. This is where you are stationed. You can't pick and choose where you want to be, you should know that.'

She dropped her head to hide her fury as he continued.

'It's unfortunate that this is your first case with us. Yes, it's demanding and maybe you're feeling a little homesick, but this is your post for the next twelve months at least, so I suggest you get used to it.'

Homesick? Really? Patronising git, she fumed, feeling the veins in her temples begin to pulse.

'Sir,' she replied, doing her best but not quite succeeding to keep her tone level, 'I am *not* homesick. It's particularly hectic and I'm concerned that with all this toing and froing something will get missed. I just want to make better use of my time, but if you would prefer I didn't try then …' No sooner were the words out than she wanted to reel them back in. They sounded spoilt and petty even to her own ears.

'Careful where you tread, Fox,' he warned, cutting her short with a stinging glare that lingered longer than was absolutely necessary.

'Sir,' she acquiesced, turning her attention back to her notes, his presence an uncomfortable charge opposite her. She wished he'd leave so she could breathe again and kick herself for what had just happened. But he let their mutual silence wrestle for what felt like hours before finally getting up to leave.

'Get me the details and I'll make that call to the bank,' he said. 'See if I can make better headway.'

'Yes, sir,' she responded, not trusting herself to say any more. Standing up, she busied herself with gathering her files and let him leave without looking up.

'What the hell?' she asked herself once she was sure he was gone. Closing the door, she slumped back into her seat. This was the last thing she needed. Her first post as a DI was turning into a nightmare. What an asshole, she thought, and for a split second wondered how and why she ever thought coming to Galway was a good idea. It obviously wasn't a place she was ever meant to settle.

Half-heartedly she went back to the images of the abandoned car and prayed for something to jump out and distract her, but it was a pointless exercise. Closing the file, she grabbed her coat. She needed a drink.

Drinking alone wasn't something she did often but every now and then it was a necessary evil. Tonight, after the day she'd had and the lambasting she'd endured, she didn't fancy going back to the soulless studio apartment she had rented weeks ago but still hadn't lived in, not properly anyway.

Ordering herself a Jack Daniels and ice, she sat at the end of the bar in a small, dark and dusty pub, the kind that was extinct in Dublin but thankfully still existed in the heart of Galway city. Reflecting on her day, she thought about Moyne and how obvious it was that he wasn't her greatest fan and without good reason as far as she could tell. She knew his type: the harder she'd work to earn his favour, the more intense his disdain would become. It was a fool's errand, she knew that, but she just couldn't accept that the best she could expect was his humiliating criticism. She didn't deserve it. What the hell was his problem?

Wiping down the counter before placing the loaded tumbler on a mat the barman smiled, then occupied himself elsewhere, knowing that don't-bother-me look well.

She loved her job. Since losing Oisín, it had replaced him as the centre of her universe. She had nothing else left and was perfectly happy to let it be that way. But it was on days like this that she missed him most. She imagined him sitting at the bar beside her with his thick brown curly hair and cheerful smile. She imagined his thick eyebrows that merged when his brow furrowed the way it always did when he considered a problem. His fingers wrapped around his pint of

Guinness, slowly and unconsciously twirling as he pondered her dilemma. He'd have found the right words to steer her in the investigation. She imagined him say that she just needed to look at it from a different perspective, to remember that things aren't always as they seem. She closed her eyes and pulled his image from a part of her memory she only visited when she was emotionally able. She took a deep breath, hoping to smell his citrus scent that she missed so much but all she got was the spice of her iced bourbon and a whiff of smoke every time the door out to the yard opened.

Friends since they were kids, they grew up together on the same street, went to the same schools and were taunted by the same running joke about who followed who into the Garda training college and, while it was always Naomi's dream, as son of the then Garda Commissioner it was Oisín's destiny.

It took one too many tequila shots to catapult them over the 'Just Good Friends' line and neither looked back, wondering playfully why it took so long to get there in the first place. They were a natural fit, like champagne and strawberries, beautiful on their own but delicious together.

She had flu the last day he played for the team. It was a big game, the league decider. There was no way she could go – she could hardly keep her head up, she was that weak.

'Good luck!' she told him with a smile before he left. 'You'll walk this one no sweat.' Then curled up and slept for the rest of the afternoon.

When her phone rang she was sure it was them calling from the dressing room to celebrate the win. She didn't even look at her watch – if she had she'd have seen it was only half time.

He collapsed on the pitch after scoring the point that put them in the lead. With his teammates roaring 'Well done!' they said he just dropped to the ground. Just like that. As if his legs gave way from under him. And he never woke up. He was cold and blue by the time she got to the hospital. They said it was a sudden cardiac arrest. Is there any other kind, she remembered asking, dazed and confused by what was going on around her. It was Simon Callaghan who sat with her for hours in the jaded yellow corridors refusing to leave, sure they'd made a mistake and he'd wake up any minute.

It was hard to come back from that moment but she did, eventually, and made her work her life. And while those around her matured, got married and had children, she celebrated alongside them but had no interest in following suit. She couldn't. There was only one man for her and anyway she was too busy training, and with a different kind of fire in her belly navigated her way up through the ranks of the police service. She was doing it for both of them. And the perfectionist inside her thrived. Immersing herself completely, Fox quickly became known as the stubborn grafter, the one that couldn't let a challenge pass her by unsolved. There was no denying it was tough both mentally and physically and in what many would describe a man's world, although she never saw it quite like that, she succeeded. To her it was a job where like every other recruit, regardless of sex, she had to prove she was fit for duty. She didn't want preferential treatment just because she had boobs or because of what had happened to her. She wanted to be treated differently because she was the best and she made it her business to be just that. She was the one happy to take on the overtime when no one else would, the one to cover bank holidays, Easter and Christmas when everyone else was home with their families. Happily and comfortably, she made her job her life. And if there were times when she showed up some of her colleagues for their lack of passion, drive and integrity, it wasn't intentional – it was just the way she was and for the most part she had become a popular member of the team.

She wasn't oblivious to the nicknames they had for her, some of which followed her from post to post while others were transient and forgotten as quickly as her desk was occupied after she'd gone. Like Foxie, most were in jest, and she let them slide over her head as inconsequential banter.

But there was something different about what was going on with Moyne. It felt different and she couldn't put her finger on it. Whatever it was, it didn't bode well and she itched to know what it was that bothered him so much about her.

Noticing her empty glass, the bar man approached.

'Same again?' he asked cautiously.

'Go on then, just the one,' she replied with a shrug and a smile like it mattered.

Swirling the potent liquid, watching it chase the ice as it melted and shrank, she worried. Her job was her world, her safety bubble, in which she had total control, but outside everything else was dangerously fluid. She had never been assigned to a position where her boss wasn't anything other than one-hundred-per-cent supportive and confident of her professional ability. Moyne's negativity towards her was unsettling both personally and professionally and, for the first time since cocooning herself, Naomi felt exposed.

Finishing her drink, she left the bar and walked home, unable to ignore the tightening feeling in her chest. It felt like she was suffocating, like she couldn't pull enough air into her lungs. Feeling her pulse throb and her body begin to overheat, she stopped and closed her eyes. It was years since she'd had a panic attack like this. Focusing hard on her breath as it entered and left her body, she worked hard to corral the hysteria that threatened to topple her. No one stopped or paid her any heed as she leaned against the wall – they rushed past, heads down and blinkered, afraid they might get sucked into someone else's shit. She was as good as invisible to everyone else – they had their own issues. She accepted that there was no one to help her but herself.

Chapter 12

If she were a religious churchgoing woman, she might have thought her prayers were answered because one by one the pieces of the jigsaw began to reveal themselves, her hard work began to pay off and the challenge of piecing events and people together began.

'You'll never guess who's called in here to see you!' Callaghan said before she'd even said hello.

'Nathan?'

'The very one.'

'What did he say?'

'He's still here. Waiting. Says he'll only speak to you.'

'Are you surprised? I am the boss after all,' she teased and smiled when she heard him scoff. 'And, anyway, you scared the crap out of him yesterday.'

'I did, didn't I!' He laughed.

'Give him a coffee and keep him there, I won't be long.'

She hung up and pressed down on the accelerator, enjoying the rush as the speed increased. Refusing to think about yesterday's conversation with Moyne or her disconcerting realization that still niggled like an irritating itch, she focused instead on Nathan and the strategy needed to deal with him. There was no doubt in her mind that he had been coerced into whatever it was he had ultimately done, and she was curious to see if he'd give up his uncle and perhaps even his father to save his own skin.

When she turned into the station Nathan was outside, puffing away on a Marlboro Light.

'You didn't strike me as a smoker,' she remarked as she approached the entrance.

'I wasn't, not for years,' he told her before taking a last suck on the filter and flicking it over the fence.

'That's an offence,' she told him, following the trajectory of the butt.

'So arrest me.'

'Don't test me, Nathan, I don't have time for this. Come back when you're willing to behave.'

'Seriously?'

'Seriously,' she repeated, marching up the steps and through the front door, leaving him standing bemused in her wake.

'Fine, fine!' he called with a real sense of urgency.

She assumed, having psyched himself up, he wasn't willing to be turned away still carrying his guilty luggage.

'Sorry. I'll go pick it up,' he said as he caught the door before it closed.

'Don't bother,' she replied, turning back to look at him for no more than a split second. Then nodding towards the interview-room door, she waited until like a bold child he scampered past her.

'I'll be back in a minute,' she told him briskly and left him alone before making her way upstairs to Callaghan.

'That didn't take long, hope you weren't speeding, sir.'

'Oh, shut up, Callaghan!' She threw her jacket on the stand before heading into the kitchen. 'Coffee anyone?'

With mugs in hand, Fox and Callaghan made their way back down to the waiting visitor.

'So, why don't we start again?' she suggested, settling herself into the chair opposite him. 'Pretend like yesterday never happened.'

'Fine by me.' He grinned widely then stood up and extended his hand, 'Detective Inspector.'

'Nathan,' she returned, smiling, with a nod at the audacity of his gesture. 'Sorry to have kept you – I only drove up from Galway this morning.'

'Not a bad drive – the new road is great, isn't it?'

She smiled. He really was a cheeky chap.

'So what's been going on?' she asked. 'Detective Callaghan here told me you've already been in to give us your sample.'

Nathan nodded, glancing briefly over at Callaghan. He took his time before speaking. Fox watched while he braced himself and knew by the depth of his breath, the slow shake of his head and the high tense rise of his shoulders that he was about to spill the whole pack of beans.

He lifted his head with a smile and she could feel the tension ooze from him.

'It's a bit of a bloody mess if I'm honest.'

'How?' she replied, resting her arms on the table.

'Before I start, can you look at it from my perspective?' he asked with a tilt of his head while pressing his nails into his palms.

'Go on.'

'They think I'm sidin' with the devil,' he huffed.

'Who?'

'My family. This is who they are. My da, my uncles on both sides, my cousins, half my feckin' family, they've just lost their jobs. And not only do I work for the woman who's done this to them, to us, I'm supposed to be her right-hand man – that's what I told them when they were proud of me for gettin' the job in the first place. I know when she eats, when she sleeps, I know what she has for dinner, I've probably bought it for God's sake. At night I go home and have to sit with them. They think I'm scum. My mam can hardly look at me. Can you even begin to imagine what that feels like, to have your own da leave the room when you walk in, your mates call you traitor? It's crap.'

'I can imagine,' Fox remarked, feeling a level of his pain.

'Can you? Really? I fucking doubt it.'

'So move out,' retorted an unsympathetic Callaghan.

'He's right. Move out.'

'On my salary, are you for real? All I am is an executive assistant, I'm still learning on the job, the pay is absolutely rubbish. I can't afford to move out.'

'So leave the job.'

'You really are clueless, aren't you? This job is going to set me up. Do you think I want to live in with my parents forever? Do you think I want to end up on the scrap heap with no other option but to work in the next scummy brewery? I don't bloody think so. I've got plans. I'm going to make something of myself. I don't want to end up like Mikey, a bitter, twisted eejit.'

'You still betrayed her though, didn't you?' Fox interjected and he nodded, dropping his head in shame. 'For all your loyalty and respect, you were the one who leaked those documents to the press, weren't you?'

'I didn't have an option. They were on my case, asking me, telling me to do something. I thought it would get them off my case.'

'Who's *them*?' Callaghan asked.

'My family, well, uncles mainly, but it's what my da wanted too. They were puttin' me through hell, givin' me the silent treatment, callin' me a traitor, said it was only gonna get worse. I'd have to push off, outta the house.'

'And this was your best foot forward, eh?' said Callaghan.

'Oh, fuck off, would ya!' he spat. 'Sitting there all high and mighty in your stupid jacket and that shite shirt. I'm not proud of what I did, all right? I didn't give them everything, nothing really important, nothing they couldn't have found themselves if they really wanted to. It was the least crappiest thing I could do.'

'Apart from saying no, you mean,' said Callaghan.

'Right, yeah, and face the wrath of Uncle Mikey – I don't think so. He's an absolute bollox. No one says no to him and gets away with it.'

'But I don't understand, Nathan,' Fox interrupted. 'What was the end game? Leak the documents and then what?'

'The press would put the pressure on, bad publicity and all that would delay things a bit, maybe even put a stop to it altogether.'

'You're smarter than that, you know that was never going to happen.'

'Yeah but Uncle Mikey didn't. He thought it was a sound idea.'

Callaghan sat back and measured up the young man. He was smart, ambitious and maybe a little devious, but he wasn't stupid, not by a long shot.

'So,' he said eventually, folding his arms across his chest, 'tell me about the notes.'

Nathan lowered his eyes.

'That wasn't me.'

'If it wasn't you, who was it?'

He thought for a moment before asking,

'Look, let's say, hypothetically, I had a good idea who sent them.'

'How good an idea?' Fox asked.

'A pretty sound one.'

'And?'

'And what happens to me if I tell you who it was?'

'That depends, if you simply knew about it or if you were actually involved in sending them. But you also need to consider what happens if you do in fact know something but don't help us. Then your trouble will be greater because –'

'Because we'll come down on you like a ton of bricks,' Callaghan finished for her.

Fox could tell Callaghan was enjoying this – he always wanted to be the bad cop – gave him a vent for his wannabe evil side.

'Detective Callaghan is right, so why don't we cut through the bullshit and get to the point?'

Having already made up his mind, he didn't need to think twice.

'I think it was Mikey. I went to his place after I was with youse the other day. I asked him straight out. He didn't say it was, but I can tell. But he just wanted to scare her, he's like that, likes to be the big man. But the whole kidnapping thing, that wasn't him. That was nuts, he had nothin' to do with it, he wouldn't go that far.'

'The ransom note was sent in support of Justice for the Workers – that's the same slogan coined by your dad and his brothers, isn't it?'

'Yeah. That was them.'

'So how can you say this had nothing to do with them? How do you know?'

'I just know.'

'Unfortunately, just knowing isn't good enough,' Fox said.

'I'm telling you they didn't.'

'You have access to Karin's diary?' Callaghan asked.

Nathan nodded.

'And you have a laptop?'

Again Nathan nodded.

'So what's to stop them taking a look while you're busy, or out?'

'It's password-encrypted, that's what.'

'Ever share it with them, give it to them to browse the net, buy something on line?'

'No, I did not. I'm telling you –'

But Callaghan didn't let him finish. 'You trust your family, don't you? Easy enough for them to look over your shoulder, see your password.'

'Even if they did they wouldn't know what to look for.'

'I think you'd be surprised. Did they never ask about her, where she lived, where she hung out?'

'This had nothin' to do with them,' Nathan stressed, his voice beginning to rise.

'Did they, Nathan, did they know where she was going that weekend? Did they think she'd be alone?'

'*Stop.* It wasn't them.'

'But you don't know that. Would they even tell you? Could they trust you? You said yourself they think you're scum. If they were responsible for the abduction and the death of Sive Collins, why would they tell you? They don't trust you, do they? So you don't know. Not for sure anyway, you don't.'

'Ah, for fucks' sake! I'm sorry I said a word!' Nathan huffed, throwing his hands in the air.

'Look, Nathan, this is serious. I'm not talking about some

170

schoolyard scrap here. This is very real. This is murder. Think about it.'

Nathan shook his head. 'Do you think I don't know that? This is fucked up. That's what this is.'

Neither Callaghan nor Fox responded but instead let the silence make him feel a little less comfortable and watched him massage his hands and shake his head, his feelings of frustration and injustice palpable.

'Remind me, Nathan – I can't remember – where did you say you were that night?' Callaghan asked, purposely hoping to compound his discomfort.

'Are you having a laugh?' Nathan questioned.

Then he closed his eyes and let his head fall back, his lower lip quivering ever so slightly.

When he had composed himself, he said, 'I told you. I was with me ma and me da watchin' the *Late Night Live*.'

'What do you think your uncle will do when he finds out you've been here talking to us?'

Nathan shrugged his shoulders. 'I don't plan on telling him.'

'He'll find out soon enough – we'll have to bring him in – he'll want to know.'

'Suppose I'll cross that bridge when I come to it, won't I? Looks like I've lost my job and I'm not sure I can go home and I'm a dead man after this so it can't get much more fucked-up than this, can it? Can I go now, please?'

Fox looked at Callaghan who nodded.

'Sure. But we may need to speak with you again, so don't go far,' Fox cautioned.

They watched him go.

'Poor bastard,' Callaghan sighed. 'He's fucked up royally. Almost feel sorry for him.'

'Really?' she asked, not believing him for a moment. 'You must be going soft – he brought it all down on himself. We'll need to get search warrants sorted today before he decides to make it up to them and warn them we're on the way.'

'His parents or his uncles?'

'Both.'

Two teams left minutes apart, bound for the Smyth households. Callaghan joined the first and went to Mikey's house while Fox went to Nathan's.

Nathan visibly blanched when he saw them. His instinct was to close the door but he stopped himself almost immediately.

Stepping forward, Fox handed him a copy of the warrant and gave him a few minutes to digest it before asking, 'Can we come in now?'

'This is fucking ridiculous – it's harassment.'

Fox didn't reply, there was no point, but waited for him to step aside.

'We'll try to be as quick and as tidy as we can,' she assured Nathan's mother who stood with one hand holding her mouth in horror and the other holding her phone to her ear, calling, Fox assumed, her husband.

But she needn't have bothered. Dessie was with Mikey when Callaghan knocked on his front door and responded much the same as his son only louder.

The search at Nathan's produced nothing beyond a small stash of weed and a ceramic pipe hidden under his mattress.

'See, I told you, I had nothin' to do with this,' Nathan repeated indignantly, as Fox and her team left the house almost empty-handed, 'and now, thanks to you, I'm definitely gonna lose my job!'

'Are you serious?' Fox turned back to the house, incensed

by his attitude. 'You leaked confidential documents to the media and your family are knee-deep in a murder investigation – that's why you'll lose your job, not because of anything we did.' Turning on her heel, she continued back to her car, muttering 'Dumb-ass' under her breath.

Her phone rang just as she started her car and pulled away from the kerb. Callaghan was on the other end.

'Where are you now?' he asked.

'Just heading back to the office, why?'

'Make your way to Mikey Smyth's – there's something you should see.'

'OK, I'll be there is a sec,' she told him, doing a U-turn.

Less than ten minutes later she pulled up behind the police van parked outside Mikey's house. She nodded to the uniformed officer standing at the front door and made her way towards the living room where Dessie sat smoking with Dolores, Mikey's wife, and Mikey himself.

'Ahh, here she comes – the boss lady, I suppose,' he snarled, not caring who heard him.

'*Would ya shush!*' Dolores hissed.

Ignoring him, Fox turned back to the officer on the door to ask about Callaghan's whereabouts. Hearing her come in, Callaghan was already making his way down the stairs and pointed down the hall.

'Out here,' he directed, leading the way down the hall, through the kitchen and out into the narrow garden to what appeared to be nothing more than a timber shed.

Her heels sank into the grass as they walked across the soggy lawn. Crossing the timber threshold, they passed two Gardaí and arrived into a space insulated and kitted out to such a degree that it was like an extension of Mikey's living room. Divided according to work and play, the front half contained what you would expect of a garden shed, a lawnmower, shovels, spades and shelves of various gardening paraphernalia. Beyond that, separated and partially hidden by a tall metal shelf, was a makeshift living space. An armchair with side table and lamp was positioned in front of a small but state-of-the-art large flat-screen TV complete with Xbox and soundbar speakers. Fox couldn't help but smirk as she knelt down and opened the small fridge by the chair to find it filled with cans of beer.

'Brilliant,' she remarked, almost envious of the self-indulgent mock luxury but curious to know what was so special about this particular man cave.

'Here.' Callaghan pointed towards a cork pin-board hung over a small workstation that was only apparent when you turned to leave. A cheap blue laptop sat unopened on the workbench connected to a small colour A4 printer on a shelf below and beside it was a green manila folder. Pinned randomly to the board with brass tacks was a collection of press cuttings and printouts.

'Really?' Fox asked as she scanned the images of Karin, profiles of her business and Seán Cusack her business partner. Some of them had her face circled over and over again in red marker. One bore the word BITCH inscribed heavily in red capital letters. An involuntary shiver ran down her spine when she picked up and opened the green folder to find aerial pictures and location maps of Wild Wind taken from what she assumed was Google Maps.

'Bloody hell,' she whispered.

'Where is he?' Callaghan asked one of the Gardaí.

'In the living room inside – I saw him when I came in,' Fox said without taking her eyes off the noticeboard pinned to capacity.

'So he knows we're in here, right?'

'Oh, he knows alright.'

'And he hasn't tried to run?'

'Nope. Not yet anyway. I reckon he's quite proud of what he's got here.'

Standing up straight, she'd seen enough, she turned to the Gardaí. 'OK. Let's take him in, see what he has to say and get this lot looked at,' she pointed to the laptop, 'and check this paper off against the ransom note and the threats. I want a conclusive result here and don't let anyone in here until we're done.'

'Got it.'

She marched her way back across the grass, through the house and into the living room.

'Mikey, that's an interesting collection you've got out there.'

'I know, I've been at it a while.'

'I can tell. Do you want to tell me why?'

'Not really, no.'

'Perhaps we could have a chat down at the station.'

She heard Dolores's sharp intake of breath.

'I'd rather not,' he replied calmly.

'But I insist,' Fox countered with a smile.

'Well, you'll have to arrest me so.'

'Seems fair enough,' she said, stepping forward. 'Stand, please.'

Mikey didn't resist and stood big and tall looking down on her, enjoying the superficial power his size exerted over her as she took his wrists and cuffed them together.

'Michael Smyth, I'm arresting you on suspicion of the abduction of Karin Bolger and Sive Collins and the suspected murder of Sive Collins.'

'*Jesus Christ, Mikey,*' Dolores whispered, bringing her hand to her mouth.

Dessie looked on, confused. 'What have you done?' he asked his brother.

He followed as far as the door as Fox escorted his brother by the arm out of the house and into a Garda car waiting outside.

At the station Fox stayed to make sure Mikey was processed properly before printing off his picture and leaving again. She called ahead before pulling into the car park of Karin's office.

Escorted once again to the boardroom, she couldn't help but notice Nathan's now empty desk and wondered had he left of his own volition or if he'd been asked to leave.

'Do you recognise this man?' Fox asked Karin when she joined her in the vast and beautiful room.

Taking the picture into her perfectly manicured hands Karin sat down, closed her eyes and took a breath before looking at it properly.

'Have you noticed him at all, anywhere?' Fox asked her, watching her face as she scrutinised the image. 'Maybe where you get your coffee, at the shops, in the gym, beside you at traffic lights, anywhere at all?'

Karin took her time, not really listening, just letting her eyes rest on his face, staring into his static eyes that looked back at her, mocking her.

'Who is he?' she asked.

'His name is Michael Smyth. He's an ex-employee of the brewery and one of the protest ringleaders. We suspect he may have had some involvement in your abduction.'

Karin looked up, wide-eyed. 'Really?'

Fox nodded. 'He and half his family worked there for years. We arrested him this afternoon and I'd hoped you might recognise him.'

Karin shook her head vigorously. 'I don't think I've ever seen him before.' She handed the photograph back. 'Do you think it's him, the man who took us?'

'We don't know. Maybe. Would you be happy to take a look in person?'

'But I never saw his face! How will I know?'

'To be honest, Karin, I'm not sure but we have good reason to believe that Mikey may be involved so it's worth a shot. Maybe the way he stands or the way he walks – something might connect. We'll have his face covered and see where we go from there.'

'Will he be able to see me?

'No. You'll be behind a screen. I promise you'll be perfectly safe. Is that all right?'

Karin nodded.

'Sure?'

'Yes,' she replied calmly. 'I'll give it a go.'

'Brilliant, I'll set it up.' She already knew it wasn't likely that Mikey was the man in the CCTV footage – he was too big – but that didn't mean he wasn't involved at some point along the journey either at Silene Cottage or their holding location at the abandoned cottage near the Cork–Kerry border.

When Karin arrived the following afternoon she was perfectly composed in yet another elegantly tailored outfit. Like royalty her presence commanded esteem, her chic stiletto heels announcing her arrival. There were no nerves and, eager to get down to business, she marched into the viewing room, put her bag on the chair and stood, arms folded across her chest, waiting for the men to be lined up in front of her.

'Just like you see in films,' she remarked almost excitedly to Fox, who gave the signal she was ready and dimmed the lights. In the next room the light, despite the frosted diffuser, was glaringly bright with a sickly yellow hue, which wasn't helped by the magnolia paint on the walls

In single file, dressed in the same dark tracksuit bottoms, hoodies, caps and neck warmers, their faces concealed and heads held down, the five men slowly stepped up and took their appointed positions on the plinth underneath the oversized digits mounted on the wall.

'They can't see you,' Fox assured her, hoping to allay any fears she may have had.

'I know,' Karin replied with apparently no fear at all.

Fox bit her lip, watching Karin's expression as one by one she took her time to study each man.

'Can you ask them to turn around?' she asked.

Fox repeated the instruction into the microphone. Immediately each man turned and Karin looked again.

'Can I see them walk?'

'Yes.' Fox called into the microphone for the men in turn to step down from the plinth and walk a length of the room.

Again Karin watched intently, with Fox focusing on her body language, looking for any sign or expression that might be a hint of recognition. Slowly Karin walked the length of the glass, carefully observing the men one by one. Twice she walked back and forth but no one man made her stop in her tracks.

'I'm sorry,' Karin huffed with a slow turn of her head. 'They … they all look the same. I can't tell …'

'I know,' Fox told her quietly, 'that's the point. You've got to look, I mean *really look* to see if you recognise anything at all about any of these men.'

Karin looked again.

'Take your time, Karin.'

'I'm sorry, but I can't … really I can't tell.'

Fox felt her heart sink a little.

'Don't be sorry,' she said, trying to hide her disappointment. 'It's better to be sure.'

With the job done, Karin smiled tightly and turned to retrieve her bag.

As dramatically as she arrived she left with a firm handshake and an over-the-shoulder last-minute instruction. 'Call me if you need anything else.'

Chapter 13

Knowing she only had so much time before she'd have to either release or charge him, Fox cursed the technical team.

'How long do they bloody need?' she vented, aware she was being more than a little unreasonable, her frustration sparked by the fact that they didn't appear to share her sense of urgency.

But they'd only had the car a day and on initial inspection it appeared it had been wiped clean of all prints, leaving her no option but to wait and see what the deeper analysis would uncover. On the upside there was hope – as expected they were able to harvest a significant number of both hair and fabric samples. But with that came a downside: analysing that number in the hope of finding a conclusive match would slow their discovery down.

'How long will that be?' she asked through gritted teeth, having called them first thing to see how the forensic processing was progressing.

'As long as it takes,' the agent, obviously used to being pressured on all sides, told her.

'But this is urgent!' Fox implored.

'Show me one case that isn't, Detective Inspector.'

'Look,' she tried, 'this has the eyes of the Commissioner all over it.'

'That's what they all say.'

'No, really, it does. I swear.' She heard the agent huff down the phone. 'Check with your superior. Superintendent Moyne has your team's assurance this won't take long.'

'OK, let me see what I can do.'

'Thanks. Genuinely, I appreciate it,' she said and hung up, recalling Moyne's reiterated earlier instruction to 'find something that places him at the scene, otherwise we have to let him go'. Like she needed to be reminded. The pressure was definitely on.

She had delayed the interview with Mikey long enough and her time was running out. Sitting over coffee, preparing for the interview, she debated the tactical approach with Callaghan.

'He has an alibi for the night,' Callaghan reminded her.

'Yeah, but it stinks to high heaven. Playing Xbox in the shed while your wife is inside watching *Late Night Live* doesn't count. He has both the motive and the opportunity – he left work at four and didn't go to the pub – even he admits that was unusual. She doesn't see him for hours but knows he's out there? Can't remember what time he got to bed? Bullshit.'

'But she said she saw him through the kitchen window when she made the tea at the break, and the lights were on in the shed all night.'

'The lights being on doesn't necessarily mean anyone is home,' Fox shot back.

'True, but we've checked the cameras around the area and there's no sign of him on the streets.'

'What about the Xbox?' Fox suggested. 'Does it log you

in and out, is there any way of knowing from it if he was actually playing anything?'

'Sorry, it's not my thing. I've no idea but I'll check.'

Finishing her coffee in one final gulp, she checked her watch and sighed.

'OK, let's do this.'

Mikey sat with his arms folded, head tilted to one side and a self-satisfied, malevolent grin smeared across his face. He was delighted to be there. Like some kind of anti-hero, he was fighting the cause. But there was something about him that was unnerving. Despite the malice that he exuded, he had an animal magnetism that she couldn't help but be drawn to. And he knew it. Sitting opposite her, he pinned his eyes on her and refused to look anywhere else. It was a technique she was used to: absolute defiance. Rarely did she pay heed to it but Mikey had something else going on that amplified the intensity of his stare tenfold. He made her nervous and she had to work hard not to let it show but also not to let it get to her.

'When we searched your house we came across this.' She pushed a picture of the workstation and notice board in his shed towards him.

'And?'

'We also found this.' She passed the loose leaf of white notepaper towards him. 'Coincidentally, this paper is a match to the paper used to make these.' She held up the two threatening letters, now safely packaged in plastic, in front of him before placing them on the table.

'Yeah.'

'Can you explain the connection?'

'Seems pretty obvious to me.'

'How so?'

'Do you expect me to spell it out for you? Do your job, like?'

'Actually I do expect that.'

He leaned forward and lowered his head so he could look up at her with squinted eyes.

'Because they're mine.'

Instantly his appointed solicitor was on alert. He stopped scribbling and looked first at his client then at Fox.

'Which are yours?'

'All of them, they're all mine.'

'So you made these two letters out of this paper?'

'I did.'

'And then you sent both letters to Karin Bolger.'

'OK, that's enough,' Mikey's solicitor intervened, lifting his hand to pause proceedings. 'I'd like to consult with my client before he answers any more questions.' He threw a look of caution at Mikey.

'I'm OK,' he replied with a shrug.

'I really suggest you –'

'I suggest you shut up,' Mikey told him with a grin that was anything but pleasant and, turning back to Fox, answered her question. 'Yep, that too. I sent them both to the bitch.'

'Do you understand the implications of what you're admitting to?' Fox asked, feeling the pain of his solicitor who had put his pen down and sat back. This was too easy. Incredulous at Mikey's ease of response, wondering if he was serious, she almost laughed.

'Yep,' he replied, maintaining his composure, enjoying the confusion his unusual honesty was creating.

'So, you're admitting to the sending of these threatening letters?'

'I am.'

'OK. So what about the ransom note – was that you too?' she asked, feeling more like the mouse than the cat.

'Does the paper match?' he asked her.

She paused uncomfortably. 'No, it doesn't.'

'Well then, what do you think?'

'I think you've got form, Mikey. I think you're one pissed-off man. I think you sent those threats and when they got you nowhere, when Karin ignored them and decided not to be bullied by some spineless, nameless bully, you decided to up the ante. Am I right, Mikey?'

'Maybe.' He sat back into his original position, folding his arms, tilting his head and smiling.

Even though she knew damn well he was playing with her, she could feel the frustration build.

'Maybe? Either you did or you didn't. Which is it, Mikey?' she asked. 'You see, I don't think you like being ignored, especially by a woman, do you? You wanted to make sure that next time she'd take notice. So you used your nephew to find out where she'd be and you took her. But you didn't bank on her having company and, not only that, you probably didn't bank on that company being ballsy enough to make a run for it.' She stopped and used the moment to watch his face. Unfazed, he simply shrugged with a smile and an unsettling wink intended to intimidate and provoke.

She could feel Callaghan tensing beside her, itching to have a go, but her instructions to him had been clear: let her do the talking until they got a sense of him, his behaviour and his attitude. Then she'd have a pretty good idea of what he was about.

Doing her best not to let her agitation show, she made a

point of observing him that little bit longer, playing him at his own game by matching his stare and smiling at him as if she'd figured it all out.

She continued in a more conciliatory tone. 'But you're not a killer, Mikey, not purposely anyway. So with Sive lying dead in the ditch you got scared and I'd be scared too because you messed up. I really don't think you meant to hurt Sive but there wasn't much you could do, was there? She ran and you had to stop her, isn't that right? Is that what happened?'

'If you say so.'

'This is only going to get worse. You've got to help us here, help us help you.'

'*What a load of balls!*' he suddenly roared. 'Help me? You must be joking. You're no more interested in helping me than I am in helping you, so I'm just going to sit here and watch you fuck it all up.' His raucous laugh filled the room.

Preempting Callaghan's reaction, she stepped on his foot as a warning and, pressed on as if Mikey hadn't spoken.

'Who helped you, Mikey? You didn't do this on your own, you couldn't have. I'm assuming you were the brains of the scheme but who did the legwork for you? Who drove the car, Mikey?'

Mikey sat back in his chair with his arms back across his chest and that smug smile rooted firmly on his face. They were getting nowhere.

'You previously said to Detective Callaghan that on the night Karin Bolger and Sive Collins were abducted, you were at home playing computer games in your shed. Is there anyone who can verify that for us?' She locked into his stare which in his silence spoke volumes. Turning to his solicitor, she asked, 'Mr O'Fee, please instruct your client to answer the question.'

Taking his cue, O'Fee sat forward with a huff. Having waited patiently for his moment, now that it had arrived he behaved like he wasn't that pushed.

'Actually, Detective Inspector, I'm not sure that's actually in his best interests. He's already unwittingly implicated himself so I'm going to take a moment with my client. This interview is over.'

Fox shook her head. 'Just to remind you, your client *has* admitted to intimidation and threatening behaviour.'

'I am well aware of that, Detective Inspector.'

'We'll figure this one out with or without your help, Mr Smyth.' Fox stood to gather up her case file and terminate the interview.

'Good luck with that!' Mikey replied, laughing at her as both she and Callaghan left the room.

Outside, once the door was closed, she leaned against the wall and breathed a deep and frustrated sigh of relief.

'Oh, my good God!' she swore. 'What a prize asshole!'

'He certainly got under your skin. Why wouldn't you let me have a go?'

'Because that's what he wants – he wants to have us both chasing his tail,' she replied, feeling his frustration. 'Now he knows me like I do him, but he doesn't know you – you're our surprise reserve. He'll get tired and slip up. They always do. That's when you'll step in to close him off.' She smiled at him with as much confidence as she could muster but inside she doubted her own prediction.

'Do you really think he's our man?' Callaghan asked.

'I really don't know. If you'd asked me earlier I'd have said no way. But now … Jesus, he's weird.'

'What we've got isn't enough to get a conviction,' Callaghan warned her unnecessarily.

'We need to place him in the car – that'll wipe that stinking smile off his face.'

This time it was Callaghan's turn to put a stop to her potentially unprofessional reactions. 'Careful now, you're making this personal.'

'I know, I know!' she cried, rubbing her eyes, frustrated by the disconcerting effect Mikey had on her, sure he'd be delighted if he knew and fearful that he already did.

'So what do you want to do?' Callaghan asked. 'Keep him or let him go?'

She thought for a minute, quickly weighing up her options.

'Let's hang on to him. Charge him with intimidation and we can see where we go from there. I'll go take a look at the car and see what pressure I can put on forensics.'

Silently she prayed it was him, just so she could take him down and lock him away herself.

Chapter 14

Big enough to hold at least three double-decker buses, the central bay of what could easily have been an airfield hangar made the car seem minute. Pristine and clinical with large glass bucket-lights dropping at metre intervals overhead, the place looked like something from the set of a science-fiction movie.

All of the car doors were open, the interior mats spread out in a neat row behind it and the contents of the boot along with random other items laid out alongside them.

'*Hello!*' she called out as she approached but couldn't be sure she was heard above Stealers Wheel's 'Stuck in the Middle with You' which was blaring out over the speakers and amplified by the echo that bounced off every wall.

She couldn't help but smile to herself as a lone technician emerged from the bowels of the car, dressed head to toe in white overalls, the only flesh visible his shiny pink face peering out from under the hood of his suit. Oblivious to her presence, he shimmied in time to the music between the car and the organised chaos on the work counter.

'*Hello!*' she shouted again as she got a little closer, almost sending him into orbit.

'Jesus, you shouldn't sneak up on people like that,' he

188

huffed dramatically, bringing his hand to his chest.

'Sorry about that,' she replied, entertained by the flush that crossed his face. 'I figured you couldn't hear me above the music.' She took her ID from her pocket and showed it to him. 'I'm DI Naomi Fox. I'm here to look at this Volvo.'

Putting the part of the car he was inspecting down on the bench, he peeled back the hood of his suit.

'Oliver Begley,' he said, smiling. 'I have to admit I expected to see you sooner.'

'Have I been that bad?' she asked, referring to the multitude of calls she'd made during the course of the last few days.

'I'm not saying a word,' he said with raised eyebrows, holding his hands up defensively, his smile widening.

'Well, don't worry, I'm not here to hassle you. I just want to take a look at it for myself.'

'We've pretty much stripped the inside down,' he told her, turning back to the car. 'She's an old lady and isn't as easy to put back together but we're going our best.'

'Was there much damage from the fire?' she asked, wandering over to take a look inside.

'Nope. Hardly any, damage mostly on the exterior.' He walked her round to where most of the damage could be seen.

'What did they use to set it alight?'

'Petrol but only a bit – obviously thought it would spread without too much accelerant. Probably too scared it'd go up too quickly and attract attention. We see that a lot. Idiots.'

Seeing her cautiously circle and peer into the car, he told her, 'It's OK. We're done. There's nothing in there that we haven't captured.'

'Is it safe to sit in?'

'I think so. Might be a bit wobbly, not sure we've fixed the bolts in properly so be careful.'

She sat in tentatively with no motive other than to see it, to sit in it and to feel it. Having mapped its route, watched it drive out of petrol stations and past traffic cameras, it was a relief not only to establish they were watching the right car but also to get close enough to examine it physically herself. She scanned the front compartment about which there was nothing remarkable, then turned towards the back, its seats yet to be properly fixed in position.

'I know, I know,' Oliver said as she got out of the car and approached him again, mouth open ready to speak. 'I've already had your man Moyne on the phone. We're going as fast as we can, I swear.'

Her immediate instinct was to be cross at Moyne for interfering. Why didn't he trust her to do her job? She could just as easily have made the call – she didn't need him to do her work for her. But promptly she took it back with a hint of shame – she should be more appreciative of his support.

'And we're sure this is the car?' she asked.

'As sure as we can be at this stage – it certainly matches the description. But we found this which might help you be one-hundred-per-cent sure before we get our sample results back.' Reaching over to a metal tray on the counter, he grabbed a small clear plastic bag and handed it to her. 'It's a lady's bracelet. If you're lucky it might have come from either victim. Then you'll know for sure.'

'Pretty,' she remarked, inspecting it through the plastic. 'Can I take it?'

'Please do. We're done with it. I was going to get it over to you today anyway so the paperwork is ready to go – you just need to sign for it.'

'No problem. Where was it?'

'Under the front passenger seat,' he told her, taking her over to point out exactly where it had been.

More like a cuff than a bracelet, black studded with rows of pearls and diamonds, it was edgy, bohemian almost. It didn't look like something Karin would wear.

'I believe you managed to get a lot more samples?'

Oliver nodded. 'We sure did.' He turned back to the workbench. Flicking the monitor of his computer towards her, he pulled up a spreadsheet. 'We collected over three hundred and fifty different samples which in itself is a challenge – they all need to be analysed and that takes time.' He scrolled down the numbered list as if to prove his point. 'This is an old, old car – God knows who's been in it. We might only achieve one relevant result –'

'That's good enough for me,' Fox interrupted.

'I appreciate that, but it could be the first or it could be the last sample we test that proves to be the one – needing only one doesn't make this happen any quicker.'

'I appreciate that.'

'The guys in the lab are working on it as we speak.'

'Even if you can feed the results to me as they come through?' she asked.

'I'll say to you the same thing I said to your boss. We're on it. You'll have it as soon as we're done. We're not sitting on this, we have a whole team working on it.'

'I know, I'm not suggesting you're not, it's just I'm under pressure …'

'We all are but this is a slow, methodical process that just takes time. Patience.' He was obviously used to dishing out the same advice on a regular basis.

Deciding it was better to take it than to leave it, she left

Oliver to do his job and made her way back to her car.

Behind the wheel she took the bracelet out of the bag. It wasn't an expensive piece – more like costume jewelry, something to wear casually and every day. Taking it out of the bag, she touched the rows of crystals and pearls set on individual strands that were stitched together at their ends. Instinctively she guessed it belonged to Sive.

She hadn't spoken to Gordon in a while, he'd been remarkably quiet and this she felt was a good reason to pay him a visit. If the bracelet was Sive's, hopefully he'd recognise it.

Gordon's practice was located in the heart of the city. The receptionist smiled nervously as Fox announced herself.

'He's fully booked for the afternoon,' she told her. 'He might not have a minute between patients till after the last appointment of the day.'

'This will only take a few minutes,' Fox assured her.

'Why don't I check with Mr Collins once he's finished with his present client and we can see what he says,' she replied with a smile, happy to delegate the responsibility of saying *no* back to the dentist himself.

Fox took a seat in the almost full waiting area where pictures of cute kids and frolicking families beamed down from the walls with their flawless straight and brilliant white photo-shopped teeth. She closed her mouth with its full complement of fillings.

Operating alongside another dentist specialising in orthodontic treatment and a resident hygienist, the practice appeared to be booming with almost every teen and self-conscious adult within a twenty-mile radius attending. This, according to their website, was the clinic of choice for those looking for the perfect smile and if the reviews were anything to go by then they weren't wrong. It was, they claimed, a sophisticated business that relied as much on the reputation of their practitioner as they did on referrals from their past and present clients. Sitting in the bright and airy waiting room, with not a fish tank in sight, she had to admit things had moved on since her days as a wire-mouthed teenager and even found herself considering whether or not it was time to have her teeth whitened.

In the absence of doors between the waiting area and the treatment studio, she could hear the chatter of activity and a poor boy being told off for not wearing his night-time retainer: new braces was the conclusion.

'That's what you get now,' his mother chastised him when they were done, pushing him through the doors to reception, no doubt counting the cost of her son's idleness in her head.

A nurse with a disposable mask hanging loosely around her neck came into the waiting area with a smile.

'Ms Fox?' she enquired, scanning the room.

As she stood, Fox felt the glares from the patients wondering how she got to waltz straight in when they'd been waiting ages. Amid audible huffs, she returned the cheerful nurse's smile and followed her down the short corridor and into a small office on the edge of the treatment area. She noted that the nurse hadn't used her official title but let it pass.

'Mr Collins will be with you shortly,' she said and went out, closing the door behind her.

Fox looked around the small but bright room and wondered how appropriate it would be for her to show him her gnashers and see if he'd do her a deal on some invisible braces of her own. Smiling to herself, she stood suddenly when the door opened as if caught in the guilty act of having a small joke with herself. Dressed in smart navy slacks with a yellow shirt and coordinated tie, he too wore the signature mask around his neck and extended his hand to her with a curt smile.

'Gordon. Sorry to bother you at work,' she said, taking his hand, his handshake firm, formal and fast.

'That's all right,' he said although she could tell he was just being polite. 'Please, take a seat. What can I do for you?' He took the seat opposite while getting straight to the point.

'How are you?' she asked politely.

'Fine. Just trying to get back some sense of normality, which is difficult. So many people just want to talk about her.'

She could feel his stress and felt he was including her in that group of irritants.

At a first glance he had appeared calm but the quick jitter of his knee and unconscious squeezing of his hands while they were clenched tight in his lap said otherwise.

'How can I help you, Detective Inspector?' he prompted with an undeniable level of impatience.

'If you don't mind, I have something I'd like you to look at.' She took the plastic bag from her pocket, removed the bracelet from it and handed it to him.

Taking it in his hand he closed his fingers around it and inhaled deeply before lifting it to his nose.

'I can still smell her. Jo Malone. It was her favourite. Never mine though.'

For a split second she thought he might buckle but, pulling his shoulders back, he composed himself then placed the bracelet carefully on the table between them.

'It's Sive's?' Fox asked quietly.

'Yes, it is. Harry bought it for her last Christmas.' He smiled as he spoke. 'She was delighted. I think she liked it more than my gift at the time. I wondered where it had got to. Harry wanted her to wear it when we … well, when we buried her. Where did you find it?'

'We found it in what I think we can now safely assume was the car used in the abduction.'

Gordon nodded, looking warily at it as if it might jump up and bite him. 'Can I keep it? I think Harry would like it back.'

'Not just yet, I'm afraid, but I'll keep it safe for you.'

'I understand. Thank you, if you would.'

She waited for him to hand it to her but when he made no move to retrieve it she leant over and picked it up herself.

'So, you're making progress then?' he asked awkwardly as they both stood up.

'Yes, it's always a bit slow at the beginning – things can take a long time to process – but hopefully, soon, I'll be able to give you some positive news.'

'That would be great,' he replied, holding the door open for her.

'And how is Harry?' she asked.

'Fine. Back at school.' He seemed anxious for her to leave.

She put it down to the almost full waiting room which was in earshot and respectfully taking the hint followed him in silence through to reception.

He shook her hand at the door, thanked her for coming and before she knew it she was out on the street.

'Wow,' she muttered getting into her car, feeling suitably dismissed and not quite sure what to make of what just happened.

She checked her watch – it was just after four. She was

exhausted, it had been a long day. She was glad it was Friday and promised herself a real rest. She'd stay in Dublin, maybe head to the gym to burn off the stress that the week had given her and maybe get a take-away – she deserved it. Immediately she felt her shoulders relax.

Traffic was light and she made it back to HQ in no time at all. With her team clocked off, the incident room and surrounding desks were empty. Taking Sive's bracelet from her pocket she locked it in the drawer of her desk in the incident room. As she turned to leave she caught sight of the smiling picture of Sive pinned to the whiteboard. Without wanting to, she imagined her lying unconscious across the back seat of the Volvo, her arm falling to the floor and the bracelet falling off. She shivered. It was time to go home.

Chapter 15

She hit it hard, left then right, bouncing toe to toe, waiting for the bag to come back for more. It had been a while, she was out of practice. Sweat trickled down her brows and her heart hammered in time to the beat that blasted in her ears. It felt good, all that pent-up frustration finally finding its release. The bag was everything and everyone that kept her from her sleep. It was Mikey and his nauseating grin, Gordon and his nervous disregard, Moyne and his misogynistic condescension, and everything else in between. The pain of her fist connecting with a hard thump against the tough leather was masked by the power it gave her. Here she was in control, no one looking over she shoulder telling her what to do or how to behave. This was her zone where no one else had a voice.

Although tired beyond belief, from somewhere the adrenaline kept coming and she kept going. The pain felt good, the release empowering, the sweat a testament to her muscle. When she could go no more and her body eventually gave up, she slumped against the wall to focus on settling her bursting breath. She scanned the trendy studio while letting her heart resume it natural rhythm, its bright lights and arsenal of equipment enough to attract the die-hard gym bunnies on a rainy Friday night. Looking at them push, heave, drag and sweat, she wondered how sad it was that they had nothing else to do. The fact that she was there too seemed irrelevant.

Forty-two and perfectly happy in her own skin, she didn't consider her situation to be in any way mournful. She didn't consider her situation to be in anyway akin to theirs. She was perfectly comfortable working out alone on a Friday night.

Checking her watch, she saw it was almost ten. She pushed herself off the wall to head towards the shower. The music in her head changed to a ringing in her ears. It took her a confused moment to realise her phone was ringing through her headphones.

Not now, she thought, grabbing her towel from the floor. But having rejected the call, it rang again. Callaghan wasn't going to take no for an answer but what was he doing calling her on a Friday night?

'Where are you?' he asked abruptly.

'I'm sorry?'

'Are you near a telly?' he asked, ignoring her tone.

She looked around at the screens mounted on the walls showing the latest from Sky News.

'Yes. Why?'

'Switch over to RTÉ, the *Late Night Live* – it's Bolger, she's on it.'

'Seriously?' She turned on the spot to look for someone who might have the remote control.

'You've got a few minutes,' said Callaghan. 'They're on the ads but she's up next.'

'Right. I'll call back.'

She recognised the guy at the bars – he'd given her the initial tour and set her up with a programme.

'Excuse me, Jason,' she said.

'Hi, Naomi, how are you getting on?' he enquired cheerily.

'Any chance we change the channel?'

'Well, not really, it's our policy to keep it neutral,' he apologised with a well-meaning smile.

'Sorry, Jason, but this is urgent. I need to switch over to *Late Night Live*. It's a work thing – please, just for a minute.'

He looked around the almost empty studio.

'Don't see the harm,' he told her and went into the office to return a minute later with the remote control which he pointed at the screen and scrolled through the channels.

'RTÉ, right?'

'That's it – thanks a mill, you're a star,' she told him.

A very dapper Chris King in a three-piece navy-blue suit with pale-pink shirt and cerise-pink tie, complete with matching pocket square, was standing in front of the fake-brick set, clasping his hands while bobbing from one foot to the other.

'My next guest is a woman who in the past few weeks has gone through a life experience that only nightmares are made of. Drugged, gagged and bound she, along with her life-long friend Sive Collins, was snatched from her weekend retreat and held against her will for almost a week. Following a tip-off to the Gardaí, the women were located. Unfortunately, her friend Sive Collins didn't make it but we are delighted to have businesswoman Karin Bolger and her husband Finn with us this evening to honour Sive and tell us their tale. Ladies & gentlemen, please, put your hands together and give a warm welcome to Karin Bolger and Finn Ellis.'

'I don't believe it,' Fox whispered.

As the audience clapped, Chris walked across the set to greet the couple as they emerged from around the screen. Grasping Karin's hands, he kissed both her cheeks before turning his attention to Finn.

Fox called Callaghan back.

'Jesus Christ,' she said into the phone.

Karin looked tall, confident and well.

'She could have warned us,' said Callaghan.

'She should have,' Fox remarked vacantly, watching the screen overhead and the welcome unfold.

'She's looking great,' Callaghan commented in her ear.

'Is that the woman who was kidnapped?' Jason asked.

Fox had forgotten he was there.

'The very one.'

'Wow!' he whistled. 'Brave move but to be honest she kinda looks like she'd be the one to beat the crap outta you.'

The crowd continued to clap as they made their way across the set to the leather couch, with Chris taking up his spot behind his mahogany desk.

Karin looked fantastic. She was dressed in a beautifully tailored blood-red dress fitted to the waist which showed off the best of her curves before kicking out into a pleated skirt. But it was her killer LaCroix heels that stole the show.

Fox smiled. Karin had picked them well.

'Can I just say,' Chris was announcing, tapping his cue cards on the desk, 'that we are genuinely pleased to have you here.'

The audience again erupted.

'You look wonderful. You don't look like a woman who's been through the ordeal you've been through.'

And so the interview sobered and Karin nervously pushed loose strands of hair behind her ear.

200

'It would be wrong of me to start without first mentioning your friend Sive Collins,' Chris said.

Karin let her eyes drop and nodded sadly.

'Tell us about her.'

'Do you think Gordon knows she was going to do this?' Callaghan asked.

'Somehow I doubt it,' Fox replied, unable to take her eyes from the screen as the camera zoomed in on Karin's face hoping to leverage emotion as she launched into a generous eulogy to her dead friend.

'She'd been a good friend to me over the years, kind, loving and so passionate. She had real heart,' she told Chris sadly.

'You're going to miss her,' he prompted.

'I am. She had so much still to give. It wasn't her time.'

'Can you tell us what happened?'

As soon as his question was aired Fox felt the phone vibrate in her hand and glanced quickly at the screen. She had a call waiting and didn't need to guess who that was, the sick feeling in the back of her throat an immediate response to her intuition. Moyne was going to go ballistic.

'I'm not really sure I should say anything, to be honest – the Gardaí are still investigating,' Karin was saying.

Wisely she was giving nothing away, but the fact she was on the show in the first place was guaranteed to enrage him.

'So they haven't found out who did this?' Chris continued gently.

Karin shook her head.

'And how did you feel? Did you think you were going to die too?'

'I didn't know she was gone until after it was all over.'

'So all the while you were held you didn't know what

happened to her? That news must have been a terrible shock,' Chris expertly probed, leading her gently back into the days after the event.

Karin picked up her water and sipped. All credit to the woman, she was holding it together well.

'It was. It was like nothing I've ever experienced before. I was sure she was safe. She ran away and I thought she'd made it.' She swallowed hard.

The camera shifted back to Chris who nodded sympathetically.

'Did you ever expect something like this could happen to you?'

'I'm a wealthy person and so I know I'm a target, but that's a concept that my head of security owns, not me. To me until that moment I woke up in that dark, horrible place it's always been a notional threat, not a real one.'

'But it's a real one now, isn't it?'

She nodded. 'Yes, very real.'

'You must have been terrified.'

Again Karin nodded. 'I was the most scared I've ever been.'

Chris turned his attention to Finn.

'And what about you, Finn? It must have been a pretty harrowing time for you?'

Like a rabbit in the headlights Finn nodded, his eyes wide and blinking wildly. Shifting in the chair, he cleared his throat. 'Yes. It was difficult waiting and not knowing anything. We didn't know what was going on. But the Gardaí were very good – they talked us through what we should expect.'

'And how was it when you found out Karin was alive?'

Finn paused before answering. Fox knew it was because he had two stories to tell with two conflicting sets of emotion. Viewers would have been forgiven for thinking he was struggling out of joy that Karin was alive rather than grief that his lover was dead.

'It was a relief,' he choked. 'We were thinking the worst all along, so it was an enormous relief when they found her.' He turned to his wife and smiled. Karin reached out and covered his hand which held tight to the arm of his chair. He glanced at it and faltered. 'Karin is a strong, intelligent woman. It hasn't taken her long to get back to normal.'

'And what about Sive? That must have been hard, knowing she didn't make it?'

'That was tough.' He sighed. 'Sive was a very special lady – she didn't deserve this to happen to her.'

'Poor fecker,' Callaghan muttered. 'I don't think I'd be able to sit there like that.'

'He's got a lot to lose,' Fox offered.

'No more than he's already lost.'

'True,' Fox replied, wondering if Karin knew – had Finn told her what had been going on with her friend? And, if he had, was this just a performance for the cameras? She thought about Gordon and Harry – how were they coping? She'd be furious if she were him.

Dragging herself back to the moment, she watched as the cameras and Chris shifted the attention back to Karin, asking her, 'Do you think what happened to you is connected to your business and commercial interests?'

'I do, Chris. People don't like what is happening in the local community and so I am an easy target.'

'But this is your plan, is it not? To close Kings Brewery and put so many people out of work, knock it down and develop it to make a hell of a lot of money?'

Proficiently Chris had turned the tone of the interview from one of empathy to hardline questioning.

'If it's not me it will be someone else,' she objected. 'This is a facility that's going to close anyway. It's losing money hand over fist, it simply can't go on indefinitely. This way the brewery facility moves – granted to a smaller place but at least some jobs can be saved.'

'So does that make it right?' Chris asked.

'No, it makes it fair. This is about progress, it's about creating new homes and lifestyles that some might not ordinarily be able to achieve…'

Fox felt sick, realising that the interview was nothing more than a party political broadcast on behalf of Cusack and Bolger's Spiro Capital, looking to get their great project back on track. Had Karin no shame?

'This development will improve the area tenfold, it will reduce crime and build communities, it will bring a value and a pride back to the places we live …'

You could feel the energy, Fox thought. There was no denying her passion and her drive. This was real Karin.

'I believe in it. This is a great, great opportunity and those shortsighted people who lack the vision to see what's coming can knock me over again and again but I'll keep getting up because this is what I believe and I won't be bullied. Not by anyone.'

Remarkably, applause ripped through the studio, her passion infectious.

Chris took control again. 'And do the Gardaí think that someone from the community, from Kings even, was responsible?'

'I don't know about them but personally I don't. These are ordinary people – yes, they aren't happy with me, but this?' she asked with an incredulous shrug. 'I don't think so.'

Fox couldn't believe what she was seeing or hearing. If

this had been a collaborative effort, part of the investigation strategy, she wouldn't have minded, but Karin, without warning and with total disregard for the entire investigation as well as her personal safety, had gone rogue.

'So, how do you feel now? What would you say to your detractors?'

'I feel great. I'll never forget what happened to me or to Sive and out of respect to her memory I'd say I won't hide from you. *Here I am – come get me!*'

Chris smiled. This was obviously what he was looking for: she made great TV and so he pushed her further.

'Aren't you afraid these guys, whoever they are, will come back for you? You paid what, five million euro? Aren't you afraid they'll come back for more?'

'Let them,' she said, full of bravado. 'Let them come – only next time I'll be ready and there will be no more money. I won't be threatened. Next time they can have me!'

Chris raised his eyes in mock alarm.

'But they'll be left with me because there's no more money coming out of this house. *That* I can guarantee.'

The camera closed in tight on her face, like a cage fighter calling the game before it was fought. They gave her a full five seconds before switching to Finn whose eyes were lowered and cheeks flushed.

Fox shook her head in disbelief and, while the audience seemed to lap Karin up, the self-serving nature of the interview wasn't lost on her.

'What the hell is she doing?' came Callaghan's voice.

Fox had all but forgotten about him, still connected at the end of the phone line.

'I have no idea,' she said, 'but we'll need to speak to Williams – she's all but put a bounty on her own head.'

Her phone shuddered again in her hand.

'I have to go, that's Moyne trying to get through.'

'Shit.'

'I know.' She sighed. 'I'll give you a call later.'

With Callaghan gone, she counted to five before answering the still ringing mobile.

'*I assume you were watching that charade!*' Moyne shouted down the phone at her.

'Yes, sir, I was.'

'*What the hell is going on, Fox? I thought you had this under control!*'

'I do,' she said a little too quickly, a little too desperate.

'Really? Well, that's not what it looked like from here.'

'Sir, even I can't stop what this woman does.'

'No, I agree you can't, but did you tell her not to speak to the media until after the investigation was done?'

'I did, sir, but –'

'But nothing. This is an unmitigated disaster.'

He was being melodramatic and she knew it. Karin had revealed nothing that wasn't already in the public domain. Sure it wasn't great that Karin was so vocal, especially without their cooperation, but Moyne was obviously looking for any excuse to reprimand her and she simply wasn't prepared to accept it.

'I disagree, sir. I briefed Karin and her husband as well as her head of security. They understood perfectly well. This isn't about the investigation, this is about her commercial interests. She's looking to revive her project.'

Moyne wasn't listening.

'This stops now,' he told her. 'Rein her in or I'll take matters into my own hands.' And, before Fox had a chance to reply, he was gone.

Immediately aware of her surroundings and a gob-smacked Jason who had, she assumed, overheard everything, she turned to leave. She felt awkward and embarrassed – it's not every day you get taken down by your boss while dressed in lycra and she wished the ground would open up and swallow her.

'Are you sure you don't want to have another go?' Jason asked, nodding towards the punchbag.

'Thanks, Jason, but I think it's time I went home.' And mustering as much confidence as her bruised ego could manage, she made her way to the showers.

Chapter 16

It seemed that at every turn she took she was greeted with a brick wall. And they were becoming harder to overcome. Some she could get over easily enough, but others needed to be taken apart brick by brick.

When the forensics email finally came through she nearly wept and closed her eyes in silent prayer before opening the folder, in dire need of good news.

Double-clicking the report on screen, she scanned the opening summary. It confirmed what she already suspected, that the interior and exterior of the car had been wiped clean of prints and it was likely this happened before the crime had been committed and the last occupants had worn gloves. But the car had played host to over fifty unique DNA profiles that were generated from skin and hair samples harvested from it. Fox felt her heart quicken. Over fifty! Had she the time or been so inclined she might have romanticised about the provenance of the car's relatively short seven-year life and the stories behind the people who had sat in its seats. But she wasn't and she didn't. She was only interested in its last journey and the passengers who took it. Skimming down through the list, she searched for a name she recognised, specifically Mikey Smyth or any other member of the Smyth family.

As expected, DNA from both Karin and Sive was found on the back seat of the car, Sive's on the left, Karin's on the right. Both women's DNA was also collected from the boot of the car and the front passenger cabin. Despite the finding of Sive's bracelet, there was always the chance that this wasn't the right car – but this evidence made the result conclusive. Silently she congratulated AJ and his team, making a mental note to congratulate him in person.

With the exception of three names, all other samples were attached to people unknown to the Gardaí and much to Fox's disappointment there was no sign of Mikey, Dessie, Nathan or any other member of the Smyth family.

Alan Fitzpatrick and Patrick Wilson were two petty criminals who had each done time for burglary and had spent long enough in the car to leave their DNA behind. Fox wondered if there could be any connection between them and the Smyth family. It was a long shot but worth a look.

But it was the last name on the list that was most intriguing. It was neither inexplicable nor surprising for Finn Ellis's name to appear on the list. After all, cross-contamination was a known and mitigated risk associated with DNA forensics and, as husband to Karin and lover to Sive, his DNA was bound to be present in that car. And while it wasn't hugely alarming it was definitely something she'd have to follow up and that, she knew, wasn't going to make her very popular either with him or his wife.

Pulling out her phone she first rang the lab then rang Callaghan's number.

'Hey,' she greeted him. 'Have the Smyth clan been in to give their DNA sample?'

'They have indeed,' he replied confidently.

'And we processed Mikey's, didn't we?'

'Yep, late last week.'

'Do you think there could be a delay? I mean, I know we pushed forensics for their report – is there a chance the Smyth DNA profiles weren't uploaded into the system in time for the report?'

'There's a chance alright – it's slim but possible – why do you ask?'

'We got the report back on the car and there's no sign of the Smyths in there. I'm just making sure there's nothing we've missed.'

'Well, it makes sense if you think about it,' he reasoned. 'We've already established he wasn't the driver so maybe that's it – he just didn't get in the car – doesn't mean he wasn't involved.'

'*Hmmm*, true,' Fox mused, considering the best approach to her next move. 'I'll send this to you. Check out two names: Alan Fitzpatrick and Patrick Wilson. See if there is anything that can link them to Mikey, Dessie or Nathan or even the brewery deal.'

'Will do. Anything else?'

'Yeah. What they did find in the car was Finn Ellis's DNA.'

'Now *that* is interesting.'

'I know.'

'Before you go tell me, how was Moyne?'

'Pissed off – he's at a conference today so I can breathe.'

Callaghan laughed, thinking she was joking.

'No, seriously, he's driving me mad – you'd swear I booked the woman onto *Late Night bloody Live*.'

'Don't take it to heart, I doubt it's anything personal.'

'Honestly, I actually think it is,' she said with a heavy sigh.

With Finn Ellis on her mind, Fox sat down in the conference

room and turned on the TV. Scrolling through the menu, she navigated her way to the RTÉ Player and pulled up Friday night's *Late Night Live*. Enduring the thirty-second ad that went on for what felt like an hour, she found Karin and Finn's segment and let it play, only this time as much as was possible from the camera angles she focused all her attention on Finn.

Dressed in black jeans, white shirt and a black blazer that was just that little bit too big across the shoulders, he unwittingly bore the look of a lost boy that she very much doubted he was trying to achieve. With his thick head of hair brushed to a glassy sheen, he was the support act to Karin's defiant survivor and looked like he wanted to be anywhere else but there. The distance between them seemed vast. Buried into the corner of the sofa, he leaned away from her with his legs crossed and his hand balled into a fist partially covering his mouth. Fox wondered if his body language was as telling to everyone else as it was to her, betraying the distance between this husband and wife.

The focus was all on Karin but when Finn did speak his words seemed rehearsed and impersonal and, when Chris ultimately asked how he felt upon his wife's safe return, his declaration of apparent delight was flat and unconvincing by comparison to the emotion he displayed when he was asked about Sive.

Over and over Fox watched the segment from the show. While she was sure that Karin's intention was to show strength, a purposeful display of grit as well as a defiant stand against the principles of their attackers, instead she came across as a cold heartless bitch more concerned about the success of her business than the loss of her dear friend.

'What are you looking for?' Callaghan asked, coming up to lean on the table beside her. Lost in the performance she hadn't heard him come into the room.

211

'I'm not sure – anything, I suppose.'

'I can practically hear the cogs moving inside your head – go on, tell me, what are you thinking?'

'Watch this, see what you make of it.'

Scrolling back to the beginning, she made him watch it through, glancing at the key moments to see his reactions.

'She's some woman all right – they're chalk and cheese, aren't they?'

Fox nodded, waiting for him to say it.

'He's not her biggest fan either by the looks of things. Not sure I see the attraction either to be honest.'

'Exactly!' Fox exclaimed triumphantly. 'Why is he with her at all? He's more or less told us he's only there because it's a pretty cushy number. What if Sive was never meant to die,' she said. 'What if Karin was the one we were supposed to find in the ditch?'

'It's definitely possible. He has motive and no concrete alibi and …' he paused to search out the CCTV picture, '… under the cover of layers of hoodie, cap and neck warmer it could be him, don't you think?'

'Definitely possible,' she repeated with a grin, feeling like finally they were making good headway.

'And worth a closer look?'

'Definitely.'

'I'll give the lab a shout to see if they've an update on where exactly they found his DNA and we'll see where we go from there.'

With the warrant secure in the breast pocket of her jacket, she drove up the steep hill towards Wild Wind, behind her a cortege of Garda cars and vans, enough to make the residents of the upper-class neighbourhood chatter wildly. She did, but

212

only for a brief minute, consider warning Karin that they were coming but decided against it. She couldn't risk any possibility of her warning Finn and handing him both the opportunity and time to dispose of any incriminating evidence, if there was any to be found.

For some reason she felt deeply uncomfortable but, as Callaghan reminded her for maybe the millionth time, in most cases it's the husband that did it. Maybe he had planned it all along, maybe Sive was an accident and it was Karin who was never meant to come home. Makes sense, she reasoned, thinking again about the five-million euro that had almost become a secondary issue to the main crime. And as Finn was both the husband and the lover his was a double motive, so to speak.

It was early, the sun was still thinking about whether or not it would make an appearance and already she'd had two coffees. It was never nice surprising someone with a search warrant and as always it had the potential to become nasty very quickly, especially if there was something to hide.

She had been clear during the team briefing over an hour earlier: this was a big house and they needed to be thorough but the main focus would be around Finn's personal space and the areas that were accessed infrequently, like the attic, outhouses or sheds, somewhere someone might hide something that either they weren't ready to dispose of or else getting rid of it was risky and keeping it for a while made sense.

'Above all, guys,' she warned, 'be respectful and neat. I don't want to read in the papers that we made shit of the woman's house. Remember Karin Bolger *is* the victim and this is her home and, whether you like her or not, she's been through enough.'

They nodded their understanding before leaving the station and agreed that Fox would stay close to Karin, and Sam Reilly, still their appointed liaison, would stay with Finn.

Pulling up to the gate, she got out of the car and rang the intercom, giving the thumbs-up to the team pulling up behind her. She had to buzz three times before a gravelly Aggie answered.

'Yes, who is it?' she asked, the irritation of being woken before seven apparent.

'Good morning. This is Detective Inspector Fox here to see either Ms Bolger or Mr Ellis.'

'But they're still asleep,' Aggie protested like they should know.

'Please wake either of them,' Fox instructed politely.

Aggie didn't immediately respond, obviously trying to decide what she should do.

'Aggie, I suggest you go get him, now.'

'Wait a minute.'

Fox imagined her slippered feet scampering down the polished hallway and up the stairs to Karin's room – she was the boss after all. And she wasn't wrong. Within minutes the gates whirred into action to slowly draw back, and the front door opened. Fox put a hand up to the guys to indicate they should stay put while she approached the front door.

'What is this?' Karin asked, tightening the belt of her long satin dressing gown.

Taking the warrant out of her pocket, Fox presented it to her.

'Karin, this is a warrant to search your house.'

'*What? This is outrageous!*' Karin shrieked, whipping the document out of Fox's hand.

214

'Karin, this is just procedure. If you can let me in I can run you through why this is happening.'

'Tell me here. *Now*,' Karin demanded.

Rarely did implementing a search warrant go well, especially not at the beginning, so Fox was well prepared.

'Karin, I really think it's best if I come inside. I'm sure you don't want your private affairs played out in the open.'

'I don't give a fuck who sees!' she spat angrily. 'The neighbours, the press, they despise me anyway. Give them something to talk about.'

'I wasn't thinking of them, I was thinking of you. Karin, we have received the forensic report on the car. If we can sit down I'll talk you through it.'

'What part of *no* don't you get?' Karin asked furiously.

Realizing she wasn't making progress, Fox reluctantly acquiesced. Let shock be the thing to put her in her place.

'Karin, the report has shown that Finn's DNA is in the car.' She gave her a moment to process what she was saying.

'What do you mean?'

'Exactly that: evidence to suggest that Finn, your husband, was at some point in the car that was used in your abduction.'

'That's ridiculous!' she scoffed, grasping the lapels of her dressing gown, tight-lipped.

'I appreciate how it seems, but it does mean we have to follow it up.'

'And how exactly does ransacking my home help you with that?'

'We're not here to ransack your home. We're just here to look, to find something we hope will reasonably explain how Finn's DNA came to be in the car.'

'I'm not stupid, Detective Inspector. What could you possibly find here that would explain that?'

215

There was no pulling the wool over her eyes.

'We'll also be looking for something that might connect him with the crime,' Fox admitted uncomfortably.

'What do you think you'll find – a bloodied baton perhaps?' Karin asked smartly but the bite was gone from her tone.

'I don't know, nothing probably – but, as I've said, we just need to make sure we investigate all leads fully.'

'Was there anything else?'

'Look, Karin, why don't you let me and my team in so we can get this over with. I can talk you through the report and the guys can carry out the search. Is Finn here?'

'Yes. Asleep, I assume. In his room, I suppose.' She shrugged and turned back into the house, leaving the door open behind her.

Fox went back to her car and parked it on the cobblelock driveway, giving way to the twenty officers who filed silently past her into the house.

She signalled to Callaghan who gave the nod for the search to proceed, each of the five teams knowing where they were to go.

Aggie stood bewildered with her mouth agape, watching the crowd of uniforms disperse through the house. Quickly realising her place like a mother hen, Aggie ushered Karin into the kitchen.

'Come on,' she clucked, guiding her to the table. 'I'll make you some tea.'

'Coffee, Aggie, I'd prefer coffee, thanks,' she responded quietly, her voice having lost its earlier edge.

'You might as well sit there too,' Aggie puffed with a sideways glance at Fox as she entered the kitchen behind them.

Aggie bustled around the kitchen, preparing coffee and toast.

'So, tell me, please, what is going on?' Karin said.

'As I said, the forensic report shows that traces of Finn's DNA were picked up in the car that we believe transported Sive and yourself the night you were abducted.'

'But how can that be? He was here. Aggie will tell you that, won't you, Aggie?' She turned to her housekeeper who kept her head down.

Not wanting to sound dismissive of either Karin's claim or Finn's alibi, Fox nodded as if Karin's observation had merit. She knew how to keep her powder dry, to say only what was needed and at all times maintain control of her investigation.

'That may be so, but we have to investigate as best we can, to rule him out and that unfortunately means conducting this search.'

'Finn wouldn't do this – he's my husband for God's sake!'

Right on cue Finn entered the room, dressed in navy checked pajama bottoms and a plain white T-shirt, his hair dishevelled and a night's worth of stubble on his face.

'What the hell is going on?' he asked, his expression a mix of confusion and fury.

'They're ripping my studio apart – you can't do this! *Why* are you doing this? You don't think I had anything to do with … with what happened?'

Fox stood up in response. 'As I was explaining to Karin, we found samples of your DNA in the car that was used in the abduction.'

'Well, your intelligence is wrong – there is no way that's even possible because I wasn't anywhere near any car other than my own. It's not mine. There has to be another explanation.'

217

'There could be,' Fox assured him, trying to keep him calm. 'It could very well be cross-contamination – you know, your hair may have transferred to Karin and could then have transferred to the car.' What she didn't say was that his hair was found on both the headrest and the driver's seat of the Volvo, making her alternative scenario less likely.

Agitated and confused, he seemed to dance on the spot, obviously torn between sitting down or walking out.

'This is routine,' she assured him. 'If you've nothing to hide then you've nothing to worry about.'

'Of course I haven't!' he spat.

'Well, then, why don't you sit down and let the officers do their job?' Looking to lead by example, she sat back down at the table.

Finn considered her proposition, twisted and turned on the spot before shuffling like a tormented teenager towards the table. Karin still hadn't lifted her head.

'You believe me, Karin,' he asked her quietly. 'You don't think I have anything to do with this mess, do you?' His voice lacked the confidence of his indignant display only minutes before.

Karin shook her head silently but refused to meet his gaze.

'This is bullshit!' he spat.

'Sit down now and have your coffee,' Aggie ordered, slicing through the tension and marched to the table with a plate of freshly buttered toast. 'Come on now, sit yourself down,' she urged, returning to the table seconds later with mugs of steaming hot coffee.

Fox's phone beeped in her pocket. Excusing herself, she extracted it and read the text.

You'd better come up. Finn's studio.

Putting the phone back in her pocket, she smiled up at

Aggie who declined to reciprocate and pushed the sugar bowl towards her with a scowl.

'Milk?' she then asked, jug poised, having poured the milk for the others first.

'Please,' Fox replied with a smile. She was waiting for the right moment to arise when she could leave the table without causing alarm.

Although her team was well trained and searched in relative silence, only talking as was necessary, their noise was amplified by the tension in the room. She could track their progress by the scrape of the drawers, the lugging of furniture and clatter of footsteps, every creak making her cringe.

'*I can't bear this!*' Karin burst out when the ground-floor group arrived into the kitchen. 'I'm going to work.' Turning to Fox, she asked, 'You don't need me here, I assume, do you?'

'No,' Fox replied honestly, not sure if she'd have had the nerve to ask her to stay even if that was needed.

'And my bedroom door will be locked!' she called over her shoulder as she left. 'I'm sure you can wait to search it till I'm gone!'

Finn sat at the table, his head resting in his hands and the mug of coffee going cold in front of him. He looked like he might just cry.

Fox's phone pipped again in her pocket.

'Why don't I go and see how they're getting on?' she said, happy to leave him be.

She made her way to Finn's studio, a large open-plan extension that overlooked the gardens and sea beyond. No wonder he stayed so long. She'd be reluctant to leave this place too: how many other aspiring albeit talented artists had a work space like this to enjoy? To her dismay, the room had been respectfully turned upside down. Canvases were moved from the walls, drawers pulled from cupboards and dressers and the contents of the closets lay scattered on the floor.

'Jesus, guys, I asked you to go easy – this place is a mess.'

'To be fair,' Callaghan interjected, 'it doesn't look any worse than when we arrived – most of this chaos wasn't us.'

'Be prepared to put this to rights before you go,' she warned, looking around, stepping over boxes and clothes strewn across the floor before asking with hands on hips, 'So what have you got?'

'This lot,' Callaghan said, walking over to a neatly folded pile of clothes beside an empty rucksack in the middle of the floor. He handed her a pair of gloves that she put on before hunkering down to lift and scrutinise each item one by one. First a pair of Nike tracksuit bottoms, then a matching hoodie followed by a baseball cap with the Boston logo, a black fleece neck-warmer and finally a bottle of cheap spray deodorant. Taking off the lid she smelt the can: strong and musky, its tang was enough to sting the back of her nose and throat. Putting everything back in the bag she stood up and took a step back. She exhaled a long and deeply disappointed sigh, realising she had been wishing it wasn't him.

'Where were they?' she asked without taking her eyes off them.

'Up there,' he pointed to a now-open trapdoor in the roof above her head. 'It's a small enough attic, not much in there except a few boxes and bags but this lot was pushed in between the joists. He tried to pad it over with the insulation but sure it stood out like a sore thumb.'

She glanced over and sighed again, clicking her tongue against her teeth just like her mammy used to do. Having hoped and initially believed this situation had nothing to do with Finn, her frustration was as much with herself as it was with him. Normally her instinct was a sharp as a blade – nothing passed her easily. This was pretty basic stuff and while he was of course a suspect and an obvious one at that, he just didn't seem like he had it in him. But with all the evidence stacking up neatly against him, evidently she was wrong.

She pushed her disappointment aside. 'OK, well, bag this lot and get it to forensics. What else have we got?'

'We've a laptop, nice one too, some paperwork and a box of files taken from the cabinet there.' He pointed to the small box cabinet under the desk.

'OK, well, keep going and see what else you can dig up.'

'Are you happy we've got enough to arrest him?' Callaghan asked.

'Unfortunately, I think so.'

'Jesus, don't sound so disappointed! It's a serious breakthrough – we have him.'

'You're right, I know, it's just …'

'Just nothing, Foxie. He's our man.'

'You're right. I know, I'm just unsettled, that's all.'

'You're just disappointed it's not Mikey, aren't you?' he teased. 'Speaking of which, where does this leave him?'

'Exactly where he is. Could be they know each other. Anyway, we have him for intimidation for sure but after that, well, let's see where this leads us.'

Downstairs Finn was sitting still at the table. He looked like he hadn't moved since she left. Aggie was nowhere to be seen. The search done, she had put the kitchen back to its pristine order before disappearing.

Hearing Fox come in, he looked up.

'Are you done?' he asked.

'Almost.'

'Can I get dressed now?'

'Not yet a while.'

'I need to get dressed,' he objected, 'I'm not sitting here like this all day.'

She called in one of the officers.

'Take Mr Ellis upstairs, accompany him to his room to get his clothes, nothing more, then bring him down here.' Turning to Finn, she said, 'You can get dressed in the loo down here.'

Dawn had well and truly broken to spawn a dull grey day. Looking out of the expansive window at the spectacular view of the sea, Fox felt no envy of either Karin or Finn. For all their wealth, their super cars and the beautiful things that surrounded them, at that moment she felt far richer than them. Never in her career so far had she ever taken pleasure from charging a husband for the murder or attempted murder of his wife. There was nothing to celebrate, especially not the waste of two lives no matter how unloving. And while Finn and the likes of him sought to end the life of their lovers, she would give anything, everything, to get hers back. She closed her eyes to see him and his beaming, goofy smile. That image was all she needed to recharge her waning spirit: it was her treasure chest. And yet here was Finn … what had he been thinking? She doubted he ever realised how lucky he was. His response seemed so extreme. Why didn't he just leave? Weighing up the pro's and cons of leaving versus murder should have had only one logical result. Again she asked herself what the hell was he thinking and how did he think he was going to get away with it. And then, where did it all go wrong? How and why did Sive end up in the ditch?

After Finn had dressed she would need to explain to him what he was facing.

She didn't have long to wait long. When he returned to the kitchen it was with thunder in his voice and Callaghan in his wake.

'*What the hell is going on?*' he boomed. 'Your guys have just walked off with my laptop and half my stuff. You have no right!'

Fox nodded to Callaghan who approached Finn from the door.

'Finn, we'd like you to come down to the station to answer a few more questions,' he said, standing tall with his chin held slightly forward.

'*Fuck you!*' Finn spat furiously. 'I'm not going anywhere. I've done nothing wrong.'

'Finn,' Fox explained calmly, 'we found some clothes in your studio that links you to the abduction of your wife and Sive.'

'Really? Well, show them to me! I'll tell you if they're mine or not,' he demanded, waving his arms. 'Show them the fuck to me *now*!'

'We will.' Treading cautiously, she approached him. 'But we would like to do that at the station.'

'Did you not hear me? What part of fuck off don't you understand? I'm not going anywhere. This is crazy.'

'Finn, you can either come with us willingly,' Fox said, 'or we can arrest you and take you that way.'

'Well, you'd better arrest me, because I'm not going anywhere.'

Shaking her head, she watched Callaghan unhook his cuffs from his belt and take hold of Finn's arm. Turning him around, Callaghan put his wrists in the handcuffs.

'Finn Ellis,' he said, 'I'm arresting you on suspicion of the abduction of Karin Bolger and the murder of Sive Collins …'

'This is nuts! Really I had nothing to do with this.'

'You are not obliged to say anything unless you wish to do so …' Callaghan continued.

'Karin!' Finn yelled.

'But whatever you say will be taken down in writing and may be given in evidence.'

He finished just as Karin waltzed in, looking perfectly polished, in a classic black-and-white Chanel suit.

'What the hell have you done?' she immediately asked, looking at Finn.

'I've been arrested for your abduction,' he told her.

'I beg your pardon?' she asked, visibly faltering. Turning to Fox, she asked, 'You've arrested him?'

'That's correct.'

'Tell them, tell them this had nothing to do with me!' Finn pleaded desperately.

Karin looked at Fox, her face aghast, then back at Finn but her words failed her. She couldn't or wouldn't say a word.

'Karin?' he beseeched as Callaghan guided him by the arm out of the kitchen into the hall. *'Karin!'*

She took a step back as they passed her in the doorway and, rooted to the spot, watched him go. With each step he took Finn's voice grew a little louder until he was gone from sight but she could still hear him roar.

Turning, she looked to Fox.

'What just happened?'

Fox couldn't help but feel sorry for her – standing in the hall dressed to kill but confused as hell.

'Come on,' she invited, 'let's sit down.'

Taking her by the arm, she led her through to the sofas in the lounge.

Placing her bag carefully on the coffee table Karin slowly lowered herself onto the edge of the plump cushions.

'I don't believe this,' she whispered, leaning forward and massaging her temples.

Fox sat, angling herself so she could look directly at Karin but respecting her need for silence. She watched her struggle to understand but with nothing constructive to offer let her work through it alone until eventually the silence stretched out too far and needed to be broken.

'All of this – the car, the clothes – it could be coincidental,' she said.

'Please don't patronise me,' Karin replied quietly. 'You know it's not and so do I. Jesus Christ, this isn't happening. It can't be.'

'I'm so sorry, Karin, really I am.'

'What the hell are you sorry for? You didn't do bloody anything.'

Appreciating the devastating blow that had been delivered and its certain effect, Fox let that slide, almost getting used to Karin's caustic tongue.

Shifting back into the sofa Karin crossed her legs, folded her arms and let her head fall back to rest on the cushions. She stared up at the ceiling as if admiring the detail of the delicate stucco overhead.

Such an intense gaze, focused and unblinking, Fox wondered if this was some kind of learned coping mechanism. Every emotion in transition was evident through the expressions on her face, from disbelief to rejection to acceptance. As the time passed the tension in the room abated, her shoulders relaxed and calm was restored.

As Karin's focus, bordering on meditation, continued, Fox structured the questions in her head that needed to be asked, the most significant being Karin's knowledge of Finn's relationship with Sive. It wasn't one she was looking forward to asking.

'Sorry,' Karin eventually said, pushing herself back up. 'I'm not sure I understand what's just happened. I can't believe it. Finn? Why? Why would he do this? To me, to Sive?' Dropping her head, she held it in her hands. 'Why Sive? What had she ever done?'

'You don't need to apologise. I understand but I do need to ask a few questions if you're ready.'

Karin nodded and Fox, shifting slightly, cleared her throat. She was reluctant to ask her straight out. No matter how thick-skinned or hardnosed Karin was, there was no way she wasn't feeling the effects of the morning's events. If she was lucky she might not have to. Maybe Karin already knew.

'Finn and Sive, how would you describe their relationship?'

'He didn't hate her if that's what you're asking. From what I could tell they got on just fine.' She shrugged, the innocence to her response dousing Fox's hopes of a reprieve.

'Do you think there was anything more to it than friendship?' Fox coaxed.

'Finn and Sive? Good God, no! Sive would never … she wasn't his type.' Her face squashed in exaggerated disgust.

'Karin, we believe it *was* more than just friendship. They were … involved.'

'Don't be ridiculous!' Karin scoffed. 'I'd know if they were at it. Or if I didn't Tom would for sure – he knows everything that's going on even before it happens.'

'It was Tom who brought it to us.' Then, not wanting to get Tom into hot water, she qualified, 'We asked him not to say anything until we were able to establish what was going on.'

A deep scowl crossed Karin's face, her brow furrowed and lips tightened.

'Tom knows? He should have told me. You had no right to ask him to keep this from me.'

'I'm sorry, Karin, but we had no option.'

'And now you've arrested Finn. Can I assume you now, as you say, *know what was going on?*'

'Not quite, but we're getting there.'

Karin got up and walked to the window where she stood in silence, her arms wrapped protectively around herself.

''How could they? I never ... I just never, ever would have thought he was capable. As for Sive ...' she huffed but said no more, leaving the sentence hang unfinished. 'Can this day get any bloody worse?'

Fox could see the deep rise and fall of Karin's shoulders and the slow, short shake of her head as she processed the events of the morning. There was nothing she could say to console her. In such instances she had learnt it was best to say nothing.

'Have you spoken to Finn about this?' Karin asked her, without turning.

'We have.'

'What did he say?'

'Finn has admitted the affair,' Fox told her quietly.

Now she knew. But now she wanted the detail.

'When?' she demanded. 'When did he admit it?'

'At the funeral.'

Karin nodded. 'How long had it been going on?'

Fox paused, debating how involved she needed to be. This was swiftly turning into a domestic.

'You'll have to ask him that.'

Karin turned her back on the view to sneer at Fox.

'How convenient that you have him now, so I can't, can I? Maybe you can hang on to him and I can forget them both.'

She was hurting, Fox could see that, and so excused her behaviour. To the best of her knowledge Karin had no one else to turn to. She'd lost her friend, her ally and now her husband. But it was important that she had someone on her side right now and Williams might well be that person. At least she trusted him, he could confirm what he saw and if he was up to it he could show her the footage.

An involuntary sob escaped Karin's lips, which she immediately covered with her hand.

'I'm so sorry, Karin.'

'Oh, for God's sake, will you please stop saying that!' Karin growled, her sadness morphing quickly to anger and aimed squarely at Fox. 'It's utterly pointless and a complete waste of time. Why the hell are you sorry? You've got your man now, haven't you? He's it. Sive's murderer. You can go home now, your job is done.' Her voice cracked as she spoke. But Fox doubted if anyone had ever seen Karin Bolger cry and didn't think Karin would want today to change that.

Resuming control, Karin fixed the waistband of her skirt and marched across the room to sweep her bag from the table.

'Right. Well, I have to go to work – unless there is anything else?'

Getting used to Karin's rhetorical questions, Fox interpreted this as her invitation to leave and stood to leave.

'Why don't I give Tom a shout, maybe get him to come over, give you a lift into the office?'

'*I'm not a child!*' Karin hissed. 'I don't need him. I don't need anyone. At this stage of my life I've had more disappointments than you've had walks in the park. I got over them then and I'll get over this now. So, if you don't mind …' She moved out of the room and extended her arm towards the front door.

Back at her Dublin-based desk, Fox knew she should call Moyne to update him but she didn't have either the inclination or the emotional energy needed to deal with him. Predicting his obsessive need for detail and knowing she still had to prove to him that she was a competitive and intuitive officer who didn't need him to tell her how she should do her job, she decided instead to send him an email. Taking her time, she outlined in short concise bullet points what had occurred that morning and what her resulting plan of action was. Even as she read and reread it, she knew he wouldn't be happy but there was only so much trying she could manage without becoming desperate.

She could hear Callaghan's footsteps in the corridor, probably looking for her to start the interview. She checked her watch and smiled – he was playing football later and obviously wanted to make sure he got out on time.

'Are you ready?' he asked, sticking his head around the door.

'Almost, just need to finish this.'

'How was Karin?'

'Shit,' she told him with a sigh before biting the bullet and pressing *Send*.

She stood up and stretched, ignoring the skittish butterflies that danced inside.

'Didn't take it too well then?' he asked.

'What do you think?' she replied sarcastically, arching her back.

'Tough one. Bad start to her day.'

'God, yeah.' She paused, chewing pensively on the inside of her lip.

'We're almost there – come on, let's finish this one off.'

'I know, I know,' she agreed, 'but …'

'But nothing. He's guilty. We have all the evidence we need to charge him. This interview is a formality.'

'I'm not sure.' She scowled. 'Does it not seem a bit easy, like it's been all wrapped up ready for us to find?'

'It doesn't always have to be difficult – some people just aren't made to be criminals and they make mistakes. Sometimes it is that easy. And this is one of those times.'

'So why don't I feel like celebrating?'

'Maybe you fancy him,' he said with a cheeky grin. 'He is an attractive man after all.'

'Don't be crass, Callaghan, it doesn't suit you,' she retorted, sweeping past him and down the hall towards the interview room.

Chapter 17

Finn raised his head from his hands when they entered the room.

'You've made a massive mistake,' he told them confidently as Callaghan set up the recorder and Fox set out the case file and notepad in front of him. 'Please. This isn't right.'

'Why don't you start by telling us what happened?' Callaghan suggested, settling into his seat.

Finn sat forward with his elbows on the table and his head held in his hands.

'I don't care what you say you have, you're reading it all wrong. This wasn't me. I didn't do anything like that. Why would I? I loved her.' Looking up, he caught Callaghan's eye.

'Who? Who did you love?' Callaghan asked defiantly.

Finn hesitated, realising his claim, and dropped his head back into his hands.

'Both of them, I suppose. I loved both of them. You don't understand.'

'Try me.'

'I didn't set out to fall for Sive, it just happened. She was sweet, funny, smart …'

'And Karin?'

'And I never wanted to hurt her either, she's been good

to me. And I do love her, despite everything, I do.'

'That's not the impression you gave us last time we spoke.'

'Yeah, well, that was before I was under suspicion for her kidnapping. You guys came to me, you made me think you were on my side. I was honest with you, I was feeling … I don't know, vulnerable maybe.'

'How about unguarded?' Callaghan said. 'You thought you'd slipped under our radar, didn't you? But what I'm curious about is which of them was never meant to come home? Karin or Sive?

'You're nuts. Neither. I mean both. I don't know. Why the hell would I? Seriously?'

Callaghan shrugged. 'I don't know. That's what I was hoping you would tell us. Why? Why you did it.'

'But I didn't.'

From the case file Fox pulled out a bundle of pictures held together with a paper clip. One by one she laid them on the table in front of him.

'Do you recognise these clothes?' she asked him.

Finn took his time, looking at each picture then nodded, 'I think they're mine, yes. Why?'

'Let me show you this,' Callaghan said, nodding towards the screen built into the wall. As he pressed play on the remote control the CCTV footage from the service station appeared almost immediately.

Finn realised what he was looking at and what it was supposed to mean.

'But that's not me! The clothes, they look like mine, but they're not. You don't think that's me?' Finn asked desperately.

'You've already told us they're your clothes.'

'*They're* my clothes,' he stressed through tight lips,

pointing at the pictures in front of him, 'but *they're* not!' He pointed at the screen. 'That could be anyone but *it's – not – me*. Got it?'

'Really?' said Callaghan. 'Surely you have to admit then that it's a crazy coincidence that you own *exactly* the same outfit as the person who kidnapped your wife and murdered your lover. Odd that, isn't it?'

'Half of Dublin wears this gear, not only me.'

'And why did you have them hidden in your attic?'

'I didn't.'

'Do you always keep your clothes in the attic, Finn?'

'No. Of course not.'

'So how did this lot get in there then?'

'I don't bloody know, do I?'

'Well, I think you put them there.'

Finn shook his head wildly. 'Nope. Wasn't me.'

'If it wasn't you, who was it?' Fox asked.

'How the hell do I know?'

'And that's where the problems begin,' she told him, leaning forward. 'Can you see why we're having difficulty believing you?'

'But you're not listening to me. I'm telling you I had nothing to do with it. I mean, why? Why would I do it?'

Callaghan leaned back to consider Finn through squinted eyes and pursed lips.

'Contrary to our very patient DI here,' he nodded towards Fox, 'I don't think this was an accident. I think you set out to do serious harm – maybe not from the get-go but certainly as things got complicated you shifted gear. Am I right?'

Finn grimaced and shook his head.

'You said it yourself – extracting yourself from the

lifestyle you've created wasn't going to be easy. Let's face it, you enjoy the luxury and the pampering. I mean, how many other artists work from such lavish surroundings? Not many, I'd guess.'

Finn stared at him without blinking, moving his head slowly from left to right, his face filled with anger.

'But to go it alone you needed money. That's where the five mill came in. Originally that was your way out but then things with Sive went pear-shaped and the money wasn't as important as shutting her up. So for what it's worth, I think your original scheme was to kidnap your wife, extort enough money to set yourself up and release her unharmed, eventually. I think you were always going to point the investigation in the way of the protestors – they were an excellently convenient decoy.' Callaghan paused, looking at him with questioning eyes. 'How close am I?'

'You're so far off the mark.'

'I'm not so sure.' Callaghan smiled, lifting his eyebrows playfully. 'You and Sive, you had a fight. I'd put money on it she was having doubts, maybe thought about it and decided she preferred Karin over you. Was she having second thoughts?

'You're so wrong!' Finn spat. 'You think you know everything but you know nothing, not a damn fucking thing!'

Callaghan looked at Fox with a grin. 'I suspect he may have tried to kill two birds with one stone.'

The childish pun wasn't lost on Fox who had to consciously stop herself from throwing her eyes to heaven.

'Maybe you should rethink the day job,' Finn suggested sarcastically. 'You're obviously not very good at this because you're miles off, fathoms in fact.' Turning to Fox he enquired,

'I'm assuming you're the one who knows what you're doing – so please, will you listen to me?' He banged the table hard with his fist.

She jumped, embarrassingly so, like a nervous bird. Collecting herself quickly, she made no reference to his sudden action but simply asked, 'May we have access to your bank accounts, any log-ins and online passwords. Please.'

He looked startled. She had said very little thus far, letting Callaghan take the lead. She didn't think he expected her to be so direct.

'If, as you say, you've got nothing to hide you won't mind giving them to us, will you?'

There was no denying the flush or the fleeting panicked look that crossed his face but, as quick as it appeared, it was gone.

'Sure,' he replied, taking the pen and notebook that Fox passed across the table to him and with a scant glance up at her he wrote down a sequence of numbers from memory then pushed it back.

'Is that it? One account?' she asked.

'There are two, but they're linked – this lets you see both.'

'Is that it? No more?'

He shook his head.

'You sure? You don't look sure. We will check, you know.'

Again he shook his head. A little too quickly, she thought.

She nodded to Callaghan, a signal to wrap things up. But he wasn't quite ready.

'Before we go, you still haven't answered my earlier question. Which of the two was supposed to live? Because, depending on which way you look at it, you've got a motive for both.'

'You're an arsehole, do you know that?'

'That's enough,' Fox interjected calmly, placing her palms on the table.

'Motive?' Finn persisted, 'I don't have a motive. For fuck sake, Karin has more motive than I do.'

'How so?'

'Look at them. It was hardly an obvious friendship, was it? More like the odd couple.'

'But isn't that one of the fundamentals of friendship – opposites do attract,' said Callaghan.

'Maybe, but these two, they had bugger all in common. Sure, Sive respected her but she didn't like her very much.'

'So why did she hang out with her then?' Fox interrupted.

'Why do you think? Money. It was her cold hard cash that Sive loved.'

'That's a pretty harsh statement about someone you're supposed to love.'

'It's the truth.' He shrugged. 'Doesn't mean I have to like it.'

'So, what?' Callaghan asked. 'Karin paid Sive to be her mate? A bit desperate, don't you think?'

'I suppose, but Sive had something over her, something from when they were in college together that Karin didn't want anyone else to know, not even me.'

'What? Sive was blackmailing her?' Fox asked.

Finn thought about it for a minute. 'Maybe, yeah.'

'And how do you know?' Callaghan asked sceptically.

'Sive told me.'

'Can you prove it?'

'All you have to do is look at the track record – ten failed businesses in as many years. What more proof do you need? Karin's a savvy businesswoman, we all know that, so why do you think she threw so much money at Sive?'

'To be honest, Finn,' said Callaghan, 'to me this smells of nothing more than a pretty feeble attempt to distract us.'

'Don't believe me? Ask her. Go on. Ask her.'

Callaghan stood and Fox followed suit.

'Oh, we will,' Callaghan said as they left. 'But it's no distraction. We'll be back to you and your story in no time.'

'So what do you think?' Fox asked as they made their way upstairs. 'Do you believe him?'

'Not one bit. He's just buying himself some time, time to figure out what to say next, craft his next story, paint his next picture, that's all. He's a chancer, shacked up like some candy-coated toy boy …' His distaste was evident on his distorted expression.

Fox smiled at his analogy, 'Jealous, are we?' she asked.

'Nah. Wouldn't for love nor money. Do you?'

'What? Believe him? I don't know. It certainly answers the question about Karin and her free money. And, I mean, does he really have motive? Why wouldn't he stay? With Karin he had all the money he could ever need – what other artist can say that?'

'But he's a kept man – surely the novelty runs out and it becomes a little embarrassing, doesn't it?'

'I dunno, but to be honest, it's a little irrelevant, isn't it? It doesn't give us any further insights into Finn beyond the fact he's a kept man, which we already knew. Maybe this big secret has something to do with him?'

'Maybe,' Callaghan replied, unconvinced. 'Are you not heading back to Galway?'

'Not tonight.' She was about to say she was going to try and get an early night when the duty sergeant called.

'You've got a visitor,' he told them. 'Karin Bolger is downstairs asking for you.'

'Thanks, sarge,' she said with raised eyebrows and, turning to Callaghan, she smiled. 'This is where it gets interesting.'

Downstairs in the waiting area Karin hummed with unspent energy that was bursting to escape. Both Fox and Callaghan felt her charge as soon as they walked through the door. She stood as soon as she saw them and immediately set about explaining why she was there.

'I've spent the whole afternoon racking my brain, trying to think why Finn would do such a thing and I think I know why.'

Fox ushered her into the adjoining interview room.

She sat down at the table and Fox purposely sat beside as opposed to in front of her while Callaghan didn't sit at all but leaned against the wall with his arms folded across his chest, hoping for a quick exit.

Agitated and restless, Karin appeared to have difficulty focusing.

Callaghan stole a glance at Fox who was wondering if the affair and the fight and the desire to escape weren't motive enough.

'You know why?' said Fox.

'Yes, well, I think so. It's the best I can come up with, to be honest. I think it's because of Sive and me.' She paused and dropped her eyes to the floor. 'And what happened in college.' Her demure demeanour seemed totally out of character.

'He did mention something all right.'

'So he's told you?' said Fox.

'All he said was that Sive had some kind of secret she was holding over you and that this was the reason why you've been bankrolling her businesses over the years.'

Karin looked at Fox, her face a twisted expression of confusion, but as the seconds ticked by it seemed her brain-fog began to clear and a smile slowly filtered across her face.

'That's what he told you? Oh, for God's sake!' She began to laugh, slapping her hands into her lap. 'And you think he's telling you the truth?'

'At the moment we don't think anything. But I'm curious to know if he's right.'

'I'm sorry,' she said, bringing her laughter under control. 'It's just … well, it's ridiculous.'

'So, she wasn't blackmailing you then?'

'It's complicated.'

'Perhaps you could try to simplify it for us?' Callaghan invited, his fuse diminishing by the second.

Taking a deep breath and exhaling slowly, Karin clasped her hands tight in her lap. 'Sive and I were in college together. It was our final year, nineteen ninety-two I believe. One of the top 'A' students in our year, I was in line to get the Alice Redmond Gold Medal of Distinction. There were two of us in contention, myself and Darina Mulhearn. But I wanted to win, I mean *really* wanted to win. That award was mine.' She smiled wistfully, having travelled back to the moment and the memory. 'I supposed Darina was the favourite – not to win, just the favourite, she was the one everyone hoped would win, she was so much more popular that I was or ever could be. Our last exam was economics, which wasn't my best subject overall and I suppose I wasn't willing to leave anything up to chance so I broke into my professor's office and copied the paper.'

'You *broke* into his office?' Callaghan repeated, astounded by the admission.

She nodded.

'How?'

'Does it matter?'

'Not really, I'm just curious.'

'Well, not really *broke* in. Professor Scanlan was a forgetful old goat and was forever leaving his key in one place or another so he had a spare, hidden. Nothing too convoluted. His was the office at the end of the corridor in the old building. There was a big old window with a sill deep enough to sit into. It had these heavy timber shutters. No one ever used them, there was no need, so Prof hung his *just-in-case*y key on the back of the shutter. He never remembered telling me about it, I'm sure. It was halfway through second year and he had to use it on the day of my specialization tutorial. I guess he didn't have me down as the dishonest type and never thought to move it. See, nothing too sinister, I'm afraid.'

'It's always the one you least suspect,' Callaghan joked, then checked himself following a sideways glance from Fox.

'Anyway, Sive found it, the paper I mean. I left it under a pile of papers on my desk the morning of the exam. I planned to burn it that afternoon once the exam was over. I have no idea what she was doing in there in the first place. I never bothered to ask her. Anyway, she promised not to tell and true to her word never did, or so I thought – till now – pillow talk, I suppose.'

'To be fair, I don't think Sive actually told Finn anything specific,' Fox defended her.

'Well, I suppose that makes it all right then!' Karin snapped then checked herself. 'I'm sorry. But the money I gave her had nothing to do with that. I gave her the money because I wanted to.' She paused to glance briefly first at Fox then at Callaghan still leaning by the door. 'That's what you do for people you love – you help them, you share. Maybe she saw it differently, but that's the way I looked at it anyhow. I wasn't looking for anything in return.'

The air hung tense with the question that begged to be asked. They both heard her say it but neither was sure they quite got the undertone.

'And do you? Did you? Love her?' Callaghan tested tentatively.

Karin smiled sadly. 'Yes, I suppose I did. That's what I told him anyway.' She sighed. 'That's what has caused this. It's all been my fault. Me and my big mouth.' Neither Fox nor Callaghan said a word, letting her explain fully.

'You see, I told him one night a few months ago. We'd had a fight – things hadn't been great between us and, well, I suppose I was angry and hurt by his rejection. He simply didn't want me any more. So in a fit of rage I told him about Sive and me.'

'Are you and Sive …' Callaghan paused, looking for the right words. 'Were you together?'

She laughed. 'Typical man. You'd love that, wouldn't you? Think what a story that would make. The press would guzzle that one up for sure. No, we weren't together, not now anyway, but in college, yes, we had a *thing*. A short thing. But it came and went in a semester. Everything seemed, well, possible – like nothing was impossible – so we explored a little. It seemed harmless at the time, exciting but harmless.'

'How did Finn take it?' Fox asked, glaring at Callaghan whose mouth hung open – she could almost hear him whistle inside his head.

'Well, he wasn't pleased, that's for sure. Said I was being spiteful, that I'd made it up and just said it to hurt him.'

'Did you suspect he was having an affair with Sive?'

241

'No. Not with Sive. I kind of knew there was someone. No disrespect,' she threw a filthy look at Callaghan, 'but I believe a man will travel to find what he's not getting at home. But not for a minute did I think it was *her*. I should have guessed, though, he was so … wounded by what I'd said. And he doesn't love me enough to be hurt by something I did when I was nineteen years old. How could I have been so blind?'

'But you said it yourself – it was years ago. Why do you think he'd react so violently now?'

'Maybe he was afraid that weekend we were, you know…'

'Rekindling old flames?'

She nodded.

'And were you?'

'No!' she exclaimed. 'It was a working weekend, that's all.'

'Seems a bit extreme, don't you think?'

'He's an artist, passionate and fiery and so incredibly intense. Most of the time he's the perfect gentleman and so laid back he's almost horizontal but push the wrong button at the wrong time and …' she shook her head and closed her eyes, 'well, let's just say he can get pretty agitated, especially when things don't go his way.'

'Has he ever been violent?'

'Towards me? Never, but I've replaced a few doors and repaired a few walls over the years.'

Fox nodded. This was something she needed to see for herself.

'She's some woman,' Callaghan remarked when Karin had left. 'She's got some balls, I'll give her that.'

But Fox wasn't listening. '*Hmmm?*'

'I said she's got balls.'

'She does, doesn't she? I wonder about Finn. What on earth was the attraction in the first place? Why did he marry her? Would you – marry her, I mean?'

'Not in a month of Sundays,' Callaghan scoffed. 'She'd eat me for breakfast, lunch and dinner with her bare hands.'

Fox smiled. He was right, she would. 'So, is this it? Is this our motive?'

'Maybe this was what Finn and Sive were fighting over? Maybe Karin's right. Maybe it was jealousy with the fear of being replaced or pushed out even that pushed him over the edge?'

'Perhaps,' Fox replied, unconvinced but listening.

Chapter 18

No one was surprised when the tech team returned with evidence of a third account. A simple Internet history search on his laptop offered it up immediately. It had to be the worst cover-up in the history of Fox's career, if he'd even tried to hide it.

'Why didn't you tell us about this one?' Fox asked when they presented the evidence to him.

Having left him stew overnight she was as anxious to question him as he was to be released. Still protesting his innocence, he was restless and uptight. She could see he was trying to contain his anger, but she predicted it wouldn't take long for his simmering frustration to explode. She hoped Karin was exaggerating about Finn's temper but, experiencing his demeanour for herself, she didn't think it would be long or take much for him to erupt. She felt his tension as he sat almost rocking on the edge of his seat, rubbing his temples.

'Because I knew exactly what you'd think,' he told her.

'And what's that?'

'That it was me, that I killed Sive.'

'And did you?'

'No! I've told you a million times it wasn't me,' he hissed, his nails digging deep into his palms, 'but you just won't listen.'

'Did you not think we'd find out about it?'

'Maybe, maybe not, I had nothing to lose.'

'What about honesty and trust?' she said. 'How do you expect us to believe you now when you've already lied so convincingly? Your credibility's shot. You had a lot to lose and you've done it.'

'I only lied about the account, not about anything else, I swear, and even then I didn't lie. I just didn't tell you about it.'

Both Fox and Callaghan laughed simultaneously.

'Seriously, Finn, we're not in junior school now. You didn't lie?' Callaghan mocked.

'Why don't we start again?' Fox suggested, adopting a conciliatory tone. 'But you need to be totally honest with us.'

Finn nodded and took a deep breath, his face pinker than a boiled lobster.

'Take your time,' Fox encouraged. 'Why not start by telling me about your relationship with your wife.'

'I've told you all this before.'

'I know, but I want to hear it again. Look at it this way, I'm giving you a second chance to convince me this wasn't you.'

He nodded, the tension abating, and for the first time that morning he met her gaze.

'When Karin and I met she was a different woman. While I was naïve and a little bit blinded by her kind of celebrity status she was confident and, well, gentle, I suppose. I thought she'd be good for me, you know, for my art. So I went for it. For the most part we were happy enough. It was never electric, there was no passionate love affair but I was happy enough and I think she was too.' He shrugged his shoulders. 'She's generous and smart and she knows good art, she's my best critic and mentor. I loved her, really, I did. And I trusted her. I still do, but beside that there's not much else really.' He looked at them, his mouth turned down.

'You told us that she had accused you of having affairs before. Was your affair with Sive your first?'

'Yes, it was. I genuinely wasn't interested in anyone else despite what she thought.'

'And in the lead-up to the kidnapping, how were things between you two? Did you fight? Were you talking? How did you get through your days with her if things are that bad?'

'It's funny really,' he told them with a small chuckle. 'It's like we've both realised it's over but neither of us has the guts to admit it. We do talk to each other, at least we did, all the time. She'd come to my studio and we'd talk about my work, we'd have dinner together but we just weren't *together*.'

'What about sex?' Callaghan asked bluntly.

'None of your bloody business!' Finn snapped.

'But I think it is.'

'Finn, do yourself a favour and answer the question – it's all relevant,' Fox advised.

'Well?' Callaghan prompted.

'We don't, not anymore,' Finn replied defiantly, holding Callaghan's stare.

'Does she try?'

'Not really, no.'

'Not *really*?' Callaghan tested.

'Not at all.' Finn qualified with hate in his eyes.

'Even recently?'

'What the hell are you getting at? I've already said no,

haven't I? What more do you want me say?'

'I'm just trying to get a sense of what was going on in your house, that's all,' Callaghan teased with a shallow grin designed to provoke rather than reassure.

'We used to have sex, all the time. Good sex. But not recently. I don't fancy her anymore. I don't fancy her, alright? That's not a crime, is it? And that doesn't mean I would harm her. Ever. I wouldn't do that.' He made a point of looking each of them in the eye. 'Sive and I ...' he paused to swallow, his hands fidgeting in his lap, 'we were going to leave together, well, that was the plan anyway. But I knew Sive wouldn't come with me unless I had money so I've been saving ...'

'Saving or skimming?' Callaghan threw at him.

Finn sneered with poison in his eyes, his nostrils flared and his breathing deepened. Having confessed his plan he didn't appreciate being chastised like a child. Yet he didn't argue, how could he?

'I set up my own account and every now and then I'd deposit what I could. Anything I'd made on my paintings. I got a few commissions and did a few classes and instead of spending what I earned I just lodged it. Nothing wrong with that.'

He was right, there wasn't anything wrong with it but the deceitful intent of his actions spoke volumes about his frame of mind that warranted deeper and sceptical scrutiny.

'Did you tell her – Karin – did you tell her you were leaving?'

'No. I wanted to, I didn't like deceiving her but Sive said she wasn't ready.'

Fox had been waiting for the right moment to establish if he was aware of the true relationship between the women.

'Why do you think that was?' she asked, hoping to lead him to it.

Finn huffed with a derisive chuckle. 'I'm assuming it was the money. I don't think she was ready to let go of Karin's purse strings. She said it was the last time, that she deserved to give it one last go.'

'And you think that was it, nothing else?' she enquired.

'Why else?' he asked tentatively.

'Were you aware that Sive and Karin were involved?' she pushed.

'Yes, of course I was, you know that! I told you Karin was financing her business notions!'

'No,' Fox corrected, 'I mean personally. While in college, for a time, they were intimate.'

'They were having their own little fling,' Callaghan told him bluntly.

Fox glowered at his unnecessary and insensitive interruption.

In any normal circumstance Finn's laugh could have been described as vivacious but in the formal environment of the interview room, in the context of their conversation, it felt wrong and inappropriate.

Yet on he laughed as if he'd heard the most deliciously hilarious joke.

Straight-faced, Fox and Callaghan let it run its course without taking their eyes off him.

'Are you guys for real? he asked as his laughter subsided. 'Sive and Karin?'

Fox nodded.

'That's bullshit!' he spat, a dark veil coming over him in an instant. 'Absolute bullshit!'

'That's what we've been told.'

'By whom?'

'By Karin herself.'

'Well, she's lying,' he persisted, his face a twisted scowl.

'And why would she do that?'

'How am I supposed to know?'

'She says she told you and you were pretty pissed off,' Callaghan told him.

'That's bullshit and you know it. You're trying to trick me here – do I look stupid?'

'I'll bet you didn't like that one bit,' Callaghan continued with a malicious chuckle.

'Were you jealous, didn't like the idea of your mistress heading off for a filthy weekend with your wife? Imagine that, dumped by your lover for your wife.'

'Stop!' Fox warned, putting a hand on his arm but he was on a roll.

'Not true, I said, not true – are you deaf or something?'

But Callaghan continued, ignoring both Finn's and Fox's protests. 'I'd be pretty upset if it were me. Betrayed by the two women I trusted – in fact, I think I'd be fit to kill!'

'*For fucksake!*' Finn shouted, banging his fists on the table. 'No. I said *No. No. No*. It wasn't me. Why the hell isn't this getting through to you? As you thick as well as fucking ugly? Why would I do that? I loved Sive, I loved them both I've already told you what the fight was about – yeah, I didn't want her to go, but not because of this imaginary fling!'

Ignoring his denials, Callaghan picked up his notes and read, '"*I wanted her to stop but she said no, said it was none of my business and actually accused me of being jealous. How ridiculous is that?*" Those are your words, Finn. Why would she accuse you of being jealous? What else did you have to be jealous about if not her little college fling with your wife?'

249

'Oh Christ!' Finn dropped his head into his hands and clenched fists full of hair, his frustration palpable. 'I've told you already there was no bloody fling. Yes, she accused me of being jealous, but why would I tell you that if I'd done anything to her, to either of them?'

'Maybe you're just not that bright, Finn?'

Finn looked up with fury in his eyes. 'Who the hell do you think you are?' he demanded, his voice louder and deeper than before, his frustration having turned to malignity. 'You don't know me. You have no idea.'

'Now, now, calm down,' Callaghan said with a smile, infuriating him further.

Pushing his chair back violently, Finn lunged over the table and made a grab for Callaghan who only just escaped his grasp by pulling back quicker than he could dive.

Finn spat across the table.

'You're a walking prick, do you know that?' he shouted with venom.

'Let's take a break – cool off a bit,' Fox said, suspending the interview. She nodded at Callaghan and left the room.

'What the hell was that?' Fox whispered when O'Callaghan joined her outside the room.

'Well, you said you wanted to stretch him to his limits,' Callaghan defended himself.

'You certainly did that,' she told him, marching up the corridor.

'At least we got to see him blow,' he said, marching after her. 'So, what do you think?'

'I'm not sure.'

'Seriously?' He gawked. 'After that performance? He's as guilty as sin and you know it.'

'Let's wait and see, shall we?'

'Seriously? Look at the evidence. We have everything we need – it's pretty obvious he did it.'

'I know, it's all stacking up quite neatly around him, but …'

'But nothing. He's our man. We'll give him a few more minutes and go back in.'

Fox sighed, unconvinced, and made her way towards the canteen, wishing they served something stronger than coffee – she could do with a drink.

They gave him fifteen more minutes before re-entering the interview room. Fox was carrying her laptop. Placing it on the table, she opened it up and refreshed the preloaded homepage for IntroBanks website. A purely Internet-based bank online was the only way to access any individual account, no matter who or where you were. Clicking on to the log-in page, she turned it towards a much calmer Finn.

'Log in for me,' she asked.

He pulled the computer towards him and without a second glance tapped in his code and waited for the second screen to load before typing in the password. When he was done he turned the machine around and pushed it back to her.

'There,' he said, without looking at the screen, 'see for yourself.'

'I don't need to,' she replied politely without taking her eyes off him and waited for the on-screen page to fully populate.

'Who is John James?' she asked.

'That's me. Finn John James Ellis,' he replied like a child caught with his hand in his mother's purse.

'Why not use your own name?'

'It *is* my own name,' he replied smartly.

'I mean the name you are known by. Anyone ever call you John James?' she asked with raised eyebrows.

'No.'

'So why not Finn Ellis?'

He didn't answer and she didn't ask again. She already knew why.

'This is your savings account,' she asked, 'the one you don't want Karin to know about?' Reaching, she took back the laptop.

'I never said that.'

'You mean you're happy for her to know you've been secretly saving up ready to run away?' she said while clicking into the on-screen menu to display the balance. Then, without waiting for his reply, she asked, 'Do you know what the balance of this account is?'

'Twenty-five thousand six-hundred and twenty-five euros,' Finn replied without hesitation.

Quiet until now, Callaghan raised his eyebrows and asked, 'When was the last time you checked?'

'I don't need to, I just know,' Finn replied. 'I keep track.'

'Not that well it seems,' Callaghan returned sarcastically.

'It better be all there,' Finn warned. 'If it's not it's because someone's taken it. One of you guys. Well, is it?' Anxiety-driven panic was evident in his voice.

'Not quite,' Callaghan told him, turning the screen around towards him again. 'Take a look for yourself.'

Squinting, Finn leaned towards the screen only to leap back suddenly as if bitten.

'*Holy shit!* Where did that come from?'

'Funny that, but we were about to ask you the same question,' said Callaghan. 'Five million twenty-five thousand six-hundred and twenty-five euro.' He pretended to do the math. 'That makes a five-million-euro error. Now where do you think that came from?' Folding his arms across his chest, he turned to Fox with raised eyebrows as if she might have the answer.

'Why don't we take a minute?' Fox suggested and, standing up, she snapped closed the laptop.

'No, wait, that's not mine!'

But they weren't listening.

'Listen to me!' He stood up as Fox gathered up the case file while Callaghan glowered at him. 'You have to listen to me! That's not my money!' he shouted as they left the room.

Despite his protests of innocence, Finn was charged with the abduction of Karin Bolger and murder of Sive Collins.

'They all do that,' Moyne remarked when Fox called to give him the update. 'Only in the movies do they confess as they're carted away – you should know that. Think about it – O'Malley, Kennedy, Liston – they all protested they were innocent, probably still do but they were all convicted. Even on appeal they failed to have those convictions overturned. And rightly so.'

He was right and she knew it, but it didn't silence the sceptic inside her head that kept asking *what if …*

'I suppose,' she mused as Finn's desperate cries of innocence echoed from the cells.

'*You've made a massive mistake! It isn't me! I didn't do it! I swear, this is a goddam set-up. I'm being framed!*' he protested vehemently from behind the locked doors.

'You've done a good job, just make sure the evidence is sound enough to stick,' Moyne warned. 'We don't want his to be the first successful appeal.'

Distracted and thinking much the same way, his compliment washed over her unnoticed.

She went back to the incident room and stood back to inspect the evidence they'd gathered and the journey they'd meticulously worked up. With no spare space to scribble, Fox ripped blank sheets off the flip-chart in the corner and, sticking them with Blu Tack to the wall, made herself a blank canvas to draw on.

'Can we just go through this one more time, just to be sure we've missed nothing,' she said to an increasingly impatient Callaghan who entertained her only because she was his superior and he usually trusted her judgment.

'Go on then,' he conceded and, sitting back into his chair, folded his arms and watched her step back, tap the marker against her nose and considered the blank pages stuck to the wall. Stepping forward eventually she began her clinical unravelling of the assumed scenario.

Scribbling on the pages, she recounted the journey as if voicing a trailer from a thriller, constructing a picture that wasn't so different from the one Callaghan painted earlier in their interview with Finn.

'An unhappy man in a loveless marriage has an affair with his wife's best friend. Unhappy about the continuing friendship his frustration is further compounded when he discovers his mistress was his wife's one-time lover. Jealous and worried he's about to be exposed and made penniless, he stages the kidnapping using the very public Justice for the Workers campaign as a decoy, demanding a halt to the Kings Brewery development. Greedy and stupid, he tacks on a ransom for money using his own online account which he foolishly thinks is untraceable as the destination for the money. Using his known reaction to rich red wine as his alibi, he sets off early and drives to the house in Galway in the car he'd bought weeks before for cash. Staging the break-in at the cottage, he dopes the wine which Karin and Sive drink, making it easy for him to bundle them into the car and take them to the abandoned cottage and secure them both before they regained their strength.'

She paused and looked at Callaghan.

'How am I doing so far?' she asked.

'Good, yeah.' Callaghan shrugged patiently.

'Any questions?'

He shook his head.

'What about why he staged the break-in?' she asked, circling the action on the makeshift whiteboard. 'Why draw attention to himself? Why not just drive down, let himself in, dope the wine and leave as if he was never there? Why draw attention to it?'

'No idea,' Callaghan replied, having considered the question for the umpteenth time.

'Neither do I,' Fox said decisively and with a red marker redrew the circle. 'Let's park it for the time being.'

She picked up the story where she left off.

'So, Sive escapes and Finn gives chase. She falls and the blow to the head kills her – but rather than hiding her he just leaves her there in the ditch where anyone can come across her. Why?'

'Heat-of-the-moment decision? Maybe he got scared? Maybe the plan was to take the money, release them then disappear into the sunset, happy out. So, when she fell, he knew he'd fucked up.'

'That's the question really and one we can't answer: did he intend to kill them both? In which case, why wait? Why hang about keeping them alive? The longer he stayed around, the more dangerous for him.'

'And the more risk there was of them recognising him.'

She stared at him. He was right. 'Absolutely. How could he even risk being in the presence of these two women who knew him intimately? Why *didn't* they recognise him?'

'Maybe Sive did,' Callaghan shrugged. 'Maybe that's why he left her there.'

'And why he didn't come back,' Fox made her second red circle. 'Perhaps if he didn't plan for Sive to die, if it was an accident, he panicked, not sure what to do. After all, between the abandoned car and the hardly hidden clothes, we already know he's not the sharpest criminal in the world.'

'Yeah, but there's another thing,' Callaghan said with a frown. 'Why in God's name did he hide the clothes? Why didn't he dump them, burn them, whatever?'

'Doesn't make much sense, does it?' She looked at him, eyebrows raised. 'No more than "hiding" five million euro in plain sight.'

Callaghan sighed. 'True.'

'And why kill one woman and keep the other alive? Well, the answer is obvious – because Sive's death happened by accident or impulse. It was not premeditated.'

'But, with Sive dead, maybe he didn't come back because he didn't want Karin to live either. Perhaps he wanted her to suffer and die slowly,' Callaghan proposed dramatically.

'Oh, come on!' Fox rolled her eyes. 'But that raises another question. After all, she *could* have died – she was fading by the time we found her. So why didn't he just let the women go after he had secured the ransom money? I mean, phone in a tip? Why was he prolonging the whole thing – and prolonging the risk? God, we still have more questions than answers!'

'Hang on a sec,' Callaghan objected. 'Let's take a minute to look at what we *do* have.' Counting on his fingers, he started: 'First we have multiple motives, second we have a picture of our abductor dressed in the clothes which we found hidden in his roof —' He paused and raised his eyebrows, waiting for her to agree. She nodded. 'Then we have the footage of the fight, his confession he was preparing to run and we have his DNA not only in the car but on the driver's seat and finally we have the ransom money in his account. Seriously, Foxie, what more do we need?'

She shook her head. 'I know all that, yes. When you put it like that it seems pretty airtight, I admit, but what about all this?' She pointed at her case examination that with all its scribbles and lines had become its own work of art.

'Look. Take it to Moyne, see what he says, and if he says go we go. Right?'

'OK,' she agreed.

'Well, if you're happy with that then we need to talk about Mikey.'

Chapter 19

So sure was she that Moyne would see the case through her eyes and agree that they needed to investigate further, she took Callaghan with her to Galway so he could hear Moyne's instructions for himself. He'd never let it rest otherwise. Even if she had tried she couldn't have hidden her bewilderment when, having presented Moyne with the facts, he agreed with Callaghan.

Behind flushed cheeks she defended her position.

Sitting behind his desk, Moyne listened to everything she had to say but in the end he ruled against her.

'I hear you, Fox, but the evidence speaks for itself. Take it to the DPP, get it done today and unless they say otherwise this goes to trial. It'll get the press and the Assistant Commissioner off my case.'

'Yes, sir,' she replied, hoping to avoid Callaghan's eager face that she knew had *told you so* written all over it.

'Before you go,' Moyne asked as they turned to leave, 'what about this Mikey Smyth fella?'

Fox shook her head. 'He's in the clear – well, for the abduction and murder anyway.'

'How can you be so sure?'

'He's too cocky, he has no fear, the only offender with no

fear is the one who didn't do it.'

Mikey had sat opposite her in the interview room with a self-satisfied grin fixed rigidly on his face. He had denied nothing, impervious to her accusations. He actually wanted them to believe he did it if for no other reason than to waste their time. Fox was sure he had a perfectly good alibi up his sleeve beyond the playing-video-games-in-the-shed that he originally offered. But, she reckoned, he was holding out till the very last minute and an ultimate showdown reveal, serving not only to make fools of them but to feed his perverted fantasy that little bit longer. The worrying aspect was that Mikey really did hate Karin. A man obsessed, the display in the shed confirmed that, it was likely that he had plans of his own for Karin and his single regret was probably that he didn't get in there first. But having charged Finn in custody Mikey was demoted to nothing more than a bully and a nuisance.

On Moyne's instruction she set about preparing the case file to brief the DPP's office. It was past ten by the time she closed down her laptop and got up to leave. Yawning, she left the building through the side door and made her way to the car park. I'll sleep tonight, she thought, pulling her keys from her jacket pocket, her hold-all slung heavily on her shoulder making her walk at a slight angle from her hips.

'Fancy meeting you here,' a distinctly deep and gravelled voice spoke out in the darkness, making her stop dead in her tracks. She recognised him as soon as she heard him. His wasn't a voice she'd forget in a hurry

Turning slowly, she faced Mikey Smyth standing under the awning of the bike-park, hands in his jeans pockets and a sneaky smirk shaping his lips.

'What are you doing here?' she asked, thinking quickly

about who was left inside the building and how she might get their attention. Clutching the keys in her closed fist, she let one drop to between her middle and index finger like they taught her in self-defense classes.

'I was in the area an' thought I'd stop in to say hi.'

'Well, here I am, but it's been a long day, I haven't slept in almost forty-eight hours and I smell like a dog. I'd like to go home, so make it quick, Mikey.'

'You smell just fine to me, Detective Inspector.'

He leered at her, making her skin crawl.

'Thanks for that.'

'I hear you've picked someone up.'

'I beg your pardon?'

'The Bolger woman, the lad who took her, you've got him. Here.'

The arrest was public knowledge but the identity of the accused was not and she was anxious to keep it that way. Not until she was good and ready.

'Good news travels fast,' she remarked, eyeing her car in the darkest part of the carpark.

'I've come to shake his hand.'

'Have you now?' she asked, glancing at the door back into the building, wishing someone to walk through it. 'And why would you want to do that?'

'Two reasons,' he smirked. 'First to tell him I admire his balls and the second to tell him next time make sure he finishes the job properly, maybe give him a few tips.'

'Not sure I'd advise that,' she replied, less worried about his feelings towards Karin than the risk he might actually want to do her harm right there in the carpark.

'I'd have gone down for that bitch. She deserved it – only sorry it's not her six foot under, eh?

Fox shook her head, deciding he was only showboating, and continued her trek to her car, calling over her shoulder, 'Go home, Mikey!'

'If yer man in there isn't up to it maybe I should have a go – ya know, finish the job meself.'

He was provoking her and she knew it. *Don't react*, she told herself firmly, *it's exactly what he wants.* But she was tired and cranky and just couldn't help herself. Carefully, as if carrying a most precious cargo, she placed her bag down beside the car and turned slowly but purposefully towards him and his face that silently dared her.

She took a first step and didn't stop until their noses were almost touching.

'You go within a mile of her and I'll have you arrested for harassment. Got it?'

'Oh, I've got it all right. But I don't give a shit. I'd gladly do time just to see that smug bitch face down with the last breath of air sucked outta her.'

'You're all talk, you know that? But I'd like to see you try if only so *I* can see *your* face on the other side of those bars in there.'

'*Whuuuu!*' he jeered, taking a step back and holding his hands up in mock surrender. 'I'm so scared.'

'You should be, Mr Smyth, you should be,' she replied, cutting him she hoped with the sharp edge of her glare before dismissing him with a forward thrust of the back of her hand, and marching back to her car without a second glance. Picking her bag up off the ground, she threw it in the back seat, got in and locked the doors.

Her phone rang just as she pulled out of the gates without giving Mikey second glance.

'Well, that was interesting.'

'What?' she bit, not in the mood for Callaghan's small talk.

'You and Mikey, outside there. I saw you talking.'

'Well. thanks a bunch! Did you not think to come down and help me?'

'From where I was standing it didn't look like you needed much help – you seemed to be doing a good job all by yourself.'

'Very funny, Callaghan.'

'What did he want?'

'He was just being an asshole, that's all.'

'Go home, get some sleep,' he told her. 'You need it.'

Chapter 20

Thinner, greyer and a little smaller, if that were possible, Gordon opened the door a changed man to the one they'd met only weeks before. Even his eyes seemed to have lost the spark that had patronised them so blatantly. He led them through to the conservatory and, unlike before, politely offered them tea. Like the weather, the mood in the house was grey and heavy and sucked every ounce of joy from them as they waited for Gordon to return with the tray of tea.

The rain pelted down outside and crashed against the glass roof overhead, making it difficult to hear him speak.

'There has been some progress,' Fox told him, trying hard not to show her shock at his personal deterioration. 'We've made an arrest.'

'I know, Sam our liaison told me,' he said quietly. 'Do I know him? Sam wouldn't say.'

Fox nodded.

'You do. We charged Finn Ellis with your wife's abduction and murder.'

'Finn Ellis?' he echoed the name, pulling his head back in shock. 'My God! Finn? I don't believe it. That spineless little bastard.' He dropped his head.

She could see his hand quiver as he brought it to his temple.

'A sad, sad day,' he said. 'Has he confessed?'

'No, but the evidence is very strong and we're satisfied that we'll get a conviction,' she told him, careful with her choice of words.

'It'd be easier if he confessed though, wouldn't it?'

'Of course, yes, it would be and maybe when he sees sense and with the right advice he will.'

Gordon closed his eyes.

They let the silence stretch out.

'Well, thank you for telling me,' he eventually said and made to stand up, assuming their business concluded.

'There is something else we think you should know,' Fox said, staying put, knowing that telling Gordon about his wife and her past liaison with Karin would be difficult but was necessary. Apart from anything else it was the right thing to do. No one should learn such intimate details about their deceased wife in open court or through the press. As a motivating part of their evidence against Finn it was bound to come out.

Appearing a little startled, Gordon lowered himself back into the chair.

Fox had thought about little else over the course of the last twenty-four hours, with concerns that he might not believe her. Having seen him today she thought that it might push him over the edge.

But Gordon didn't need much convincing nor did he appear that shocked.

'Why doesn't it surprise me?' he asked, looking like he'd eaten something foul, his lips turned down and his brow furrowed into deep grooves of bulging flesh. 'I always knew there was something repugnant about that woman.'

For a split second Fox wondered who exactly he was talking about, only for it to become clear when he continued.

'Sive was always captivated by her, obsessed almost, as if under some kind of enchantment. She'd dress like her, walk like her and I'm sure recently she'd started behaving like her. If I didn't know better, I'd say she wanted to be her. The clothes, the husband, and now it seems the woman herself. It's not normal, is it? I suppose I should have seen it coming. What was I married to? How on earth am I going to tell Harry?'

Fox sat in silence while he wallowed.

'It's quite the cliché, isn't it?' he said, pushing himself out of his chair and standing to attention. 'All roads lead to the husband, don't they say? It's a shame, I liked him.' He sighed. 'You know, I think I should thank you. I hear this and it makes my grief that little bit more bearable.' He turned away from them and took the few steps towards the window to look out into the garden. He stood with his shoulders slightly stooped and hands stuffed in his trouser pockets. From behind, he looked like a broken man.

Fox felt his pain but she had to push on. 'I have a couple more questions to ask if you feel you're up to it.'

He turned back to them and nodded.

'Of course,' he said and retook his seat.

'We spoke previously about how Karin consistently invested in Sive's businesses over the years and I know I've asked you this before but are you sure you have no ideas, no matter how wild, about why that might have been?'

'If I knew that! No, I don't, and at this stage I don't really care,' he huffed through flared nostrils.

'Did Sive ever talk to you about their time in college?'

'Not really, no.' He shook his head, getting visibly agitated and upset. 'If you don't mind, if that's it, I'd like to rest.'

'Certainly.' she replied and immediately stood.

Shaking his hand briskly, they left.

'Why are you asking about Sive and Karin in college – we already know what that's about.' Callaghan quizzed when they got into the car.

'I know, but I'm just curious to know what everyone else knows.'

'Curious or nosey?'

'Just curious, that's all.'

'Nosey more like.' Callaghan scoffed.

'That's what makes me good at my job. You should try it sometime.'

'What, being nosey or good at my job?'

'Both.' She pulled out into the traffic.

Chapter 21

Usually, preparing the evidence for the trial team was a cathartic exercise. Cataloging and putting everything in sequential and logical order, so someone else could follow and understand it, was usually deeply satisfying – all that hard work coming to a final conclusion. The effort needed to make sure that their hard labour worked for the next team, whose task was only just beginning, was tremendous, and ensuring the evidence was robust enough to secure the conviction was critical.

Fox had stood earlier in the day behind the Commissioner while he delivered his press briefing. He had commended her team's hard work in making the arrest and had singled her out as a key contributor to the case. Keeping the briefing short, he also stated that it was inappropriate for him to comment further as the case had been handed to the courts system to decide what course it would take.

It felt like she should be celebrating but instead Fox found herself nervous and distracted on the long drive back to Galway and it had nothing to do with the case. She didn't like giving up but it was obvious Moyne neither rated nor liked her and that was not an environment she was happy to remain part of. She knew what she had to do, it was inevitable. She was even prepared to accept the ribbing she would no doubt endure from her colleagues for the shortest posting in the history of her career so far. She had thought she was made of stronger stuff and could handle the likes of Moyne.

Disappointed in herself, she completed her drive in a punishing silence.

That afternoon, standing with her shoulders back and stomach in, facing Moyne, her hands clasped tight behind her back, she swallowed to grease the inside of her throat that had suddenly dried up.

He looked up at her expectantly from behind his desk and, leaning back in his chair, held his pen at each end and twisted it slowly.

Fox imagined it was her neck slowly being wrung between those fingers. Having practised in the car over and over what she might say, in the end she went with the simplest of opening statements,

'Sir, I would like to apply for a transfer.'

But she wasn't prepared for the jaw that dropped or the eyebrows that lifted in response to her request.

'I don't believe I have your confidence or your trust and I think it would be best if perhaps a different officer, perhaps a male, filled the post.' It was a well-placed and intentional grenade aimed at letting him know she wasn't happy with being treated, as she thought, differently because of her sex.

She tensed and waited while Moyne continued to scrutinise her through squinted eyes, as if silently planning her demise. She wished he'd just get on with it and put her out of her misery. Already she was considering the consequences of her actions. This decision would follow her, news of it would spread like a virus across the force, not because she was anyone special but because Moyne was notorious. It had the potential to blemish her impeccable career and could make her less attractive as a subordinate or even delay her next promotion. Already she felt the fleeting feelings of doubt flutter to her stomach and then to her knees but the principle of her decision held her upright.

'I'm surprised,' Moyne said eventually, still twisting his pen. 'I was obviously wrong about you.' His lips clenched tighter as he continued to silently observe her.

Fox could feel her cheeks burn and hated herself for it because her flush didn't reflect how she felt. She was neither embarrassed nor anxious, more like pissed off and determined. She'd made up her mind but, true to his nature, he was insisting on prolonging the excruciating pain of it all.

'Sorry, sir, I don't know what you mean.'

'That I was wrong about you? Seems like a pretty obvious statement, don't you think?'

'I got that bit, I just don't understand why you would say it.'

'I was wrong. I thought you were a tenacious ambitious detective who could stand with the best of them. I was wrong, it seems, to think that you would work under fire as well as under scrutiny.' He put the pen down carefully on the desk and sat forward. 'I was also wrong to think that you could ignore the ignorant misconceptions about certain senior members of the team.'

His words made her feel small, insignificant and petty.

'When you were presented to me as one of my senior officers I wasn't pleased not to have the ability to choose myself, but I was relieved to have someone who I thought wouldn't hold back, who'd take on this position with vigour. Who would add to my already solid team. Yet here you are requesting your transfer with this *sexist* card.'

'I apologise if that's how it came out. It's not what I meant.'

'Yes, yes, it is. You can't go back, not now. Having said it, you should at least have the wherewithal to follow through. You think I have a problem with you because you're a woman.'

'Well, do you?' she asked audaciously, believing herself to be so deep in the shit, what's another few inches?

'There are many in this organisation who will openly contest that this is no place for a woman, no matter how able.' Pushing his chair away from the desk, he stood and walked around to sit on its edge in front of her. 'Against these odds we have become obsessed with political correctness without truly taking up the gender-balance position. It's unfortunate.'

Fox felt like the collar of her shirt might strangle her. God knows where this was going, she wondered nervously.

'That said, sexist is one thing I am not, although I know I have a name for being that.'

Fox remembered her 'Break in Case of Emergency' gift and did her utmost to keep her mouth shut.

'I believe I would be wasting my time to dispute it,' Moyne continued. 'People will think what they will and the more I protest the stickier the accusation becomes. So I don't bother.'

Without noticing it, Moyne's tone had changed. He had shifted from the disappointed accuser to the patient counsellor.

'What I do believe, for the record, is that only an officer capable of doing the job should get the job, regardless of age, gender or sexual inclination. I'm not interested in giving any job, junior or senior, to a woman just because she is one. But this incessant push for gender balance is placing women in roles they simply aren't up to, not because they are female but because they aren't good officers. Full stop. And good men miss out, because they're men.' He paused for a minute to let the impact of what he was preaching hit home, never letting her gaze go. 'Now that, in my opinion, is sexist. But that's my problem.'

Lecture over, he stood up and retook his original position behind the desk.

'So, when you came up – you, I thought, were a woman with courage, intelligence and ability. I jumped at the chance to have you on my team and it just so happened you ticked all the boxes: female and able. Perfect, so to speak.'

It was a bizarre experience, standing there listening to her boss who only minutes before she had assumed was her antagonist while in fact it appeared he was her greatest advocate. But, despite his laudatory and somewhat unsettling words, she was more confused than flattered. What was she supposed to think? He was right, she was well able, more able in fact than most of her colleagues both male and female, and like him she did not approve of the drive to deliver gender balance. She would like to think she earned her promotion because of her ability and experience, not because of her sex.

'Thank you, sir, I'm flattered –'

'I sense a *but* coming.'

'Well, yes. If you think I'm so capable then why do you choose to tell me how to do my job? You know I'm able, well able, so I don't need you to tell me how to do it.'

'That's just my way. That is one of the disadvantages of being better known for only one thing. They say I'm a sexist bastard, but they forget I'm a micro-managing egotist as well – not as sexy, I can only assume.'

Fox couldn't help but smile.

'I would like you to reconsider your decision for transfer because you're an excellent officer and, although I was asked to take you, I would be very sorry to lose you.'

Fox remained where she stood, not sure how to respond, her face blushing now for the right reasons.

'Think about it.' He turned his attention back to the paperwork on his desk and without looking up said, 'And close the door on your way out.'

AJ looked up from behind a stack of boxes in the almost completely dismantled incident room.

'How did that go?'

'Surreal, AJ, just surreal. I think he's mad.'

'Join the club.' AJ chuckled quietly, 'So when are you leaving?'

'I'm not sure I am.'

'Worked his magic then?'

'Seems so.' She sat down under the pretext of completing her report which would form part of the book of evidence against Finn. But in her head she went over the conversation she'd just had with Moyne.

'AJ, can I ask you something?'

'Fire away.'

'Just there Moyne said something odd. He said that I wasn't his first choice for this job, that he was *asked* to take me. What do you make of that?'

AJ stood up from the box he was sealing and stretched his back.

'Well, for what it's worth I know he had a call from

Commissioner Fenlon,' he told her, bending backwards with his hands supporting his lower back.

'Really?' she asked with wide eyes. 'Are you sure? But he's retired years now.'

'Yes, and sorely missed if you ask me.' AJ nodded. 'He's a lovely man, always liked him.' Both were aware of her relationship to the ex-commissioner and both understood the implications of his call but neither chose to elaborate, AJ out of respect, Fox out of embarrassment.

Turning her attention back to the still incomplete report on her desk, Fox pondered this nugget of information while AJ returned to his boxes.

'It's been relatively easy one this, hasn't it? It's all fallen into place nicely,' he said, opening up a fresh box to fill.

'Yeah,' Fox replied but she wasn't really listening.

She wasn't left long to her brooding thoughts, the ring of her phone bringing her right back to the moment. A glance at the screen told her it was Amanda Stynes calling. Fox wondered why.

'Hey, Amanda, how are you?' she answered, glad of the chance to be distracted from her thoughts.

'Not bad – you?'

'Good, yeah, what can I do for you?'

'A couple of things. I hear congrats are in order. I believe you arrested the husband in the Bolger case.'

'Yeah, a great result,' she replied and for the first time realised that, even though it was Sive Collins who had died, everyone continued to refer to it as Karin's case. Was Sive really that insignificant?

'Well done. So, this may or may not help your case but they've taken so long to come through I thought I'd best get them to you myself.'

Frantically Fox wondered what she'd missed.

'We did the analysis on the sedative used on the women.'

'Ahhh yes, I remember now,' Fox replied, recalling the frustration of the brief and curt conversation with the lab technician weeks ago, and thanked God it was obviously nothing too significant to the outcome of the case. With the constant movement between counties it was one of her biggest fears that something would be missed. 'So what did you find?'

'Well, it's a standard enough sedative – Ketamine – not the usual or favoured date-rape-style drug used by predators but it works just as well and it's pretty accessible which is what makes it attractive, They give it to asthmatics and it's used for small emergency procedures or dentistry.'

'Dentistry?' Fox repeated.

'Yep, I'll pop the results in the post and you'll have them in the morning.'

'That'd be great. Don't suppose you've any influence with the guys in the lab at the hospital? We still haven't got their report back. It'd be good to get corroboration from the blood tests and samples they took from Karin.'

'I'll see what I can do.'

Still vehemently protesting his innocence, Finn wasn't exactly a forthcoming defendant – he was giving nothing away. Knowing now precisely what drug was used would make it easier for them to trace where it might have come from and hopefully prove it was Finn who acquired it. More evidence to convince a jury of his guilt.

She thought of Gordon.

'He's a dentist,' she reminded AJ. 'Can't think of a better place to start. He should be able to give us an idea about how Finn may have got his hands on the stuff.' She picked up her phone and called Callaghan – it made sense for him to go ask the man, he was nearer. But his phone went straight to voicemail and within seconds a text came through.

Hot date. Gorgeous redhead. Call me tomorrow.

She smiled and replied with a smiley face emoji. At least someone was having fun. It wasn't urgent – she'd go herself tomorrow.

The following day she returned to the capital and dealt with the day's business before heading to see Gordon. She turned onto his road to see him pull out of his driveway and accelerate down the street. Instinctively she slowed and let him turn at the end then followed him, keeping a safe distance behind. If anyone had asked her what made her do it, she wouldn't have been able to construct a definitive answer. Intuition was the best she could come up with or, maybe as Callaghan had accused, it was just that she was plain nosey. Regardless of why, having followed him for the first few kilometers she figured out exactly where he was going and shivered as the voice of warning that had niggled at the back of her head all day began to shout a little louder.

He was in no rush, driving carefully and blissfully unaware of who was following him. Turning onto the coast road, she told herself it was normal for him to call on Karin – they were, after all, two victims of a horrendous crime and were bound to want to support each other. It was nothing to be suspicious of.

Daylight was fading when they arrived at Karin's house. Gordon turned into the gateway and, without his getting out of his car, the heavy timber gates began to pull open.

Relieved but curious that he was obviously expected, Fox pulled in a little further up the street and got out of her car to run back to the gates of Wild Wind just in time to see Gordon get out of his car and approach the front door that opened almost immediately, by whom she couldn't see. Slipping through the electronic gates as they rumbled and dragged themselves closed, she tucked herself in behind the bank of shrubs that lined the perimeter wall. Only then did she ask herself just what the hell she was doing.

Her phone vibrated in her pocket. It was Callaghan calling. She didn't answer. Seconds later she felt it vibrate. This time it was a text.

Where are you?

Karin's. Don't ask.

Can you talk? Report in from lab.

Good woman, Amanda, she silently cheered. Why hadn't she thought of her sooner?

Not really

You need to. Call me.

Huffing and flustered, she rang his number.

'What's up?' she whispered, bending down further into the shrubs.

'The report is in from the lab,' he told her, unnecessarily whispering too.

'And does Ketamine show up?'

'Oh yes, and more,' he replied with glee. 'Are you with Karin?'

She paused, deciding how best to answer.

'Ehhhh … technically yes, but no.' She explained the situation.

Realising her predicament, Callaghan cut straight to the point.

'The night Karin was taken to hospital they did a raft of tests, including a rape test.'

'Yeah, tell me something I don't know,' she whispered impatiently.

'The results –'

But she didn't give him the chance to go on as the penny dropped.

'*Shit, no!*' she groaned heavily.

'Shit, yes.'

Chapter 22

Pools of light from the windows splashed across the ground to light the route towards the side gate and the rear of the house. Conscious of the cameras and aware that anyone could be watching her, she lifted the latch carefully so as not to make a noise. Deftly she made her way around the side of the house to the back garden which was swathed in light from the kitchen. Her heart racing, she skirted around the periphery, sticking to the edge of the darkness. She moved to where she could see in through the kitchen window and thanked contemporary styling for the lack of curtains. Keeping camouflaged and out of sight like some kind of stalker, she watched the couple inside the window.

Her phone pipped in her pocket.

En route, Callaghan texted.

OK. Text when you're in situ.

Crouching down, confident they couldn't see her, she risked taking a few steps closer and watched Gordon through the window. He seemed ill at ease, fidgety and uncomfortable, while Karin appeared to chat away unperturbed. If she noticed how terrible he looked, she showed no signs of concern or worry.

And he looked awful, like he hadn't eaten or slept in days.

His clothes hung loose on his frame and his eyes wore dark circles like glasses. He stood at the island and pulled the cork from the bottle of wine without taking his eyes off Karin as she dished two plates of food from the pan. Watching him move woodenly to the table, Fox wondered if it was grief or guilt that was affecting him so badly.

The implications to the investigation were significant. Had they arrested the wrong man, was that what had set her conscience on high alert? Or could it be that Gordon and Finn were a team acting together? That would explain the evidence and might help to explain some of the unsettling gaps. How would that even have worked, she silently debated. What role had they each played and why, if they were in it together, hadn't Finn yet exposed Gordon's involvement? What bind, she wondered, did Gordon have over him? They were good, she thought, recalling their first meeting. They played it cool. She never would have guessed they were partners in crime. She replayed the encounter in her head from start to finish, remembering the strange awkwardness of their company, and suspecting now it was nothing more than a well-deployed act infuriated her. She didn't like being taken for a fool.

She had so many questions – like who was the brains of the plan and how did they come up with it? Who approached whom? Was one more involved than the other? And while neither in her eyes seemed to fit the bill of a conniving killer, one of them surely had to be. Stranger things had happened, she reminded herself. Finn, although smothering and a little spineless, didn't seem the type, while Gordon – well, the old Gordon and not the depleted one she was looking at now – he'd had both the brains and the audacity. Could it be that Finn was Gordon's puppet?

Watching Gordon, she felt a profound sense of futility, her faith in humanity taking yet another knock. That was one of the perils of her job but sometimes those knocks felt harder than usual.

Why? she asked herself silently from the bushes, thinking about what he might have done to both women, alive and dead.

Her phone pipped again.

Ready to go whenever you are, Callaghan texted from around the corner.

I'll be out in a mo, she replied and carefully retraced her steps back towards the entrance. Afraid that the opening of the gates from the inside might activate some kind of alarm inside the house, she scrambled through the shrubs and bushes to hoist herself over the wall.

Callaghan was waiting at the end of the street with three uniformed officers in an unmarked car. Giving him the thumbs-up, she stood at the gates to Wild Wind, pressed the intercom and waited for Karin to answer. It didn't take long.

'Come on in,' she said, activating the gates and a few minutes later appeared at the front door.

'I'm popular this evening, I have no visitors from one end of the week to the other and this evening I have two. Gordon Collins is here – we're just about to eat, compliments of Aggie. I wouldn't inflict my cooking on anyone. Will you join us?' She led the way into the kitchen.

'Thanks, but no, it's a flying visit. I was actually hoping to chat to you in private.'

'Oh,' Karin replied, looking slightly taken aback and glancing towards Gordon.

Obviously nervous and flustered, Gordon raised both hands.

'No problem,' he said. 'I really should be going anyway – we have a Lions Club meeting tonight at the Golf Club.'

'Don't be ridiculous! Stay,' Karin protested, 'The Detective Inspector and I can go to the living room, can't we?' She looked at Fox for confirmation.

'Absolutely,' Fox replied, confident that Gordon would decline.

He didn't let her down and was already slipping into his jacket.

Fox waited in the kitchen while Karin saw Gordon to the door.

'Sorry to intrude,' Fox apologised once she'd returned.

'No problem. To be honest, I'm not sure why he called. And I'm starving!' She offered Fox the already filled and now spare plate of food. 'I haven't eaten all day and couldn't wait.'

Despite the delicious smell, Fox declined.

'Do you mind if I do?' Karin asked.

'Not at all, please do. Does he call over often?'

'Every now and then. It's very sweet of him really. I think he's checking up to see if I'm OK.' She laughed, taking a mouthful of her dinner.

Having experienced Gordon's venomous opinion of Karin first-hand, Fox very much doubted her assessment of his intentions.

'Are you sure you won't have some? A glass of wine maybe?' Karin insisted.

'Thanks but no. Do you mind if I ask you a few questions?'

'As long as it doesn't give me indigestion, fire away!'

'I appreciate this might be painful but I'd like to ask you a few questions if I may about the night you were brought to the hospital, when we found you.'

281

Karin's swallowed her mouthful of pasta.

'OK,' she replied tentatively, placing her cutlery down on the plate.

'That night, do you remember having a conversation with your doctor?'

'Not really to be honest – the whole thing is a bit of a blur.'

Fox paused, choosing her words carefully. 'Please don't be alarmed,' she cautioned, 'but the doctors have told us that when you were admitted they carried out a series of routine tests. They also checked to make sure there was no signs of any attack or rape ...'

Karin leaned back in her chair, her expression difficult to read, the furrowing of her brow indicating worry while the panic in her eyes suggested fear.

'Do you remember?'

'No. No, I don't, and I don't remember giving permission either,' Karin declared, her defensive instincts kicking in immediately.

'It's a routine test in these situations, especially when drugs and sedatives are involved. It assists them in figuring out how to treat you and helps us piece together what happened while you were held. It's likely Finn signed a consent form on your behalf when you were admitted for them to carry out whatever was necessary.'

'A little ironic, don't you think?'

Fox couldn't help but agree and nodded while swallowing hard.

'So, they carried out the test and thankfully there weren't any signs of a violent attack. Everything was as it should be.'

Karin's relief was palpable as she released the breath she was holding.

'I think I'd have noticed if it wasn't,' she responded smartly but her cocky recovery was to be short-lived as a cringing Fox continued.

'That's true, but they did take an internal swab for examination.'

'And?' Karin asked, the returning tension visible in her tight lips and taut shoulders.

'Well, they found traces of semen,' Fox told her with difficulty. This definitely wasn't a part of her job she enjoyed.

Karin visibly stiffened, her face blanched and blanked any expression.

Fox's heart thumped inside her chest, beating as fast as her mouth was drying out.

'Finn and I, w-we –' Karin stammered, trying to process what she was being told.

'Karin, it wasn't Finn,' Fox interrupted as gently as she could.

'If it wasn't Finn, who was it?' Karin asked, her eyes narrowing along with the pitch of her voice.

'Gordon. His DNA is a match.'

Karin's eyes opened wide in response then closed tight as her face contorted in horror.

'What the … *Gordon?*' She yelped, every muscle in her body tensing in disgust. Holding her hands up, her fingers splayed as if to protect herself, she cried out, '*This isn't possible! It's just not, I mean how* …' As she spoke the words it began to dawn on her exactly how it could have happened and she cursed. 'He was there. It was him. That bastard, that absolute steaming pile of horseshit!' she swore, enunciating every syllable in every word. Pressing her lips together, she stood up abruptly, snatched her unfinished meal from the table and marched around the island to the sink. There was no denying the indignity and tortured pain she felt. It was written in the way she clutched at the kitchen counter and let her head hang with her back to Fox.

'So you think he raped me?' she asked, her tone flat and calm.

'Well, unless it consensual then ...'

'*No, it bloody well wasn't!*' Karin barked at her.

'Then, yes, we do.'

'And Finn?' she pressed, busying herself with scraping the plate into the bin before dropping it into the sink with a clatter.

Fox assumed she was trying to be normal, trying not to let herself be seen as being helpless, defiled or vulnerable.

'We're not sure yet – we're looking at the possibility that Finn and Gordon were working together.'

'Finn and Gordon? Now that's a hilarious concept.' A manic burst of laughter escaped Karin's lips as she turned to face Fox.

'Why so?'

'Seriously? You've met them, haven't you? They're chalk and cheese.' She rinsed out a dishcloth and wiped the counter down.

'So you don't think they could have pulled this off?'

She shook her head. 'I don't know what to think.'

She looked awkward moving around the kitchen, tidying things up, loading the dishwasher, setting things to right, the everyday activity seeming a little alien to her.

But Fox had to admire her composure. If it were her she'd be baying for blood but Karin obviously, not used to being out of control, wouldn't let that happen, not in front of her anyway.

Karin returned to the table and sat down with a heavy

slump. She let her head drop back, closed her eyes and took a deep breath.

'Why would he do it?' she asked with a sigh.

'I don't know, revenge perhaps, control?' Fox shrugged.

'Filthy bastard,' she whispered. 'He has come to my house, eaten at my table …' She shook her head. She wasn't a very likeable woman but watching her go through the motions, Fox felt deeply sorry for her.

When eventually Karin came back herself there was an undeniable air of defiance about her. Taking a breath that filled her chest, she straightened out her shoulders and smiled a small but determined smile.

'Sorry. What was the question?' she asked.

'Has Gordon ever given you any reason to feel uncomfortable? Was he threatening at all?' Fox asked.

'He can be bit creepy alright – a couple of times he's been here, waiting for me outside the house when I got home from work. Then I'd turn and find him watching me. It made my skin crawl a little but I never thought any harm of it.'

'Why didn't you report it?' Fox asked, remembering his intense look which she had seen for herself this evening.

'And say what? What are you going to do? Ask him to stop freaking me out? Have you not got better things to do? No. I felt I owed it to be nice to him. It's my fault Sive is dead, isn't it? It's the least I could do, to be nice, to afford him the time of day, but …' she let the words drift off.

'But what?'

'He believes we have a connection and I agreed, I thought we'd shared a pretty monumental trauma. It's a natural response, I get that, I assumed he missed his wife and I was the last person with her before she …' Karin swallowed hard before continuing as if excusing herself. 'Look, don't get me wrong. I understood what he was saying and I thought we could be a good support for each other but I didn't need that support as much as he seemed to. He seemed fragile and vulnerable, I couldn't just turn him away. But now I know why.' She cringed and looked intently at Fox. 'He's bonding a little more than me and I'm afraid he may be getting a little too attached.' She flinched as she said it. 'Isn't it hilarious that I should feel like this all the while that man … *ugh*!' She shivered, her face contorting into an unrecognisable grimace.

Fox shifted in her chair. 'You're safe. Gordon is being arrested as we speak. He won't bother you again.'

'What about Finn?' Karin asked with what seemed like hope in her voice.

'Neither man will be free, not until we know what happened,' Fox told her and at the same time asked herself, amazed: did Karin actually want him back? After all he had done?

Chapter 23

Callaghan waited until Gordon had stopped at the lights before making his approach. Having had his rights read to him without question or protest, and with his hands cuffed behind his back, he allowed himself to be placed in the back of the police car. At the station his photograph and fingerprints were taken and, after calling for his solicitor, he was placed in a cell to await interview. He sat quietly, his head held high as if ready to face his accusers, his expression defeated and worn. He oozed shame. Gone was his past arrogant confidence. Now he looked straight ahead instead of down his nose, now he was a much smaller man no better than the array of grubby criminals who had previously occupied the bench on which he sat. Still, he looked out of place in the stark surroundings – as if he didn't belong there – but now everything had changed. To Fox, looking at him through the security mirror, this wasn't an overnight change. It had to have happened over time, starting she guessed from the very moment he committed his crime. Like his ill-fitting suit, he didn't wear his guilt well and, just like Finn, he wasn't made to be a criminal – it didn't rest easy and, if the bags under his eyes were anything to go by, he probably hadn't slept in weeks. Curious about what it felt like to bear the weight of that much guilt, she was equally curious to know how it would feel to have it lift in an instant.

They escorted him into the interview room where he sat in the chair bolt upright, staring straight ahead, his face vacant and expressionless with his hands joined and resting on the table.

'I'd like a word with my client in private, please,' his solicitor, Veronica Garvey, asked when she arrived before attempting to brief him on what he should and shouldn't say.

'Did you do this?' she asked calmly as was her job. 'Were you involved?'

But Gordon refused to answer, staring blankly ahead.

'Gordon, if you don't help me I can't help you. You're in a world of trouble here and you need to listen to me,' she told him firmly but she was wasting her time, Gordon appeared to have disconnected himself from the reality of his situation. 'OK,' she conceded with a shrug and, powerless to help, knocked on the door to indicate they were ready to return to the interview room.

She sat beside him uncomfortably, crossing then uncrossing her legs. She had been in situations like this so many times but never with someone like Gordon. He was what she would describe as a pillar of society. What on earth had happened to him?

Gordon sat calmly and unmoving in his seat when Fox and Callaghan entered the interview room. Taking their seats, they settled themselves, arranged the case files and prepared the recorder.

Having announced the interview commencement for the purposes of the tape, Fox asked, 'Gordon, how are you feeling?'

'Fine,' he answered quietly, averting his eyes nervously for a split second before catching Fox's gaze.

'Do you know why you're here?'

'I suspect so,' he replied clearly.

'Good. Well, let's get going and see if your suspicions are correct,' she replied without taking her eyes off him. 'On the night Karin was found and admitted to hospital a routine rape test was carried out and samples were taken from that test for DNA testing.' She watched his face, searching for a reaction. 'Do you know what we found?' She kept her tone level and matter of fact.

Gordon closed his eyes and smiled with an almost inaudible huff.

Pulling a sheet of paper from the file, she placed it in front of him and pointed to his name underlined and highlighted in neon yellow marker.

'Do you see that, Gordon?' she asked. 'It was your DNA we found.'

His solicitor took the document and scanned it quickly. She handed it to Gordon but he declined to even look, pushing it aside gently, seemingly disinterested.

'But you know that already, don't you?' Fox concluded from his reaction.

He smiled again, a small smile that was heavy with emotion.

'Do you know what that means?' she asked.

Gordon made as if to reply but Fox wasn't waiting for him to answer.

'It means that we know you were there, Gordon, in the cottage. We know what you did. We know you murdered your wife and raped her friend, but what we'd love to know is why. Why, Gordon? What did they do to deserve it?'

'You think I raped her?' he asked.

'Yes, we do, Gordon.'

Unblinking, he stared into the corner, opening his mouth as if to speak but closing it again without saying a word. Unlike Finn, there were no abject denials, no defensive and flaying arms or raised voice, no angry protests of innocence or demands to be heard. And although he sat with a vacant, expressionless face, his shoulders slumped and his head drooped slightly forward, creating an air of resigned acceptance.

Conscious of every other sound in the room, her own breathing, the hum of the computer and the air conditioning that churned the air at an even nineteen degrees, Fox waited patiently for Gordon to speak.

He took his time, focusing hard on that spot in the corner, silently working out, Fox assumed, exactly where and how to start. Sensing his wavering conscience, she gave him the nudge he needed.

'We can sit here and speculate till the cows come home about why you were there and what happened, or we can avoid all the bullshit and you can come right out and tell us. How about it, Gordon?' She leant forward with her elbows and arms on the table, hands clasped together. She looked at him expectantly. 'What do you think?' She was hoping to lure him with a friendlier approach.

'I think I'd like to consult with my client,' Garvey said eventually, breaking the silence that stretched out uncomfortably between them.

'Absolutely,' Fox replied and made moves to take them back to the private meeting room.

'It's OK,' Gordon interrupted, lifting his palm to stop her.

'Gordon, really, I insist,' Garvey urged, placing a hand on his arm.

Smiling, he turned and covered her hand with his own.

'It's OK,' he told her with a serene smile. 'It's time to put this charade to bed. It's gone on long enough and I'm tired.' Sitting back, he looked at Fox, his chin lifting as he mustered up his remaining pride. 'I'm ready.'

Garvey sat back down. A panicked look crossed her face as helplessly she glanced from Gordon to Fox.

'Please, Gordon,' she implored, 'talk to me first.'

But he ignored her and, taking a fortifying breath, confessed.

'I'm not a criminal,' he said. 'I was an idiot to think I could live with myself. I'm not and I can't.'

'What happened, Gordon?' Fox encouraged him, holding his stare. She could almost see the cogs turn furiously behind his eyes as he put events in sequence.

'They were making fools out of us,' he eventually said. 'Out of both of us. Finn and Sive, gallivanting like a pair of lovesick teenagers. They didn't think we knew but we did.'

'We?'

'Karin and I.'

'And what did she think about it?'

'She was as disgusted as I was. She was too good for him.'

'You've changed your tune,' Callaghan interrupted sarcastically. 'Only a week ago you were telling us you couldn't stand the woman.'

Gordon couldn't control the colour that deepened on his already flushed face.

'Well, it wasn't her fault, was it? She's not responsible for her husband's behaviour, is she?'

'And what about the money that she threw into Sive's failed businesses, have you forgotten about that?' Callaghan enquired. 'That was her fault, you said it yourself.'

Putting a hand up to stop him, Fox interrupted. 'Gordon,

I'm not sure you've been altogether honest with us. I don't think you despise Karin as much as you'd like us to think, do you?'

'Think what you like, it is what it is.'

Callaghan made to challenge him but Fox threw him a look that stopped him in his tracks.

'Let's move on for the moment, shall we?' she said. 'So, what did you do?'

'I lived with the humiliation for a while, watched them pretend and lie and sneak around for weeks and weeks before I'd had enough and all I wanted to do was wipe the smile off their faces, teach them a lesson. I followed them a few times. They were shameless. They came to my home and fornicated in my bed.' His fists clenched tight as he spoke. He paused, wisely letting his rising anger simmer down. 'That was the last straw for me. There was no respect anymore, taunting us like that.'

'Do you think they, Finn and Sive, were aware you knew?'

Gordon shook his head.

'But you still think they were taunting you?'

'Yes, flaunting themselves, they had to know they'd get caught and every day they didn't was a flagrant slap in my face.'

They listened intently as he spoke clearly and calmly, his mood almost serene, his relief palpable.

'It started out as a simple idea, a *what if*, with a beginning and an end, and all I needed to do was fill in the *how to* in the middle. I thought about it for weeks but all I knew was that, however it panned out, I wanted him to suffer the way he had made me suffer. I didn't want him to die, I wanted him to be helpless, as helpless as I was. I wanted him to know something had been taken from him and he would never get it back and there was nothing he could do. The only downside was that I wouldn't be able to tell him it was me who did this to him, not directly.'

'He?' Fox asked, needing him to admit it on tape.

'Finn. I knew all I had to do was present enough evidence to suggest he was there and you lot would do the rest.'

For a minute, thinking about Finn still behind bars, Fox experienced her own moment of shame. If, as Gordon suggested, he had manipulated the system so simply then she wasn't as good at her job as she thought.

'I got into Finn's studio and took his clothes and once I was done I went back in to plant them in the attic where I knew you'd find them. I bought the car off that buffoon Baxter and drove to Galway, making sure I stopped along the way to have my Finn caught on camera. And when I got there I broke into the house, I was setting the scene, for Finn. It had to seem like he was setting up his decoy.'

'Justice for the Workers?' Fox asked.

'That's correct. I was worried it was a bit simplistic, not very credible, but then it was Finn's decoy not mine and he's not the sharpest knife in the block.' He stated this plainly like it made perfect sense.

'Once inside, I replaced the wine put on the table by the housekeeper with one of my own vintage. Then I waited.'

'What if they didn't drink it?'

'We are talking about Sive here, aren't we? I knew she'd drink it.' He smiled at the apparent absurdity of the suggestion. He recounted his journey as if reporting his experience of buying groceries on any given day. It was clinical and impersonal. There was no way anybody tuning in by accident could have guessed that the subject of his story was murder.

'It was ironic really. In the beginning I fully intended Sive to die, I wanted her gone.'

'Why, Gordon, why did she have to go? It seems a bit extreme. Why not just leave her and get a divorce like a normal person?' Callaghan asked, giving voice to the question Fox had asked herself over and over again.

'I wasn't going to stay with her, not after this. I wasn't going to put my practice through that. And I don't want my patients knowing my private business. But when it came down to it I didn't want to follow through.' He sighed heavily, his energy draining fast.

'What changed your mind?' Fox enquired curiously.

'It just happened.' He shrugged, averting his eyes.

'You just changed your mind? This isn't like changing your mind about what to wear or what to eat, Gordon. This is murder. It doesn't just happen like that.'

'*Well, this did!*' he shouted, raising his voice for the first time. They could feel his frustration build. 'Just like that!' He snapped his fingers. 'She ran. But then she stopped, she had to, she couldn't go any farther. She turned and knew it was me. She said my name. She looked at me and I didn't like that look. Confused, like she didn't understand why, like she didn't deserve it. Like it was my fault, my doing. I suppose it was for the best really ... what happened then.' He followed this with a wistful, 'There could be no going back,' as if convincing himself all over again that it was the only conclusive end and it had to be done.

'She fell back into the ditch and hit her head.' Unconsciously he lifted his hand to the back of his head. 'She wasn't moving but I knew she was still alive.' He paused and gulped hard, tears filling his eyes as finally his remorse began to swell and overflow. 'I wanted to put her out of her misery, but I couldn't do it.' Heaving a deep breath, he continued. 'My father, when we were young, he did it to Trixie, our dog, she ran in front of a car and my dad had to do the same. I saw him do it. I knew what to do, but I couldn't do that to Sive. So I watched over her till she was gone. I let her die.'

His ability to reason was beginning to merge with irrational logic. Fox threw an astonished glance at Callaghan. How could he be likening his murder of his wife to putting a childhood pet out of its misery?

'But it wasn't me, it was Finn, I was Finn. He was going to take the blame for this so it belonged to him, his crime.'

'And Karin?' Fox prompted.

He shook his head. The tears that he so valiantly fought back flowed freely and unashamedly down his cheeks.

'Does it really matter?' he cried. 'I've just told you about Sive, is that not enough? I killed my wife. My once lovely sweet wife, the mother of my son!' He wept into his hands.

'Gordon, we need to know. You need to tell us,' Fox insisted but he shook his head.

'I can't,' he sobbed.

Fox watched him disintegrate in front of her eyes. Here was a man who had just murdered his wife but felt, it seemed, greater remorse for raping her friend.

'I didn't mean to, I– I don't know what came over me.' He let his head fall into his hands, his previously manicured fingernails now bitten to the quick. 'I feel so ashamed,' he sobbed. 'She was lying in the filth on the floor. She looked so peaceful, her skin was so perfect. She was so quiet. She's different when she's quiet. I just wanted to see what it would feel like, what it would be like on my own, no words to stop me, no pressure to get it right, just me being me. I bent over her and touched her skin – she was like velvet, so smooth and soft.' He took a sharp breath, his exhale a quiver of emotion. 'I couldn't help myself.' His body shook. 'I didn't mean to hurt her. I didn't think she'd ever know.'

'I'm sorry,' his solicitor interrupted, her face pale and shocked, 'but I need some air.'

'Let's break for a bit,' Fox said.

'I'm tired, can I sleep?' Gordon pleaded.

'When we're done,' Fox told him, nodding to Callaghan. 'Half an hour?'

Fox and Callaghan spent the half hour analysing everything they had been told.

'I just don't believe he could do this,' she said, 'I mean, look at him. He's a bloody mess.'

'Do you still think Finn is in the frame?

'If he is, then Gordon is covering for him but I don't see why. Likewise, why would Finn want to protect Gordon? The whole thing feels fake,' she told him nervously. 'We need to get under the detail.'

'Well, you had this from the start, Foxie. Listen to your gut because I'm all ears.'

When they re-entered the room half an hour later Gordon jumped, his head jerking forward from his short-lived snooze.

Rubbing his eyes, he looked around, slightly disorientated.

Garvey stood by the window, her arms crossed protectively across her chest.

Callaghan handed both of them a fresh, cold bottle of water before resetting the recorder.

Fox sat and opened her notebook that had a raft of questions scribbled in it.

Focused and professional, she had a specific job to do and was itching to get going.

'OK. Are we ready?' she asked once everyone was sitting and the recorder hummed into action.

'So, Gordon, how did you get into Finn's studio?'

For a minute he looked startled, his eyes blinking, unprepared for this direct line of questioning.

'Keys, I used the keys.'

'Where did you get them from?'

'Sive had a set – he must have given them to her.'

'And where are they now?'

'I don't know,' he answered, shaking his head. 'Somewhere.'

'And the alarm?'

'It wasn't on.'

'So you walked right up to the house and walked straight in?'

'Yes!' he snapped.

'Where was the housekeeper?'

'How the hell am I supposed to know?'

'Well, how did you know she wouldn't be there?'

'I was careful. I checked. She wasn't there.'

'And how did you know what clothes to pick?'

'I don't know, I just did. I picked what I thought he'd wear.'

'Did you know beforehand what you were going to take or did you select randomly?'

'Randomly, I guess …'

'You guess or you did, which is it, Gordon?' she interrupted sharply.

'I did. I did.'

'Are you sure?'

'Of course I'm sure, I've just said so, haven't I?'

'And then you went back and put everything back in the attic of the studio?'

He nodded while his solicitor did her best to keep up, following the volley like a spectator at Wimbledon.

'So how come we didn't we find your DNA on the clothes, Gordon?' she asked and wasn't in the least bit surprised when he opened his mouth almost immediately to answer but nothing came out. She didn't wait for him to reply, instead she shot off her next round of questions in quick succession.

'What kind of a bag did you use to put the clothes in, Gordon?'

'I don't remember.'

'A plastic bag, a rucksack, a hold–all? Surely you remember that?'

'I've told you no.'

'Was it brown, black, red?'

'How would I know that if I can't remember what bag in the first place?'

'What else did you put in the bag with the clothes?'

'What do you mean *what else*?' he asked, his agitation beginning to show.

'Simple – what else was in the bag?'

'I don't know.'

'If you put the stuff in there then you should know.'

'Well, I don't.'

'Think about it. There were the tracksuit bottoms, the jacket, cap, what else? Take your time, we've got as long as you need.'

'I don't remember.'

'You don't have a very good memory, do you?'

'Not when I'm being interrogated like this, I don't.'

He shrugged and she again changed tack.

'So you put the bag back in the attic.'

He nodded.

'Can you remember how many windows there were in the studio?'

'This is bloody ridiculous! What kind of stupid questions are these? How many windows, like I noticed. I had other things on my mind.'

'Windows, Gordon. It's a simple question really. If you'd ever been in there you'd have noticed one very large window, impossible to miss, difficult to forget and a view to die for.'

'So what?'

'I don't think you were in there at all, were you?'

'What? You don't believe me?' He laughed. 'I've just confessed and you don't believe me?'

'Oh, I believe you all right for the most part, but this part, no, I don't.'

Chapter 24

The front door was wide open when she arrived.

Tentatively crossing the threshold and closing the door behind her, she called out, 'Hello?'

Her voice bounced against the polished surfaces but no one replied. The house was quiet. Cautiously she made her way down the hall and called out again. Walking into the kitchen, she scanned left and right but it too was empty. Through the double glass doors, she saw her sitting out on the stone terrace basking in the afternoon sun. Despite the time of year there was still a little heat left in those rays. A bottle of red wine sat beside two glasses, one full, one empty. On the glass table alongside was an ashtray, lighter and a twenty pack of Marlboro Lights.

Fox pulled back the heavy door and stepped outside. Karin lifted her head, shielding her eyes with her hands and smiled, nodding towards the empty glass.

'You know your front door was wide open? Fox asked, admiring the luxury of the beautifully appointed terrace with its potted trees and shrubs and low-lying wall dividing it from the sloping lawn below.

'Sit down,' Karin invited, pushing the empty chair beside her back with her foot.

'Expecting someone else?' Fox asked, nodding towards the empty glass.

'No. Just you,' Karin replied.

'How so?' Fox asked as she sat down.

'Well, you did interview Gordon this afternoon, didn't you?'

'I did,' she replied with a nod.

Karin was dressed casually in jeans and a red-and-blue checked top with her hair tied up in a single high ponytail. She lifted the glass and took a generous sip of her wine, letting the liquid linger in her mouth, eyes closed, savouring the taste before swallowing.

'Won't you join me? It's a wonderful Bordeaux, definitely one not to miss.' She poured wine into the second glass and handed it to Fox without waiting for her answer.

Taking the glass without having any intention of drinking it, Fox knew that to refuse would only add to the already heightened tension that sizzled around her.

'I've been saving this one for something special,' Karin told her, raising her glass to the sun to inspect the beautiful burgundy colour. 'It was a gift from a client and it's a good one, worth I'm told about nine hundred quid.' She brought the glass to her nose and inhaled deeply. 'You're supposed to breathe it in before you swallow – apparently you get better flavours when you do it that way. Smells divine, doesn't it?'

Fox had to admit it certainly did, the aroma of deep oaky tannins wafting up to tempt her to one small sip.

She watched as Karin took a cigarette from the pack, lit it up and sucked hard then let the smoke billow from her mouth.

'I didn't realise you smoked,' she remarked.

'I did but don't anymore, not until earlier anyhow – it's

the first I've had in years. Stress, I suppose. Want one?'

Declining with a shake of her head and apologetic smile, Fox noted the peculiar mood and braced herself for what was to come.

They sat in silence, listening to the birds chirping, and watched the flotilla of boats that dotted the sea beyond, out for one last mid-week race of the season,

'How is Gordon then?' Karin asked eventually, staring out to sea.

'He's had finer moments, I suspect,' Fox replied with a sigh.

'Did he admit what he did to me?'

'He did.'

'Did he say why?'

'Does it matter?'

'Of course it bloody does – *the man raped me!*' she spat, the precarious calm sucked immediately from the air as she twisted sharply like a viper, sending a spray of wine mixed with saliva unintentionally across the table.

'I'm sorry,' Fox said, 'I didn't mean to –'

'Yes, you did! I know what you're thinking, what you're all thinking – you think I should be grateful I'm alive. Never mind him raping me – I got off lightly, didn't I? Look at Sive. She's dead. I'm not, isn't that it?'

Silently Fox counted down from ten but didn't respond, there was no point.

'Was it him then, is he responsible for all this?' Karin demanded with a dramatic sweep of her arm.

Fox took her time before answering, deliberately and obviously assessing her through slightly squinted eyes, making sure Karin knew that her performance despite its theatrical quality didn't impress her. With every muscle in her body clenched tight she chose to bide her time and held Karin's glare, the polite conversation descending into a spiky exchange.

'Yes, we believe he was involved, he's said as much but he's confessed, I think, to more than he's actually guilty of. I believe he's covering for someone.'

'Finn?' Karin shot, turning her head back to the boats that moved elegantly through the water in the glorious sunshine.

'Maybe, although Gordon says he had nothing to do with it.'

'Does he now?' Karin laughed silently into her glass, giving a hint that there might have been a bottle before this one. 'Will he be released?'

'Finn? Not yet, not until we can piece together what happened. Gordon is insisting he was the one who set Finn up, he was the one who manipulated the evidence that placed him at the scene.'

She stopped to see how Karin would react but she continued to stare out to sea, listening without comment.

'That said, it simply doesn't add up. He's just not very convincing. The devil is in the detail, I always say, and he just doesn't have the detail.'

'*Gobshite!*' Karin whispered, leaning forward to pour herself a top-up, the bottle almost gone.

'He says he got into your house, into Finn's studio, took his clothes, then when he was done went back and planted them where we found them. How possible is that, do you think?'

'How should I know?'

'I'm not asking how he did it – just if you think it was possible.'

'If he had the codes to the gate and the keys then, yes, of course it's possible.'

'But there's no evidence that Gordon wore them, no sign at all, not a hair or a flake of skin, nothing.'

'Maybe he didn't wear them – maybe he had a second set?'

'Possible, but he didn't say that – why wouldn't he say if he did? But it's a good explanation. What about Gordon himself? Do you think he has the nerve to do that? Breaking and entering, is that the way his mind works?'

'Look at what he did to me. The man is obviously unhinged. Himself and Finn, they're obviously in this together. I mean, look at them. What a pair of idiots!'

'But that's the point, isn't it? Whatever about executing it, neither seem like the type to conceive something like this, do they?'

'What the hell are you talking about? Hasn't Gordon confessed? And you've got Finn's DNA all over the place – of course they're the type!'

'I'm not so sure. I think there's someone else.' She looked straight at Karin. 'I think someone else is the mastermind here, Karin. Gordon, if he's telling the truth, is nothing more than a puppet and, as for Finn, I don't think he had anything whatsoever to do with it. I think he was intended to be the fall guy and I think Gordon and whoever else he's been working with almost got away with it.'

'You think too much, that's your problem!' Karin sneered.

'That may be the case but I can't figure out who. Who he's covering for? What do *you* think?' When she got no answer, she continued. 'He says you both knew about the affair.'

'Did he now?'

'He did. He said you've both known for some time.'

Karin drained her glass.

'But you told us you didn't know anything about it – you made it seem like I was the one to break the news.'

Karin shrugged.

'He's lying.'

'I don't think so.'

'He's infatuated and deluded. You can't trust anything that comes out of that man's mouth.'

'Who do you think he's covering for? Is there anyone else we should be looking at? Tell me again about your relationship with him.'

'There's nothing to tell. He's a man obsessed, nothing more, nothing less.'

'I don't think that's altogether true, is it?'

Chapter 25

They came together by accident, having followed their respective unfaithful spouses. Both, curious to see if their suspicions were correct, collided in the foyer of the seedy Majestic Hotel where, stunned and embarrassed, they realised their unusual relationship. Their mutual heartbreak and disgust was aligned, Sive being Karin's supposed best friend and Finn the husband of his wife's greatest distraction. Both betrayed and humiliated, they found comfort in a friendship that made the knowledge of the affair easier to stomach. They agreed not to interfere, to let whatever that attracted them in the first place run its course, neither one wanting to force the hand of their spouses for fear of the potential permanent result. Despite his own anguish, Gordon sympathised with Karin, recognising the double dose of betrayal she had suffered at the hands of both her husband and her friend.

'How will you ever trust again?' he asked with compassion.

She couldn't bring herself to admit that, whatever about Finn, she had never trusted Sive. How could she? For years Sive had been siphoning money from her in plain sight and with her consent. The threat of her revealing what happened in college was always there and Sive made sure Karin never forgot the danger of letting her down. Each cash request seemed always to be accompanied by a random comment or reminder of a character, a face or an event from their past. And, contrary to what she may have said or how she may have behaved, it irritated the hell out of her. It wasn't so much the funds she had dished out but rather the senseless manner in which it was squandered. Her hard-earned money became one failed venture after another. Sive never tried, she didn't have to. *Bank of Karin* it seemed was always open. And even though it was nothing short of extortion, it seemed like a small price to pay for the continued silence of her very own sleeping dog that she considered to be more a niggle than a headache. But when the money was no longer enough, when she wanted more, the sleeping dog became the bitch that took her husband. Shrewdly, very early on, Karin had established that while friends come in various shapes, sizes and sorts, Sive was the dangerous kind, a wolf in sheep's clothing. *Keep your enemies close*, was the best piece of advice she'd been blessed with many years before, so she did. Very close.

But more than anything else Karin found it impossible to overcome her profound sense of ineptitude. How could she have been so stupid as to let something like this happen, especially knowing what she did about Sive? She should have seen it coming, should have known Sive would do something like this. Karin blamed her completely. In her eyes Finn may have fancied Sive but he wasn't the type to instigate an affair. He didn't have the balls. On the other hand she had no difficulty imagining Sive pursuing him like an animal. She was sure Finn would tire of her – they had nothing in common – after all, she didn't know her Monets from her Manets and certainly wasn't the brightest light on the tree – but he didn't. And as the affair refused to fizzle out, as it instead grew stronger, Karin's fury intensified and they became a humiliating everyday reminder of her stupidity. She couldn't get them out of her mind, picturing Sive in her house, drinking from her glasses, eating with her cutlery and sleeping with her husband. Incensed with herself for being so foolish as to think Finn could actually love her, Karin wondered pitifully how he had survived their last ten years together. And oblivious to the fact that their relationship was being tracked, Sive and Finn snuck around like teenagers.

Throughout their ten-year relationship Karin and Finn had maintained their own personal space in the house. It was an unconventional but practical choice they made right from the start. They didn't need to live in each other's pockets all the time and, while it was intended to be their key to a happy and healthy relationship, in the end it became the stick she used to punish herself with. He used to come regularly to her room. Sometimes it was impulsive and carefree, other times his knock was uninvited but welcome and she never turned him away – but when he stopped knocking, her confidence dashed, she stopped inviting him, deciding that if she didn't ask she couldn't be humiliated by his potential rejection. Her only comfort was that he chose to stay with her – surely that meant something?

The brick that toppled her tower came on one of the rare weekends when Finn was at a weekend artist's retreat in the Burren and had left the house at the crack of dawn on the Friday morning. She had planned to drive to the cottage but the weather had turned in the late afternoon and rain fell heavily outside, making the journey less palatable. Lonely and cold she arrived home to an empty Wild Winds, missing the homely fix that Silene Cottage gave her at the end of yet another tough week. Even in the coziness of her room she couldn't find comfort. Despite Finn spending most of his time in his studio, she liked the assurance of him being in the house. His presence was enough, it was too big for her to be on her own. That evening she missed him too. Without a good reason other than curiosity, dressed in her pajamas, dressing gown and slippers, she wandered into his studio that as usual was in a state of organised chaos. She loved the smell of the paint mixed with the musky odour of his aftershave.

Resisting the urge to tidy, she explored his room, running her hands over the jumble and leafing through the random layers of paper that were strewn every which way on his desk. Finding an open pack of cigarettes, she picked one out and lit it. She hadn't smoked in years but still loved that first sniff of nicotine as it hit the back of her throat. Pulling on it but without inhaling, she let the smoke drift from her mouth as she cruised the room. She pressed *play* on the Sonas player and David Bowie's uniquely sultry voice instantly filled the room mid-song, picking up right where Finn had paused it. She felt him in the room singing to her and smiled, a fitting choice to be inspired by, she thought, as she continued to peruse.

Reaching the unfinished canvas she imagined Finn confronting it with his paint tubs and tubes chaotically cast on the shelf, table and floor and smudges of colour staining the reclaimed timber floorboards.

Somewhere under the mess on his desk his phone rang. She let it ring and go to the answer phone – she'd forgotten he had a landline and was surprised anyone used it anymore.

'*Hey, buddy, sorry to ring you so late, tried your mobile but it's*

309

ringing out.' Josh, Finn's agent, spoke out to the ether.

She had brought them together years before. It was a good match. Josh was as flamboyant as one of Finn's paintings, they connected instantly and Josh soon became his friend as well as his representative. Karin liked him, he was a smart guy, and made to pick up the handset buried deep in the piles on the desk to say hi, only to remind herself it was Finn's private line and she'd have to explain what she was doing in his studio. So instead she stood still and listened.

'*Listen, great news, mate. I have a buyer for Celestial Mania and he wants to commission another. Apparently even at their size he has the perfect wall for two.'* Josh laughed at the idea that was somehow hysterical. '*Anyway, just wanted to let you know. Another few grand for your escape fund, eh? Call me.'*

Scrambling through the papers on his desk, not caring that she would never be able to put things back the way they were, she searched for the phone to ask Josh to explain what he meant but by the time she found it and plucked the handset from its cradle he was gone.

His escape fund? The words echoed around her. They could have meant anything, could be a title for a show, his next commission or publication title, she silently argued. But why would he need to add a *few grand* to it? She could cut the reason any way she liked but her instinct told her exactly what Josh meant. Her last remaining hope for a future with Finn was dashed – she was a dope to even think it could work. It appeared he was leaving and not on a whim but as part of a preconceived and well-funded exit.

Carefully she replaced the handset back in its slot and tried to shift the papers back to the way she found them, even though she knew he wasn't likely to even notice. She didn't want him to know she had found him out. Didn't want him to suspect her humiliation. She felt as if a weight had suddenly been placed on her shoulders and she didn't have the strength to hold them up. This was it. He was as good as gone. And the big question: would he go alone?

Her knees trembled and she let them give way to gently place herself cross-legged on the floor. What an idiot, she cursed herself. A fool to think she could possibly hold off the inevitable, a day she had no real control of.

And Bowie sang to her. 'Is There Life on Mars?' he serenaded, his words just about audible above her heart beat that banged boisterously in her ears. Such beautiful words that did nothing but compound her sense of betrayal. Poignant words that rang so true to her ears. Would she now have to face the double humiliation of not only having him leave her but also seeing him with *her*? Did they really expect her to do that? Was that the reality of what she was facing? She wouldn't put up with this defeat in her work life so why or how could it be acceptable at home? This was her movie, she had lived it long enough and now she was bored with it, now was her time to change and spit in the eye of anyone who dared to have taken her for a fool.

The biggest difference between Karin and Gordon was that Gordon wasn't yet bitter about what had become of his marriage. Karin on the other hand was not only bitter, she was seething, and what began as nothing more than a fantastical statement, a simple '*I wish she were dead*' over time became a detailed, fully fledged scheme. The more she thought about it, the more layers she added complete with conversations, mental run-throughs and timings until eventually it not only seemed reasonable, it seemed possible. But she couldn't execute it on her own, she needed help. She needed Gordon and a plan on how to recruit him.

As it turned out, she couldn't have orchestrated it any better if she tried.

They had taken to meeting regularly for lunch or supper and sometimes just for coffee. There was no real purpose to these events – they seemed to be more about silently supporting one another, confirming suspicions and assuring each other they weren't going mad with their notions. Their relationship as it developed was purely platonic. Although Gordon was sweet, he wasn't the most dynamic of characters and Karin had absolutely no interest in him. If bland and boring was her thing, there were any number of men she could have chosen from, but Gordon wasn't one of them. It took her some time to realise that he was interested in more than just a friendship. Returning her home after a light supper and cocktails on a bright Tuesday evening, he pulled up outside the house and waited for the gates to open. Relaxed and comfortable in their mutual hell, she leaned over to peck his cheek, a friendly gesture of thanks before exiting the car but at the last minute he turned so her kiss landed on his lips that were open and eager. Pulling back shocked and horrified, she stormed from the car, slammed the door and marched into her house. For the next hour she silently ranted about his audacity – how dare he?

But when she calmed and flattery battled its way through her indignation, the final layer of her plan took shape. Could it work? It was a risk but there was something powerful and wildly exciting about the prospect of seducing an unwitting Gordon into her scheme.

The real prize wasn't how well it worked but how much she enjoyed it.

She wasn't used to using her feminine charm, she wasn't

even sure she possessed it but the confidence she got from Gordon's responses was enlightening.

Using her virtue as a married woman as the excuse to keep him at bay, then using the promise of more as his enticement, she drove him wild.

Slowly she reeled him in, starting with short kisses that ended abruptly but lasted long enough to draw him in and give him a taste of what might come. Like a dog he was easily manipulated, eager to do whatever she wanted if the reward was more of her.

'Why?' he moaned as she cut off their embrace. 'Why should we deny ourselves when they're out there cavorting?'

'Because we are better than them,' she explained with feigned sadness. 'I can't do that, I won't. We just have to be patient.'

And each day with each encounter she reminded him of Finn and Sive's betrayal, She drove home the notion that this was Finn and Sive's fault, that it was because of them that she and Gordon were each shunted out of their individual marriages. Patiently she waited for him to look for a way out, for him to come up with a plan.

'Why wait? Why not get rid of them now?' he moaned bitterly one day. 'Let's start over, pack their bags, change the locks.'

And there it was, the opportunity to plant the seed.

'And give him half of everything? Not a hope. Do you really want to hand over half of what you've earned in the practice to have her piss it away? I don't think so. No, there has to be a fairer way.'

'You can't blame me, can you? I only want to be with you.'

'It would be nice, just the two of us, we could have so much fun together,' she teased and, taking it to the next level, moved in to kiss him deeply, deeper than she had ventured so far and placed the palm of her hand firmly on his groin. Massaging him gently she waited till she felt him pull away from her mouth to let his head fall back and, once she heard him moan, she stopped abruptly with a sharp apology.

'Don't stop! Please!' he begged.

'I can't, I'm sorry!' she cried before getting up to leave the room.

The spark that ultimately lit his fuse was a call from a six-star hotel in Dubai.

'I'm sorry to disturb you this afternoon, sir, I'm calling to confirm your dinner reservations for this evening at Nico's.'

'I'm sorry?'

'Your wife dropped by reception this morning and asked for us to make the booking.'

'Sive?'

'Yes, Mrs Collins. She asked that we make a booking for seven o'clock this evening.'

'I'm sorry, where did you say you're calling from?'

'This is Franco at the reception of the Grand Plaza.'

'In Dubai?'

'Yes, sir, Dubai.'

'And how did you get my number?'

'I'm sorry, sir, I got it from our records from your last visit. Mrs Collins didn't leave a contact number and there is no answer from your suite so ...'

'My suite?'

'Yes, sir, the Presidential Suite. I'm sorry, sir, if this isn't the right time ...'

Gordon hung up the phone, feeling his blood pressure rise.

'*And who the fuck do you think is paying for that? The*

Presidential Suite, for fuck sake!'

Karin found it awkward, comical even, hearing him curse like that. The vulgar words just didn't suit him.

'They're parasites!' he spat, his voice filled with venom. 'How dare they! They're making fools of us, you do realise that, don't you? Fools!' His fists met the counter with such force the plates hopped.

Karin couldn't have manipulated it any better if she tried and silently she thanked Sive for being her usual selfish self.

If he was surprised by the fact that she had it already worked out, he didn't show it. Her plan was simple and had one key objective, to get rid of both Sive and Finn while putting herself and Gordon beyond suspicion.

For the plan to work she had to trust Gordon implicitly because the key to its success was that it should follow as close to real events as possible. She had to be sure he was as invested in it as she was. It had to look and feel real even when it was all over and, while Gordon would be the one to set it up, it was Karin who would have to convince them it was real. She had to look and sound like it had actually happened and there was no way anyone could credibly make it up. It had to actually happen. She had it all worked out and all Gordon had to do was follow her instructions to the letter, which he did, almost.

So as not to contaminate the car, dressed in brand-new clothes fresh out of their packaging, leather gloves and a hat pulled down over his head, Gordan paid cash for it and drove it to the garage Karin had rented on the opposite side of the city.

On the Friday of the kidnapping, Gordon worked as usual until four then made his way across the city. Parking in a multi-storey car park, he made his way on public transport to the rented garage where Karin had left a rucksack for him. Inside he found newly purchased tracksuit bottoms together with a hoodie, hat, neck-warmer and pair of gloves, all identical to the clothes she had taken from Finn's room. Once changed, he made his way in the old Volvo towards the West. As instructed he stopped en route at the petrol station and made sure he was picked up by the cameras before leaving the forecourt. Once he'd reached Silene Cottage, sure to wear the gloves, he staged the break-in and put the drugged wine on the table before parking no more than a couple of miles away to wait.

Just before midnight he returned to the cottage. The lights were still on and the front door off the latch. Quietly he opened the door but he needn't have been so cautious as both women were unconscious at the table. Getting them into the car was a task in itself. Sive was easy, he was used to her weight, but Karin took a little more effort, with him almost knocking her head off the door as he left. With them both secure in the car, he drove main roads and motorways all the way to the derelict cottage that Karin had scoured that part of the country for, and found during one of her supposed relaxing weekends at Silene. As they were beginning to come around but still incoherent, he gave each of them more of the sedative before securing them inside. Painstakingly following her instructions, he consulted the directions she gave and drove the car along the back roads through Limerick and into Tipperary. There, just outside Toomevara, he turned onto a dirt track and into a field where he wiped down the interior of the car, took the hair samples Karin had put in a plastic ziplock bag and placed them as she told him on the driver's headrest and seat and, taking Sive's bracelet from his pocket, placed it under the passenger seat from the back. Changing his clothes once more, he cursed the rain that fell to drench him as he walked the quiet road towards the village where he picked up a bus in the morning. Nervous but keeping himself well covered, he posted the ransom note that Karin had prepared. It felt like a bomb ticking against his chest in his breast pocket and he was glad to be rid of it.

Gordon returned early the following day. This time as planned he made sure when checking Sive's ties that he loosened them a little, just enough for her to be able to slip her slim wrists through. In directing Gordon, Karin knew he wouldn't have to wait long before she'd run. Not doubting her, he made plenty of fuss as he unlocked the door, giving her time to prepare for her escape – then stepping far enough into the room he gave her sufficient space and opportunity to run. Still heavy under the effects of the drugs, she didn't run fast and he had to slow himself down sufficiently to let her to reach the far side of the field and the edge of the ditch. When he reached her he wasn't even out of breath. He had planned on hitting her hard on the back of the head but she turned just as he lifted the rock above his head, ready to bring it down hard for maximum impact on her skull. She turned and faced her pursuer, her hands lifting to protect herself. And she recognised him. He hadn't banked on that. Her arms dropped slowly as her expression turned from one of fear to confusion.

'Gordon?' she whispered and repeated his name as she realised her situation, taking a step backwards. But the ground was soft and slippery. He didn't have to push hard. Just a gentle shove. She lost her footing and with arms flailing she fell backwards into the ditch. The sound of her head as it made contact with the stony ground was unnerving. Like no other sound he'd heard before, a hollow pop like a coconut might make as it is split in two. He didn't need to follow her in. Nature had done the job for him.

He squatted down for while and watched her, almost leaning over her, his breathing heavy and heart racing as he watched her slip away. She didn't take her eyes off him and she made no sound, no dying gasping breath, no twitching or moaning. She simply never moved again.

As the rain fell then stopped, the blood first pooled before soaking into the mud.

It was a different man that returned to Karin. There were very few who could say they watched their wife die by their own hands.

'Is it done?' Karin slurred, struggling to sit up, still foggy.

Gordon, standing in the doorway, nodded and went to her. He held the last glass of water to her lips. From somewhere inside his head, his conscience chastised him for what he had done. He was supposed to leave now, close and lock the door, walk the few miles back to his car and drive back home. He was supposed to leave her there, untouched. That was the plan, that was what she told him to do. Turning, he sat on the floor beside Karin, knees to his chest and back against the wall and waited quietly for the voice to stop. The rain beat down on the patched-up roof, poured in through the holes and bounced off the already sodden ground, the smell of damp and dirt heightened in the darkness. Turning to her, he thought she looked peaceful and serene.

It's never going to happen, the voice in his head told him as he stroked her hair. Not a chance.

Gently he touched her cheek with the back of his hand and then her neck.

'You promised,' he whispered and let his hand trail

beyond her neck to her chest and, placing a hand on her breast, let it rest there, feeling it rise and fall with each breath she took. It wasn't part of her plan but he couldn't help himself. This was his plan and she didn't have to know.

He returned twice after that. Parking his car, he walked the distance to the house then stood outside, listening. But he never went back in. And then he never went back at all but waited for her to be found, dreading the moment he'd have to face her and hoping they didn't find her soon. Maybe they wouldn't find her at all.

It was a good plan made better by real events that Karin had no hand in making. The security footage found by Tom was a gem that set the scene beautifully – she couldn't have manipulated better substantiation of his motive and the bank account he'd set up was the perfect vehicle to track the ransom back to him. She knew one had to exist, he had to have somewhere to put his pathetic escape funds. And she wasn't wrong. Finn wasn't devious at heart and didn't know how to hide these things properly. How was he to know he needed to, how was he to know what his wife was planning? He could never remember anything and had to write things down. All Karin needed to do was look. It didn't take her long to find them in the only drawer in his studio: account numbers and codes written in a small unassuming notebook alongside all the other important details and passwords in his life. With good planning and plenty of time, setting up the seemingly untraceable offshore bank account she needed him to credibly have in order to accept the ransom was simple. Used to signing contracts for joint-asset deals, Finn never read them anymore, he just signed away on the dotted line. Slipped in amongst many forms to sign, his signature on the account application was simple to obtain.

And once the money arrived she transferred it almost immediately into his perfectly named Escape Fund.

Yes, it was a good plan, a brilliant plan, that if it had been carried out as it was conceived would have without question succeeded. Her attention to detail was exact and her performance brilliant. Even Gordon stepped up to the mark with his feigned revulsion of Karin but ultimately it was his guilt, not to mention his lack of control that let her down.

Poor Gordon, Karin mused, a lumbering fool. Once she got over the revolting thought of him inside her she was perversely flattered that he wanted her so much that he just couldn't wait. She never had any intention of ever giving him what he wanted. He was her means to an end and maybe he knew it, maybe that's why he did it. She couldn't have predicted how her plan would backfire and how sweet now it was that he was trying to cover for her. But he didn't have the detail to save her. She had kept it from him on purpose but only because she didn't think he needed to know. Had she been less supercilious and shared her entire strategy with him, not just the bits she thought relevant, maybe he might have been able to save her and, after what he'd done to her, it was the least he could do.

But he didn't know about the distinctive spray deodorant that she'd put in the bag along with Finn's original set of clothes before planting it in the attic even before she left for work on that Friday morning. How else could she explain not being able to recognise her own husband who always smelt divine? He'd never set foot in Finn's studio, for Christ's sake! How the hell did he think he'd be able to describe how or where he'd put the evidence? Did he think they wouldn't ask? That they'd take his confession at face value? Poor, stupid Gordon, but at least he tried.

Karin knew her game was over and all that remained was to decide how and to what extent she told the truth.

'I don't suppose there's any point in telling you that Gordon made me do it?'

'Not really. Sure you said it yourself, he's not really the type, is he?'

Karin smiled and stood up.

'More wine?' she offered, taking the empty bottle from the table.

Holding up her still full glass, Fox shook her head.

'No thanks, I'm good,' she replied and watched Karin go inside to fetch another bottle. 'It was a pretty slick plan!' she said when Karin returned. 'You had me fooled and you almost got away with it!'

'Thank you,' Karin replied, returning to the table and filling up her glass. 'It was pretty good, wasn't it? It's only flaw really was Gordon.' She grimaced. 'I shouldn't have trusted him. Every time I think of him ...' She shivered, leaving the sentence hang. 'He was always the risk that I thought I had under control,' she mused. 'But I suppose I pushed him too far, didn't I? He has a weak soul and instead I created a monster, my very own Frankenstein.' She laughed bitterly.

'Not everything can be manipulated, Karin.'

'It's worked pretty well for me so far. I manipulated you, didn't I?'

Fox let her head drop and a sardonic grin cross her face. She certainly had.

'And I manipulated Gordon, right until the end. He didn't know about Sive and me – he was pretty shocked, you know.'

'I can imagine.'

'So I told him it was a lie.'

'And was it?' Fox asked, fully expecting her to say yes.

'No. That was real. We had our moment, or two.' Karin smiled wistfully. 'It was quite an intense moment that I'll always remember fondly.'

Fox shifted uncomfortably in her chair, not because of how she felt about Sive and Karin's affair, but more because Karin just couldn't help herself.

'Why go this far though, why not just kick Finn out, be done with him, stop hanging out with Sive? There are plenty of lawyers who'd be chomping at the bit to get him out of your life and all it would cost is cash, definitely less than the five million you spent on this, and more. Why did it have to be so dramatic? You've already said you knew it was a risk – was it really worth all this? You're facing a pretty long time in prison. Can you honestly tell me it was worth it?'

Karin sighed and looked far out to sea.

'You're not so different to me, you know – a woman, not just any woman but a strong woman with a sense of purpose surviving in a man's world where one sniff of weakness and they're out for blood. You have to be at the top of your game all the time – there's no prize or forgiveness for vulnerability. It's so bloody tiring. I'm tired.' Her voice was no more than a whisper.

Fox believed for the very first time she was seeing the real side of Karin, the stripped-back human version and it was terrifying because she seemed almost normal, whatever normal was.

'Put me in a boardroom and I'll easily battle my way through but somewhere between my office and my home I just lose it, my confidence vanishes. I don't know what it is or why, it just goes.' She snapped her fingers, making Fox jump.

'You know those moments at night when you're totally alone, neither awake nor asleep and everything seems bigger, more intense, like a tightrope between waking and sleeping with nothing underneath to save you if you fall. You're paranoid and helpless, so helpless that the harder you try the worse it gets and there is no answer.' She looked at Fox, her stare intense, pleading to be understood.

Nodding to Karin with wide eyes, Fox acknowledged that she'd been there often enough, in that hypersensitive consciousness that like a bad trip she had no control of. It was in those moments of sleep limbo where she'd try to work through the why's and the what if's of Oisín's death. She understood her completely.

'Well,' Karin responded, 'that's what it feels like to be me, all the time.'

It was a moment of disturbed realisation for Fox who admitted that, but for a few small differences, it could be her standing in similar shoes to Karin, her world slowly falling apart around her.

'I almost feel relieved.' Karin laughed with a meek embarrassed squeak. 'This has been a tough few weeks, watching Gordon disintegrate, constantly having to think two steps ahead ...'

'Well, if it were easy everyone would be doing it,' Fox replied and standing up signalled it was time to go.

Chapter 26

The key was where it always was, under the hydrangea pot by the porch. Taking it, she opened the front door and replaced it before closing the door behind her.

'*Only me!*' she called out as she entered the bright four-bedroom detached house that smelled of burnt toast and polish. She never understood how he managed to do it – even with a toaster the bread always came out singed and stinking. The house was as always neat and tidy and she was pleasantly surprised to see fresh flowers on the hall table. She walked the short hall to the kitchen, past the family portraits that hung proudly with all four children represented on their very own wall of fame. She slowed but didn't stop as she passed Oisín's. Taken at his passing-out parade, he looked so smart and handsome in his blue uniform and so excited for his future. Her heart hurt when she thought of him and his bright, bright future extinguished so young. She always liked this house – it had a heart – and, even though Oisín had passed so many years before, she still felt welcome here. It was still her home too. In all the time she'd been coming here, it hadn't changed one bit. It still smelt and looked the same – if anything it just seemed that little bit emptier. That was one of the disadvantages of being stationed so far from Dublin –

it meant she could now visit less often. And even though she knew Paddy of all people understood her long absences, she still felt guilty. Since Margaret died it was just him in the house on his own. Fox reckoned she had died of a broken heart – no mother wants to bury her son. And she understood because it nearly killed her too and she wondered how Paddy managed to survive. At the time he had his work colleagues – they were like an extension of his family and supported him when Oisín died, and then again when it was Margaret's turn they were there to help and comfort him. Of course he had his remaining children but, scattered across the globe, they returned to their homes almost as soon as their mother's funeral was over. She wondered how long he would stay in the house on his own but was afraid to ask.

'*In here, pet!*' Paddy called, the term of affection putting a smile on her lips. They got on like a house on fire from the first time they met – they had the same quirky sense of humour and strong principles that often made Sunday dinners very lively events. She could see where Oisín got his handsome good looks, not to mention his charm. It was no surprise that he was a great father as well as a hugely respected member of the Force. Paddy always said she brought the best out in Oisín, making the final days of his short life the best he had ever known, and promised to look after her after Oisín died, making her swear to stay in touch, no matter what. Which she did and, true to his word, both he and Margaret treated her like their own daughter. She also knew he kept a distant eye on her as she climbed the ranks. He always seemed to know the cases she was working on and the challenges she faced.

'Stop pestering the girl!' Margaret would tease when he

appeared to test her when she'd visit. 'Let her eat her meal in peace, for God's sake!'

And his interest didn't wane even after his retirement – it just became less obvious. He was like her very own Guardian Angel in disguise.

She found him sitting alone on the long side of the French-polished dining table in an open-neck cream shirt and khaki-green cardigan with his glasses perched at the end of his nose. In front of him, set on a giant piece of timber, was the biggest jigsaw she'd ever seen.

'Holy shit!' she exclaimed. 'Where on earth did you find this one?'

'*Ha!* I knew you'd like it!' he replied with a cheeky grin, 'Good, isn't it? I bought it online, some weird site for nerds I think you'd call it.'

'How long has it taken you to get this far?' she asked in awe, slowly sitting down, and immediately getting sucked into the challenge she picked up and inspected one of the two thousand pieces that Paddy had organised into structured groups.

'Oh, about a week so far I'd say,' he said placing another piece in its right place with a satisfied grin.

Laughing out loud, she scanned the picture of Washington crossing the Delaware and the unfinished puzzle and prepared to get stuck in.

'Still burning the toast, I smell,' she said, picking up piece after piece and returning them to their group.

'Still stating the obvious.' he retorted playfully, taking a piece from her fingers and clicking it in place.

'*Touché!*' She finished with a smile.

'So, how's the new job?' He ventured, picking up and trying out a new piece.

'Interesting,' she replied, sneaking a glance over at him.

'He's a piece of work alright, that Moyne fella,' he said with a knowing smile. 'Don't let him push you around.'

'Oh, I won't,' she told him although she reckoned he knew that already.

'I worked with him years back when he was just a young sergeant, always knew he'd be one to watch – balls of steel and pigheaded to boot.' He chuckled to himself.

'Don't think he's changed much so,' Fox sighed.

'That bad, eh?'

She grinned. 'I hear you made a call to the station before I joined.'

He pursed his lips and nodded with a sheepish grin. 'I did.'

'You know, Paddy, you didn't have to …'

'I appreciate that,' he told her with a shrug, 'but when you told me you were going for promotion outside of Dublin, well, there are a lot of idiots out there and I wanted to make sure you landed the right idiot. Moyne's a tough nut, but he's a good nut.'

'The problem is that your help could be misconstrued.'

'I'm flattered that you think I still have that much influence. You got that job on your own merit, I just gave him a verbal reference, nothing more. But I get it, stop interfering, is that what you're trying to say?'

'Interfering is a strong word but, kind of, yes,' she said, hoping her smile would take the edge off her request. 'I have to do this by myself.'

'Fair enough so,' he conceded. 'You're going to stay then?'

'Looks like it,' she said, giving him a look that told him she didn't earn her detective stripes for nothing, and realising that his conversations with Moyne were obviously more frequent than she had first guessed.

'Good.' He smiled. 'But I'll miss your visits, rare and all as they are. Don't go forgetting about me altogether now, hear?'

Fox smiled. 'Of course I won't. It's not Timbuktu, you know. I'll be back every couple of weeks – sure I'll probably see you more now that I'm not in Dublin.'

Focusing on the puzzle, neither said a word for a while, each lost in their world.

'Any other news?' Paddy asked, breaking the silence.

Fox could tell his question was leading and he was opening the conversation on purpose.

'Nothing at all, work has taken over my life!' she laughed, 'You?' She looked at him expectantly.

'No,' he replied nervously. 'Just curious to see if you've made any new friends?'

'Friends?' she repeated with a smile, recalling the fresh flowers in the hall. 'Can't say that I have.' And, after a slight pause, asked, 'You?' She was surprised to see the colour rise in his cheeks, confirming her immediate suspicion. 'It's about time you met someone,' she said, cutting immediately to the chase. 'Margaret wouldn't want you to be alone – in fact, I think she'd hate it.'

'Thank you,' he replied gratefully.

'Just don't wait too long to introduce me.'

He smiled again. 'I won't. I think the same applies to you.'

'Me, I don't have anyone for you to meet!' she scoffed.

'Well, maybe it's time you did.'

Her phone vibrated in her pocket.

'Speak of the devil,' she said, excusing herself from the table, grateful for the distraction.

In the kitchen she listened as Moyne spoke, nodding intermittently and offering the odd 'Yes, sir' and 'Right away, *sir'* before hanging up and heading back to the dining room.

'Sorry, Paddy. I have to go.'

'Checking up on you already? Paddy asked.

'Not quite.' She smiled. 'They've found a body.'

'Really, where?'

'Up at Blackheath Woods about twenty miles from Galway. But it seems that this corpse has died once before already.'

'What?'

'He's been positively identified as a fisherman who drowned over two years ago and is buried up at the old forge cemetery.'

'What are you going to do?' he asked, wide-eyed and curious.

'Dig him up, I suppose.' she said and, spotting a piece of the puzzle, picked it up and popped it into the centre of the picture.

THE END

Now that you're hooked why not try
Blood & Water
also published by Poolbeg?

Here's a sneak preview
of the prologue.

Blood & Water

Prologue

They carried the coffin into the crammed church, two abreast and three deep, their footsteps falling in time to the sombre drone of the organ. In silence they offered up the polished rosewood casket at the front of the altar. A long display of white lilies was placed on its top, then one by one they genuflected and turned to take their places in the pews reserved for the family at the top of the church. The three brothers stepped into the first pew beside their sisters and mother. From behind they were a unified force, standing tall, shoulder to shoulder, all dressed in black for the occasion.

Here the siblings were in familiar territory: this was where they had come as children to pray each week. It was where their parents had married and where they were each christened, all five of them. However, on this day they were burying one of their own earlier than they could ever have expected, and under less than usual circumstances.

An enormously well-respected family with almost celebrity status, this deference was evident in the numbers that gathered to mourn alongside them, with sympathisers spilling out the doors onto the gravel square outside. Government ministers standing side by side with local dignitaries, friends and neighbours. To the outside world, spectators to the event, they were solid. This, they reflected quietly in their seats, was a close-knit family that didn't need the emotion of grief to be united. They were the family that was referenced around other folks' dinner tables, the '*Why can't you be more like Sebastian Bertram, so polite, so smart?*' or '*Cormac Bertram, he's handsome, so entertaining*'. The tactless statements that every other child dreads to hear: the comparison and the disappointment. Today that admiration and respect was amplified.

Together they stood tall, heads bowed: a fine and imposing example of family unity. A family any parent would be proud of.

Detective Inspector Milford stood at the end of his carefully chosen pew in the west transept and watched them standing together. The opening hymn ended and they took their seats, heads down, eyes focused on the floor, each lost in his or her own grief.

From the pulpit, one of the celebrating priests welcomed the congregation, calling it a day of great sadness, a day of enormous loss not just for the family but also for the community and the county – the loss of a true statesman and long-serving politician who gave his service to the county and the cause he so obviously loved. He bowed his head in sorrow as he extended his sympathies to Barbara, the grieving widow, who without lifting her gaze from the floor shook her head as if to deny the reality of what was happening. Poignantly then he invited them to join him in prayer for the repose of a soul that was taken so prematurely, so violently, from them.

Milford didn't take his eyes off the front pew, noting their every move, every nod of their heads and shift in body pressure. He didn't miss a budge or nudge or a single word, their incantations and their hymns, their participation and their expressions. He watched them from start to finish and admired their staunch, stoic performance. And when they spoke from the rostrum their voices boomed through the vaulted church, the readings and prayers delivered so beautifully and with such perfect pitch and diction. And, like the rest of the congregation, he found himself thinking how extraordinary they were but for reasons different to those of the grieving onlookers.

As funerals go it was almost perfect. It had mood and humility; it spoke of greatness in this life and rewards reaped in the next. Extolling the life lived and celebrating great achievements, the priest rejoiced not just in the deceased, but also in those that he had influenced around him. And the music: what an impressive arrangement – sentimental when required yet uplifting as the words declared a welcome into heaven.

Heaven: do we really still believe in that concept, Milford wondered while he watched and listened. He was more of a live-for-today kind of a guy – Carpe Diem and all that – happy to leave the caretaking of heaven to God, if one existed. And while he wasn't so sure about heaven he was certain of a final judgment, and not in heaven but here on earth, in the here and the now. Sceptically he scoffed as the creed warned: *'From thence He shall come to judge the living and the dead.'*

Yes, apart from his own heathen wonderings, the service was almost faultless and that, for Milford, was the quandary. If the priest hadn't regularly mentioned the name of the deceased throughout, it could have been anyone's funeral. It was textbook stuff. Definitely not his preference.

Curiously, for someone who died so suddenly there were

no tears, like it was a relief or a long time coming, Milford surmised, then silently admonished himself for stepping ahead of the investigation, a classic error he often had to reprimand his overly eager juniors for. But his instinct wasn't often wrong.

As the service reached an end, again the men took up their positions at the elaborate casket to lift and bear its weight on their shoulders. Slowly, arms bracing each other, they followed the three celebrating ministers down the aisle, passing through the heady scent of burning oils and incense. The church bell tolled loudly, once for every year of his life, its ring sounding a bleak and sorrowful pulse into the crisp autumn morning.

Barbara, dressed elegantly in an expensive fur coat and hat ensemble, flanked on either side by the girls, stood to take up her position as chief mourner behind the coffin. Someone, she wasn't sure who, handed her a single long-stemmed lily which she held loosely in her hand. Why, she wasn't sure. He always hated lilies, she thought as they paraded down the red carpet towards the glaring brightness of the open doors. She did her utmost to ignore the well-meaning but, in her mind, patronising stares that honed in and watched them like hawks as they moved. She felt exposed, on display. Not sure what to do or how to behave she kept her eyes, like raging fireballs in their sockets, focused forward. She wished she'd had the foresight to take her sunglasses from her bag before leaving her seat. There should be tears. Why are there no tears, she asked herself. Taking assurance from the hand that gently squeezed her arm, she briefly entertained the urge to wring one out, for show if for nothing else. What must they think of us? But she simply didn't have the energy and instead did her best to ignore the audience. The stinging sun assaulted her eyes as slowly they stepped into the sunshine. Shielding herself from the burning rays, she let Ciara take her bag and dig out her glasses for her. Putting them on, she smiled and nodded politely, relieved by the privacy they afforded.

Reverently the coffin-bearers navigated the steps into the crowds outside: the late arrivals and the ones that couldn't squeeze into the packed church. Parting biblically, heads lowered, the gathering made way for the procession that snaked around and alongside the old majestic granite church, then headed up the gently sloping path to the graveyard where the open grave and an unsettling pile of freshly dug clay awaited. Perfectly timed, the last toll sounded as they reached the graveside where the coffin was awkwardly lowered on to the banded pulleys that would drop William Bertram's rigid bulk into the ground.

How had it come to this, Barbara asked herself, hardly able to remember the past few days, never mind the last few decades. Was there a point in time that she could actually mark, a point from which it had all spiralled so wildly out of control? This wasn't a spontaneous thing, she knew that. Things like this didn't *just happen*. It had been building for a very long time. Our finest hour, she mocked silently. She wished she could say it wasn't, wished she could say that it had been an impetuous act of frustration that just got out of hand, went too far. But that would be a lie. This, she acknowledged rationally, was a culmination of years of actions. No one was more cognisant of that than she.

Hilarious, she thought, watching as the coffin was lowered and somehow one of the inexperienced pallbearers managed to almost let slip his end of the pulley into the hole. She imagined William standing beside them, glaring at them, infuriated by their inability to co-ordinate and get it right. '*Why do you insist on being such idiots?*' she imagined him roar, always the perfectionist. Always himself imperfect.

'Our family,' she said aloud. She hadn't meant to, but it had come out involuntarily, quiet but audible nonetheless. If the girls were surprised they didn't show it. She knew they had heard: she felt them flinch. But they looked neither up nor at her.

She stole a glance at each of her children standing to her left, her right and directly in front of her across the grave. Silently this time she spoke to her dead husband. *Look at them,* she told him. *Our family, connected by blood, but divided by personalities. We were supposed to nurture them, to teach them how to experience each other, to tolerate and care for each other.* Outwardly she shook her head. This was the conversation she didn't have the chance to have with him in person. These were the words she needed him to hear. *Look what we have done to them. Look what you have done to me.* Now she felt the tears that had been so obviously absent freefall down her cheeks. But they weren't tears of grief, rather they were tears of frustration and shame. She had watched it happen and did nothing to stop it. She let it happen. Her body shook.

Ciara, of all people, put an arm around her shoulders and let her head rest against her shoulder. How ironic, Barbara mused, that this child should be the one to offer her comfort, their roles reversed, their lives changed. She felt the strangely welcome pressure of her fingers on her upper arm. She was free now to feel, as she should, waking finally from years of inertia, the sensation of Ciara's embrace peculiarly exceptional.

His mouth was moving but she couldn't hear the priest's words. She watched him flick oil at the polished timber and bow solemnly but she wasn't listening. Way over his head she watched the trees sway gently against the clear blue autumn sky, their leaves discolouring beautifully, just waiting to be carried to the ground to decay and complete their life cycle, just like the coffin that was without doubt a coffin fit for a king, now resting in the rectangular hole which was its final destination, primed to decay and rot. It was nature's way.

'Mum,' Enya prompted from her left, waking her from her evanescent thoughts and nodding to the flower in her hand.

The lily: William's least favourite flower. Barbara cast it from her hands and waited for its quiet, comical thump as it hit the wooden box below. If she could have chortled aloud and got away with it she would have, but it just wasn't appropriate for the grieving widow to snigger at her husband's funeral.

Around her, one by one, her children reached down to cast still-moist handfuls of clay on to the coffin. The organic, wet smell of it made her stomach lurch and her skin prickle. She didn't need to look up to know how they appeared or how they would behave. In the silence of the past few days she had come to know them well: the distinguished leader, the careful diplomat, the amusing joker, the rebellious doer and the sensitive carer. The remaining line-up of her team.

Order the full book online at Poolbeg.com

Also by SIOBHÁIN BUNNI

Dark Mirrors

*A missing husband . . . and a journey towards the truth
about a man she never knew*

Esmée Myers, once an impassioned woman, is living a life
where her only excitement is the laundry and the children.
Her relationship with her husband leaves a lot to be desired,
but she is content to focus on providing emotional stability
and security for her two young children.

For her husband, Philip, she is no more than a housekeeper,
childminder and cleaner, easy to betray but not so easy to fool
. . . When Esmée becomes convinced that Philip is having an
affair, she secretly plans to leave him and set up a new home
with the children. Finally making the break, she feels she can
look forward to a bright and fulfilling future.

Then Philip disappears without trace, leaving only his car
standing on a clifftop. Though no body is found, the police
deduce he has committed suicide. Esmée, however, thinks
otherwise.   What begins as a carefully planned escape from
a maudlin and tedious relationship descends into something
much darker as layer by layer Esmée strips back the last ten
years of her life with a man it turns out she never really knew.

ISBN 978-184223-6192

Published by Poolbeg.com